Dear Reader,

One of the things t[...]do
please keep them co[...]ear
from you all!) is how much you enjoy the variety of
Scarlet characters and storylines. That's why choosing
the month's books is always such an exciting challenge for
me. Will readers prefer the ups and downs of married life
to a story about a single woman finding happiness? What
about books featuring children?

This month all of these themes appear. The heroines of
Clare Benedict's *A Bitter Inheritance* and Margaret Call-
aghan's *Wilde Affair* are both, in their very different ways,
prepared to make sacrifices for the sake of a child's
happiness. *The Second Wife*, by Angela Arney, highlights
the problems involved when two single parents fall in love
and decide to combine family forces. In *Harte's Gold*, by
Jane Toombs, the no-nonsense single heroine faces a
different sort of family problem: how to protect her
susceptible grandmother from being conned when a film
company rents their ranch and she has her doubts about
the attractive leading man.

Whatever your taste in romantic reading I hope that you
enjoy this month's *Scarlet* selections.

Till next month,

Sally Cooper

SALLY COOPER,
Editor-in-Chief – *Scarlet*

MARGARET CALLAGHAN

WILDE AFFAIR

Enquiries to:
Robinson Publishing Ltd
7 Kensington Church Court
London W8 4SP

First published in the UK by Scarlet, 1997

A copy of the British Library Cataloguing in
Publication data is available from the British Library

ISBN 1-85487-983-9

Printed and bound in the EC

10 9 8 7 6 5 4 3 2 1

CHAPTER 1

She disliked him on sight. Tall, too good-looking to be true, and the laughing, smiling centre of attention. Dark hair, brushed straight back at the temples, with one long, rebellious lock falling casually across his forehead, giving a rakish look to his appearance that was much too casual to be anything but contrived, Stevie decided waspishly, and with the sort of heavy-lidded eyes that would lull the unwary into a sense of false security. Not that Stevie Cooper was unwary. Twenty-six and convent-qualified, should she ever feel in need of taking up the option, she wasn't so much pitied by her friends as the focus of their well-meaning though misguided attention . . .

'Stevie, be a darling. Come and meet James . . .' Or John, or Jeremy, or Jake. Even their names seemed to blur into sameness. The same build, the same uninspiring grey suits, the same fleeting hope in their eyes that their luck would have changed and tonight they'd 'score'. A quick

1

fumble of fingers along with that snifter of brandy, a hot, wet mouth covering hers, and then wham, bam, thank you ma'am.

Only Stevie wasn't playing. Ever. Not a difficult resolution, given the tangible reminder of Rosa, tucked up safe and sound in bed by now, Stevie decided, automatically checking her watch and smiling at the thought. Easy to make, easy to keep, despite the optimistic meddlings of her friends. Dinner parties . . .

Stevie scowled, didn't realize she'd focused her mind on the dark-haired man until he glanced up, his gaze crossing to Stevie, looking through her rather than at her, she decided. The jolt to her stomach was a physical blow, and, more unnerved than she'd care to admit, she tossed him a glance of pure defiance before spinning on her heels and following her nose.

'Need a hand?'

'Stevie! Thank heavens.' Hot and flustered, Lorna swung round, the relief in her eyes tangible. 'Take your pick,' she entreated, waving a frantic hand. 'The starters are ready for the table, the potatoes need creaming and the water in the steamer is sure to be boiling dry. But no –'

She pulled up, absent-mindedly offered her cheek for the kiss Stevie obligingly gave. 'On second thoughts, grab yourself a drink and pop upstairs and rescue Tom. Little madam, Kelly, is refusing to go to sleep,' she explained. 'And the doting father has promised another story. I could

2

wring his neck,' she tagged on evilly. 'He knows full well I'm useless at making gravy, so if he doesn't show his face in the next five minutes, you can tell him from me, I'll be forced to open a packet.'

'An empty threat if ever I heard one.' Upstairs Tom grinned, completely unrepentant, when he heard the message. 'Convenience food at a Lorna Deighton party? She'd never live it down. Five minutes,' he told the shiny-faced Kelly as he leaned across to kiss her, 'and then Aunty Stevie is coming down to eat. Five minutes, miss, and then sleepy-byes.'

Chance would be a fine thing, Stevie decided, logging the angelic smile Kelly bestowed on her father. Yet as the story unfolded, and Little Red Riding Hood's future began to seem secure, leaden lids began to lose the battle.

Stevie slowed down, allowed her voice to trail away, pulled her mind back to reality. Dinner parties. Purgatory. Small talk. And as for the man she'd soon be sitting next to . . .

A Tom find or a Lorna find? she mused, hoping for the first. More lively. More likely to be simply passing through, a couple of days on business and he'd never be seen again, unlike the stream of Lorna's young hopefuls, who seemed to view Stevie as the cream in the after-dinner coffee.

Swirling her wine around the glass, she let an image take shape. Dark-haired, dark-eyed, and the laughing, smiling centre of attention. Certainly lively, she would allow. Attractive too, if you liked your men to come with a hint of Latin blood. But, since Stevie didn't like men at all, period, not worth worrying about. Only she was.

Disconcerting. Illogical too. And, banishing the image with a massive surge of will, she took the steady rise and fall of the bed clothes as a hint that she should move.

Standing, stretching, listening, *stalling*, she supposed, more than happy to sit and watch, sit and think, she reached across to kiss the warm forehead and then froze, the hairs on the nape of her neck rising like the hackles of a cat.

'I was reliably informed you'd be hiding away up here.' A strong voice, velvet undertones. But she'd been wrong about the Latin influence. British through and through, and well-heeled British at that, she realized, wheeling round to face him.

The sudden surge of heat as their eyes locked was an absurd overreaction. 'Oh?'

He grinned, stepped forward, offered his hand. 'Jared Wilde. Or in this case, Miss Cooper, the Big Bad Wolf himself. There's a glaringly empty place at the dinner table and the pleasure of seeing you down has fallen to me.'

'Thank you.' Ignoring the outstretched hand, Stevie swung past.

The touch on her arm pulled her up short and she dropped her gaze to the fingers that detained her, long, tapering, tanned, standing out against the cream of her freckled skin. For a wild, illogical moment she saw the same hands cupping her breasts, and blushed to the roots of her hair.

Smothering the panic, she angled her head in enquiry.

'My aftershave?' he queried dryly. 'Or, let me guess, Little Red Riding Hood prefers her men on the meek and mild side?'

'Maybe Little Red Riding Hood prefers men who don't stand and eavesdrop,' Stevie told him curtly, annoyed he'd been listening, watching, and even more annoyed to discover that her early-warning system had for once let her down. 'Maybe,' she told him crisply, 'Little Red Riding Hood prefers to choose her own men. Maybe Little Red Riding Hood doesn't need a man, any man, and furthermore, I can assure you, she doesn't need escorting down the stairs of a house she knows almost as well as her own.'

'Why?'

'Why what?'

'Why reject the hand of friendship? Good food, good wine, and a hour or two of pleasant conversation.' He shrugged. 'If I can make the effort for Tom and Lorna, surely you can.'

A lesson in manners? And from a perfect stranger at that. It was Stevie's turn to shrug. 'You're right. My apologies, Mr Wilde. It's good of you to make the effort. But then Lorna,' she informed him crisply, pointedly shaking free, 'has a habit of twisting the unwary around her

5

little finger, along with one or two other endearing traits I'll leave you to discover for yourself. In the meantime, since we're keeping Tom and Lorna waiting, lead on.'

'You don't like me.'

Statement, not question.

Stevie blushed again at the expression on his face, part amazement, part amusement, because either way, she realized, he didn't give a damn. Well, he wouldn't, would he? she silently derided. Tall, powerfully built, too good-looking to be true, he'd be used to women falling at his feet, would view the one that got away as the exception that proved the rule. And, with the female world his oyster, no need to waste time on lost causes.

A lost cause? Stevie? One of Lorna's waifs and strays? she wondered, hearing the words in her mind: '*Poor Stevie. It's not that she doesn't like men, you understand. And you'd be doing me a favour, darling . . .*'

A taste of her own medicine. If it was true. If. She shrugged again. Like this devastating man, she really didn't care one way or the other. But, since he had asked a question, it would be the height of bad manners not to respond.

'*Like* you?' she challenged dryly. 'With the sum total of our acquaintance adding up to a whole five minutes, I haven't had time to form an impression. Whilst *you*,' she couldn't resist needling, 'have the advantage of five minutes' covert observation.'

6

'Hardly covert, since I was standing in the open doorway large as life,' he demurred, spreading his hands. 'Believe it or not, I was simply biding my time. Children – and the perils of moving too soon. I've done it myself often enough – didn't want to spoil your efforts by even breathing out of turn.'

'How very considerate,' Stevie scorned, relieved to discover he was married. No ring, her darting eyes noted. A trusting wife? Now if he was Stevie's –

Impossible thought, purged in an instant.

'If you like,' he agreed tersely. 'But, with that exquisite meal of Lorna's rapidly getting cold, we can argue the finer points of my motives from the comforts of the table. Come along, Stevie,' he urged politely, offering an arm. 'If we linger any longer, that roomful of people might just begin to wonder why.'

'Hardly,' Stevie bit out, but, since they *were* horribly late, she placed her hand gingerly in the crook of his arm and matched him step for silent step across the landing, down the stairs and the interminable length of the hallway.

'Stevie! Jared! At last!'

A dozen sets of eyes swivelled in their direction as Lorna crossed to meet them, linking arms with each of them and drawing them back across the room.

A knowing smirk from Jared, a smile of defiance from Stevie, who took the seat that he held with an ungracious murmur of thanks.

Shaking her napkin onto her lap, she glanced the length of the table, caught an envious glance from another of her friends and swallowed a wry smile. Poor Dee, itching to catch Jared's eye and yet forced to listen politely while the man on her right held forth. How did it go again? 'Good food, good wine, and an hour of two of pleasant conversation'? Well, two out of three wasn't bad, wasn't even for the want of Jared trying – trying to provoke her, she quickly discovered, refusing to bite – and yet Stevie's curt replies didn't throw him in the least.

'More wine, Ginge?'

Ginge. A childhood nickname she'd early learned to ignore. She forced a smile. 'Thank you, Jet. Or was it Joey?' she mused, with an exaggerated play at concentration. 'Jason? Jacob? Jeremiah?' she added, wrinkling her brow. 'Joseph? Japeth? Goodness, how annoying. How embarrassing,' she lied, completely unrepentant, and then, green eyes dancing as they locked with his, 'Sorry, Jet, I guess it's clean slipped my mind.'

'You're right, I deserved that.' A surprise concession as he filled her glass, angled his own in a toast. 'To first impressions?' he suggested, black eyes oozing challenge. 'And the delights of proving them right – or wrong.'

'Heads you win, tails you can't lose, huh?' Stevie drawled, catching his drift.

'I never lose,' he informed her solemnly. 'But

8

you're a bright girl; you'll work it out for yourself in time.'

My, my – compliments from Jared. Things were looking up. 'Since you won't be around for me to judge,' she retorted matter-of-factly, 'I'll just have to take your word for it, hey, Jet?'

'Jared. And if I hadn't intended sticking around in the first place, believe me, Stevie, wild horses wouldn't stop me rising to that particular challenge.'

'What challenge?' Stevie asked, instantly wary, taking a sip of the crisp white wine and allowing it to sit on her tongue.

He grinned, spread his hands. 'Like I said, you're a bright girl; you'll –'

'Work it out for myself?' she interrupted dryly, crumpling the napkin into a ball and dropping it casually on the table. 'Well, maybe I could at that – always assuming I could be bothered.'

'Oh, but you will,' he informed her, eyes bottomless pools Stevie could happily drown in. 'And you shall. On both counts.'

Promises, promises, Stevie jeered, only silently, swinging away. Paired for dinner they might have been, but as far as Stevie was concerned the pleasure was all Jared's.

Determined to escape before Lorna could chivvy them into shuffling around the minute square of parquet mockingly dubbed the dance floor, Stevie headed straight for the garden. Antisocial, maybe, but a welcome snatch of peace – and if footsteps inevitably followed at least they were familiar.

'You should be so lucky,' Dee chided lightly, taking a long and satisfying pull on a cigarette, her most recent resolution to 'pack it in once and for all' having gone the way of the previous dozen. 'A hunk like Jared Wilde on the loose and I draw the short straw. You can take it from me, Tom's new business partner could bore the salt and pepper into submission.'

'Prospective new business partner,' Stevie corrected, shuffling across to make room on the swing chair. 'And if I'd known I'd have happily traded places. Still, next time hunky Mr Wilde homes into view, I'll count it a pleasure to make the introductions. But a word of caution in your shell-like. He'll eat even you for breakfast.'

'Here's hoping,' Dee retorted, blue eyes dancing. 'Well, come on, then,' she chivvied brightly. 'Don't keep it to yourself. What have you discovered?'

'About Mr Popularity? Hardly a thing,' Stevie conceded. 'Just a hint that he's not as footloose and fancy-free as he'd have a girl believe. Oh, yes –' She smiled grimly. 'He's convinced he's God's gift to women.'

'Here's one who wouldn't be complaining. Engaged?' Dee probed, eyes narrowing. 'Not married?' she groaned as Stevie's smile broadened. 'Oh, Stevie, are you sure?'

'Well, not in so many words,' Stevie allowed. 'But –'

'Precisely. And he wasn't wearing a ring –'

'Not that you'd made a point of looking,' Stevie cut in dryly.

'Since a girl can't afford to look a gift horse in the mouth, it doesn't hurt to be prepared.'

'For what? A quick kiss and a fumble if he condescends to see you home? A tumble between the sheets if you fall for the age-old patter? Oh, Dee,' Stevie wailed good-naturedly, 'will you never learn?'

'Nothing ventured, nothing gained,' she pointed out tartly. 'And it wouldn't hurt you to let a man into your life once in a while.'

'Nothing ventured, nothing lost,' Stevie contradicted. 'And that definitely goes for my self-respect.'

'But it isn't your self-respect you're terrified of losing,' Dee reminded her slyly.

'So it isn't,' Stevie agreed, smiling widely. 'But in a democratic society, Dee, that's one decision that's mine and mine alone. No man, no sex, no complications.'

'Precious little fun, too,' Dee pointed out.

'I'm happy enough,' Stevie declared, draining her glass. 'And don't forget, there's Rosa to think about.'

'Exactly. And maybe Rosa needs a man about the house just as much as you.'

'You're not seriously suggesting I grab myself a man, any man, to provide a father for Rosa?'

Dee shrugged. 'It's – just a thought,' she allowed. 'But I should have known better than to voice it.'

'Delia Fields, you're impossible. For two pins I'd –'

'Smile sweetly and make the introductions as promised,' Dee hissed, driving an elbow into Stevie's ribs and all but robbing her of speech.

A shadow fell over them – six feet three inches of dynamism.

'Hiding away in the shadows, Stevie?' Jared drawled, with barely a glance at Dee despite the obscene flutter of lashes. 'Lorna was wondering where you'd got to.'

'And the Big Bad Wolf offered to track me down? How kind. But you needn't have worried. As you can see, Dee was looking after me. I don't believe you two have met – Delia Fields, Jared Wilde.' Jumping up, she waved a hand to the space left behind on the cushions. 'Sit down, Jared,' she entreated silkily. 'Duty over, why not make yourself comfy and swap a few notes with Dee? Believe it or not, you two have one hell of a lot in common.'

And with Dee's latest marriage heading for the divorce courts, hunky Jared Wilde might just have met his match. Irresistible thought.

Stevie grinned, skirting the lounge, with its shuffling, dancing couples, and heading instead for the peace and quiet of the kitchen.

'Stevie.' Lorna swallowed the nugget of cheese she'd been nibbling. 'There you are. You must have missed Jared. He was afraid you'd gone without saying goodbye.'

'Which I might, if a certain so-called friend doesn't stop meddling in my love-life.'

'Love-life? Hmm. Sounds hopeful. You and Jared hit it off, then?'

'Like oil and water. Sorry to disappoint you, but it was daggers drawn before we reached the table. And I'd thank you to remember what happened the last time you tried your hand at the dating game.'

'Ah, yes, Peter.' Lorna looked thoughtful. 'A moonlight serenade from the garden. Very romantic. You should have been flattered.'

'Hardly. And in the middle of December the poor chap nearly froze to death.' Literally, as it happened, since he'd been carted off to hospital with mild hypothermia. 'And since this man's married,' Stevie reminded her, scowling, 'you of all people ought to know better.'

'Married?' It was an absent-minded echo, and the task of hooking bits of cork from a newly opened bottle was a temporary diversion and not entirely successful, Stevie observed, fishing the offending debris from the glass Lorna slid in front of her. 'What on earth gives you that idea?'

'Are you telling me he's not?' Stevie enquired, the hem of her dress riding up as she hitched her bottom onto one of the high-legged stools. Daringly short to start with, it fitted like a glove, hugged the curve of breast and waist before skimming hips and thighs and ending an anything but demure six inches above her knees. Red, to match the colour of her short, feathered hair, and just the sort of vivid shade she ought to avoid like the plague. But a girl had to live dangerously sometimes, and since she had ruled men out of the equation . . .

'Not according to Tom. He's as eligible as you are, and just as picky, apparently.'

'Wrong, Lorna. I'm not picky; I'm just playing safe. Men – and men like Jared Wilde in particular – simply don't figure in any of my plans.'

'No.' Lorna shrugged, smiled, shrugged again. 'But you can't blame a girl for hoping.'

'You and Dee both. Talking of whom . . .' She paused, shrugged and grinned in turn. 'Going on the evidence so far, I'd say they're well matched.'

'Oh, Stevie, you haven't –?'

'Thrown them together? Why not? It's no more than you were doing to me.'

'Ah, yes, but you're not about to ditch husband number two.'

'Sounds a perfect match. He's a predatory male; Dee's an optimistic female.'

'While you –'

A sudden blast of noise from the lounge swallowed Lorna's retort. Unrepentant, Stevie grinned and raised her glass at Tom as he quickly closed the door behind him.

'Oh, yes? Time for a gossip?' he enquired good-naturedly giving Stevie's shoulders an affectionate hug as he squeezed by *en route* for the fridge. 'And whose ears are burning this time?'

'Not yours, my pet,' Lorna assured him pertly. 'Which is all you need worry about. And for your information, it wasn't so much gossip as girls' talk.'

'"A rose by any other name . . ."' he pointed out tartly. 'But I know when I'm not wanted. Give me a couple of minutes to open some extra bottles and I'll pop upstairs to check on Kelly.'

'No –' Stevie was down off her perch in an instant. 'Let me. You're busy with guests, and at this time of night, five minutes' peace with my goddaughter is my idea of bliss.'

No noise, no small talk, no effort. Yet, put like that, kind of selfish, Stevie decided, standing at the end of the bed and watching the steady rise and fall of the duvet. Selfish? Self-contained maybe, with Rosa giving her life its focus, but selfish? Surely not.

Rosa. Stevie sighed. A man about the house. Given Rosa's recent spate of questions, it had been a strangely perceptive remark from Dee. Just the first of the hurdles, Stevie supposed, a child's natural curiosity. And, since the other children in her class at school were blessed with the full complement of parents, it was hardly surprising Rosa was confused. But for Stevie to find herself a man, any man, to provide a father for Rosa was nothing short of absurd.

15

'I thought I'd find you hiding away up here.'

She swung round, glad of the subdued light to mask the sudden surge of colour to her cheeks.

'I – simply came to check up on Kelly,' she pointed out coolly. His uncanny knack of sneaking up on her was beginning to turn into a habit.

'A broody female, no less. Am I supposed to be impressed?'

'No more than I am with your arrogant assumption that everything a woman does is with the sole intention of impressing a man.'

'You mean it isn't?'

'Strangely enough, Mr Wilde, no. Not this woman, at least.'

'No.' He smiled, moved away from the door where he'd been lounging and joined her at the foot of the bed, his nearness unnerving. 'But you were hiding.'

Statement, not question. Those heavy-lidded eyes switched from the sleeping child to Stevie, in a strange, probing glance that touched a chord somewhere deep inside.

'Just snatching a moment's peace,' she acknowledged. 'Five minutes and then back to the serious business of enjoying life. How does it go again – good food, good wine and an hour or two of pleasant conversation?'

'Which you find irksome?'

'Let's just say, it all depends on the company. Now, left to my own devices –'

'You'd avoid me like the plague? But the lovely Miss Fields –'

'Mrs, actually, for the next few weeks at least. And what Dee does is Dee's concern. She's a big girl; she can take care of herself.'

'And you can't? Is that what you're saying?'

'Hardly, Mr Wilde, since I'm holding my own with the Big Bad Wolf himself – your description, not mine,' she reminded him sweetly.

'I simply took my cue from the story you read so prettily. Now had it been Goldilocks –'

'You'd be giving Dee the third degree instead of me?'

'Hardly the third degree, Ginge. But you're sure as hell one prickly little lady. Now why, I wonder?'

'Then wonder no longer. Just take it from me, it's nothing personal, *Jet*.'

'Fine. No offence taken. But you stick to Jared and I'll stick to Stevie. Agreed?'

'For the whole of the next five minutes?' Stevie shrugged. 'Sure. Why not?'

'And then?'

'And then what?' she stalled, instantly wary.

He checked his watch. 'It's five to twelve. What happens when the clock strikes midnight?'

'Why, Cinderella's coach shrinks out of sight and the handsome prince turns back into a toad.'

'Not my problem,' he insisted. 'I'm the Big Bad Wolf, remember?'

17

Stevie smiled despite herself. 'So you are.'

'So?'

'So?'

'Does Little Red Riding Hood disappear in a puff of smoke at midnight?'

'You're the expert on fairy tales,' she reminded him. 'You tell me.'

'With my luck,' he conceded wryly, 'I'd be the one going up in smoke.'

'Or losing your head to the axe-man.'

'Ah, yes. But then this wolf is a very rare Italian breed. You can take it from me, all those run-of-the-mill endings simply don't apply.'

Italian. She'd been right, then. Despite the perfect British accent there was more than a hint of the Latin about him.

Stevie stiffened, her lips tightening in unconscious disapproval. He had it all. Lashings of money, going by the surfeit of evidence: hand-tailored suit, hand-made leather shoes, solid gold cufflinks peeping from the sleeves of a shirt that had probably cost a month's worth of Stevie's money. Good looks. And even more lashings of charm.

Italian. Somewhere along the way. No wonder she'd disliked him on sight. A hot-blooded Italian.

'The most wonderful lovers in the world,' Mae had insisted – beautiful, clever Mae, who'd had the world at her feet and could have taken her pick of men. Until she'd made the fatal mistake of giving away her heart. The most wonderful man in the world: handsome, rich – and married.

Stevie closed her eyes, squeezing back the tears. The memories were washing over her: the weeks of hell persuading Mae to come home, her sister's shock appearance, the once beautiful face ravaged by hate and neglect, the hellish three months following Rosa's birth, and then –

'Stevie? Stevie? What is it? Stevie, tell me what's wrong.'

A hand on her arm; a man's hand. Skin on skin, the touch searing. 'No!' She shrank from the touch, her voice echoing round the room, disturbing Kelly who murmured, turned, settled, giving Stevie a precious few moments to pull herself together. The past. Over and done with. She'd rebuilt her life and she was happy, and yet right now she hated this man with every fabric of her being.

Dashing the tears away with an impatient sweep of her hand, she angled her head, caught a hint of concern in those dark velvet pools and returned his gaze with a glance of pure venom.

'No,' she repeated frigidly. 'Leave me alone. Don't say a word and most definitely don't touch me. Are you listening, Mr Wilde? Don't *ever* touch me again. Understand?'

He shrugged, the handsome features hardening, his lazy gaze sweeping the length of her, down over the swell of breasts that tightened with an ache she stubbornly refused to acknowledge. Down again, logging the cut of the dress, the generous expanse of skin beyond the daring hemline; down one long, slender leg, back up the other in a slow and insolent appraisal every bit as devastating as the touch of skin on skin. And Stevie trembled, felt a sudden dampness at her groin, and wanted to shout her denials from the rooftops.

No. No. No. It couldn't happen. Not to Stevie. Not in an instant. Want. Need. A body's needs. The needs that must have sent Mae to her death. Stevie's need. No!

'No.' Generous lips curled in contempt. 'As it happens, I don't understand. Unless – ah, yes! Why not?' Another long, lazy appraisal. Stevie's breasts tightened, nipples jutting through the fabric of her dress as she fought the urge to fold her arms. 'I can look, but I can't touch, is that it?' he asked. 'Stevie Cooper's warped idea of a game. Flaunt the goods in the flimsiest of wrappings and then scream blue murder when a man misreads the signals? Look – but don't touch?'

An eyebrow raised in silent enquiry, a grim smile, a nod. 'Well, for your information,' he sneeringly conceded, 'touching you was the last thing on my mind. You can take it from me, I like my women to dress with a degree of restraint you clearly wouldn't recognize if it hit you in the face.'

'Only I'm not.'

'Not what?'

'Your woman. Never have been, never will be.'

A careless shrug of powerful shoulders. 'Never have been, never will be,' he parodied cruelly. 'Suits me.'

'Maybe so, Jared Wilde,' Stevie acknowledged tightly, crying inside but damned if she'd let it show. 'But it suits me even better. For your information, *mister*,' she all but spat, 'I like my men to come with a touch of finesse you clearly wouldn't recognize if it was delivered to your table on a solid gold plate.'

'Men? As in plural, Stevie?' Another raised brow, another insulting sweep of her body with those mocking dark brown eyes, a pursing of lips as he whistled under his breath. 'Yes, I suppose it would be. In which case, my dear, the men around her must be sadly lacking in taste.'

'You bastard.'

'A compliment from Stevie? My, things are looking up. Touched a nerve, did I?' he hissed, closing the gap between them in two easy strides. 'Look, but don't touch. And who the hell do you think you're kidding?'

And before she had a chance to fathom his intentions, Jared reached out, snatching at her arms and pulling her against him, the heat of his body driving the breath from her lungs.

Devastating. A river of molten lava flooding her veins. No, no, no! her mind shrieked as Stevie battled for control, clamping her lips together in an effort to deny him. Only Jared knew, and Jared

21

responded, the growl in the back of his throat both thrilling and shocking, and yet providing the spur Stevie needed to resist, to repulse, to deny.

Deny. How to deny when Jared was stronger than she? And Jared was simply playing games, scoring points – unlike Stevie, who, fool that she was, hadn't the sense – or the shame – to curb her reactions. Because she wanted him. Because she hadn't the guile to pretend, the strength to deny.

Yet as Stevie slumped against him, parted her lips, craving the touch of his hands, his mouth, his tongue, her need was so exquisite that Jared's gasp of surprise simply didn't register.

CHAPTER 2

'Stevie?'

Tom's voice, part query, part concern, with a hint of something else Stevie couldn't quite place – would have placed in a trice had it been Lorna sitting in front of her. Speculation. Pure and simple. Only she wasn't, and it wasn't. But at least the idea served to banish the shadows.

'Sorry, Tom. I must have been miles away.'

'So I gathered. A late night?' he probed slyly. 'Or did Rosa's cough keep you awake?'

'Neither. Would you believe a headache from too much wine the night before that?' she riposted, catching his drift. Speculation indeed. She might have known. Stevie swallowed a smile, returned his gaze without so much as a shimmer of an eyelash.

'Hmm. I don't suppose you and Jared managed to hit it off well enough to –?'

'No, Tom,' she cut in dryly. 'Since the male of the species doesn't normally show an interest, I don't suppose you *do* suppose. Which means that matchmaking wife of yours is fishing.'

'An innocent enough hobby, surely?' he teased, having the grace to look ashamed. 'And, heaven knows, Lorna needs something to occupy her mind, keep her from spending my money as fast I can earn it.'

'Your problem, not mine,' she reminded him lightly. 'And you don't need me to point out the answer to that one.'

'No. With Kelly settled at school, Lorna's bored rigid, and it shows.'

'So?'

'So . . .' Tom shrugged, pulled a wry face. 'It's not as easy as it sounds. Mummy and Daddy don't approve of their only daughter being forced to earn a living like the rest of us.'

Stevie's eyebrows rose. 'In this day and age?'

'You know the Hunters. It's a family tradition. The male of the species earns enough to keep the lady of the house in the style she was born to, and since Lorna wouldn't dream of hurting so much as a fly —'

'Heaven forbid she'd risk rocking any boats. Pity she doesn't apply the same logic to her friends,' she added tartly. 'For if it's a wedding, bedding and christening she's planning, yours truly is about to jump ship.'

Tom grinned. 'I'll break it to her gently, then.'

'If you like. But while you're at it, do us both a

24

favour, hey? Tell her once and for all she's wasting her time?'

'And spoil her fun? Oh, no! One of us has to live with her, remember?'

'You should be so lucky. Which brings me neatly to the point. You and Lorna. Eight years into a marriage and as much in love as the day you first met. But when it comes to fairy tale endings,' she reminded him, 'the rest of us aren't so lucky.'

Fairy tales. Little Red Riding Hood fighting off the Big Bad Wolf. Leastways, that was the theory. Only prissy Stevie Cooper had fluffed her lines completely, kissing Jared, touching Jared, wanting Jared . . .

Jared's mouth on hers, his tongue sweeping through into the secret, sensitive corners, swirling, entwining, the currents of heat pulsing out from every point of contact. And Stevie drowning, her mind refusing to function, just her body, each and every inch, reacting to the touch, the taste, the smell of him.

'Stevie, oh, God, Stevie,' he'd moaned, nibbling the corners of her mouth and moving down, with devastating kisses that feathered the stem of her neck, nuzzled the hollow of her throat. Stevie's head had swayed from side to side like a swan performing a love dance.

Madness. A flare of emotion, a haunting sound that had come from Stevie herself, she'd realized, whimpers of pleasure and pain in the back of her throat. Pleasure because his hands were ranging her body, stroking the soft underswell of breasts that needed no support yet ached for the touch of a man's hands, a man's fingers. Exquisite pain – the fleeting brush of thumbs against her nipples a bittersweet denial of her need.

No! No! No! Her mind had screamed as the hands moved on, into the curve of waist and over the swell of hips, with an impatient Jared tugging her hard against him. Hard. Oh, God! Jared wanted her every bit as badly, she'd realized, and the mix of desire and fear had been an intoxicating cocktail.

Hands and lips exploring, touching, branding. Jared's mouth nuzzling the valley at the vee of her dress while a shameless Stevie had prayed he'd reach for the zipper, allowing hands, fingers, mouth the access she craved. And craved. Jared enticing, denying as his mouth moved on, the long, lazy journey back to her mouth driving her insane.

Pause to nuzzle the hollow of her throat, delicious excursions around the stem of her neck, the trail of devastation all-consuming. Ear to ear and back again, feathering the line of her jaw and then upwards, less a journey than a pilgrimage. Stevie's mouth the grail, the cup of pleasure – pleasure denied, pleasure to come. Kiss, taste, savour, kiss again, and oh, God, how she'd wanted him.

A surge of panic as Jared had pulled away. Stevie's eyelids snapping open in alarm. The panic subsiding as their glances had locked, the message flowing between them, currents of heat flowing between them.

Not a word, not a sound. Just the soft, gentle rhythm of the sleeping child, and man and woman alone – alone with a knowledge too shocking to admit. She wanted him. Heaven help her, this man she barely knew, yet hated with an instinct as sure as life itself, had touched a secret chord, and, like a genie emerging from a bottle, the woman within the woman had blossomed into existence.

Only she mustn't. Allow a man close enough to touch, to hurt, to wreak havoc in mind and body? Follow Mae down the long hard road to ruin? Impossible. Pitifully easy, she was beginning to think, but that didn't mean she had to give in to the impulse. All she needed was the strength to deny, to resist.

Easier said than done with her body tingling from the touch, the taste, the feel of him, and yet the moment Jared had dropped his gaze, dipped his head to kiss her again, Stevie had seized her chance.

'No!' Hands snapping downwards, breaking the hold, the force of impact knocking Stevie off balance. Thrown against the wall with its frieze of fairy tale characters, Stevie had smiled, an ironic twist of lips that Jared had caught, misconstrued, condemned, his own features hardening into granite.

'You teasing little witch.'

'My, my – compliments from Jared.'

Scorn. The key to survival. Stay strong. Deny him, deny herself the luxury of slumping to the floor, pulling up her knees, dropping her head onto those knees and crying as she'd never cried before.

Scorn from Stevie, contempt from Jared. Because she'd denied him? she wondered. Or because Jared had proved his point? Look, but don't touch? Only Jared had looked; Jared had touched; Jared had tasted.

A careless shrug of shoulders. 'Like I said, lady, it's all a matter of restraint. You don't look it, you don't dress it, you sure as hell don't act it.' He gave a contemptuous snap of the fingers. 'Jail bait.'

'Trust a man to read things that way,' Stevie jeered, the need to repay the insult keeping her strong. 'And how typical, how boringly predictable. So much for progress,' she sneered. 'On the eve of the third millennium the old double standard rears its head.

'Nice girls don't – is that what you're implying? Don't breathe, don't live, don't respond. Don't give in without an elaborate show of resistance – or the dubious promise of a shiny band of gold? But if that makes me a tramp,' she acknowledged tersely, 'at least my reactions were honest. Talking of which, where does that leave you? Or doesn't it count when it's the male of the species in danger of losing control?'

'Lose control? With you? No chance,' he sneered.

'Oo-oh! A liar as well as a cad,' Stevie drawled, more hurt than she cared to acknowledge.

'If you were a man, I'd knock you flat on your back for that snide remark.'

'A liar, a cad and a bully, no less,' Stevie countered coolly. 'But if you were even half a man, Mr Wilde, you wouldn't force your attentions where they're clearly not wanted.'

'So who's lying now?'

'Not me, and that's for sure, since I'm the one who called a halt.'

'Ah, yes. So you did. Eventually.'

'Meaning?'

'You responded. And sooner rather than later, I seem to recall.' He smiled grimly, pointedly checked his watch. 'Time. Amazing how it flies when you're enjoying yourself.'

'If you say so.'

'I don't need to. You gave yourself away, Ginge.'

'Your opinion, or mine?' she queried politely.

'Irrelevant. The evidence speaks for itself.'

'And the mighty Jared Wilde is judge, jury and prosecution lawyer all rolled into one? Let me guess. Guilty on all counts?'

'Only one. You wanted me. Fact.'

'Hogwash. You kissed me. If I responded – *if*,' she repeated, 'it was an easy mistake to make. After all, you're quite an expert.'

29

'Thank you.'

'It wasn't said to flatter you.'

'I didn't think it was. But you can't have it all ways. And, since it takes one to know one . . .'

'I'm not sure I like what you're implying.'

'I bet you don't. Expertise,' he reminded her slyly. 'You're not exactly lacking in practice yourself – hey, Stevie?'

'Are you asking me or telling me?'

'Simply making an observation, my dear.'

'Precisely. An opinion. Your opinion. Well, *that* for your opinion,' Stevie scorned with a contemptuous snap of her fingers.

'Fine.' Jared shrugged. 'Dodge the question by all means. But you can take it from me, it doesn't look good.'

'It doesn't have to. I know the truth and your opinion doesn't bear repeating.'

'I wouldn't waste my breath. Not that I'd need to.'

'Meaning?'

'Kiss and tell. That sort of news travels fast enough without . . .'

'Speculation. Gossip. Tittle-tattle. What a boring life you must lead. You surprise me, Jared.'

'Not half as much as you surprise me.'

'I can't imagine why.'

'Can't – or won't even bother trying?' he retorted.

'Same difference,' Stevie insisted. 'I don't

know, don't care, don't intend wasting time by giving it a second thought. Disappointed?' she queried slyly.

'Let's just say, mildly curious. You're stalling.'

'And you're peeved. Stevie Cooper's changed the rules of the game and that fragile male ego's been stung.'

'What game?'

Stevie waved an airy hand. 'This. You, me, the insults –'

'The kisses and cuddles?' he interrupted slyly.

'No, Jared. Not the kisses and cuddles. Believe it or not, this little lady doesn't enjoy being mauled by a perfect stranger.'

'Mauled? *Mauled*?' he repeated incredulously. 'Lady, when it comes to hitting a guy where it hurts, you sure don't miss any tricks.'

Only she did, and she had, because now Jared was teasing, his lightning change of mood lifting the hairs on the back of Stevie's neck. Dangerous. Just like the expression in those dark velvet eyes. Because Jared had moved, had closed the gap between them, his eyes fastening onto hers and refusing to allow her to look away.

And he was touching her, yet not touching, just the merest hint of connection as his hands slid into the curve of her waist and over the swell of her bottom. The swirl of thumbs at her groin was almost sheer imagination, tantalizing, teasing, tormenting. And Stevie closed her eyes, shutting out the man but not the need. Because she wanted him. Hated him, hated herself just as badly. And, oh, God, he was kissing her, kissing, touching, enflaming, and Stevie was drowning, the battle fought and lost, drowning, floating, soaring . . .

'Stevie?'

Disappointment scythed through her, Jared's features dissolving as Tom's worried face swam back into focus.

'What is it? Is it Rosa?' Tom asked. 'Is there something you're not telling me? Because if Lorna finds out you're bottling things up when she's aching to help, we'll both be facing the firing squad. Come on, girl, spill the beans, hey? Tell me what's wrong.'

Stevie smiled despite herself. 'Nothing, Tom.' Nothing she'd care to reveal, at least. 'Rosa's fine. Everything's fine. Honestly.'

Such a little white lie to cover a moment of madness. A kiss that wasn't a kiss, a touch that didn't amount to a mauling. Devastating. Yet if Stevie had been shaken, she hadn't been alone. Jared. The shock of recognition in his eyes. And if Kelly hadn't chosen that moment to cry out in her sleep –

'Hmm.' Tom looked doubtful. 'Well, if you're sure . . .'

'No need to take my word for it,' Stevie reminded him, reaching for the box file Tom had just set down. 'Since Rosa's at your house for tea, you'll be able to judge for yourself.'

'Tea? Ah, hell! The birthday party. How could I have forgotten?'

Stevie grinned, flipped open the lid, turned a critical eye on the batch of glossy photographs. 'Fair's fair,' she pointed out. 'The grown-ups had their turn on Saturday.'

'Well, that settles it,' he pronounced grumpily. 'I'm working late. And if you've half the sense you were born with, Stevie Cooper, you'll do the same.'

'And neatly back up your alibi? No can do. And if *you've* even half the sense *you* were born with, you wouldn't dream of upsetting that mild-tempered wife of yours.'

'Hell hath no fury, hmm?' Tom grinned. 'You're right. When Lorna blows, she goes up like Vesuvius. Luckily for me, it's a very rare occurrence.'

There was a knock on the door and Tom's secretary sidled in with another set of files. 'Your ten o'clock appointment has just arrived, Mr Deighton. I thought you might be busy so I've settled him in the visitors' room. Shall I show him through?'

'No, don't bother. It's one of Lorna's lame ducks, unless I'm very much mistaken, so it shouldn't take long to weigh up his potential. Women!' he muttered, heading for the door. 'Can't live with 'em, sure as hell can't live without 'em. Heads they win, tails I lose.'

Shades of Jared. And, since that was the last

thing Stevie needed just now, she pushed thoughts of Saturday evening to the back of her mind as she spread the contents of the box file across Tom's enormous desk.

She gave an unconscious nod of approval. The photographs were good, and since she'd taken them herself she was humming lightly as she sifted them into piles mentally labelled 'probable', 'possible', 'doubtful'.

Sicilian Casserole – the first in Deighton's Italian Impressions range and a far cry from the plates of watery greens and obligatory cold meats Stevie had faced day after day as a child. And, since money had been tight, turning up a fastidious nose and leaving the food to congeal had never been an option for Stevie and her sister.

Thank heavens for ready meals, Stevie decided, shuddering at the memory. But if Stevie had hated the greyness of the food, it had been Mae who'd suffered most, Mae who'd pushed the food around her plate meal after tense meal, gagging when the same untouched, unpalatable mess had been served up for breakfast, lunch and tea. Hardly surprising she'd developed anorexia. Hardly surprising –

But no, Stevie had work to do – work, ironically enough, centred on food. Stevie's own interest clearly having been triggered by the aversions Mae had never come to terms with.

Sicilian Casserole. Italian Impressions. If she could finish the mock-ups this morning, Stevie realized, pulling pencil and pad towards her, she could spend the rest of the day feeding the designs onto the computer. Italian Impressions. A taste of the Mediterranean. Sun-dried tomatoes, vibrant red and yellow peppers, baby courgettes and tiny button mushrooms with a smattering of imported olives to give the all-important flavour of authenticity.

Italian Impressions. First impressions. Jared.

Stevie smothered a sigh, allowed the pencil to drop from her fingers. It was no good. Italian Impressions. Jared Wilde. Not one of Lorna's lame ducks; she'd known that instinctively. So, given Tom's flair for marrying business and pleasure, his invitation to Jared had to have been a means to an end. Only which end? And why did that leave Stevie feeling vaguely uneasy?

Too much to do to allow thoughts of Jared to intrude. Stevie pressed on, was just putting the final touches to the layout on the page when the door swung open behind her.

' "The taste of Sicily",' she murmured, without glancing up. ' "A bouquet of flavours from the sun-kissed isle." How does that sound?'

'Perfect. But then naturally enough, Ginge, I'm somewhat biased where Italy's concerned.'

'You!' She swung round, cheeks on fire, her startled gaze colliding with Jared's vaguely amused one.

'Don't sound so surprised,' he scoffed. 'You work for Tom. It must have crossed your mind that my invitation for Saturday's party wasn't totally altruistic?'

'As it happens, no,' Stevie retorted coolly. 'With Lorna and Tom generous to a fault, I wouldn't dream of eating their food and drinking their wine whilst secretly probing their motives.' She angled her head, eyes nuggets of ice. 'Friends don't, you know.'

'A lesson in manners?' Jared probed, with more definite echoes of Saturday evening. He grinned. 'You're right, Ginge. Guests are guests, come business, pleasure or both.' Double-checking the nameplate over the door, he lazily crossed the threshold. 'Tom's expecting me. I'll make myself at home – if you don't mind?'

Stevie did, but didn't suppose it would make a ha'p'orth of difference if she said so.

Business or pleasure? she wondered, as Jared hitched a chair in much too close for comfort. And, since Tom had slyly said nothing to Stevie about Jared dropping by, his conspicuous absence, coupled with that earlier spot of fishing, bore all the hallmarks of Lorna's machinations.

'May I?' He was carefully polite, and Stevie's nod of assent was equally civil as Jared leaned across, rifled through the photographs, and unerringly matched the best with the mock-up she'd been working on. 'These are good. First rate,' he acknowledged. 'Your work, Ginge?'

Stevie nodded, too overwrought by his devastating presence to object to the use of the hated nickname.

A pursing of lips, a whistle of approval. 'I'm impressed.'

'Why?' Bristling, searching for the barb in the innocuous-sounding words.

'Why what?' he queried mildly.

'Why the surprise?' Stevie needled. 'Or don't the women in your part of the world have an input in business?'

'Since my "part of the world", as you so quaintly phrase it is – was – London,' he informed her, 'that remark couldn't be further from the truth, and furthermore it smacks suspiciously of bitchiness. But in the interests of peace I'll let it pass. This time.'

Big of him, Stevie needled, only silently. A sudden thought was occurring. Business or pleasure, client or guest, Jared's appearance spoke for itself, and in the cut-throat world of business Deighton Foods needed all the friends it could muster.

'Sicilian Casserole,' Jared echoed, flipping the photograph back onto the pile. 'How did it go again – "a bouquet of flavours from the sun-kissed isle"? A meal after my own heart,' he conceded, twisting round, pinning his gaze on Stevie. 'But in the interests of authenticity, tell me, which particular Sicilian came up with the recipe?'

'Ah.' Like a child caught out in a tiny white lie,

Stevie felt the blush rise. 'Never heard of research?' she tossed out defensively.

'I sure have. And you can take it from me, the easiest way to research this particular subject is to hop on a plane to the sun-kissed isle itself.'

'Maybe so,' Stevie agreed. 'But follow that through to its logical conclusion and there wouldn't be time to develop and market the product. Believe it or not, there are cunning little aids called books – recipe books.' Not to mention a whole host of computer software, videos, cooking demonstrations and 'secret' recipes handed down the generations by word of mouth. Though not in her particular family, Stevie recalled, scowling.

'Logic, huh? A rare female attribute. If I wasn't impressed to start with, I'd be impressed now.'

And if I wasn't immune to such blatant soft soap, Stevie silently derided, I'd be flattered.

'Tom's running late,' she murmured crisply, scraping back her chair and shuffling the photos back into the box. 'If you'll excuse me, I'll put these away and tell him you've –'

'There's no need to bother on my account.'

A hand on her wrist. The heat of his fingers searing.

'I –'

'In a hurry?' Jared probed, 'Or running away?'

'At the risk of sounding rude,' she pointed out coolly, 'one of us has work to do.'

'All work and no play,' he teased. 'And another

five minutes won't hurt. Unless you really are running away?'

'From you? Don't be ridiculous.'

Jared nodded, black eyes loaded with challenge. 'Fine. In that case, Stevie, why not sit down and prove it?'

'Nothing to prove,' she pointed out sweetly, willing herself to believe it. 'But if it makes you happy . . .' Pulling free, she flounced down into the chair, rubbing at her wrist where his fingers had bit. 'Coffee?' she offered belatedly, spotting the jug simmering on the side. 'Or, since the sun's high in the sky, a snifter of something stronger? Brandy?'

'Only if you'll join me,' he murmured politely.

'I never drink in the middle of the day,' she countered primly.

'Never, ever?' he challenged incredulously. 'Not even when you're on holiday. Stevie?'

'I –'

'Let me guess – you don't believe in taking holidays?' he interrupted dryly. 'And that's just the latest in a line of intriguing admissions. So what have we learned so far? Doesn't like men,' he mused annoyingly, raising a hand and counting on his fingers, 'or holidays. Or dinner parties. Or alcoholic drinks in the middle of the day. On the other hand, despite a figure to rival a beanpole, the lady enjoys her food. Has a soft spot for kids, too, yet is definitely single, going by the ringless fingers. And as for her dress sense . . .'

39

He paused, allowing his eyes to travel her body, over the tailored suit she wore to work, the crisp white blouse beneath the lightweight jacket that served to hide the give-away thrust of nipples that had a life of their own where Jared Wilde was concerned, and on to the calf length, front-buttoned skirt, which clearly met with his approval, despite the expanse of leg glimpsed through the vent. Tip to toe and back again. Jared's eyes searched her face, exploring the angles and planes with slow and deliberate thoroughness, until, inspection over, all ship-shape and satisfactory, he nodded.

'Very restrained. Very understated,' he teased, eyes dancing as they locked with hers. 'But believe me, Stevie, oh, so sexy. All in all, quite an enigma.'

'Disappointed, Mr Wilde?' Stevie challenged, unnerved to find that this man's approval should matter.

'Jared, Ginge – the name's Jared,' he lazily entreated. 'You avail yourself of mine and I promise to carve yours in words of stone upon my heart. And, no, Stevie, I'm not in the least disappointed – so far. How about you?'

'H-how about me?' she stammered, his train of thought baffling.

'First impressions,' he reminded her. 'And the delights of proving them right – or wrong. Time for a progress report. Ladies first?' he suggested politely.

Stevie shrugged, angled her head, made a pretence of considering. Stalling, she realized, her insides in a churn. Because Jared was playing games. Dangerous games. The sort of games that Mae had played. Mae and Dino. Man and woman. Love. Sex. Want. Need. Only Stevie wasn't Mae, and Stevie had no intentions of falling into the pit. Ever.

Assuming an air of concern, she leaned forward, lowered her voice, fluttered her lashes. 'Much better to wait a while,' she advised confidentially. 'I should hate to put a dent in that fragile male ego.'

'Progress indeed,' Jared allowed, a hint of a smile at the corners of his mouth. 'Two short days ago concern for my ego was the last thing on your mind. Now if you really wanted to make amends –'

'I'd be certifiably insane. You insulted me – remember?'

'A moot point, given the speed of your riposte. So why not call it quits and start again?'

'Start what again?' She was wary now, the angle of her chin unwittingly defensive.

'Us. You and me. Little Red Riding Hood and the Big Bad Wolf straight out of reform school.'

'Once a wolf, always a wolf,' she pointed out sweetly.

'Oh, no.' Jared shook his head. 'First impressions,' he chided softly. 'Either stick with them and say so, or keep an open mind. Only fair, wouldn't you say?'

'Since life isn't fair, never has been, never will be,' she pointed out, 'that's clearly a matter of opinion.' First impressions? No holds barred? Now that *would* put a dent in his ego. 'Worried, Jared?' she tossed out slyly. 'Afraid you're losing your touch? Trust a man to need constant reassurance –'

'Trust a woman to need to hedge her bets. Give a simple answer to a simple question? That'll be the day –'

'Those insecurities are showing again,' she interrupted tartly. 'But if it helps to reassure you, I'll promise to keep an open mind if you'll promise to stop hassling me.'

'Hassle? Hassle?' he repeated incredulously, pushing that rebellious lock of hair out of his eyes. 'Ah, yes, but is that hassle as in tease, torment, badger, worry, bait?' he challenged, with a lightning change of mood. 'Or hassle as in touch, stroke, caress –'

' "Maul" is the word you're looking for.'

'My definition or yours?' he bit out.

'Mine,' Stevie snapped, jumping up and towering over him – an overreaction, she knew, but if the anger and the hate helped to keep him at a distance then so much the better. 'My definition, my life, my body,' she reminded him. 'You don't look, you don't touch, you don't –'

'Precisely.' Generous lips curled in derision. 'I don't. End of conversation. You can take it from me, Miss Cooper, your life, your body and your

42

raging feminist views don't interest me one jot.'

'Which makes us quits, because you and chauvinist ways don't impress me in the least.'

Stalemate.

Not a sound, not even the tick of a clock. Just Stevie's heart thumping wildly in her breast, the noise filling her head but not her mind.

God, how she hated him. Hated Jared, hated the thought that he could hurt her. And he had. Touching her, kissing her, touching her again. And then tearing her apart with his sneering words. Jared Wilde. Devastatingly good-looking, devastatingly sharp. Dynamite. And he'd insulted her, kissed her, roused her, roused frigid Stevie Cooper, who'd vowed never to let a man close enough to steal so much as a whiff of her perfume!

Frigid Stevie Cooper, who'd discovered by chance that the man-eating mantle of the siren was a godsend. Outrageous clothes, an outrageous hairstyle and the boldest of men would instinctively back away. She'd been safe. Until now. Until Jared Wilde had walked into her life and turned it upside down. Two days. Five or six hours of turbulent give and take and he was inside her head, inside her mind.

Only she wouldn't. Follow Mae along the pathway of disaster? Oh, no. One fool in the family was more than enough.

Choking back a sob, she swung away.

'Stevie –'

'No! Don't –'

Too late. Jared had out-thought her, out-paced her, his powerful form filling the doorway, and like an animal caught in a trap Stevie froze, raised her face, caught the scent of danger and instinctively backed away.

'Stevie –'

'No!' Folding her arms, she dropped her gaze, tracing the faded pattern of the carpet beneath her feet. 'You promised. No hassles. Ever. You don't remember? Me and my feminist views don't interest you in the least. Now practise what you preach,' she hissed. 'And leave me alone.'

'If that's what you want?'

'It is, but I don't expect a man to believe it. Take a woman at her word? That will be the day.'

'My God, you're bitter,' he railed. 'Heaven knows why, unless some man's let you down –'

'No chance,' Stevie jeered. 'And that's another misconception. Sorry to disappoint you, but as far as the average woman's concerned, there's more to life than men and sex.'

'Fine.' He cut the space between them in three easy strides. 'So why the hate, the barbed wire fence around your heart?'

'As if you know – or care,' she bit out. 'Face it, Mr Wilde, you know nothing about me beyond my taste in clothes, and even that's open to debate.'

'Maybe, maybe not, but at least I'm making the effort. A complete waste of time since you refuse point-blank to meet me halfway. Stubborn, prickly, suspicious as hell – damn it all, woman, you're not being fair.'

No. Stevie swallowed hard, the anger draining away. The knowledge that Jared could be important to Tom put the past twenty minutes into perspective. She was alone in her boss's office with Jared Wilde, a powerful man, a man with influence, since he hadn't felt the need to knock. And she'd blown, could well have blown an important contract. And with business in the doldrums . . .

Emotions in turmoil, she swung away, crossed to the simmering pot of coffee.

'I'm sorry,' she murmured thickly, the words almost choking her. 'I'd no right to rant and rave. It was – rude and inhospitable,' she conceded awkwardly, pouring the coffee into delicate china cups. 'Now, let me –'

'Make amends?' he suggested softly, and Stevie gasped, froze, silently cursed his uncanny knack of moving without a sound. 'Tender a pretty apology along with that cup of coffee – strong, black and sugarless,' he informed her confidentially, with not a trace of anger or hate in the lightly spoken words, 'and maybe, just maybe, since the sun *is* high in the sky, maybe a certain fiery lady will join me in a brandy'

'But I don't –'

'Hush,' he urged as Stevie's taut nerves reached breaking point, because Jared was standing behind her, not touching, by any means, but close enough for the currents to bridge the gap – and they did, filling her with heat, filling her with dread.

Madness. The man's very presence was enough to turn her world upside down. And Stevie was afraid. And Stevie was trapped, the warm flutter of breath on the back of her neck paralyzing mind and body.

'Hush,' Jared said again. 'Just this once,' he all but crooned, 'break the habit of a lifetime and let yourself go. Forget the time and place and do what you want to do. *Want*, Stevie,' he emphasized, long tapering fingers closing round her shoulders, just as Stevie had known they would, just as Stevie had craved.

And she closed her eyes, praying for the strength to deny him, the strength to break the spell of Jared's words, Jared's devastating presence, Jared's lips nuzzling at the nape of her neck.

'Relax,' he urged. 'I won't hurt you. I promise not to touch if that's what you really want. But, oh, hell, woman,' he groaned, his arms closing round her as the last of her resistance drained away. 'Hell, woman,' he repeated, gathering her fiercely to him. 'That's one resolution I was hoping I'd never have to make.'

CHAPTER 3

'Wine, Stevie? Red or white?'

'Thank you, Tom, just a small –'

'Good heavens, no,' Jared interrupted, features impassive. 'Have you forgotten? Stevie makes it a rule never to touch alcohol in the middle of the day.'

'Is that so?' Tom's speculative gaze switched from Stevie to Jared and back again. He pursed his lips. 'Strange,' he mused. 'In all these years I've known you, Stevie, I can't say I've ever noticed.'

'Never having dined in style with me in the middle of the day,' she pointed out calmly, shooting a glance of pure defiance at the man across the table, 'that's hardly surprising. And thank you, Tom. A small glass of white would be lovely.'

Not to mention soothing. Break the habit of a lifetime and resort to drink to calm her down. Break the habit of a lifetime and let a man close enough to touch, to bruise her heart. And, since

47

the man in question was a virtual stranger, madness.

Devastating. Sipping the wine slowly, she allowed the conversation to ebb and flow around her, watching Jared through the veil of her lashes. Jared Wilde. As much of an enigma to Stevie as she seemed to him.

A business lunch, supposedly, or Tom's way of making amends for keeping Jared waiting. For dining in style it certainly was. The Prince of Wales, Southport's premier hotel, an eye-opener for Stevie, who dropped in for a drink in one of its bars semi-occasionally but had never ventured as far as the restaurant.

And, flanked by two such imposing men, was it any wonder heads had turned as she'd crossed the threshold?

Tom Deighton, her boss of the past four years, tall, blond, ruggedly good-looking, his love affair with food just beginning to show in the slight loosening at the jawline, a slackness of muscle, an expanding waistline.

And Jared Wilde, the most devastating man she'd ever had the misfortune to meet. Too good-looking for his own good, she decided, openly scowling. The thought that he'd touched her, roused her, pierced the iron shell she'd built around her heart, was anything but reassuring. For if letting any man come close was a hard fact to swallow, having this man, with his determination and his charm and his undoubted

Italian connections manage it so easily, was unthinkable.

'Isn't the wine to madam's taste? A mite too acidic, perhaps?' It was Jared, slicing through her musings, velvet eyes dancing as they locked with hers.

'On the contrary,' Stevie demurred, taking a larger sip this time and savouring the taste on her tongue. 'The wine's perfect.'

It was the company she couldn't cope with – the man opposite, whose sharp eyes missed nothing, whose sharp tongue had locked her emotions onto permanent red alert, whose hands –

But no. She needed to keep her wits, couldn't afford to allow her mind to drift as she focused on that scene cut frustratingly short by Tom's return. A tactful return? Stevie wondered.

Tom's voice, over loud and drifting through the panel long before the rattle of the handle and the subsequent creak of the hinges proclaimed his arrival – plenty of time for Jared to stifle a curse, release her, move away, giving her space easily enough but doing nothing for the turmoil in her heart. And, since he hadn't even kissed her, that was all the more ridiculous.

And, taking her cue from Jared, Stevie had swung round, proffered the rapidly cooling coffee, strong, black and sugarless, the giveaway rattle of cup on saucer thankfully going unnoticed under the bustle of Tom's arrival, Tom's apologies, Tom's unexpected invitation to lunch and point-blank refusal to allow Stevie to wriggle out of it.

Lunch with the boss – and Jared. A working lunch, and yet, with the conversation anything but, not so much a working lunch as a chance to relax. Relax? Some hope. But Jared had been right about one thing. Beanpole figure notwithstanding, Stevie enjoyed her food – wasn't about to allow overwrought nerves to come between her and a first-class meal.

First-class prices too, she would imagine – had to imagine, since her leather-bound menu didn't boast them. The feminist in Stevie was vaguely amused, vaguely annoyed and half toying with the idea of testing the maitre d's reaction by insisting on footing the bill herself. Shock. Horror. Outrage, she decided. Doubtless the same shock-horror Stevie would feel when presented with an obscene amount she couldn't hope to pay without taking out a mortgage.

But since this was Tom's treat, was clearly tax deductible, she'd savour each and every mouthful. Despite the devastating company.

'It's a seaside resort, why not try the oysters?' Jared suggested blandly, instinctively aware that Stevie was spoilt for choice. 'Florentine oysters. Oven-baked on a bed of spinach and lightly coated with a rich cheese sauce. Parmesan, naturally.'

'Oh, naturally,' Stevie echoed, shockingly afraid Jared was back to playing games. But at least with Tom cast as unofficial referee – or maybe that should be chaperon – Jared would be forced to behave. 'Heaven forbid such a prestigious hotel would resort to common or garden mousetrap,' Stevie mocked. 'Now a generous dash of Lancashire . . .'

'I wouldn't know,' Jared conceded. 'Never having sampled it. But later, perhaps. After all, when in Rome . . .'

Rome. Florence. Sicily. Was there no escape from the Italian connection? And with the great man himself a larger than life reminder, just a table width away, it was hardly surprising her nerves were in shreds.

Outwardly calm, she angled her head. 'The oysters sound divine,' she conceded. 'But I make it a rule never to touch oysters unless there's an R in the month.' And then, sensing she'd rendered him speechless, she chose to put him out of his misery. 'One of Grandma's little foibles,' she explained – only didn't explain, her features impassive.

'You are joking?' he queried politely.

'I only wish she was,' Tom conceded wryly. 'In the good old days seafood was considered a risk in the summer months and, unfortunately for business, it's a myth that refuses to lie down and die.'

'Better safe than sorry,' Stevie reminded him. 'And, with that in mind, I think I'll settle for a melt-in-the-mouth ham and cheese soufflé.'

Melt-in-the-mouth indeed. A tiny ramekin with a dusting of paprika, served on a bed of basil leaves and leaving plenty of room for the main course. Stevie stored away each and every detail: her own duckling roulade with fresh peaches, and a fan of avocado and steamed baby vegetables, Tom's ever-predictable medium rare steak, and the marinated turkey with asparagus selected by Jared.

If not traditional local fare, at least the ingredients were fresh and cooked to perfection, the service superbly discreet, and the next time Stevie consulted her watch she was amazed to find the afternoon had flown.

'Hardly worth going back to the office,' Tom decided, signalling the waiter for a second large brandy. 'Might as well call it a day and head for home. What about you, Stevie?'

'Tempting, Tom, but duty calls. The mock-ups for tomorrow. But don't let me stop you. I'll give it till six and then head over to your place to give Lorna a hand.'

'Lorna – oh hell!' He clamped his hand to his head. 'How could I have forgotten? How could you let me forget?' he railed. 'The chimpanzees' tea party. That's all I need.'

'Birthday party,' she corrected mildly. 'Your only daughter's birthday, at that. And who does the doting father think he's kidding? Besides, it wouldn't hurt to arrive home early for once.'

'I'm game if you are,' he countered.

'No can do,' Stevie insisted, completely un-repentant. 'I'm a working girl remember?'

'And I'm –'

'Heading for home like the big-hearted guy we all know and love. You can drop me off on the way,' she added automatically.

'There's no need,' Jared insisted. 'I'm heading for Preston – practically passing the door.'

'I –'

'You don't want to deprive the doting papa of a single moment of pleasure, hey, Stevie?' he reminded her, features impassive. 'Just let me settle the bill –'

'My invitation – my treat,' Tom interrupted.

'Your invitation maybe,' Jared agreed plea-santly. 'But this one's on me. My way of saying thanks for Saturday evening. Besides, it can go on my room bill.'

But of course, a mere bagatelle, a trifling matter of a cool hundred pounds or so to add to a hotel bill that would stretch as long his arm, Stevie acknowledged sourly as, ever the gentleman, Jared moved to hold her chair before leading the way back to the marble-tiled foyer, with a reluctant Tom bringing up the rear.

Pausing at the huge revolving doors to allow Tom to catch them up, Stevie caught the gleam of amusement on Jared's face and stiffened.

'Worry not, Stevie,' he teasingly reassured her. 'You won't come to any harm. The Big Bad Wolf promises not to touch.'

53

'Good. Because the Big Bad Wolf might just discover that Little Red Riding Hood has teeth. And, furthermore, she knows how to bite.'

'She knows how to kiss, too,' he tossed out absurdly. 'I don't suppose –'

'You don't suppose right,' she hissed. But, annoyingly enough, Jared simply smiled.

'No, Lorna, he hasn't asked me out. And he didn't ask me to lunch either. I don't know what that man of yours has been saying, but you can take it from me it's mere speculation – speculation, I might add, cunningly fuelled by his matchmaking wife. Understand?'

'Perfectly.' Completely unrepentant, Lorna smiled, folded her arms, and assumed an air of superiority. 'He hasn't asked you out and you're miffed,' she expanded. 'In your place I'm sure I'd feel the same. But I shouldn't let it worry you. The man clearly goes around with his eyes closed.' Leaning across, she patted Stevie's hand. 'Take my advice. Forget him. Stevie, he isn't worth the effort.'

'Lorna Deighton, you're impossible. For two pins I'd –'

'Smile for the camera,' Tom interrupted, zooming in on Stevie's scowling face. 'You know how much you enjoy parties.'

'Twenty or thirty seven-year-olds, maybe,' Stevie agreed, locating Rosa's dark head among the running, skipping, laughing brood careering

54

round the garden. 'It's the grown-up version I find wearing.'

'But a cosy dinner for two is something else.'

'It certainly is,' Stevie allowed sweetly. 'But, at the risk of boring you rigid, Lorna Deighton, I'll say it again. The lady wasn't asked.'

'And if she had been?'

'Irrelevant. Why meet trouble halfway?' And Jared Wilde was trouble all right, trouble with a capital T.

'Hmm.' Wide blue eyes narrowed suddenly. 'I don't suppose –'

'No, Lorna,' Stevie cut in sharply. 'I don't suppose you do. Safer that way.' For if a cosy dinner for two was out of Lorna's hands, an almost as cosy foursome wasn't. And yet Lorna was too shrewd a hostess to risk a less than cosy threesome when Stevie pleaded toothache, headache or a dozen and one minor ailments tendered too late to challenge.

It wouldn't stop her plotting for long, though, Stevie realized, collecting Rosa and giving an over-excited seven-year-old an extra special hug. But by the time Lorna came up with Plans B through to Z, Jared Wilde would have moved on. And as for that Saturday night threat to stick around for a while, Stevie would believe that if and when it happened.

'Can *I* have a party, Mummy?'

Settling her daughter in the back of the car, logging the plea in a set of black eyes, Stevie's heart sank. The thought of even half a dozen kids careering around the stark but stunning whiteness of her apartment was enough to trigger a fit of the vapours. And with Andrew due home by the end of the year, there was all the more reason to keep it as a thought.

'Of course you can.' She gave a smile of reassurance, less for Rosa than for herself. She was just beginning to realize that her unexpressed reluctance to allow anyone but Kelly across the threshold had managed to filter down to Rosa. 'Soon. Very soon, I promise.'

A hug, a sticky kiss – another twinge of conscience as two small arms crept up around her neck. The age-old dilemma. So much love, so little time to spare. The need to pay the bills, save for the deposit for a place of their own, ensure that Rosa wanted for nothing. Time or money and no easy answer. And, whilst Tom wouldn't stand in the way of Stevie working part-time, part-time work meant part-time wages. Time or money? An uneasy compromise. But once they were settled in a place of their own, Stevie vowed, Rosa would never lack for company her own age.

Pulling into the car park behind the exclusive block of flats that currently served as home, Stevie edged her way into the only remaining space, a narrow gap between the garage wall and a plush black car that had no right even to be there, let alone take up so much room. A Rolls-Royce. Just like that Roller she'd earlier been whisked back to work in. Decadence on wheels. A rich man's plaything, she'd decided then, unconsciously disapproving.

'I work hard, Stevie,' Jared had pointed out, uncannily reading her thoughts. 'I am allowed an indulgence now and again.'

Now and again? Exclusive hotels, expensive taste in clothes and cars, not to mention solid gold cuff-links and wristwatch. Oh, yes, and who was Jared trying to convince?

JLW 1. She aimed another scowl of disapproval at the personalized number plate, the thought that it was Jared, taking the trouble to track her down, was enough to make her cheeks flame. Wishful thinking? Not unless she'd taken leave of her senses, she decided waspishly.

Rosa scrambled out as Stevie held the door carefully away from the gleaming paintwork. 'Suzy's daddy has a big black car,' Rosa volunteered thoughtfully.

'Does he, poppet? And who's Suzy?' Stevie asked automatically.

'You know. Suzy Waterson. She sits next to me in the dining room,' Rosa explained a mite tetchily.

'Oh, *that* Suzy,' Stevie agreed mildly, aware that Rosa was tired, that the excitement of the party, on top of a hard day at school, was beginning to take its toll. And since John Waterson, Suzy's father, was one of the town's leading lights, it might even explain the car.

'And it's Suzy's birthday on Sunday, and guess what?' Rosa breathed. 'She's having a real party with clowns and magicians and a bouncy castle in her own back garden. And Suzy's mummy's had special invitations printed at a shop and the postman's bringing mine,' she confided, almost tripping over the words in her haste to explain. 'And I can go, can't I, Mummy?' she ended doubtfully, a small sticky hand creeping into Stevie's.

Glancing down and logging the excitement, the hope, the unspoken concern that the usual visit to Nanna might be given priority, Stevie felt the sudden well of tears. Quick as a flash, she gathered Rosa close and whisked her off her feet, whizzing her round and round until the world spun dizzily.

Having banished the clouds with the happy sound of laughter, Stevie blew against Rosa's ear and whispered loudly, 'Of course you can. And guess what? I've been thinking. How about we book McDonald's for *your* birthday and then you can invite the whole class?'

'All of them?' Rosa queried, falling into step, her smile spreading as the truth dawned. 'Even the boys?'

'Even the boys. But only if you want to, mind,' Stevie conceded solemnly. 'After all, it's your party, your decision. And on Saturday we'll pop into town and choose some special invitations. Agreed?'

Rosa nodded, her expression more than enough to compensate Stevie for the expense of keeping thirty or so children entertained. Not to mention the ubiquitous 'party bags' – the young hostess's way of saying thank you for the presents. A slice of cake, a few sweets and an inexpensive toy. Usually. Doubtless Suzy Waterson would break new ice.

On the subject of which, there was plenty of time to buy a new dress for Rosa. A fiercely proud Stevie was determined to ensure her daughter never suffered the shame of second-hand clothes, the taunts of other children when the same 'best' dress did for each and every occasion. More money, but worth every penny just to see the light in a set of shining black eyes. Black eyes. Italian eyes. Jared's eyes –

Stevie pulled her thoughts up, checked the time, and took Rosa's hand as they stepped out of the lift and laughingly hop-skipped the final ten yards to the solid front door, with its spy hole, security panel and sophisticated locking system. Not that burglars stood a chance of breaching the high-profile security in the foyer downstairs, but, with the end apartment empty, better safe than sorry.

Into the spacious brightness of Andrew's flat, automatically kicking off shoes. White. Stark and unrelieved. The walls, the carpets, the sumptuous leather furniture. Impractical at the best of times, but with a normal healthy six-year-old an absolute nightmare.

'Bath-time, miss.'

Sweeping Rosa straight to the bathroom, she noted the blinking light of the answer phone in passing and filed it away at the back of her mind. Time enough later, when Rosa was settled and Stevie had a moment to herself.

'Face first,' she reminded her, rinsing the flannel in the clear warm water and handing it across before adding a hint of bubble bath. The intense concentration on Rosa's shiny face brought a smile to Stevie's lips.

Rosa glanced up suddenly. 'There will be time for a story, won't there, Mummy?'

'We-ell –'

'Just a teensy-weenie little one,' she cajoled, eyes wide as saucers. 'And it *is* your turn to choose.'

'We'll see,' Stevie stalled, racking her brains for the shortest she could think of.

Rosa nodded, innocently aware that 'we'll see' meant yes, that if Stevie had really intended saying no she'd have said so in the first place.

The phone rang. Aware she hadn't switched off the answer phone, Stevie ignored it, but opened the bathroom door a crack in case it proved important.

Important? More like cataclysmic.

'Playing hard to get, huh?' A familiar voice, an amused voice, and the hairs on the nape of Stevie's neck were rising like the hackles of a cat. 'Come on, Stevie,' Jared lazily entreated,

velvet tones bouncing the length of the hallway, echoing in her mind. 'Be a devil, pick up
the phone. Please? Pretty please?'

A long pause, not a sound, and then a throaty
chuckle. 'No? Ah, well, I guess I'll have to try
again later. Unless, of course, Little Red Riding
Hood would care to return my call? After all, it's
the height of bad manners not to, hey Stevie?
And, since you do know where to find me . . .'

The click of disconnection and then silence,
just the sound of the blood pounding in her
ears. Damn Jared Wilde. How dared he intrude? And, since her number was ex-direc-
tory, how on earth –?

How? *How*? she repeated silently, incredulously. Not so much the sixty-five-thousand-
dollar question as glaringly obvious. But there
was no time to breathe fire and brimstone down
the phone line to a traitorous Lorna, and definitely no time to return the irritating man's call.
Not that Stevie intended to.

Rosa, bedtime and bedtime rituals.

'Kiss for Ted, kiss for Loopy Loo, kiss for
Tiggles –'

'Bed,' Stevie insisted. 'It's late and you've got
school in the morning. And if you really want to
hear that story . . .'

Unabashed, Rosa grinned, climbing under the
duvet and arranging her collection of bedtime
friends on the pillow around her.

'Good girl.' A smile from Stevie, a nod of

approval. 'Now. Story-time. You choose, but make it a short one, hey, poppet?'

'Oh, yummy. *Little Red Riding Hood*,' came the prompt request, and Rosa's eyes were full of curious challenge.

'Why?' Stevie snapped, feeling frazzled, beginning to feel trapped and aware she was being paranoid.

'Oh, Mummy, because you said *I* could choose,' Rosa reminded her huffily. 'And *Little Red Riding Hood*'s my very favouritest story.'

'That's news to me,' Stevie declared lightly. 'But I guess you know best. *Little Red Riding Hood* it is – the short version, understand?'

Thumb in mouth, Rosa nodded, sinking back against the pillows as Stevie began the tale in the age-old tradition. 'Once upon a time there was a little girl who lived on the edge of the woods . . .'

Escape. A glass of chilled white wine. Another nightly ritual, with Stevie stretched out on the sofa, scanning the headlines on the teletext pages and indulging in a precious half-hour of peace before starting the chores – a never-ending set of chores with a child in the place. Only tonight, of course, the peace had been well and truly shattered by that man, and the single glass of wine was doing little to calm her frazzled nerves.

And, since she knew she wouldn't settle until she'd purged his voice from her mind, from the answer phone memory, she snatched the open bottle from the fridge and flounced into the hallway to cancel that blinking red eye. Only she couldn't. Since the machine had been blinking when she arrived home, she could hardly cancel Jared's mocking tones without destroying all her other messages. Her message. Singular. And, surprise, surprise, no prize for guessing who'd been calling.

'Just your friendly neighbourhood wolf, footloose and fancy-free and wondering if you'd care to join me for a drink. And before you trot out another rule from that vast northern repertoire, you can take it from me, one drink won't hurt a single hair on that pretty little head of yours. I'll be seeing you.'

Just that. Oh, and the time of the call – a mere twenty minutes before she'd arrived home, less than an hour between calls. *I'll be seeing you.* Innocuous-sounding words, yet uttered in Jared's assured tones curiously menacing. *I'll be seeing you.* And, since he'd clearly extracted her number from a conniving Lorna, what price her address? Lorna wouldn't. Lorna would. Lorna hadn't. According to Lorna at least.

'Stevie, darling!' Lorna protested, her doleful tone wasted on Stevie. 'As if I would.'

'You gave him my number,' Stevie reminded her coolly.

'Exactly. A number where he could reach you. And, since he's clearly interested –'

'Fiddlesticks,' Stevie interrupted rudely. 'I

don't want to be reached, not by him. The answer phone's on and it's staying on, and you, Lorna Deighton, have been purged from my Christmas card list as of now.'

And, gamely resisting the urge to slam the receiver, Stevie deleted the offending messages before heading back to that dwindling bottle of wine.

The phone rang. And rang. And rang.

Damn and blast, she'd forgotten to reset it, and, suspecting a thoroughly repentant Lorna, Stevie flounced back into the hall in a whirl of indignation and snatched up the handset.

'No, I do not forgive you,' she barked. 'It was irresponsible and inexcusable. And if I never hear from you again, *ever*, as far as I'm concerned it will still be too soon. Are you listening to me?'

'Yes, ma'am!' A different voice, a man's voice, the last voice in the world Stevie wanted to hear, she realized, stifling the groan but not the scowl and glad they hadn't developed the vision to go with the phonics – in this part of the world at least.

'Kind of difficult not to,' Jared conceded lazily. 'With the message bouncing the length of Lord Street. But, in the interests of fairness, Ginge, shouldn't you be saying this to my face, and spelling out precisely what it is I've done to offend you?'

CHAPTER 4

'Oh, hell!'

'Oh, hell, indeed,' he agreed solemnly. 'But worry not, Stevie, I accept your gracious though curiously unspoken apology.'

'I –'

'Just say yes,' he cut in smoothly. 'Nothing more, nothing less.'

'Yes, what?' she queried warily, catching sight of her reflection in the mirror on the wall. Her face was white and pinched but for the high spots of colour in her cheeks. Tiredness, she swiftly conceded. Nothing more, nothing less.

'Try, "Yes, thank you, Jared. It's kind of you to ask and a drink would be lovely."'

A moot point, since she'd practically polished off half a bottle already, but she wasn't about to tell Jared that. 'Thank you, Jared,' she obligingly echoed. 'It's nice of you to ask but a drink is out of the question.'

'Why?'

'Why what?'

'Why is a drink out of the question?' he repeated patiently – too patiently, Stevie decided, instinct telling her that Jared wasn't renowned for that particular virtue.

'I don't have to supply a reason,' she pointed out coolly. 'You've asked nicely, I've just as nicely declined. Any gentleman worth his salt would leave it at that.'

'Ah, yes, but any lady worthy of the name wouldn't breathe fire and brimstone down the phone line,' he riposted. 'So it stands to reason: a certain fiery little lady owes me.'

'Not in my book,' Stevie retorted. 'And it wasn't you I was sounding off at.'

'Oh, but it was. A case of mistaken identity, perhaps, but yours truly still caught the full six barrels.' He gave a throaty chuckle. 'Heaven help the poor guy you really wanted to blast. Anyone I know?'

'I doubt it,' Stevie snapped. 'Since you're new in town. And what makes you so certain it's a he?'

'You mean it wasn't?' he queried slyly. 'Oh, good. I should hate to come between a guy and his gal.'

'Don't worry, Jared, you won't. Now if you don't mind . . '

'And if I did?'

'Too bad,' she told him crisply. 'Because I'm hanging up anyway. Believe it or not, Mr Wilde, one of us has work to do.'

'Jared. The name, lady, is Jared. J-A-R-E-D,' he enunciated slowly. 'Now, repeat after me –'

'Goodnight, Jared,' she cut in swiftly. '*Good-bye*, Jared.' And, without giving him time to reply, she cut the connection.

Smiling grimly as she swung away, she'd barely taken a step when the phone began to trill. Sorely tempted to ignore it, Stevie snatched it up at the fifth ring.

'Now what?' she snapped.

'Just calling to say goodnight,' he explained placidly. 'Goodnight, Ginge, sweet dreams.'

'Stevie,' she ground out grimly. 'S-T-E-V-I-E. Not so difficult for an intelligent man to commit to memory, surely?' she queried saccharine-sweetly. 'Along with this well-known phrase or saying I'll leave you to rearrange at your leisure. Night. Good. Jared. Now. Alone. Leave me. Please. Get it?'

'Loud and clear. And on that cheerful note, I guess it's over and out.'

Jared's turn to cut the connection. And an out-of-sorts Stevie was irrationally annoyed that it was Jared who'd had the last word.

As she reached the door to the lounge, the phone rang again. 'Don't you ever take no for an answer?' she bit on, suppressing the guilty stab of pleasure.

'Stevie? Stevie, is that you?'

'Andrew? Andrew, darling!' she called delightedly. 'Oh, Drew, it really is good to hear you.'

'Missing me, Stevie?' he laughingly probed.

'Like hell,' she conceded, a picture of her tall, handsome cousin flashing into her mind, all laughing black eyes and strong white teeth in a sun-bronzed face.

But it was true. Andrew was family, all the family she had apart from Nanna and Rosa, and she missed having someone to confide in, to share the burden of Nanna's frailty. And yet she couldn't be selfish in wishing Drew home. He'd given so much already – providing a roof over her head for a start. He would have made it rent-free but for Stevie's insistence on paying her way. Yet with Hong Kong now returned to China, it was only a matter of time before Andrew's job folded and he'd be heading for home. Until somewhere equally exotic beckoned, Stevie amended, swallowing a smile. And on the subject of places exotic . . .

'Heavens, Drew, it must be the middle of the night over there. Is something wrong?'

'Breakfast-time. An early breakfast, admittedly,' he conceded with a smile in his voice. 'And, no, Stevie, nothing's wrong – unless you count having a house guest for a week or two.'

'You're coming home? But that's wonderful. When?'

'Next month maybe, though nothing's settled yet. But if it's too much trouble,' he added doubtfully, 'I can always check in at the Scarisbrick.'

'Trouble? If you dare to cross the threshold of the Scarisbrick for anything as innocuous as a drink in one of the bars, Andrew Roxton, I'll give you trouble. This is your home, remember?'

'Your home too, Stevie.'

For now, she silently qualified, mentally rearranging Rosa's bedroom to make space for the put-you-up bed, leaving the master bedroom free for Drew – just a temporary inconvenience while Stevie stepped up the search for a place of their own.

A house, she decided. With a garden for Rosa and room for a rabbit and a cat or two. Home. All hers. Hers and Rosa's, with nothing and no one to come between them. All the more reason to keep men, and men like Jared Wilde in particular, firmly at arm's length.

In the meanwhile, there was Andrew to think about. 'Just come home, Drew,' Stevie ended wistfully. 'Today, tomorrow, next week, next month. Everything's ready and waiting.'

Too much excitement for one day: lunch at the Prince of Wales, Jared's tormenting presence, Jared's tormenting words, and now the wonderful news from Andrew. An overwrought Stevie poured the last drop of wine into her glass and silently weighed the consequences of opening another bottle.

Unwise, she told herself, wandering from room to room with a critical eye and double-checking that there'd be nothing for Andrew to fault on his return. Much better to settle for a mug of hot chocolate and a good book, she decided, halting in front of the bookcase, her fingers climbing the spine of a well-thumbed, leather-bound volume that had been an eighteenth birthday present from Mae. *Pride and Prejudice.* Jane Austen at her best. The spirited Elizabeth Bennett, whose first impressions of Mr Darcy had turned out so disastrously wrong.

First impressions.

Tall, too good-looking to be true, and the laughing, smiling centre of attention. And Stevie had disliked him on sight. Only she'd been wrong. She didn't dislike him at all. Which was precisely what was playing on her mind.

'Lorna said to say hello.'

'I'll bet,' Stevie agreed vehemently, and then she relented, softened the words with a smile. After all, this was her boss's wife they were discussing.

Tom rubbed his chin with the back of his hand, his normally placid features strangely drawn. 'She, er, said she might drop by on her way into town. She needs to have a word, apparently.'

'I can't think why,' Stevie murmured off-handedly, shuffling a heap of papers into a pile and returning his gaze with unblinking innocence.

'No.' Tom grinned. 'But I wouldn't mind listening in on this one. It's not often I have the pleasure of seeing Lorna squirm.'

Stevie's turn to grin. 'She told you?'

'What with Jared's cajoling at the start of the night and your dulcet tones an hour or so later, she didn't need to bother. Lorna had been meddling and it showed.'

'She'll learn,' Stevie insisted brightly. 'The hard way. Stevie Cooper, spinster of this parish, has no intentions of falling for the charms of a sweet-talking man. Any man, full-stop.'

Subject closed. She swung away, scowling, remembering, and was brought up short by a hand on her arm. She glanced up to find Tom's solemn gaze fastened on hers and smothered a twinge of premonition. 'Tom?'

'Don't be too hard on Lorna,' he entreated softly. 'She meant no harm, and, just between the two of us, things haven't been going too well just lately.'

Stevie's lips formed a silent O. 'Anything I can do?' she asked, swallowing hard, racking her brains for a clue to the problem – not marriage problems, surely, since Tom and Lorna were two of the nicest people she knew and suited one another down to the ground. And there'd been no hint of any strain between them at the weekend, she recalled, relief washing over her.

Tom shook his head. 'Just carry on as normal. And don't breathe a word to that wife of mine or she'll skin me alive. But if you could –'

'Let her off lightly?' Stevie supplied, smiling despite herself. 'What do you think, Tom?'

'Oh, no.' His shook his head emphatically. 'Where women and the minefield of their minds are concerned, I never presume to think. Safer that way.'

Humming thoughtfully under her breath, and landing back in her office ten minutes later, Stevie pulled up in the doorway, the exquisite plant arrangement in the centre of the desk knocking the breath from her body. Now who on earth —?

'Don't be cross, Stevie. You know I didn't mean any harm, and, cross my heart and hope to die, I'll never meddle in your love-life again. Ever.'

Stevie spun round at the words, caught the hang-dog expression on Lorna's plump face as she emerged from behind the door and was forced to swallow a smile.

'Until next time, Lorna Deighton,' she reminded her coolly. 'Though for two pins I might still refuse to reinstate you on my Christmas card list.'

'But you won't, hey, Stevie? After all you are my best friend, not to mention my daughter's godmother. Or should that be my goddaughter's mother?' she queried absurdly, frowning, giggling.

Stevie's own smile spread at the pun. 'Exactly. Family in all but name, and you of all people ought to know better.'

'Yes.'

'But you just can't resist meddling.'

'No.'

'And you know perfectly well how I feel about men.'

'It's – just beginning to dawn on me,' Lorna conceded sorrowfully.

'And, cross your heart and hope to die, this is positively the last time you play cupid?'

'Well –'

'You promised,' Stevie reminded her sternly. 'No promise, no forgiveness, no best friends.'

'No contest. I promise. I won't invite a single unattached male to dine at my table again. Ever. Satisfied now?'

'It will do for starters,' Stevie conceded, relenting and waving Lorna to a chair. 'Coffee?'

'Coffee would be lovely,' she agreed. 'But I should hate to keep from your work, and Tom says –'

She pulled up sharp, and Stevie's highly tuned antennae prickled in alarm. 'Tom says?' she prompted casually, logging Lorna's flush of colour, the flash of dismay she couldn't quite hide.

'Oh, you know . . .' She shrugged, waved an airy hand. 'Men. Time is money and that sort of thing. And you *are* heavily involved in the new line.'

True enough, Stevie conceded, pouring the coffee, giving Lorna time to pull herself together. It was a worrying enough event taken on its own. Put it with Tom's worried face and his enigmatic words and the reasons didn't bear thinking about. But, since she had promised Tom, there was nothing she could say unless Lorna gave her an opening.

'So . . .' Stevie forced a smile. 'What's on today? The designer hall at Broadbent's or Chantelle's exclusive creations?'

'Just a spot of window-shopping,' Lorna conceded vaguely. 'You know, something to fill the time.'

'You wouldn't need to fill time if you went back to work,' Stevie hazarded, feeling her way around a churn of ideas. Not marriage problems, she quickly decided, and with Kelly the picture of health, nothing to worry about there. Which left money – or business.

Business. Deighton Foods. A long-established family firm, but, with competition fierce, it was hardly surprising Tom had been toying with the idea of taking on a partner. Adam Marriot, a bit of dry stick from all accounts, and, recalling his presence on Saturday evening, not Dee's cup of tea at all. Would he be anyone's cup of tea? Stevie mused, those vague rumblings on the factory floor beginning to assume gigantic proportions. Because if Tom needed a partner as badly as it seemed, something was drastically wrong.

Lorna's smile faded. 'I know. And, since Tom's been dropping hints, it's high time I did something about it. Only –'

'Only?' Stevie probed.

Lorna shrugged, pulled a wry face. 'Mummy. She doesn't approve. And since she's never approved of Tom –'

'Precisely. You can't win. And you're a big girl now.'

'Decision time?' Lorna mused doubtfully.

Stevie nodded. 'Decision time. But if it's any consolation, you'll have Tom's backing every step of the way.'

'But it isn't Tom's backing I'll be needing,' Lorna tossed out enigmatically, at the same time reaching for her handbag. 'Still, nothing ventured, nothing gained. And, given the way things are, I'd say it's now or never.'

Curiouser and curiouser, Stevie decided, replaying the gist of the conversation in her mind. And, illogical though it seemed, she couldn't shake the feeling that whatever the problems at Deightons, they were all tied up with Jared Wilde's appearance out of nowhere.

CHAPTER 5

'You are joking?'

Afraid she'd misheard, more afraid she hadn't, Stevie angled her head, eyes flashing ice as they rested on the man who filled the room, made the four walls of Tom's office appear to close in with suffocating menace.

'Believe me, Stevie, I couldn't be more serious.'

'But –' She broke off, searching his face for some hint of emotion, some clue to his thoughts. That curiously bland expression gave nothing away, but hinted at a confidence Stevie found galling. Because Mr Arrogance himself was convinced she couldn't turn him down.

Only Stevie could, and she would, and she did.

'Thank you, Mr Wilde, but the idea's out of the question.'

'Any particular reason?' he drawled, just the sharp narrowing of jet-black eyes betraying his surprise.

Stevie smiled grimly. 'My decision, my reasons,' she told him coolly, reaching for her bag and coming slowly to her feet though her insides were churning. 'You've made the offer: I've turned it down. End of discussion.'

'I don't agree. We've barely exchanged a dozen words. Why not sit down and let me explain?'

'Why not simply accept that no means no?' she countered sweetly. 'And save us both a lot of time.'

'But you haven't heard my terms yet.'

'Irrelevant. I have a perfectly good job here.'

'For now.'

'Meaning?'

'Meaning all good things come to an end – eventually. Why not jump before you're pushed?'

'By whom?' she asked, glancing round, scanning the office that was as familiar as her own – Tom's office, with its well-worn carpet and fading paint work, the solid oak desk that had been Tom's father's, and his father's before him, the faded photographs of both among the batch of silver frames dominated by smiling images of Kelly and Lorna. Her gaze moved on, sliding beyond the cluster of family snapshots to the man sitting large as life and twice as brash behind then. 'By you?' she challenged incredulously. 'Or by Tom?'

Tom. Just where was he? she wondered, suppressing a frisson of alarm. Tom's office, Tom's business, Jared Wilde's devastating presence. Unless –

'Worry not, Stevie. Tom knows I'm here, and furthermore he knows exactly why.'

Poaching. Better than that other dreadful scenario that had popped into her mind. But only just.

She nodded. 'Fine.' Only it wasn't. Something was wrong, and if forewarned was forearmed Jared Wilde had the advantage. Stevie suspected, but Jared knew, and he was using that knowledge to make her squirm. She forced a smile. 'As I said, the answer's no.'

'Fine.' Jared's turn to nod. 'You're an intelligent woman. Your life, your decision. You'll change your mind once you've heard all the facts.'

'I doubt it,' Stevie bit out, swinging away. 'I'm happy at Deighton's, and Tom's more than happy with my standard of work.'

'Which is precisely why he'll let you go.'

'But he doesn't want to let me go,' she pointed out coolly, halting, half turning, cold green eyes locking with his. 'Remember?'

'Ah, yes, but maybe he can't afford not to.'

'In which case, Mr Wilde, I'm sure he'll tell me so himself in time.'

'Assuming he's still in business.'

'And what the hell is that supposed to mean?' Stevie demanded, horribly afraid that other scenario had been banished a mite too soon.

Jared smiled, spread his hands. 'Take a seat,' he insisted pleasantly. 'And all will be revealed.'

Damned if she did, damned if she didn't, Stevie

decided, still half inclined to turn on her heel and flounce back to the safety of her own office.

Too late. Jared smiled, rose from the chair where he'd been lounging – Tom's chair, Stevie noted huffily – and closed the space between them in three easy strides.

Stevie froze, afraid he was going to reach out, take her by the shoulders, twist her round, steer her to the chair and urge her to sit, more afraid that he'd smile again, turning her insides to water. Only it was worse than that. A single finger slid beneath her chin, tilting her face upwards while a lazy thumb stroked the angle of her jaw.

'You're one hell of a suspicious woman,' he acknowledged lightly. 'Prickly, loyal, hard-working – and too bright to walk away without weighing all the options. Business, Stevie. Purely and simply. Nothing more, nothing less. So why not sit down and relax while I pour the coffee? Please, Stevie. Pretty please,' he added, black eyes dancing.

Stevie flushed. He was teasing, tormenting, baiting, and so supremely sure Stevie would fall in with his plans – and sooner rather than later – that she was sorely tempted to raise a hand, wipe away the smile with a lightning flick of her wrist. Only she wouldn't. Allow Jared to goad her? Give him the satisfaction of provoking a rise?

Stifling the panic, she pulled away, retraced her steps, took the chair that he proffered and angled her head in enquiry. 'So?'

'Coffee,' Jared insisted, reaching for the jug simmering at his side. 'Sugar and cream? Or does m'lady have a figure to watch?'

'Given my obvious love of food,' Stevie scorned, 'what do you think?'

'With the female of the species unpredictable at best, I wouldn't care to say. So, sugar and cream it is?'

Stevie nodded, silently cursing the give-away rattle of cup on saucer as she took the cup from him. And Jared noticed. And Jared swallowed a smile. But at least Jared regained his seat, keeping the solid lines of the desk between them.

Silence. Not a sound. Hardly a drawn breath. A rigid Stevie waiting anything but patiently, an exasperating Jared making it anything but easy.

Hoping he'd take the hint, she pointedly checked her watch, saw the smile playing about the corners of his mouth and bristled. 'You said you'd explain.'

'Very true,' he acknowledged lightly.

'So?'

'It's very simple. There's an opening tailor-made for you in the ALITANI organization and Tom's agreed to let you go.'

'And I'm supposed to be flattered?'

'And could at least consider the idea before dismissing it out of hand.'

'But surely there's nothing to consider,' Stevie purred, irrationally hurt that Tom should discuss something as vital as her future with this man, this stranger, without so much as a hint to Stevie herself. 'It's all signed, sealed and delivered, by the sounds of it – cunningly arranged between you and Tom. Lot one, Miss Stevie Cooper, employee. Sold to the highest bidder.'

'Hardly, since slavery's abolished –'

'Good heavens,' she exclaimed. 'You're not going to let a mere technicality stand in the way of progress? After all, what's an employee or two between friends?'

'Precisely. Tom and I are friends. Friends, Stevie. We talk, we socialize, we listen, we help. We try not to rock any boats. Why raise your hopes if Tom isn't happy?'

'Manners, Mr Wilde. Common courtesy. This is my life you're calmly rearranging, and without so much as a by your leave. And, just for the record, if and when I need a change of job, I'll find one. Understand?'

'Your reaction? Perfectly. You're angry. You think Tom's let you down and naturally enough you're feeling rejected. Only you're wrong.'

'Am I? And why is that, precisely? Because Jared Wilde's decided to take what he wants and if one or two lives are trampled in the process, then tough?'

'Hardly take,' he pointed out mildly. 'Given the salary on offer.

'On offer? Oh, I see! That makes everything all right, then. Not take, *buy*.'

'Head-hunt, actually,' he retorted, folding his

81

arms and leaning back, regarding Stevie from under heavy-lidded eyes. 'And perfectly normal business practice.'

'Not in my part of the world,' she snapped.

'Debatable, since you work for a living like the rest of us. But if that's your only objection, let's scrub the whole conversation and start again.'

'Wipe the slate clean, you mean? Difficult, I'd say, since the damage has been done.'

'Yes.' He smiled. Not the mocking, teasing, goading smile Stevie was expecting but a strangely tender smile that tugged at her heartstrings, sent eddies of heat swirling through her body.

Fool, she inwardly derided, allowing a reaction, any reaction, to this man who took what he could, bought what he wanted, sweet-talked or bullied according to whim.

Arrogant. Overbearing. Insufferable. Insensitive. Calmly assuming he could turn up out of nowhere and create waves in her ordered world, and not just Stevie's world, in Tom's and Lorna's, and countless dozens more who depended on Deighton Foods: market gardeners, farmers, delivery men, packers, food technicians, office staff. The list was never-ending.

And yet with business precarious enough to start with, the awful thought just beginning to dawn was that Jared's offer, coming on top of recent hints, shouldn't be dismissed out of hand. Desert the sinking ship? Stevie mused. Only

Deighton's wasn't sinking, was simply weathering the storm like everyone else.

Or was it?

Jared moved. Slipping round the desk before Stevie had time to react, he dragged a second chair across and positioned himself in front of her, prised the untouched cup of coffee from between her rigid fingers and held on, his solemn gaze unnerving.

Stevie flushed, acutely conscious of the man, the subtle fragrance of his aftershave, the unique body smell. Jared Wilde. All man. Six feet three inches of dynamism. Six feet three inches of power. Power. The power to arrange, to rearrange, to destroy.

But not this time. Stevie stiffened. 'I –'

'You need time to think,' Jared insisted. A second hand captured hers, cradling, not holding, because Stevie could pull away at will, no overreaction, no offended snatch, just a gentle freeing of fingers. Nice and easy. Only she didn't.

The currents of heat swirling through, the shock waves of pleasure that gathered speed began to build, spreading outwards and inwards, and as idle thumbs began to brush the backs of her hands velvet eyes began to travel the length of her in an intimate appraisal of a body that refused to behave. No reaction, outwardly at least, or at least that was what Stevie was praying. No reaction on the surface and yet turmoil inside. Because this man had done what Stevie had vowed no man ever would. He'd looked, he'd touched, he'd provoked a reaction.

It was Friday. In less than a week he'd destroyed the control she'd spent years acquiring. No love, no trust, no involvement, no commitment, no hurt – ever. And if the effort nearly killed her, she wasn't about to allow Jared Wilde to become the exception that proved the rule.

'No!' Brusque, shattering the moment along with the silence. 'You're wrong. I don't need time to think.'

'Stevie –'

The phone rang; Stevie seized her chance to pull free and Jared openly scowled, reached for the handset, remembered, belatedly, that it wasn't his place to take the call and passed the receiver to Stevie before striding to the window where he stood staring out, feet planted wide apart, arms folded across his chest, the body language speaking volumes.

'Stevie? Thank heavens, I thought you might have gone for lunch.'

At this time of the morning? Stevie mused. Tom's distraction was unnerving.

'What is it, Tom? Has something happened? Is it Lorna –'

'Yes! No! It's her mother,' Tom exclaimed. 'A heart attack, apparently. We're heading north the moment we've packed. Can you –?'

'Look after Kelly?' she cut in swiftly. 'No problem.'

'Thanks, Stevie, but we've already phoned school and we're picking her up on the way. She'd only worry if we left her behind, and with her little cousins for company, she won't have time to brood. No, it's you I'm worried about. I could be gone for days, Stevie. Stevie, you do know what I'm saying?'

Yes. A heart attack. At least twenty-four hours before they'd know if Mrs Hunter was likely to pull through. And if not . . .

'No problems. I can hold the fort for as long as you need. Don't worry, Tom, everything's under control.'

'I didn't doubt it for a minute,' he retorted with a reassuring flash of humour. 'But, hell, Stevie, I wanted to explain about Jared –'

'No need,' she insisted, her gaze flicking over to the man himself, now propped against the wall and eyeing Stevie like a cat watching a mouse. 'Like I said, everything's under control.' Just.

'Anything I can do?' A polite enquiry from Jared the moment Stevie cut the connection.

'Apart from leave, you mean?' she enquired saccharine-sweetly, back in control and determined to keep it. 'Thank you, Mr Wilde, not a thing.'

His mouth tightened. 'Fine. If that's the way you want to play it.'

'Not at all, but I've too much to do to waste time trading insults. Tom's been called away and he could be gone for days.'

'And the super-efficient Miss Cooper is left holding the reins?'

'Not exactly,' she insisted pleasantly. 'Since the place practically runs itself. But naturally there's work to do.'

'Oh, naturally,' he echoed dryly. 'And my job, my offer?' he enquired politely. 'You will at least give it some thought?'

'I just did. The answer's no.'

'The answer's no for the moment. Like I said, think it over.'

'And like *I* said,' she repeated stonily, 'I've already made up my mind.'

'But when I want something badly, Miss Cooper, I refuse to take no for an answer.'

'Bully for you,' Stevie scorned, pulling the telephone back into reach and hoping he'd take the hint, would leave, would walk out and leave – for ever, preferably.

'Three days,' he tossed out lazily, pulling up in the doorway and reaching into a pocket for his keys, which he looped carelessly round a finger. 'You have until eleven-thirty Monday morning to come up with the answer I want.'

'And when I don't?'

'Let's just say that for every day you delay after that, the salary drops accordingly.'

'Not my problem,' she insisted tightly. 'No job, no salary, no threat.'

'Then I suggest you have a word with Tom.'

'Why?'

'No job, no salary, no references,' he scorned. 'No bread in the house. And I know how much you enjoy your food.'

'You can't.'

'Can't I? Like I said, my dear,' he lazily entreated, 'have a word with Tom.'

Cancel lunch with Dee or carry on as normal? Keeping things normal won. It wasn't the first afternoon Tom had been called away, doubtless it wouldn't be the last, and, as Stevie had pointedly reminded Jared, the place practically ran itself. If not strictly true, then nothing dire was likely to happen in a ninety-minute break from the office, and if it did Tom's secretary would know where to find her.

Normality. Stevie's treat of the week – lunch with Dee at the Café Matisse. Another misconception, she quickly discovered, joining the crowd in the Cambridge Arcade and finding that with all the upheaval she'd forgotten to reserve a table and, today of all days, the restaurant was full.

'I'm sorry, Miss Cooper, but when you didn't ring to confirm as normal, we were forced to let your table go. If you'd care to wait . . .'

Stevie shook her head. 'It's all right, Marc. It's not your fault,' she reassured him swiftly. 'But I'm a bit pushed for time. We'll leave it.' She turned to Dee, who'd come up behind her in a

87

cloud of heady perfume. 'It's not my day,' Stevie conceded, flashing her a tight smile. 'I'll explain as we're going along. How does grabbing a salad at Pippins sound?'

'Miss Cooper, excuse me . . .' A smiling Marc was pushing through the knot of people at the door. 'If it's agreeable, a gentleman dining alone has offered to share his table. Yes?'

'I –'

'We'll take it,' Dee cut in brightly. 'A lone male? Could be the best offer I have all day. Besides, I need to sit down. My feet are killing me.'

'Serves you right for wearing those ridiculous heels,' Stevie observed tartly, following Marc through the crush of tables to the cosiest corner of the room, the nook beneath the open-tread staircase.

Something about the cut of the suit and the arrogant angle of the head glimpsed between the rungs was vaguely familiar as the man rose, turned, smiled, pulled out a chair.

'You!' Stevie ground to a halt and a blissfully unaware Dee careered into her, knocking her forwards, only Jared's outstretched arms preventing a nasty fall.

'Talk about how to make an entrance,' he growled, his arms closing round her automatically. 'And to think, Ginge, I didn't know you cared.'

'I don't!' Stevie bit out, struggling to keep her

balance, with the growing suspicion that Jared was making things worse by deliberately holding on. Tight.

Pulling free and ignoring the chair that he'd proffered, Stevie flounced around the table, leaving a simpering Dee to sink with unashamed alacrity into the vacant seat, hitching her chair closer to Jared's in the process.

Catching Jared's eye, Dee preened. 'Thank you, Jared. My stomach's been rumbling half the morning,' she confided. 'And the idea of settling for a salad simply didn't appeal.'

'My pleasure. And it will be a pleasure,' he insisted silkily, his mocking gaze crossing to Stevie. 'Given the attractive company. Now, let me order some wine.'

'I –'

'Never drink wine in the middle of the day. Yes, Stevie, I know,' he interrupted mildly. 'But rules are made to be broken. Wine, Dee?' A lightning switch of gaze, a dazzling smile that set Stevie's teeth on edge. A touch of the green-eyed monsters? she mused, stubbornly refusing to believe it. 'Red or white?'

'Oh, red, please,' Dee said promptly. 'Red for danger.'

'A girl after my own heart,' Jared acknowledged, his eyes sweeping over her in one of those swift, appraising glances that Stevie couldn't help but recognize, couldn't help but inwardly rail against. And yet watching Jared behave in character was a lesson she needed to learn – and firmly commit to memory. 'Stevie?'

A pause, a quizzical expression in those dark velvet eyes – eyes she could happily drown in, Stevie realized absurdly.

'Stevie!' Dee chivvied sharply. 'Jared's waiting to order.'

'I –'

'Just a glass,' Jared insisted, a half-smile playing about the corners of his mouth. 'Nothing more, Stevie, I assure you.'

Stevie stiffened. She might have known. Jared was playing games, amusing himself at Stevie's expense. And talking of expense . . . 'Fine. A glass of white would be lovely,' she acknowledged crisply. 'But on one condition.'

'Oh?' Jared queried politely.

'The bill,' Stevie reminded him. 'Pay for the wine, by all means, Jared. But when it comes to the meal itself, Dee and I will be paying our way.'

'Lady, you drive a real hard bargain,' he acknowledged coolly. 'But, if it's a case of take it or leave it, I guess I haven't any choice. This time.'

This time, next time, some time, never, Stevie derided, adapting one of Rosa's rhymes and determined to make it never if the effort nearly killed her.

Sipping her drink slowly, she pretended to study the menu, refusing to check the daily specials on the board lest her glance should lock with Jared's. Yet with Dee's blatant monopoly of the great man himself, it was a definite over reaction.

'No oysters,' Jared noted sardonically when Dee paused for breath, paused to run her eye over the menu. 'Pity. I was about to put one of your quaint northern theories to the test.'

'Oh?' Dee queried, wrinkling her nose.

'Just the folly of risking seafood at this time of the year,' he explained. 'Bad for the digestion, so I've heard.'

'But good for the libido,' Dee informed him coyly. 'Apparently.'

'Yes.' Jared smiled and placed his menu back on its stand, raising an enquiring eyebrow. 'If you're both ready to order, the obliging Marc is about to reappear.'

Prescience? Stevie mused, since Jared had his back to the room. And since Jared was a stranger in town – apparently – how on earth did he know the waiter's name?

'House rule number one,' he explained, uncannily reading her mind. 'Hotel or restaurant, private home or palace, tip the staff on your way in and the service is guaranteed.'

'A quaint Italian custom?' Stevie queried. 'Or one of the perks of the filthy rich?'

'Neither,' he retorted, generous lips tightening. 'More a matter of common sense.'

Common sense – the Jared Wilde view. And with money no object, why not? An expensive taste in clothes, a car worth a fortune and the best hotel in town – yes, sir!

And then lunch at the Matisse. Hardly slumming it, but not in the Jared Wilde league of places to be seen, surely?

'Strange, I didn't have you down as a snob,' he drawled when Dee slipped upstairs to powder her nose.

'I'm not,' Stevie retorted coolly, annoyed she'd let the comment slip. Nerves, she realized, steeling herself for a tussle over the bill, although, strangely, Marc didn't seem in any hurry to deliver it. 'I was simply stating the obvious.'

As if to prove her point, her eyes swept the room, from the long arm of the L, with its bistro ambience, and the lively bar that hugged the inner wall, to the unpretentious marble-topped tables and green rattan chairs. Not a single vacant seat, she could allow – couldn't fail to allow, given the knot of people hovering at the doorway, noisy testimony to the restaurant's popularity.

And yet dominating the room, as far as Stevie was concerned, was the man opposite, every inch the sleek executive in his lightweight woollen suit, the rich brown material a perfect match for the velvet eyes – eyes now regarding her with thinly veiled amusement.

'The service is good, the food can't be faulted,' she acknowledged coolly. 'But it's hardly The Prince of Wales.'

'A change is as good as a rest,' he chided. 'Which is why I went for French instead of Italian. Talking of which, why not join me for dinner some time? Valentino's. Top end of Lord Street. Know it?'

'Naturally I've heard of it,' Stevie conceded, not really surprised that a man with Italian connections had managed to follow his nose, albeit straight across the road from his hotel.

'And?'

'And what?' she stalled.

'Do you have an opinion?' he needled. 'The Stevie Cooper seal of approval? And, more to the point, does madam have the nerve to take up the offer?'

'The nerve, but not the inclination,' she retorted sweetly. 'But thank you all the same, sir.'

He nodded. 'My pleasure. And it will be, Stevie, when you change your mind.'

When, not if, she noted, refusing the bait as she rummaged through the debris of her handbag in search of her purse, an electric pink plastic one, emblazoned with teddy bears, and one of Rosa's cast-offs.

Logging Jared's raised brows when she finally located it, Stevie felt her cheeks burn. 'Designer gear, it isn't,' she needled. 'But it serves its purpose.'

'I'm sure it does,' he agreed solemnly. 'But just for today it's surplus to requirements.'

'Meaning?'

'Meaning house rule number two. When I find a good restaurant, I find that it generally pays to open an account. Like it or not, this one's on me.'

'But – you promised.'

'Not in so many words.'

'But you're new in town.'

'Very true.'

'So –'

'How come I've managed to make myself at home?' he interrupted, folding his arms and regarding her from under heavy-lidded eyes. 'What's the matter, Stevie?' he queried slyly. 'What's really annoying you? The fact that I'm here to stay,' he challenged softly, 'or the fact that I've fitted in so easily?'

'Annoying?' she echoed, up on her feet in an instant. And, though she stood over Jared, she had the sneaking suspicion the advantage stayed his. 'Annoying? Now there's an understatement. I'm not annoyed, Mr Wilde, I'm livid.'

'Hot-headed, hot-tempered,' he mused. 'I guess it goes with the hair. Though heaven knows what I've done to offend you.'

'Oh, but you do know,' she breathed. 'You know exactly what you've done – walking into my life out of nowhere and calmly taking over, proposing, arranging, rearranging, manipulating, lying –'

'Oh, never lying, Stevie, I can assure you.'

'You can assure me till you're blue in the face, but it won't make a scrap of difference. I'm

94

paying my half of the bill and if you don't like it, you can take a run and jump in the lake. Though on second thoughts,' she tagged on absurdly, 'wait until the tide's in and make it a walk along the pier – a long walk. If you get as far as Ireland,' she bit out, 'I'll call it quits.'

'Stevie –'

'Goodbye, Mr Wilde. Thank you, Mr Wilde. And if I never see you again, ever, it will still be a lifetime too soon.'

'Monday morning,' he reminded her, coming to his feet as she made to push past. 'I'll drop into Deighton's at twelve.'

'Good. I'll be out. Taking lunch. Alone.'

Heading for the cashier in a whirl of indignation, she caught a movement out of the corner of her eye, registered Dee tripping lightly down the stairs and then the sudden commotion a moment or two later. Vaguely alarmed, she spun round to find Dee sprawled at the foot of the staircase, Jared's protective arm about her shoulders, half a dozen waiters dancing attendance.

'These stupid heels,' Dee wailed as Jared helped her off the floor and onto the lowest rung of the staircase. 'I think I've sprained my ankle. Goodness knows how I'll make it home –'

'No problem,' Jared cut in, 'I'll run you. Wait here while I bring the car into the service road.'

'A knight in shining armour,' Stevie sneered, relieved to discover her friend in one piece, amazed to catch Dee's broad wink as she hobbled back to their table. And then the truth dawned. Not so much a sprained ankle as a broken heel. 'Delia Fields, if you weren't one of my closest friends,' Stevie chided lightly, 'I'd wish you well of the man. As it is, I'm beginning to think you deserve one another.'

'Oh, good! Let's hope Jared thinks so. And talking of Jared –'

'Don't worry, Dee,' Stevie reassured her. 'I won't breathe a word. I won't even bother telling you I think you're crazy.'

'Not crazy, just lonely,' Dee surprised her by admitting. 'I like having a man around the place. I know it sounds feeble, Stevie, but that's the way I am. I want to be like you,' she added wistfully, blue eyes fleetingly cloudy, 'But I can't. I need a man and we might just as well both admit it.'

A man. Any man.

Not quite true, Stevie could acknowledge, aware that it was company Dee craved, male company and the flush of young love – the flowers, the candle-lit dinners, the chocolates, the gifts – and the sex, Stevie supposed, vaguely alarmed that Dee could risk her health with a string of casual relationships. Only she didn't, of course, she recalled belatedly. Too clever for her own good at times, Delia Fields rarely made the mistake of giving in to a man without first extracting a promise of a shiny band of gold on the third finger of her left hand.

A man. Any man maybe, Stevie could allow. But, deserve one another though they might, for some strange, illogical reason, the thought of Jared and Dee together wasn't the least amusing.

CHAPTER 6

A hell of a week, a hell of day. Stevie breathed a huge sigh of relief when the lift doors swung open on the tenth floor.

'This year, next year, some time, never,' Rosa chanted, skipping from circle to circle and missing out the squares on the boldly patterned carpet – a ritual she performed at least once a week as she travelled from lift to door by the longest route possible. Coming to a halt outside their front door, she turned to Stevie with a definite flash of triumph. 'I won!'

'This time,' Stevie retorted good-naturedly, inserting her key and allowing the door to swing open. 'And only because I'm loaded down with shopping. Now be a good girl and go back for one of those bags I've –'

Too late. Rosa darted through the gap, heading for the lounge and the video they'd earlier collected from the library. Stevie swallowed a smile as she struggled across the kitchen to off-load the first of the carriers before retracing her steps.

A month's worth of shopping – Stevie's way of making sure she didn't over-budget.

Six-year-old children having the knack of choosing the most expensive brands on the shelves, Stevie had evolved a routine of collecting Rosa from the childminder and then heading for the Kew Bridge supermarket and the six o'clock lull. Which meant transporting a mountain of food from the boot of the car to the lift, and from the lift to her apartment. Or making several journeys with a six-year-old in tow. Easier this way, Stevie had decided, than that other alternative. Leaving Rosa alone in the apartment was clearly out of the question.

Stevie popped her head around the lounge door. 'It's too loud, poppet. Be an angel and turn it down.'

No reply. The image on screen all-engrossing. So Stevie tiptoed in, dropping to her knees to cross Rosa's line of vision as she reached for the handset and the volume control.

'Mummy!' Indignation when Stevie's head intruded.

'Sorry, darling. But you can always rewind it. Just don't touch the vol –'

A waste of time, she decided, pulling the door to, muffling the sound, and with the apartments so well insulated, probably a worry over nothing. Stevie heard little from the neighbours, and none of them had ever seen fit to complain about the exuberance of a normal, healthy six-year-old.

Not that Stevie would recognize most of her neighbours if they were to place themselves end to end, flat on the floor of her lounge.

Peace. Privacy. Security. At a price. The sort of price Stevie could never have afforded in a million years. But she did pay her way. A nominal rent, maybe, but the favour was mutual. Andrew could be sure the place was in good hands and Stevie and Rosa had a base.

Despite the ups and downs of the day, she was humming lightly as she collected the bags she'd abandoned at the lifts. Home. A weekend ahead of her. Time to spend with Rosa. That new dress, she remembered, and Suzy Waterson's party – a party Kelly would miss now. Poor Kelly. Poor Lorna. Tom had promised to call the moment he had any news but that didn't mean Stevie couldn't pick up the phone herself. Only not tonight. Things would be clearer in the morning. So, next problem. Make another two journeys, or struggle with the four remaining bags?

Easy-peasy. Too easy, as it happened. The handle of the heaviest sagged like overstretched elastic the moment she picked it up and, instead of placing it gently down again, Stevie made a dash for her open front door. The contents bounced the length of the hallway when the seam gave way.

'Damn, damn and damn!' An inelegant scramble on hands and knees as she made a grab at the nearest – tins, thank goodness, and no real damage done. She shuddered just at the thought of her fastidious neighbours turning up their noses at the sight. Neighbour, she corrected automatically, with just the widowed Mrs Jones next door and the end flat empty – though not for much longer, according to the janitor.

Catching the sound of a door creaking open, the hinges out of practice and in need of lubrication, Stevie froze. The empty apartment. Oh, no! With Stevie's luck it would probably turn out to be the mayor himself, and what a way to greet a new neighbour!

Only it was worse than that: the muffled footsteps getting closer as Stevie toyed with idea of pretending she hadn't heard, the muffled footsteps drawing level, skirting round, coming to a halt in front of her.

'I thought I recognized that fiery mop. Well, well, well, I guess we meet again – and how!'

She closed her eyes, not believing, not wanting to believe, but sure enough, when she opened them again, a pair of elegantly shod, hand-worked shoes were planted squarely in front of her. She raised her eyes the seemingly endless length of his legs, and higher again, the casual fold of arms across a powerful chest managing to annoy her, though not as much the smile playing about the corners of his mouth or the amusement swirling in those heavy-lidded eyes once Stevie had steeled herself to meet them.

'Need a hand?'

'What do you think?' she snapped, the colour in her cheeks a perfect match for her hair.

A single eyebrow rose. 'At a guess,' he drawled lazily, 'I'd say yes. But then, that's only what I think. The lady sprawled at my feet clearly has other ideas, which is fine by me, but don't say I didn't offer.'

He spun round, swam out of view, and the sudden sting of tears took Stevie by surprise.

'But – where are you going?' she asked absurdly, sitting back on her heels.

'Going? Why, since the neighbours are hostile, home, of course. I'd ask you in,' he carelessly informed her. 'But without benefit of furniture, the place is rather bare. Some other time maybe.'

Muffled footsteps receding, a squeal of hinges, the soft click of a door, and she was abandoned along with the cans of baked beans, spaghetti hoops and pasta shapes that Rosa would live on given half a chance. Stevie sniffed, felt the hot trickle of moisture on her cheek and dashed the tears away with an impatient brush of the hand.

'Men! Neither use nor ornament,' she muttered vehemently, scrambling about on all fours. 'And I'll bet it was a man who invented carrier bags that didn't –'

'Yours, I believe?'

'Oh!'

'Yes, oh,' he echoed grimly, having silently gathered a collection of tins and stacked them into a pile at Stevie's door. And then, spotting the trickle of moisture on her lashes, his expression lightened. 'Allow me.' Dropping down beside her, he pulled a square of linen from his pocket and, before she had time to fathom his intentions, gently wiped away the tell-tale smudge of tears.

Stevie went hot, then cold, afraid he was going to kiss her, more afraid he wasn't, and she fought the urge to dip her head, nuzzle the palm that was tantalizingly close, instinctively aware that the currents swirling between them had registered in Jared's mind, that Jared's control, like Stevie's, was hanging by a thread. Impossible. She barely knew the man, certainly didn't like him or his high-handed ways, and as for anything else –

She pulled away, breaking the spell, absurdly disappointed that he allowed her to go without protest, and, looking anywhere but at Jared, scrambled clumsily to her feet.

'Thank you. I think I can manage now.'

'And I think not. Worry not,' he chided pleasantly. 'I'm simply being neighbourly. Who knows? When I'm careless enough to run out of sugar, I might even call in the favour. Though on second thoughts,' he added, eyebrows disappearing into his hairline when he noted the label on the can he was about to drop into a bag, 'I'll make it something more substantial. "Pasta shapes in a rich tomato sauce – a bouquet of flavours from the sun-kissed aisle, courtesy of the local food hall." How would you rate my chances?'

Stevie winced at the pun. 'Stick to the job you know,' she advised. 'Then at least you can pay the bills.'

'Yes.' Something struck him, eyes narrowing as his glance swept the hallway. 'A fistful of bills in a set-up like this. Correct me if I'm wrong, but I hadn't realized Deighton's paid such extravagant wages?'

'They don't, as I'm sure you must know. Not that my rate of pay is any of your business,' she pointedly reminded him.

'Just being –'

' "Nosy" is the word you're looking for.'

'As a prospective employer, I was about to say vaguely alarmed. No wonder you turned me down.'

'You mean you noticed? And here's me thinking you've never learned to take no for an answer.'

'I haven't and I won't. You'll come round – eventually.'

'I wouldn't bank on it,' she retorted sweetly, back in control and intent on hanging onto it.

'Coffee?' he suggested hopefully, palming a jar that had rolled against the doorjamb.

'I wouldn't bank on that either.' Stevie's voice was clipped as she snatched the coffee from his outstretched hand, the thought of allowing Jared across her threshold triggering fresh waves of panic.

'Another quaint northern custom?' he drawled. 'Treat thy new neighbour with calcu-

104

lated rudeness. In which case, Stevie, I'm sorely tempted to change my mind – cancel the lease on that highly expensive apartment.'

'Don't make any rash decisions on my account,' Stevie needled, the thought of living cheek by jowl with Jared enough to bring on a fit of the vapours.

'When you know me better,' he lazily informed her, 'you'll realize that once I've made up my mind, there isn't a woman alive capable of swaying me.'

'Maybe so,' she acknowledged. 'But then stubbornness is a vice, not a virtue.'

'You should know,' Jared riposted. 'Since you're foolish enough to have crossed me.'

'Turned you down, you mean. Saying yes to every man who asks isn't compulsory, Mr Wilde.'

'I'm relieved to hear it. Less relieved to note your appalling short-term memory. The name's Jared. Always has been, always will be.'

'And if I take you at your word, take the job, accept your thirty pieces of silver, what name will I call you then? Sir?'

'First things first. Take the job and we can thrash out the social niceties later.'

'No need,' she reminded him. 'No job, no problem.'

'Just the not inconsiderable problem of paying the bills. Bills, Stevie. Mortgage, gas, electricity, phone, not to mention the groceries. On the subject of which, you could feed a small army on this lot. Good heavens, woman, who are you expecting?'

'Not you, that's for sure, and that's all you're entitled to hear. Don't worry, Jared, if and when I throw a party, you'll be the first to know.'

'Promises, promises – an invitation from Stevie. My, things are looking up.'

'Wrong! Not so much an invitation as a warning to fit the earplugs.'

Jared shook his head. 'Unkind, Stevie. And believe me, it doesn't pay to antagonize the neighbours.'

'Precisely. You ignore me, I'll ignore you. An ideal arrangement.'

'Suits me,' he retorted, generous mouth tightening. 'Neither use nor ornament I may be, my dear, but I can take a hint. So long, Stevie, see you around some time. Oh, yes, and happy unpacking,' he tossed back over his shoulder. 'And if you're ever in need of a hand, don't count on me.'

'Unkind, Jared.'

'Tough, Stevie. If you don't like the rules, you shouldn't get involved in the game.'

'Jared?'

'Now what?'

'Thanks. For helping with the groceries, I mean. And welcome to Parklands.'

He halted, spun on his heels, his startled gaze bouncing the length of the hallway.

She'd hurt him, Stevie realized, biting her lip, realizing too that keeping him at a distance was the only way to survive. Better to let him go. No olive branch, no cosy invitations, no risk. But, having summoned the courage to thank him, the need to take control – and prove it – refused to go away. 'About that coffee,' she murmured softly. 'If you're not dashing off anywhere –'

'Oh, but I am,' he interrupted gleefully, his whole expression lightening. 'A date with a blonde. Would you believe, a sexy little number who fell for me at lunchtime?' The mocking smile spread from ear to ear as Jared fished a bunch of keys from a pocket and swung them up into his palm with a theatrical twist of the wrist. He shrugged. 'Too bad, huh? But then, my dear, that's the way the cookie crumbles.'

An insolent wink of an eye, another jaunty shrug of the shoulders, a much too chirpy whistle as he sauntered towards the lifts, and a fuming Stevie wrestled the urge to slam her door.

Impossible man. Revolting man. Tormenting man. And as for Delia Fields . . . Just this once, she vowed grimly, leaning back against the wood-work, the laughter rising in her throat. Just this once, and only once, words failed her.

'Nanna, darling, you're looking wonderful.'

Not strictly true, given the old lady's pallor, but worth the white lie to see the pleasure light up her eyes.

Pulling her chair in close and taking her grand-mother's bony hand in hers, Stevie ran a critical eye over the age-worn face and was horribly afraid Nanna was losing weight. Two weeks. Two weeks too long, Stevie realized with a sudden pang of guilt. Not nearly often enough for Stevie, but as much as Nanna could take if Rosa came along. No Rosa today, thanks to the Waterson party, but Nanna's disappointment was tangible despite the brave words.

'I've told you before,' she muttered almost sharply. 'A nursing home's no place for a child. And especially on a day like this. Though it is nice to see her running about the gardens,' she tagged on wistfully.

Yes. It was space to run, to let off steam, to make whoops of noise that wouldn't annoy the neighbours. Neighbours. Jared Wilde. Stevie grimaced. Was there no escape from the irritating man's presence? she wondered, banishing the image with a massive surge of will. Tea. An afternoon ritual. Nanna's first cup thick enough to make the spoon stand to attention; Stevie's, in contrast, well diluted from the boiling kettle.

Warm though the day was, Stevie tucked the rug firmly round her grandmother's fragile frame before positioning her wheelchair with her back to the sun in the open patio doorway, a tableau repeated across the four sides of the court.

Sunday. The traditional day for families to visit. And, though Stevie called in whenever she could, she was sharply aware that it was Rosa's smiling face that Nanna looked for, the bond between the two more than the tie of blood. Rosa, Stevie and Nanna. Three generations, and surprisingly enough, an entire tier missing in the middle.

It would be twelve years, Stevie realized, not wanting to remember yet shockingly aware that if she lived to be a hundred she'd never forget that knock on the door, the policeman's solemn face, Mae's tears, Andrew's solid presence. Andrew, as gutted as Stevie and Mae, and yet his own grief denied because his cousins needed his support.

Andrew. Smothering the pain, Stevie smiled, leaned forward. 'Guess whose coming home soon?'

'The man in the moon?' her grandmother scorned. 'Because it wouldn't be Andrew Roxton. But just in case it is, Stevie Cooper, you can tell him from me if he's thinking of showing his face around here, he can save himself the bother. Two years,' she reminded her. 'Two whole years and the most I've had is a Christmas card.'

'And the flowers, Nan – that huge bouquet on your birthday, don't forget.'

'Aye. He can pick up the phone and order a flash bunch of roses but can't spare a few minutes to talk to his gran. Don't tell me he's finally made the effort to get in touch?'

'Just a quick call,' Stevie reassured her. 'And it's easier said than done, given the difference in time.'

'Aye. Well . . .' A sniff of disapproval, one of

109

'those looks' that could halt a charging rhino in its tracks.

Time for a change of subject, Stevie decided, relaying the rest of her news. Kelly's birthday, Mrs Hunter's illness, the rumblings at Deighton's, and then, since the man had dominated her thoughts for the best part of the week, last but not least, Stevie's new neighbour.

'A man, hey? Young? Old? Married? Single?'

Stevie smiled at the rapid fire of questions. Age, height, weight, colour of socks . . . Hardly, she allowed, knowing full well Nanna wouldn't hesitate to ask if the fancy really took her.

'And you're sure he's not married?' her grandmother probed, steering the conversation full circle.

Stevie shrugged. 'Not as far as I'm aware. Not that it's any of my business,' she reminded her gently, cursing the give-away surge of colour.

'No. But just make sure you lock your door. Better safe than sorry these days.'

'Yes, Nan.' Another smile, another tirade from the occupant of the wheelchair, though, thankfully for Stevie, the subject switched back to Drew.

'He was always the same,' Nanna murmured crossly, the wisps of white curls on the shiny pink scalp quivering with indignation. 'Stubborn, just like his father. And, just like his father, heaven help anyone who stood in his way. I don't suppose he noticed that he broke his mother's heart taking

110

that job on the other side of the world. Singapore,' she derided. 'He couldn't have gone much further if he'd tried. Anyone would think he couldn't wait to get away. Singapore, Hong Kong . . . Why, if they opened a bank on Mars,' she scorned, 'he'd be the first to apply. Coming home? Aye. And if you believe that, Stevie Cooper, you'll believe anything. Just because he can charm the birds from the trees when he's prepared to make the effort, he thinks he can do as he likes.'

Stevie ignored the rumblings, the ramblings, the dozen and one slights that were nothing more than an old lady's fancy. Nanna was lonely, couldn't understand why the younger generation seemed reluctant to settle down, marry, raise a family, produce a clutch of great-grandchildren. And as for Andrew's job, Stevie had long since given up trying to explain the intricacies of commodity trading.

Poor Nan. Having outlived her children, outlived a crop of friends, was it hardly any wonder she was feeling neglected?

'I'll bring Rosa next week,' Stevie told her, stooping to drop a kiss onto the parchment-like cheek, hug the bony shoulders. 'Promise.'

'Aye, and that's another thing,' her grandmother stunned her by conceding. 'The child needs a father, Stevie. Not to mention brothers and sisters. I don't suppose –?'

'No, Nan, I don't suppose you do,' Stevie

interrupted cheerfully. 'But if and when I do decide to take the plunge, you'll be the first to know.'

'You've no one special in mind, then?'

'Wouldn't you like to know?' Stevie teased, and then, sensing the pain behind the casually worded question, 'No, Nan. Not yet.' Not ever, she tagged on silently, bitterly. Although, disconcertingly, a pair of heavy-lidded brown velvet eyes popped into her mind. And were just as swiftly banished.

CHAPTER 7

Work. Monday morning blues. There was no sign of Tom, not that Stevie was expecting him, but, with Jared set to show his face before lunch, Stevie was in desperate need of some moral support. Not to mention his promised explanation. Still, it would keep. It would have to, and at least the news of Mrs Hunter sounded good. Not so thoughts of the stormy scene to come, for, despite her threat to be out when Jared dropped by, Stevie was determined to stand her ground.

ALITANI. She'd almost been impressed. The rising star in the trade. No quick-frozen TV dinners or ready meals here, just the freshest of fresh food cooked to the peak of perfection and supplying the luxury end of the market: London's top food halls, exclusive delicatessens and five-star hotels, not to mention award-winning restaurants. Oh, yes. She could almost be impressed. Almost.

Twelve o'clock. Stevie braced herself and, sure enough, bang on cue came the rap on the office door – her door this time – and there was barely a pause before Jared swept in, impeccable as always, steel-grey suit this morning, the press of his trousers razor-sharp. Along with a crisp white shirt and shoes she could see her face in, the whole effect was stunning, a tribute to the sort of first-class service a hotel like the Prince of Wales could provide. Though not for much longer, she silently amended, since Jared would soon be moving into Parklands. In which case, the sooner Stevie moved out the better.

'The wrong shirt?' Jared queried dryly, having paused in the doorway. Stevie's scrutiny was clearly a source of wry amusement. Running a critical eye over his appearance, he shrugged, spread his hands. 'The wrong tie, perhaps? Or maybe I'm wearing odd socks and you're too polite to say?'

'Hardly,' Stevie retorted, colouring. 'A man with an eye for detail wouldn't,' she reminded sweetly. 'And if by some wild chance you did –'

'You'd be the first to let me know? Yes, Stevie.' Generous lips twitched. 'I think we've established that tact isn't one of your virtues.'

'And neither is compliance. You could have saved yourself a journey, Jared. The lady's not for turning.'

'Maybe not,' he lazily conceded. 'But never heard of money, Stevie?'

'I certainly have. It's the stuff that pays the bills. Mortgage, gas, electricity, phone,' she reminded him, ticking them off on her fingers. 'Not to mention a mountain of groceries. Believe it or not, since I've managed well enough without you up till now, the lady's not for buying either.'

'No? Fine.' He nodded, stepped forward, closed the door, crossed the office in four easy strides and pulled out a chair. 'May I?' he enquired politely.

'Be my guest,' she replied equally politely, the solid lines of her desk providing a barrier, a welcome barrier, as Jared made himself at home.

Silence. Not even the relentless tick of a clock. No rustle of pages, no attempt to rifle through the briefcase he'd carelessly dropped at his feet. No small talk. Nothing. *Your move*, laughing brown eyes seemed to challenge, and Stevie coloured, angled her head, clamped her lips together in an uncompromising line and waited. And waited. And inwardly squirmed. Because Jared was oh, so sure he had the upper hand, that sooner or later he'd break her.

A rap on the door broke the deadlock. Tom's secretary, Belle, pulling up in a fluster when she realized Stevie wasn't alone.

Stevie waved her in, the batch of buff-coloured envelopes Belle was clutching to her chest the perfect excuse to keep Jared waiting.

'It's mostly routine,' Belle explained apologetically, eyes swivelling automatically to Jared. 'Repeat orders, invoices, job applications and so on. But there are one or two marked "Con-fidential" and I didn't like –'

'Thank you, Belle,' Stevie cut in, logging Jared's winning smile, the woman's surge of colour. 'You did right. I'll put them to one side until I can speak to Tom. In the mean time, if you could chase up Melissa with some coffee?'

'Coffee? Oh! Yes, of course. It's no trouble. I'll see to it myself.'

Yes. Stevie didn't doubt it. And if she hadn't seen it with her own two eyes she'd never have believed that the cool, calm and unflappable Isa-belle Owen could behave like a simpering virgin. A virgin. Just like Stevie, in fact. 'Spinster' was the usual disparaging term, she recalled, wondering how long it would be before that description began to apply, and, scowling visibly, she switched her mind to Jared, switched her gaze, caught his unconcealed amusement and stiffened.

'So –'

'Worth waiting for the coffee, I'd say,' he interrupted smoothly. 'Unless, of course, you feel the need to press on? After all, with Tom away you must be busy.'

'I am. But it hasn't stopped you imposing,' Stevie snapped, shuffling the envelopes into a pile on the blotting pad in front of her.

'Guilty as charged,' he allowed, sitting back in his chair, folding his arms, a rebellious lock of hair falling across his eye and giving him a rakish look that did nothing to detract from his appear-

ance. 'But I did have an appointment,' he reminded her mildly. 'And if you'd come up with
the answer I wanted in the first place, I wouldn't
be here now.'

'But if you'd taken the answer I'd given,' she
countered sweetly, 'you'd have saved us both a lot
of time and effort.'

'More fun this way,' he tossed out absurdly.

'I –'

Another rap on the door. Jared leapt to his feet
as Belle backed into the room. 'Allow me,' he
insisted, taking the tray.

'Oh! Thank you. You're t-too kind,' she sim-
pered, coloured, paused, half inclined to linger.

A sympathetic Stevie resisted the urge to
chivvy her since it would only leave her alone
with a man whose every lift of an eyebrow
managed to bowl yet another maiden over, and
Stevie wasn't so immune to his charms that she
could afford to be complacent.

'Alone at last,' Jared mocked as the door swung
back on its hinges. 'Coffee, Stevie? Since I've
made myself at home, I might as well pour.'

'Surely you mean make yourself useful for a
change?' Stevie countered tartly.

'I generally do – at the right time and place, and
assuming the lady in question appreciates the
fact.'

'But how could any lady worthy of the name fail
to notice?' she drawled, eyes wide and innocent.

'These things happen,' he countered coolly.

'But you can take it from me, never more than once.'

'An unforgiving nature, huh?'

'Let's just say that on the rare occasion it does happen, I know when I'm wasting my time.'

'Good. You won't dream of insulting me by wasting mine, then?'

'Meaning?'

'ALITANI. The offer of a job. Like I said, thanks, but no thanks.'

'But you haven't had time to discuss it with Tom.'

'I don't need to. My job, my life, my decision.'

'And your loss,' he countered coldly. 'A company car, a hefty pay rise and the sort of security a high-powered firm can provide. Oh, yes, and the chance to travel.'

'Not interested, Jared.'

'Not even if Deighton's folded, Stevie?'

'Not even then,' she bit out with her first twinge of unease. 'Because it isn't going to happen. Understand?'

A loaded pause. Cold green eyes locked with strangely perceptive brown ones. He knows, Stevie decided, absurdly hurt at being excluded. She wasn't sure *what*, exactly, but Jared knew something Stevie didn't, was convinced Stevie would take the job on offer. Only she wouldn't. And if Deighton's and every other firm in the country went to the wall tomorrow, she still wouldn't.

Impasse. Back to that screaming silence. And then, unexpectedly, absurdly, Jared smiled, came lazily to his feet, reached for the briefcase he hadn't bothered to open and strolled equally lazily to the door.

'Now what are you doing?' Stevie demanded, braced for a battle and peeved to be cheated.

Jared paused, glanced at his watch, smiled again. 'Duty calls,' he explained enigmatically, fingers tightening their grip on the briefcase. 'Time is money, for both of us. And, since you haven't come up with the answer I want . . .

'You've finally admitted defeat?'

' "Defeat" isn't a word in my vocabulary, Stevie. When the irresistible force meets the immovable object,' he informed her matter-of-factly, 'I generally find it pays to seek an easier way round. And I will. You'll change your mind.'

'So sure, Jared?'

'About you? Strangely enough, no,' he conceded. 'But this time, Stevie, I'm prepared to back a hunch. Same time tomorrow? Though on second thoughts, knowing how busy you are, I'll give you a call instead. Eleven-thirty,' he declared. 'On the dot.'

'And the next day, and the next?' she needled.

'And the day after that, if needs be. But don't forget the penalty clause. For every day you leave it, the salary drops accordingly, and as for the perks –'

'A Mini instead of a Rolls? Or a bicycle made for two, perhaps?'

'Hardly,' he murmured, grinning in spite of himself. 'But it's reassuring to know you're giving it some thought.'

Stevie screamed – silently – screwed the piece of paper on which she'd earlier been doodling into a ball and tossed it at the door Jared had closed behind him.

No time to indulge a fit of the vapours. To coin a phrase, duty called, and with the pile of mail delivered by Belle waiting for someone – for Stevie, in Tom's absence – to deal with, no time to dwell on the tawny lights dancing in a pair of velvet eyes. No time, just a contrary inclination, she discovered, as the numbers on the page became a meaningless jumble. So, decision time. Curb the gut reaction and apply the rules of common sense.

Could she work for Jared? There, she'd done it. Not so difficult after all, she acknowledged, running her fingers through her hair and absent-mindedly feathering the strands into spikes. But phrasing the question raised the dilemma of facing up to the answer. Work for Jared. Work with Jared. Spend time with Jared. Work, not play. Not baiting, teasing, tormenting, kissing – Kissing! As if. As if Stevie would want to, as if the fastidious Jared Wilde would condescend to socialize with his staff. And, since familiarity was said to breed contempt, not such a silly idea after all.

Next question. Would she *want* to work for Jared? No shortage of excitement, she acknowledged, aware that the sparks would fly, that two strong personalities would have their share of ups and downs. Too many sparks? Probably, she told herself wryly. Which made it one for and one against and time for the casting vote.

So, leaving aside the matter of loyalty to Tom, for now at least, could she afford *not* to work for Jared? A hefty salary, company car and perks – though quite what the perks entailed, Stevie wasn't sure. Foreign travel? With Rosa to think about? Rosa. The see-saw of her mind moved downwards – and stuck. No contest. The relief was amazing. The black cloud that had been hovering over her vanished at once. She'd come up with the answer fair and square. Jared Wilde and his absurd suggestions could go to blazes.

A rigorous spring clean of the soul was clearly therapeutic, she decided, checking her watch and amazed at the mountain of work she'd ploughed through. Three-thirty. Too late for lunch; she'd settle for coffee and a biscuit and a five-minute indulgence. Three-thirty. A mental picture of Rosa coming out of school, skipping down the drive into the waiting arms of Anna, who'd promised to drop her off at the Watersons' and deliver her back home at seven.

Anna Cherwick, an absolute find – a Tom-find, Stevie recalled, aware that the childless young widow gained almost as much from Rosa's company as Stevie did. And if anyone deserved the joys of a family it was Anna.

Hmm. She would soon lose two of her charges, Stevie recalled, when the twins she looked after moved back to London at the end of the month. It was just a thought, the germ of an idea to save up for Lorna and Tom's return. On the subject of which, make it soon, she silently prayed as the phone began to ring. Jared? Please, don't let it be Jared.

'Tom! You must be psychic. I was just thinking about you.'

'I thought my ears were burning,' he teased, allowing Stevie to relax as she sensed from his tone that things were going well and he and Lorna would soon be heading for home.

'The day after tomorrow,' he confirmed. 'We'd have managed it earlier but Lorna refuses to leave until we've double-checked arrangements – day nurse, granny-sitter, that sort of thing. The old dear's fine,' he reassured her quickly. 'They're keeping her in for a few days' observation, but the doctors insist she's stable and the signs are looking good. With my luck,' he chuckled irreverently, 'she'll probably live for ever.'

No time to mention Jared, but it would keep. Because Tom would be back soon and the thorny subject of Jared could be laid to rest once and for all.

And not a moment too soon for Stevie. Dee's

ecstatic droolings less than an hour later were enough to make a girl's hair stand on end.

'Oh, Stevie! The man's an absolute dream! Chocolates, flowers, champagne – and last night –'

'He whisked you off to the moon in his private jet and you played among the stars till dawn rose over Mars?' Stevie cut in, the thought of Jared and Dee together all weekend anything but reassuring. Though when Dee didn't call, hadn't bothered returning any of Stevie's calls, she should have known.

'Chance would be a fine thing. But you're getting warm. We had a candlelit dinner at Valentino's, followed by a long, slow drive along the beach and champagne cocktails on the sand. And then we kicked off our shoes and paddled in the shallows, and later –'

'Spare me the finer details – *please*,' Stevie drawled, the knife-blade twisting in her belly.

'Jealous, Stevie?'

'What do you think, Dee?'

'Straight up, Stevie Cooper?' Dee probed, all trace of amusement banished. 'I think you've no idea what you're missing.'

'Safer that way,' Stevie reminded her grimly.

'But nothing like as much fun. I just wondered . . .'

'You wondered?' Stevie prompted, vaguely alarmed.

'Oh . . . nothing that won't keep,' her friend

informed her airily. 'I'll see you on Friday. Can't make this week's lunch, I'm afraid, but I'll see you later at the party.'

'Party?'

'The housewarming party at Jared's new place. Haven't you heard? He's moving into Parklands. The same floor as you. Which means, Stevie Cooper, you've no excuse for not coming. You can't even plead the need for a sitter for Rosa,' she gleefully underlined.

A moot point, but hardly worth debating. A party. Assuming she was invited, and even without Jared's devastating presence, it was just the sort of thing she'd normally avoid like the plague.

So much for a glossy invitation waiting on the doormat, Stevie observed sourly, stepping over nothing but a mountain of bills and feeling strangely bereft without Rosa's chattering presence. Difficult to wriggle out of if there had been one, though. Babysitting problems wouldn't wash, and as for Jared . . . Damn Jared Wilde, with his absurd suggestions and his absurd invitations – probably quality vellum, gold-edged and specially printed to boot, Stevie pictured in her mind's eye. Since parties weren't compulsory, she simply wouldn't go, and if she stuck to that short, sharp phrase Jared was sure to recognize – 'Thanks, but no thanks' – he might even get the message. On two counts.

Stepping out of her work clothes, she headed

for the bathroom. The urge to take a shower was as much the need to wash away thoughts of Jared as the need to feel clean.

The imperative trill of the doorbell. Turning the dial on the shower from hot, through the gradations of red and blue to cold and back again, Stevie ignored it. Too early to be Rosa – her new-found friendship with Suzy having blossomed in Kelly's absence – too late for the postman and that unwelcome invitation. And then something struck her.

Jared wouldn't. Knowing Jared Wilde, she wouldn't put it past him. A grim-faced Stevie shrugged her dripping body into a robe before striding to the door where someone – surprise, surprise, look who it isn't! – was clearly glued to the bell.

'Now what?' she snapped, ignoring the raised eyebrow, the glance of approval as he logged her appearance, ignoring too the surge of heat that flooded her body. 'You can't have run out of sugar already,' she derided, running her fingers through the rats' tails of her hair and planing the excess water onto the collar of her robe. 'Since I know for a fact you haven't moved in yet. And before you assume I've had my nose in the letterbox, clocking your every move, Dee phoned.'

'It's a free country,' he conceded lightly. 'And what could be more natural than a spot of gossip between friends?'

'With the dynamic Mr Wilde the subject under

discussion? Sorry to disappoint you, Jared, but she barely mentioned your name.'

'Liar.'

'If you say so,' Stevie bit out, pulling the edges of her robe together and looping the belt into a more secure hitch. 'So?'

'So?'

'So, what do you want?' she prompted tetchily. 'I'm cold, I'm wet, and if I stand shivering on the doormat any longer, I'll probably catch my death.'

'I doubt it,' he reassured her dryly. 'But if it's playing on your mind, why not do us both a favour and invite me in?'

'I tried that once before, remember, and someone turned me down.'

'Ah, yes, but as I explained at the time there was the slight matter of a prior engagement.'

'A hot date, I seem to recall. A sexy blonde who'd fallen for the dubious nature of your charms – or maybe snapped the heel of her shoe in an effort to grab your attention.'

Jared grinned, shook his head, wagged an admonitory finger. 'Accidents will happen, Stevie. Now, had it been you –'

'I'd have walked home. In bare feet. Easier along the beach than in the street, of course, but I'd have managed – alone.'

'My, good news *does* travel fast,' he drawled with a hint of annoyance. 'In which case, Stevie, you'll have heard about the party.'

'Are you asking me or telling me?' she barked, beginning to shiver, aware of a puddle of water forming at her feet, on Andrew's highly expensive carpet at that.

'Just double-checking that you'll be there.'

'Two's company, three's a crowd,' she pointed out tartly. 'And I should hate to cramp your style.'

'With Tom and Lorna taking numbers up to five at least, fear not, Stevie, you won't be playing gooseberry. But if you want to bring along a friend – a male friend,' he tagged on slyly, 'to even things out – feel free.'

'Thank you.' She nodded. 'If I've nothing better planned, I might at that. When did you say it was?'

'I didn't, and you needn't bat those luminous green eyes and pretend you haven't heard. Friday. Eight o'clock onwards at my place. And don't bother eating first; ALITANI's specialist caterers will be serving food at nine. You never know, it might even turn out to be supper with the boss.'

'It certainly will,' she couldn't resist goading. 'Supper with the boss – *my boss*,' she emphasized grimly. 'Tom Deighton, remember?'

'Maybe,' he conceded tightly. 'And maybe it's high time you talked to Tom. He and Lorna are due back –'

'Thank you, Jared,' she interrupted dryly. 'Tom and Lorna are two of my closest friends and, believe it or not, I am aware of their plans.'

'Short-term or long-term?'

'Both, as it happens. They'll be home early Wednesday evening, and with everything back to normal life will go on as before.'

'So sure, Stevie?'

'As sure as life ever can be. Now, if you don't mind, I'd like to dry off.'

'Pity,' he mused, generous lips twitching as his lazy glance reached out to touch her. 'There's something very appealing about a woman wrapped in nothing but a damp robe.'

Stevie gritted her teeth, counted to five – and smiled. 'Mention it to Dee. I'm sure she'll be happy to oblige.' Assuming she hasn't already, she added silently, sourly, closing the door without waiting for a reply.

She'd reached the welcome security of the kitchen before the sound of the doorbell halted her in her tracks.

'Jared? Back already?' she purred, not the least impressed by his ready smile. She leaned forward, glanced around, lowered her voice confidentially. 'Shocking of me, I know,' she conceded, 'but, believe it or not, I haven't had time to miss you.'

He held out an envelope, that easy grin splitting his features. 'Not so much a cup of sugar as an Italian bearing gifts – of the nicest sort, of course. I wanted to deliver this in person.'

'Don't tell me? With the soaring cost of postage these days, every penny counts?'

'It certainly does. But you should know, living in a place like this.'

'I manage to pay the bills,' she bit out. 'But if you think *you* might find it a struggle, why not cut your losses before it's too late?'

'With a six-month lease all signed, sealed and delivered? Sorry to disappoint you, Stevie, but it's too late already.'

'Your contract, your apartment, your problem,' she reminded him sweetly, refusing the bait in the innocuous-sounding words. Besides, she was beginning to shiver again, part cold, part fear, she realized, and the exchange of words with Jared was beginning to sound blatantly flirtatious.

If only poor Dee could see him now, an 'absolute dream' in casual mode – or as casual as a man like Jared would care to appear: cream polo-neck sweater, a lightweight fabric like silk, at a guess, hugging the powerful barrel of his chest, the dark shadow beneath hinting at a lush tangle of hair that female fingers would be itching to scrunch. Not that Stevie wanted to notice, she told herself primly, dropping her gaze to his waistband, and lower, to black linen trousers, creases razor-sharp as always, and thigh muscles rippling as Jared switched his weight from one impossibly long leg to the other.

Her gaze moved back, higher now, her cheeks

flaming as she reached his groin, logged the outline of his manhood. The fleeting urge to reach out and touch filled her with heat, filled her with shame, her frightened eyes darting to his face and reading the truth in Jared's smoky eyes. Heaven help her but he'd followed every glance, every thought, and Stevie bristled, snatched the envelope from his outstretched hand, spun on her heel and stomped the length of her hallway, unconsciously leading the way to the kitchen.

'Coffee?' she suggested tartly, deciding that the sooner she served it, the sooner she'd get rid of him. 'It's only instant, mind.'

'My favourite,' he insisted, smiling broadly, hitching himself up onto one of the breakfast bar stools, his back to the counter, so that, annoyingly, he could follow every move that she made.

All fingers and thumbs, it seemed to take forever. She scattered grains of coffee liberally over the worktop, and, loath to see the sugar follow suit, she took the lid off the canister and pushed it within Jared's reach.

'Milk or cream?' she queried from the depths of the fridge.

'Neither,' he reminded her, clearly amused, although for the life of her she couldn't see why. 'I take it strong, black and sugarless, remember?'

'And why should I remember, since we're hardly bosom pals?'

'Ouch,' he conceded good-naturedly. 'And

here's me thinking I'd made a lasting impression.'

'Oh, but you have. It just isn't the one you were hoping for,' she informed him saccharine-sweetly, swinging away, adding an extra half spoonful of coffee to his cup before pouring the boiling water. Strong he'd asked for, strong Jared would get, and heaven help him if he dared raise so much as an eyebrow in objection.

'Perfect,' he pronounced, with barely a pause to let it cool. 'No biscuits?' he prompted hopefully, his appraising glance sweeping the pristine kitchen. 'No home-baked cookies lurking in a jar?'

'And me a working mo –' Almost too late, Stevie pulled herself up sharp. Working mother. Nothing wrong with that in this day and age, and with half the town aware of her status why *not* come clean with Jared? Nothing to tell, she decided, lips tightening. Nothing Jared would care to know. And doubtless he'd find out for himself in time, assuming Tom, Lorna or Dee hadn't mentioned it already. Not that her friends were prone to gossip, but it might just have slipped out in the course of conversation.

In a desperate bid to cover her confusion, Stevie made a grab for the biscuit barrel, slid it across the counter and forced a smile. 'Help yourself,' she invited, hitching herself up on the stool opposite, the width of the breakfast bar barely enough for safety.

'Hmm. Malted milk animals,' he noted dryly,

her half-blurted comment having clearly passed him by.

'Not sufficiently sophisticated for sir's superior taste?' she inquired, itching to know what he made of it all, what with teddy bear-covered purses and shaped pasta faces and now Rosa's favourite biscuits.

'Not at all. The little boy inside who's never grown up thinks they're great, and I guess that goes for you too?'

'Rose-coloured memories of childhood?' A pause, a deep breath, and then, the angle of her chin unwittingly aggressive, 'If you must know, I buy them for the kids.'

There. She'd done it. She'd almost told him. Or given him the opening to mention it himself.

'Kids?' he mused as Stevie went hot, then cold. 'Kelly and her friends? You're quite an enigma, Stevie Cooper. Who'd have guessed that underneath that crisp outer shell would beat a heart of gold? Except, of course, I've witnessed it myself.'

'Kelly's my goddaughter,' she heard herself explaining, the moment for the truth, the whole truth and nothing but the truth beginning to slip away.

'Then she's a very lucky girl.'

Oh! Stevie's cheeks flamed. Jared's solemn gaze, his solemn words, were equally unnerving. Unnerving. Warm brown eyes locking with hers, a wealth of emotion swirling in their depths; warm brown eyes moving down, from her heart-shaped face – scrubbed and shiny without the ubiquitous layer of make-up, strangely vulnerable without the layer of make-up – to the hollow at her throat where he paused to linger, to savour, setting Stevie's pulse rate soaring. And down, just as she'd feared, just as she'd hoped, in an almost tangible touch on skin that was beginning to tingle beneath the fabric of the robe, pausing again at the soft swell of breast.

Stevie closed her eyes. Impossible. He was touching without touching, caressing, kneading, tasting . . . *Denying*, her mind screamed, because Jared hadn't moved and yet still he managed to stir her.

'Stevie?' Soft, almost sheer imagination, the single word was another lightning caress. 'Look at me, Stevie.'

Impossible to comply, equally impossible not to. And so Stevie allowed her lids to flutter open, gazing upwards and across through the protective veil of her lashes.

Finding Jared's eyes fastened on her face, Stevie swallowed hard, moistened her lips with her tongue, caught the naked flash of hunger on his face – and bolted.

'Stevie –'

'No, Jared!' No, no, no! her mind screamed, but it was too late. Jared had moved, Jared had shot out a hand to snare her wrist, and Jared was tugging her slowly, yet relentlessly, into the curve of his embrace.

CHAPTER 8

'Aw, hell, Stevie, I'm sorry, but with so much happening at once there just wasn't time to discuss things.'

'But –' Stevie ran her fingers through the spikes of her hair. The soft, feathered look had been abandoned in a fit of remorse that she'd allowed a man to touch her – and not just *any* man, she inwardly berated herself, the waves of shame rippling through her. Jared Wilde, with his velvet eyes, his velvet words, his velvet touch – but no! There was no time to rake through embers, not with a frantic Tom pacing the length of his office, the bombshell of his words ringing in her ears.

Close the factory? One of several options, maybe, but simply putting the idea into words moved it dangerously close to making it reality. 'But – why didn't you tell me?' she asked incredulously.

'I – kind of hoped you'd notice the way things were going,' he explained apologetically, coming to a halt in front of her. 'And, damn it all, Stevie, you must have caught the rumours?'

Rumours? Yes! Factory-floor gossip, she'd supposed, never dreaming that they'd reached the point of no return, that what Tom was spelling out could mean the end of a family firm that one way or another had been in existence for over ninety years.

And, since it was a difficult time for companies the length and breadth of the country, Stevie had blithely assumed Deighton's could weather the storm, that the injection of cash from Tom's new partner would make all the difference. Unless . . .

'Marriot withdrew his offer,' Tom supplied woodenly, slumping down into a chair and resting his head in his hands, defeat written into the lines of his body. 'Hardly surprising, I suppose, once his accountants got their hands on the books.'

'You mean – this is the end?' Stevie probed incredulously, racking her brains for that list of alternatives Tom had been hinting at.

'It's – a thought,' he conceded frankly, his face pale and drawn and suddenly looking every inch and more its thirty-five years. 'We cut our losses and concentrate production in the Midlands.'

'So you and Lorna will be moving?'

'Good heavens, no. I'd rather commute. It's barely ninety miles away. It's only a suggestion, and there's still time for a last-minute turn-up. Miracles have been known to happen.'

'With Jared Wilde's gleaming new outfit in open competition just across the park?' Stevie reminded him harshly. 'Hardly.' And then, watching Tom's flicker of hope die, 'Oh, Tom, I really am sorry.'

'Well, don't be. And you're wrong about Jared. All mod-cons it might be, but, unlike Deighton's, he's aiming fairly and squarely at the luxury end of the market. And, if the worst does come to the worst, he'll make room for some of our redundant staff.'

'A favour for a friend?' Stevie scorned, aware that Monday night's scene had probably put paid to her own job prospects with the ALI-TANI group. And if Deighton's folded she could wave goodbye to any mortgage. It would be difficult enough finding the money to pay the bills, yet with Andrew back in the country, Stevie's number one priority would be a home for Rosa.

'As a matter of fact, yes,' Tom conceded mildly. 'We've known each other for years, just haven't had the time to meet up very often. He's a friend, Stevie, despite how it seems.'

Yes. Logging the silent plea in a set of cloudy eyes, Stevie swallowed her anger. Not Tom's fault, not Jared's. Just one of those things.

'Of course,' Tom was saying carefully, 'there's still the chance of a substantial injection of cash.'

'Oh?' Stevie queried, tiny hairs on the back of her neck prickling in alarm.

136

'The – er – Italian Impressions range,' he explained awkwardly.

'But the launch is another six weeks away,' Stevie pointed out, vaguely aware that Tom had dropped his gaze, focusing his attention on the desk-tidy made from recycled kitchen roll tubes, a perfect match for the one on her own desk, courtesy of Kelly and Rosa. 'It's just not ready,' she patiently reminded him. 'Unless you want to push it through at once, take a risk –'

'Not Deighton's,' Tom interrupted with a curious lack of emotion. 'ALITANI. And they want it fast.'

'But they can't,' Stevie countered absurdly. 'It's our new range. We've registered the name. It's ours – isn't it?'

Tom spread his hands, eyes full of mute appeal as they locked with hers. 'Not any longer. Hell, Stevie, I'm sorry. I know should have discussed it with you first, but –'

'No.' The surge of anger was tempered by relief, and, suddenly weak at the knees, Stevie sank down into one of the high-backed chairs kept for visitors. 'You're the boss. You carry the can when things go wrong,' she reminded him briskly, yet she couldn't understand why Tom had dropped his gaze again. Only he had, was looking anywhere but at Stevie – at the silver-framed photographs of Lorna and Kelly, at the keyboard and mouse on one side of the desk, the printer on the other, his clenched fist speaking volumes.

Tom and Stevie both, she acknowledged as another wave of emotion threatened to swamp her. Disappointment. For Italian Impressions had been *her* 'baby', *her* idea, *her* chance to make her mark in the cut-throat world of the food business. Yet, pitched against the survival of Deighton's and everyone who depended on it, the loss of Italian Impressions didn't matter one jot. It was losing it to Jared that hurt.

'You're the boss,' she reminded him again, wishing Tom would meet her gaze, wishing for all the world that he'd glance up, allow Stevie's smile to reassure him that she didn't mind, really and truly didn't mind. Only Tom didn't, and that hurt too. 'And if selling the name to Jared helps. . .'

She broke off, and, as she caught the dull flush of colour that crept up from his neck to suffuse his face, something vital in her mind died. Unable to speak, hardly daring to breathe, Stevie could only look. And wonder. And grow oh, so cold.

A lifetime later Tom raised his head, raised his eyes, the expression in their depths unfathomable. And Stevie's racing mind sifted the clues and finally saw the naked emotion for what it was. Shame.

'What is it, Tom?' she queried softly. 'What is it you're afraid to tell me?'

Sold. Sold to the highest bidder, she acknowledged bitterly, wondering if Jared would want to go through with it, given the latest development. For with the offer on the table since last Friday, six full days ago, and that heated scene with Stevie, it could have made a power of difference. Besides, for all Jared's manipulations and Tom's capitulations, the tiny matter of Stevie's views had been glaringly overlooked. She wouldn't do it. Not even for Tom. Not even for Deighton's. Work for Jared? Sell her soul to Jared when she'd already come perilously close to selling her body? No, not selling, she remembered bitterly. Giving. Shamelessly. Passionately. Because the virgin of the year had come perilously close to becoming the virgin on the rocks, all washed up, thanks to Jared. Jared.

Driving blind, the tears forcing themselves out from between her lashes, Stevie pulled the car off the main road and into the lane that would lead her to Jared. Only not like this, she decided, sniffing loudly, turning sharp left, off the beaten track and along the bumpy cinder road to the long-abandoned quarry where they'd risked their necks as children.

Jared. A swell of tears gathering momentum. A relentless scalding river. And, though she didn't want to have to remember, to relive the scene minute by painful minute, Stevie knew that until she'd purged every touch, every kiss, each and every glance from her mind, she wouldn't have the strength to face him. For to turn Jared down once and for all, and consign Deighton's to the scrap-heap in the process, she would have to face Jared – and soon. Jared . . .

'Oh, Stevie, Stevie, Stevie,' he'd groaned, tugging her forwards, and closer, and closer still. And though Stevie had closed her eyes, shutting out the room, the man, the time and place, she'd been shockingly aware of his presence, of the subtle fragrance of his aftershave, the scent of love in the air – lust, more like, she now belatedly identified, with another stab of shame.

But, no – replay the scene, Stevie, she silently reminded herself, screwing her handkerchief into a ball as she battled for control. *Now*, Stevie. No closed mind, no ostrich-like behaviour, no futile tears. It happened. You have to face it. Face it *now*, she insisted. Purge the scene you've stubbornly refused to acknowledge for the past three days. Three days of hell because you've blocked it from your mind . . .

Jared pulling her against him, Stevie's gasp raising a throaty chuckle, Jared's low laugh reverberating in her ears, inside her head, and bouncing across the spotlessly clean surfaces of the kitchen as she struggled for control.

Impossible to keep control with his arms closing round her, holding and enfolding, fingers kneading, hands caressing the curves and convolutions of her spine through the soft towelling fabric of her robe. And if his hands had caused chaos, the whispered words, his mouth against

140

her cheek, nuzzling her neck, her ear, her lips, had sent shivers of heat the length of her body.

'Stevie, oh, Stevie,' he'd growled. 'You're impossible. You're young, fiery, beautiful, and heaven help me, woman, but you're driving me insane. Oh, God, Stevie,' he'd insisted thickly, 'I want you.'

Want, she vaguely registered, with another stab of pain. Want, need, lust. Not love. Never love. As if! she silently berated herself. As if Jared could love Stevie. As if Stevie could love Jared, could ever love any man! And yet the whispered words had been relentless, soft, persuasive, hypnotic, and she was swaying against him, the sudden weakness at her knees shaming, because, heaven help her, she wanted this man's touch, this man's mouth, simply *wanted* with a need she'd never known could exist.

'Jared! Please, Jared,' she moaned as his lips brushed against hers, soft yet bruising, denying him as he rained tiny kisses from corner to corner and back again.

Another throaty growl as he pulled her even closer, parting her lips with his tongue, sending fresh currents of heat pulsing through her veins. A kiss, man and woman, mouth to mouth, lips nuzzling, teeth nibbling, tongue exploring – and how! Oh, God. Stevie's mind sang. So wonderful, so right, so unbelievable, so – No! Never wrong, too wonderful to be wrong, she insisted, burying the truth.

No time to ponder, in any case, with Jared's hands ranging her body, skimming across the fabric of the bathrobe, sliding into the curve of waist and hip, pausing, swirling, moving on and over the swell of her buttocks, cupping her buttocks as he tugged her close.

And, straining against him, Stevie felt the hardness of his manhood straining against her, and her mind soared. He was hard, he was hot, and Stevie Cooper, virgin of the year, had managed to rouse him!

Rouse him, excite him, deny him – because, innocent in the ways of love-play, Stevie jerked away in a sudden flash of fear. Jared's growl of protest was wonderfully reassuring, and though it was Jared who pulled her back, body to body, it was Stevie who moved against him, an instinctive roll of hips that set her on fire, triggered an anguished response in Jared, his wild, shuddering reaction sending Stevie's mind soaring.

'Oh, no!' he growled as she made to pull away again. 'Oh, yes!' he insisted as she smiled, took pity, brushed against his groin, her hips describing erotic circles, the touch shocking, her own response shocking her more. Because for once in her life she was alive, so alive, felt the heat pulsing through her, felt the need cascading through her veins, and Stevie was alive, alive, alive and moaning . . .

'Jared! Oh, God, Jared,' she gasped, because his hands had moved upwards, pushing aside the damp folds of the bathrobe and homing in on the rigid buds at the centre of her aching, straining breasts, twin thumbs teasing, rubbing, stroking, caressing, teasing again as they widened the circle. And then his hands were cupping her breasts, small, perfectly formed, apple-firm yet peach-soft, and simply perfect for Jared's hands to cover, for Jared's mouth . . .

'Woman, you're unbelievable,' he told her solemnly, pausing, his eyes locking with hers in a quivering moment of calm. And he nodded, and his gaze moved on, slowly, savouring every touch, every moment, his very glance a tangible caress that turned the blood to water in her veins.

Exploring her face, languidly, thoroughly, eye to eye, eye to mouth, eye to throat, where a pulse raced nineteen to the dozen, a pulse that Jared noted, Jared smiled at, Jared reached out to stroke. An erotic stroke of his hands, a velvet stroke of his eyes. Eyes moving down, caressing, approving, assessing, appraising, approving again.

Another electric pause while Stevie shivered – part fear, mostly desire, she acknowledged – and along with the knowledge came a final understanding of the demons that had driven Mae. Man and woman. Alone. Man and woman with a need primeval and true. Man and woman from time immemorial. Adam and Eve. Dino and Mae. Jared and Stevie –

'Stevie? Stevie?' he whispered, his gaze seeking hers, fleetingly uncertain. And Stevie smiled, nodded, trembled. Because Jared had reached for her hand, was leading her away from the cold, angular planes of the kitchen to the warm, inviting niches of the lounge, across the thick pile of the off-white carpet to the centre of the room.

He paused then, a momentary hesitation, and Stevie knew with a blinding flash of instinct that Jared's control was stretched to breaking point, that Jared wanted her, and yet that Jared was giving her the space to make up her mind.

'Stevie –'

She swallowed hard, shook her head, closed her eyes, shutting out the room but not the man – never the man, she realized wonderingly, and as her lids fluttered open she locked her gaze onto Jared's and smiled. And Jared smiled. And the sun and the moon and the stars in the heavens smiled.

Without conscious thought, she loosened the belt of her robe, shrugging the fabric from her shoulders and allowing it to fall in a heap at her feet, unwanted and unnoticed. Shameless to the end, she stood naked before a man. Prim and proper Stevie Cooper, who'd vowed never to let a man close enough to touch her, to stir her, ultimately to destroy her.

No! She closed her eyes again, a desperate attempt to block out the scenario. Too late for virginal fits of the vapours, she silently berated herself. Because Jared . . .

Yes. Jared. Here. Now. Alone. With Stevie.

And Jared moved, was peeling the sweater over his head, biceps rippling in the dying glow of the sun, chest muscles rippling beneath the thick mass of hair – and she'd been right about the need to reach out and scrunch her fingers through the curls.

'Woman! Oh, hell, Stevie,' he groaned in anguish, pulling her into his arms and crushing her against him, skin to skin, the wiry curls an erotic scratch against her breasts. Breasts. Hands and fingers kneading their apple-ripeness, their peachy smoothness. A man's touch, a man's mouth as Jared dropped slowly to his knees, trailing his mouth down the long, slender column of her neck, into the hollow of her throat, tongue lapping, lips nuzzling, sucking, teasing. Teasing. His mouth was teasing her breasts, her aching nipples, while frantic hands ranged her body, creating havoc where they touched, creating havoc where they didn't.

Pausing for an electrifying moment, Jared glanced up, and Stevie gazed down at his up-turned face, that handsome face with its single, rebellious lock of hair falling across an eye, its rakish appearance that tugged at her heartstrings, and, reading the unspoken question in Jared's brooding eyes, she nodded. It was time.

Time. The antique clock in the hall began to chime the hour as Jared came unhurriedly to his feet, his gaze fastened on Stevie. One. Two. Three. Snapping the button at the waistband of his trousers. Four. Five. Six. Tugging at the zipper, the atmosphere electric, the sudden silence in her head deafening. Seven. Seven o'clock.

And then she remembered. Rosa! How could she have forgotten? Oh, God, how could she –?

'Stevie?'

'No!' Twisting free and turning away, she stuffed her clenched fist into her mouth in an effort to keep control.

'But – you can't, damn it,' he insisted, dangerously close as he moved in behind her. 'Why, Stevie? Why?' he thundered. 'You wanted me. Damn it, Stevie, you wanted me.'

He touched her, the hand on her shoulder scalding, and she whipped round to face him, eyes pools of ice in a chalk-white face. And, naked and shameless, she angled her head and steeled herself to deny him.

'We can't,' she said simply, coldly. 'Not now, not ever.'

Jared winced, the gamut of emotions chasing across his face: anger, frustration, disbelief – most of all disbelief, that Stevie could deny him, that any woman could possibly deny Jared Wilde. And Stevie laughed – hysteria not cruelty, she silently acknowledged, crying inside, dying inside. Because the truth had begun to dawn, a truth she didn't want to face, a truth she'd bury deep in her heart and bring out to savour in the long, lonely years of a shrivelled old age. She loved him.

'Why, Stevie?' he asked simply. 'Why?'

Why? Why? Why? She loved him. She wanted him. She needed him.

She glanced at the clock, imagined the whirr of the lift as Anna and Rosa arrived hand in hand, imagined Rosa hopping from circle to circle on the hallway carpet, saw Anna reach out for the doorbell – only she was panicking, of course, because the intercom would buzz first – unless the janitor had waved them through?

Time. Precious few moments to ask Jared to leave, to hope that he'd leave without a fuss. Another frantic glance at the clock . . .

'Oh, I get it,' he drawled lazily, and Stevie's head snapped up at the sneering note of assurance. 'Expecting company?' he queried softly, folding his arms across his naked chest and treating her to a blast of chill contempt from beneath those hooded eyes. 'A friend? A close friend, Stevie? Someone who wouldn't understand if he found you with me – fully dressed or otherwise?' he added slyly, looking her up and down, assessing, appraising, judging, condemning. Because Jared was hurting, and Jared was hitting out, needing to blame, to salve the pain, to salvage his pride.

And he nodded, smiled, a parody of a smile because the light didn't reach his eyes – wonderful eyes smouldering with hate when they'd so recently smouldered with passion. And Stevie stood naked before him and stubbornly refused to cry, refused to fold her arms, to cover the shame. Pride. All she had left now. Stevie and Jared both.

'What a pity you didn't think to mention it sooner,' he declared, sweeping his crumpled sweater from the arm of the chair and tossing it carelessly over a shoulder as he ambled across the room. 'Because if I'd known, I would never have given you so much as the time of day.' A pause at the door, another smile, another blast from those chill brown eyes. 'Picky of me, I know,' he explained confidentially, 'but standing in line waiting my turn with the rest is where I draw the line. Only sensible these days.'

These days. Three days. Three terse phones calls bang on the dot of eleven-thirty, with Jared's brief, if succinct, 'Well, Stevie?' matched by Stevie's equally cool rejoinder:

'Perfectly well, thank you, Mr Wilde. And no, Mr Wilde, I haven't changed my mind. Never have, never will.'

She still hadn't, she realized now hysterically, whipping out her make-up bag in an effort to repair the damage to her pride along with the damage to her face. For somewhere along the way someone else had managed that for her. Jared – with the connivance of Tom. Stevie stiffened, put the car into gear and began the slow crawl back up the track.

* * *

'Hardly connivance,' Jared insisted pleasantly twenty minutes later.

The decision to beard the lion in its den while she was in the mood had clearly been the right one. For, having walked unannounced into Jared's brand-new office, she'd caught his momentary flash of surprise and her mind had soared.

'No? So just how would you describe it?' Stevie enquired, taking a chair and crossing her legs, making herself at home without bothering to wait for Jared to issue an invitation.

Leaning back into the cushions, she raised her head, raised an enquiring eyebrow, caught a flash of emotion she couldn't quite identify – admiration? she wondered absurdly. But she dismissed the notion out of hand, and waited for Jared to explain.

'Coffee, Stevie?' he offered instead.

Stalling? she mused, the thought reassuring. 'Thank you, but no,' she demurred crisply. 'Time is money, and if you don't mind I'd rather get straight to the matter in hand – the slight matter of a two-man conspiracy.'

Another eloquently raised brow, in this case Jared's. He spread his hands. 'I don't know what Tom has been saying –'

'Oh, nothing earth-shatteringly important,' she sneered. 'Just something about Jared Wilde's personal injection of cash – and the tiny matter of the strings attached.'

'No strings, Stevie, just a favour for a friend.'

'That's not the way I'm reading it.'

'No? Well, maybe you're reading things wrong.'

'Maybe so,' she acknowledged coolly. 'Which is why I'm here. Tom's given me his side of things, so now I'd like yours.' She nodded, flashed him a tight, brittle smile before folding her arms and entreating silkily, 'Fire away, Mr Wilde, I'm all ears.'

'Big Ears? Wrong fairy story,' he reminded her.

'With the Big Bad Wolf of the food trade sitting large as life in front of me?' she bit back, not the least impressed by his cool self-assurance. 'I guess you're right – this time.'

'I normally am,' he countered mildly.

'On the contrary, Jared,' she pointed out sweetly. 'You merely think you are.'

'Progress of sorts,' he allowed, with the first hint of a smile. 'At least now we're back on first-name terms.'

'Wrong again,' she contradicted swiftly. 'You don't employ me and I'm damned if I'm dropping curtseys or tugging forelocks and generally kow-towing along with the rest of the butt-licking mob.'

Those raised brows all but disappeared into his hairline. 'Language, Stevie,' he chided lightly. 'Not very lady-like at all.'

'Well, maybe I'm not in a lady-like mood.'

'No.' A barely perceptible twitch of lips. 'I guess not. It's gloves on for battle, then?'

'Queensberry rules – or Jared Wilde's?' she challenged, visibly bristling.

'No contest, Stevie. Naturally we'll play it by the book, all legal and above board – just like my offer to Tom.'

'The offer – but not the proviso.'

'Meaning?'

'Meaning *me*. Cunningly inserted into the small print.'

'Not on my copy of the document, I assure you.'

No. Not on Tom's either. Jared Wilde was far too clever to commit himself to paper. Which made it difficult to prove, difficult to challenge. But, if the effort nearly killed her, Stevie would drag an admission from him. She angled her head, fixed him with a steely glare, returned his gaze unblinkingly.

'So, no small print, no problem,' Jared pointed out smoothly. And it was his turn to fold his arms, sit back in his chair, assume an air of blithe unconcern.

'Good. You're happy, Tom's happy, I'm happy. Only the moment I walk out through that door, of course,' Stevie hissed with a lightning change of tone, 'You're on the phone to Tom and the deal's off.'

'My, someone *has* been over-indulging in fairy tales,' he scorned. 'Standard bedtime reading, Stevie?'

'And why not? There's a moral in every story,

which is more than I could say for the average company report.'

'I wouldn't know. I've better things to do in bed than read.'

Bed. Stevie's head snapped up. Bed. With Jared. Man and woman naked on the sheets. Jared and Stevie – almost, she conceded bitterly, silently, another unremitting image running through her mind: man and woman, body to body, mouth against mouth, arms and legs entwined. Man and woman. Jared and Dee.

Caught up in a nightmare, Stevie stumbled to her feet, the sudden sting of tears catching her off guard. She shouldn't have come. She'd thought she was ready to face him, but she was wrong. Yet it served to prove one thing. She could never work for Jared. So near and so far. Together yet apart. A working relationship, a personal relationship, *any* relationship with Jared was simply out of the question.

'Going somewhere?'

'Jared!'

Unseen and unheard, Jared had moved – how the *hell* did he move so swiftly, so silently? she railed as she careered full-pelt into him, the breath leaving her body as his arms closed around her waist.

'In a hurry?' he probed. 'A prior engagement, Stevie? A business meeting, perhaps? Or, since it's nudging six o'clock,' he pointed out slyly, eyes darting from her face to the clock on the wall and back again, 'maybe you're late for a date?'

'Mind your own business,' she spat, struggling to be free and amazed to discover that the afternoon had fled. And with Rosa having tea at Kelly's she was painfully aware that in collecting Rosa at seven she'd be coming face to face with Tom.

Tom, whose cloudy blue eyes had been full of remorse, full of silent pleas. The same Tom who'd helped Stevie through the bad days when Mae had disappeared, and later, when Rosa had come along. Tom – her best friend's husband, her daughter's godfather, and a pillar of strength when Stevie had needed it most. Tom – who'd given her a job in the first place and allowed her to fit the hours she worked around the baby. Tom, Stevie's friend – a friend indeed, a friend in need. Because Deighton's was sinking and, rightly or wrongly, Tom was depending on Stevie. Sell her soul to the devil? No contest. Oh, yes, she'd do it for Tom – and for Lorna – but she'd be damned if she'd give in without a fight.

'Will you please let go of me?' she hissed, arms snapping downwards in an effort to break his grip, the sneaking suspicion that he'd chosen to release her lost beneath the groundswell of anger. 'You don't own me yet, Mr Wilde,' she icily reminded him, the choice of words an unwitting give-away. 'And I'd thank you to keep your distance.'

He raised his hands in mock surrender. 'Easy, honey. There's no need to overreact. I guess what you do with your private life is your concern –'

'The name,' she reminded him icily, 'is Stevie. "Ginge" I handle, "Red" I can allow at a pinch. But that pathetic endearment that doubtless saves a slip of the tongue when you're wining, dining and bedding the string of nameless blondes you're seemingly so fond of,' she hissed, 'is strictly off-limits where I'm concerned.'

'Fine. But that also goes for comments about my private life. I –'

'You don't have to say another word. You insulted me; I insulted you. That makes us quits. Now, if you don't mind, I'd like to get back to business.'

'Business?' he queried carefully.

'But of course. Why else do you think I'm here?'

'As a natural redhead, instead of a nameless blonde, it clearly wasn't a social call.'

'Sexism,' she castigated coolly, 'like ageism, racism and all those other isms, is bad for a company's image, Mr Wilde.'

'Our company, Stevie? Or mine?' he queried as Stevie retraced her steps and regained her seat, her raised eyebrow a clear invitation for Jared to do the same.

Jared did, though, unnervingly for Stevie, he chose to perch on the edge of the desk, an elevated position and far too close for comfort.

Maybe, she consoled herself, a fleeting smile lighting up her features, just maybe Jared's insecurities were showing, and this was his way of reasserting himself.

'Let's just say, it all depends.'

'On what?'

'On the Jared Wilde notion of fairness. The Italian Impressions deal and the teensy-weenie matter of the cooling-off clause.'

'Just sound business practice, Stevie, and it works both ways, don't forget. Tom's entitled to change his mind too.'

'Only he won't,' she pointed out tersely. 'Because someone – you,' she reminded him with a sneering toss of the head, 'have him by the short and curlies.'

Generous lips tightened. 'Another curious phrase, my dear. I hadn't realized you boasted such a colourful vocabulary.'

'No? And why should you?' she queried coolly. 'You hardly know me.'

'But I'm learning, Stevie, and believe me I'm learning fast. So – spit it out, why don't you? Before it chokes you.'

'As I was saying, the cooling-off clause. I want your word that whatever I decide today, you won't invoke it.'

'The word of a gentleman?' he sneeringly observed. 'And what makes you so sure that I'd keep it?'

'As you say, you're a gentleman – apparently.'

'Whilst you,' he swiftly riposted, 'will never pass for a lady.'

Stevie ignored the insult. 'So?'

'So?' Jared shrugged, smiled, shrugged again, then nodded. 'Agreed.'

Silence. Not a word, not a sound, just Stevie's stunned expression and Jared's mocking gaze as his eyes locked with hers. She'd done it. Heaven alone knew how, unless she'd managed to touch a chord, appeal to the better side of his nature – assuming he had one, she inwardly derided. And she was free. Free to go, free to keep her job at Deighton's. No strings attached.

Without a word, Stevie reached for her handbag, came leisurely to her feet. Yet, catching Jared's flash of scorn out of the corner of her eye, she smothered the panic. Technically free to leave she might be, but it wasn't over yet by any means.

'Decision time, Stevie,' he reminded her in a voice devoid of emotion.

'Hardly,' she countered coolly. 'Since my mind was made up a week ago. A generous salary, a company car and a list of perks as long as my arm,' she itemized, steeling herself to meet his gaze. And whilst for every day that she'd left it the offer had dropped in value, the package was still worth a fortune in Stevie's eyes.

'And?'

'The answer's no.'

Jared smiled. Or rather, she amended, there

was a flash of white teeth. 'Boring, Stevie. Boringly predictable. And very disappointing,' he scorned, folding his arms across his chest, contempt oozing out from each and every pore. 'So . . .' He angled his head. 'Purely in the interest of fairness, of course, perhaps you wouldn't mind explaining why.'

'In the interest of fairness, Jared? No problem,' she reassured him pleasantly. 'It isn't enough.'

'I beg your pardon?'

'The offer on the table,' she repeated. 'Recompense for my trouble. Recognition of my value,' she emphasized grimly. 'Like I said, it isn't enough.'

'Fine.' A rapidly beating pulse at the corner of his mouth drew Stevie's gaze, gave her something to focus on. 'You know your worth,' he sneeringly conceded, spreading his hands. 'You name your price.'

Stevie did, swallowing hard, aware from his flash of wry humour that this time she might have pushed him too far. In which case Stevie's world, not to mention Tom and Lorna's, and that of two innocent children, was about to come crashing about her shoulders. Because whilst Jared had promised, it was simply that: the word of a gentleman. Stevie's word against his.

Only Jared didn't speak, didn't utter the phrase she was half expecting, instead slipping from the desk to cross to stand in front of her. Close, so close that the familiar tang of his aftershave and the even more familiar unique body smell triggered a host of memories she'd prefer to forget – never would forget, she realized instinctively, smothering the hysteria.

Another smile, another flash of white teeth that would serve a basking shark proud. A trembling Stevie was forced to stand her ground.

'You drive a real hard bargain,' he mockingly acknowledged. 'But at that sort of salary, make no bones about it. Lady, you're selling your soul.'

'Meaning?'

'Welcome to management – senior management,' he emphasized grimly. 'And along with the perks, the responsibilities. As my right hand, you can consider yourself on call twenty-four hours a day, three hundred and sixty-five days a year. Understand?'

'Thank heavens for leap years,' Stevie retorted. And she angled her head, steeling herself to meet that mocking, knowing smile. For arrogant Jared Wilde was goading her, was expecting her to turn him down, expecting Stevie to judge the price too much to pay for the privilege of working side by side with him on Italian Impressions. Because Jared *had* given his word and he would keep that word, she was finally beginning to see. And, with Stevie's job at Deighton's no longer under threat, Jared was supremely sure she didn't have the guts to jump.

In which case Jared was about to discover that boringly predictable she wasn't.

And as for being on call twenty-four hours of the day, three hundred and sixty-five days a year, she'd worry about fitting Rosa around that technicality later.

CHAPTER 9

Working for Jared? But –'

'Jared didn't forget to tell you, Dee,' Stevie interrupted softly, catching the pain and hating herself – hating Jared more – for forcing her hand in the first place and then putting her on the spot over Dee. 'Believe me, until today there was nothing to tell. And, since the arrangement's purely business,' she reminded her, 'he's hardly likely to whisper it in your shell-like in a sudden moment of passion, now, is he?'

Dee giggled, as Stevie had intended. A nervous reaction maybe, but the tension flowing tangibly down the phone line ebbed away.

One down, one to go, Stevie supposed wryly, wondering if the pain would ever go away. Loving him, wanting him, needing him, knowing how much he despised her. Stand in line and take his turn? He should be so lucky. Not that Jared Wilde was likely to stand in line and wait his turn in anything so innocuous as a bread queue.

Poor Dee. Storing up trouble, if only she but knew it. And, whilst Stevie was horribly afraid that her fun-loving friend might well have met her match, she was even more afraid that, when it came to the crunch, that extra broken heart would be more than Stevie could handle. If Jared grew tired of Dee. When Jared grew tired of Dee. Not so much a hint of wishful thinking as a foregone conclusion. And only a matter of time.

Just like that job of Stevie's. Nine o'clock sharp Monday morning, yes, sir! And in the meantime –

'I was phoning to ask what you'd be wearing,' Dee interrupted her thoughts. 'For the party. You do intend coming, Stevie?'

'Wouldn't miss it for the world,' Stevie conceded dryly, Jared's terse words replaying in her mind:

'It's business,' he'd reminded her grimly, the true meaning of the word 'invitation' having clearly passed him by. 'You'll be paid, and amply paid, and you'll be there. Oh, yes, and, as an ALITANI representative, make sure you look presentable – hey?'

'Your definition – or mine?' she'd needled hmm, walking away, having had the last word easily enough, but certain that arrogant Jared Wilde would expect total obedience.

'So?' Dee probed, breaking once more into troubled thoughts.

'Oh – any old rag that comes to hand,' Stevie retorted flippantly. 'You know me –'

'Exactly. If it's an outfit for you or an outfit for Rosa –'

'No contest. And Rosa's wardrobe isn't exactly bulging at the seams.'

'Like daughter, like mother, huh?' Dee cut in softly. 'Which is precisely why I'm phoning. Wardrobes. Plural. I've half a dozen, Stevie, and you'd be doing me a favour if you popped across and took your pick.'

Allowing Cinderella to go to the ball in style? Stevie mused, the awful suspicion that Jared was behind the offer too ridiculous for words. Dee was generous to a fault, her barely worn cast-offs keeping a whole chain of charity shops in business, and since she rarely, if ever, wore a party dress twice, there'd be plenty for Stevie to choose from. Charity. No, not charity, Stevie corrected. Generosity. A favour for a friend.

'Stevie?' Dee probed softly. 'Please, Stevie. You know it makes sense.'

Stevie closed her eyes. Sense. For Dee? For Stevie? Or for Jared? she probed, that shadow of doubt festering. For, as Jared had been quick to underline, as an ALITANI representative she'd be flying the flag for Jared. Stevie stiffened. Damn Jared Wilde and his sly insinuations. Until nine o'clock on Monday morning he'd no right to insist on so much as the time of day.

'Stevie –'

'Thanks, Dee, but no, thanks,' she interrupted pleasantly. 'It's sweet of you to offer but, believe it or not, I've the perfect little number tucked away in the back of my closet.' A stunning little number in red, in fact. A red rag to a raging bull no doubt, but Stevie would face that if and when it happened.

'Mummy?'

'Yes, poppet?'

'Do I *have* to go to bed at half past seven every single night?'

'Nope,' Stevie conceded, draping Rosa's discarded towel over a radiator and resisting the urge to help the still damp body into fresh pyjamas. 'When you're as old as I am, my sweet, you can stay up all night if that's what you want.'

'Oh, Mummy! You know what I mean. But I am six and three quarters. And Suzy says only babies go to bed at half past seven.'

'Fine. No problem. If we read the story first,' Stevie pointed out, features impassive, 'pyjamas on, teeth clean and hair ready brushed and ponytailed, now that you're nearly seven I guess we can stretch the time for going to bed to seven forty-five.'

'Really and truly, Mummy? Oh, yummy. Wait till I tell Kelly. She's older than me and she still goes at half past. Mummy . . . ?'

'Hmm? What does Suzy say this time?' Stevie enquired dryly, running her fingers through the locks of Rosa's hair, gently teasing apart the worst of the snags before Rosa could wreak havoc with the hairbrush.

There was a sudden pause. The hackles on the back of Stevie's neck prickled out a warning and she glanced up, her eyes locking with innocent brown ones through the steam clouds of the mirror.

'She, um, wants to know where my daddy is.'

'Does she now?' Stevie stalled, automatically reclaiming the hairbrush, the slow, rhythmic strokes providing a focus for her mind. So it had come, the dreaded inquisition. Only a matter of time in any case, but oh, how Stevie had been dreading it – the thought of giving Rosa the truth almost as unbearable as keeping the truth from her. 'And what did you tell her?' she probed carefully.

Rosa shrugged. 'Aunty Lorna says I'm special,' she revealed with a fierce touch of pride. 'And special girls don't need a daddy. But it would be nice to have a daddy one day,' she conceded wistfully. 'But Suzy says –'

Stevie counted to ten. *Suzy says*. For two pins she'd wring the wretch's pretty little neck. Yet she wasn't being fair. What Suzy wondered today, the rest of the world would wonder tomorrow. So – time for the truth. Only not tonight. Her nerves were in shreds already, what with thoughts of the party and Jared . . . Simply being with Jared, watching Jared, entertaining with Jared, all in the name of business, of course. Unlike the other lady on his arm . . .

164

More torment. Standing on the sidelines and watching Dee and Jared together. Kissing, touching, smiling, sharing. Jared and Dee. Jared. Stevie openly scowled. She wouldn't go. Jared didn't need her. One starry-eyed hostess was more than enough. And if Jared didn't like it, then tough. The job didn't start until Monday, and till then Jared Wilde and his ALITANI grand plans could rot in hell.

'Mummy?'

'Yes, darling?'

'It doesn't matter about my daddy. Not really. Don't be cross, Mummy. I don't mind if you don't.'

Luminous brown eyes came back at Stevie in the glass, aeons older than their almost-seven years, and the sudden sting of tears took Stevie by surprise.

'Rosa! Oh, darling!'

Kneeling, she spun her gently round, pulled her into her arms, hugging her, holding her, loving her, almost squeezing the breath from her body as she battled for control, searched for the words to reassure – herself as much as Rosa. Guilt. For keeping the truth from her. For wanting Rosa to be hers and hers alone. For shying away from the shadow of Mae and rejection.

The truth. Better for Rosa to grow up with knowledge than have it rudely thrust upon her, Stevie was just beginning to see, and it was rubbing salt into the wound. Too late to turn that clock back. Never too late for the truth, of course, but it wouldn't be easy. Soon, she promised herself. Very soon.

'You're not just special,' Stevie insisted huskily, stroking her hair. 'You're wonderful. The best little girl in the world. And I love you, and Aunty Lorna and Uncle Tom and Kelly love you. And Nanna loves you, and Uncle Andrew loves you and everyone who knows you thinks that you're special. And if you did have a daddy,' she added fiercely, brushing a stray lock of hair out of Rosa's eyes and cupping the small, heart-shaped face in her hands, smiling down through a veil of unshed tears, 'why, he'd think you were better than special. Only you don't. You just have me. And that makes it even more special, you see. Because I need you and you need me.'

Dipping her head, she kissed the tip of the upturned nose, green eyes swimming with love and assurance and yet more love as she watched the shadows chase across her daughter's face. 'And one day when you're old enough to understand,' she told her softly, 'I'll tell you all about it.'

'Promise?'

Stevie nodded, smiling, silently blessing Lorna's inspiration as the clock in the hall began to chime the hour.

Rosa was instantly diverted, and her features lightened. 'One, two, three, four, five, six, seven.

All good children go to heaven,' she chanted automatically. 'And all good mummies must look nice. Come on,' she insisted, seizing Stevie's wrist and tugging her through the door. 'It's nearly time for the party. Let's go and choose a dress.'

Not so much a choice as Hobson's, Stevie conceded when confronted by the pathetically sparse contents of her wardrobe.

Blissfully unaware of Stevie's thoughts, Rosa dived in. 'The red one,' she pronounced, pulling the dress from its hanger and pinning it against her.

'If that's what madam suggests, then the red one it is,' Stevie agreed, smothering a pang of conscience. Hobson's indeed. The only other thing even vaguely suitable was the cream two-piece she'd worn to Tom and Lorna's wedding.

Not too late to phone Dee, take her up on that favour, she supposed, beginning to waver. The need to defy Jared was little more than sheer contrary-mindedness, and behaviour more suited to a six-year-old.

Ah, yes, but if he hadn't made that sly dig about looking presentable in the first place, perhaps she'd have been more amenable. Aye, Stevie grinned. And pigs might fly, she told herself, rescuing the dress before Rosa could crumple it.

Short. Not so much daring as bordering on the indecent, and, since Jared hadn't bothered to mask his contempt the last time she'd worn it, all the better to keep him at arm's length. A vaguely familiar phrase, and just as vaguely alarming. Stevie's mind trawled for clues. And then it hit her. 'Oh, Grandma, what big teeth you've got.' 'All the better to eat you with,' the Big Bad Wolf would droolingly reply. So for supper at the Big Bad Wolf's place, what could be more appropriate?

'Oh, Mummy,' Rosa breathed, investigating further. 'Look at this. Oh, Mummy, it's beautiful.'

Dateless, too, Stevie acknowledged as Rosa slipped the sleeveless cream lace shift over her head, the arms of her pyjamas an incongruous touch with their clutch of cavorting teddy bears. Calf-length on Stevie, on Rosa the skirt concertinaed onto the floor, and Rosa gathered the excess fabric in her hands before skipping round the expanse of white carpet, for all the world like an exquisite bride-doll pirouetting on a wedding cake.

'This one,' Rosa insisted, dancing round a smiling Stevie. 'This one. Please, please, *please*.'

Sorely tempted, Stevie shook her head. With or without the matching jacket it would easily pass for evening wear, wouldn't look out of place in a ballroom at The Ritz. Only she wouldn't. Not for Jared. Not for any man. In the liberated nineties Stevie Cooper dressed to please no one but herself, and if Jared didn't like it –

The doorbell. The internal bell, Stevie registered, jumping edgily. Anna? she mused, aware that if George was on duty, he'd smilingly wave her past. Or Jared, double-checking that Stevie's definition of presentable matched his? Jared wouldn't. Jared might, she conceded, lips tightening as Rosa scrambled out ahead of her. But if Jared valued his looks half as much as Stevie valued her pride, she hoped he'd have the sense to know better.

'Special delivery for Miss Cooper.' A click of the heels, a snappy salute, and a bemused Stevie almost dropped the box the uniformed boy had thrust into her arms.

'Is it a present?' Rosa asked, following Stevie into the kitchen. And then, as Stevie tentatively raised the lid, 'Flowers? Is that all?'

All? Wisps of gypsophila and fern and the tiniest yellow roses imaginable. Unimaginable, Stevie corrected automatically, raising the corsage to her face and inhaling its delicate fragrance. But who on earth —?

' "Gared". Who's Gared?' Rosa mused, her sharp eyes spotting the card that Stevie had missed.

'Welcome to ALITANI, Stevie,' Jared's bold, flowing script proclaimed. 'And thanks. Your presence tonight is above and beyond the call of duty, and don't think I don't know it. Jared.'

She wore the cream. Out-thought, outflanked, out-manoeuvred. Or maybe Jared was simply

169

being kind. Kind? That would be the day, Stevie decided, covering the interminable length of the carpet with all the enthusiasm of a pirate walking the plank. Reaching the door to his apartment, she halted, took a deep breath, raised her hand to the bell and –

'Stevie? Well, well. Who'd have believed it?' Jared drawled as the door swung open on its hinges.

'Look presentable, *you* said,' Stevie reminded him, the shock in his eyes so fleeting it had to be sheer imagination on her part.

'So I did. And so you are. Positively stunning, in fact. Ah, I see you got the flowers?'

'Nothing wrong with your eyesight,' she couldn't resist needling him, attempting to sweep past and brought up short by a hand on her arm. Skin on skin. Searing. Scalding. Unnerving. Stevie stiffened, raised an enquiring eyebrow.

'I wrote it on the card,' Jared murmured softly, the expression in his eyes unfathomable, 'and now I'm saying it. Thanks.'

'For what? For being here? For obeying the call of duty? Time enough for the inquest later,' she reminded him tersely. 'The evening isn't over yet.'

'The evening,' he countered solemnly, 'has barely begun. But you can take it from me, the signs are looking good.'

Just like her host, she sneeringly conceded as

Jared led the way into the lounge, with its sub-dued lighting, discreet background music and smattering of guests.

With supper planned for nine, there was plenty of time for people to arrive, and with Dee con-spicuous by her absence, Stevie couldn't decide which emotion to indulge: relief that she didn't have to witness the lovebirds billing and cooing – yet. Or panic that she didn't know a soul.

'Lorna! Thank goodness. You know how much I love parties,' she derided, as the first flurry of arrivals followed hot on Stevie's heels.

'Good heavens! It isn't? Surely not! Stevie? Is that really you?'

Tom, grinning broadly, nodding his approval at an outfit he clearly didn't link with his wed-ding. Hardly surprising, she supposed, given the dateless cut and style – his own preoccupation on the day. Eight years ago, Stevie realized, wonder-ing where on earth the time had gone. But she was glad she'd changed her mind and worn the cream; the knowledge that she could hold her own among the best was a balm to her ego.

With a give-away gesture of nerves, she smoothed the lacy folds, hitched a tiny shoe-string strap more securely onto her shoulder.

'Dynamite,' Tom conceded solemnly, blue eyes dancing as they locked with Stevie's. 'And if I wasn't already spoken for, I'd be first in the queue of young bucks beating a path to your door.'

171

'You look wonderful,' Lorna whispered, aiming a playful slap at her husband. 'Oh, Stevie, I'm so glad.'

'That Deighton's is out of the wood? You and me both, Lorna,' Stevie conceded brusquely. 'But if that gleam in your eye means what I think it does, you're wasting your time. The arrangement's business. Purely and simply. And you needn't look sceptical. Dee's on the prowl for husband number three and the great man himself is besotted. Sorry to disappoint you, Lorna, but if I was the last woman on earth, Jared Wilde wouldn't waste a second glance on me.'

'Want a bet?' Lorna challenged, her glance slipping past Stevie, focusing on a point just beyond her left shoulder.

Hating herself for the weakness, Stevie turned her head and followed the line of Lorna's gaze, her eyes crossing to Jared who was propped against the jamb of the open terrace window, hands thrust casually into the pockets of a suit that screamed Savile Row even to Stevie's unknowledgeable mind. And though the shutters came down at once over deep velvet pools, Stevie caught the swirl of naked hunger in their depths and her mind soared. He wanted her. *Want*, she emphasized grimly. The thrill of possession. Nothing more, nothing less. Because Stevie had dared to deny him – and how!

Another wave of arrivals; Dee, stunning in a slinky black outfit that fitted where it touched, had male eyes standing out on stalks. Suddenly in need of a drink, needing to watch Dee and Jared just as badly, but without giving herself away, Stevie crossed to the sideboard with its vast array of drinks.

Jared, smiling his approval as he moved towards Dee, greeting guests in passing with an ease born of practice . . . Jared, reaching Dee, reaching out for Dee, hands closing round her shoulders to draw her close . . . Jared, dipping his face to kiss her, allowing the kiss to deepen, to lengthen, the rest of the room forgotten . . . Jared, raising his head, those heavy-lidded eyes – such wonderful eyes, Stevie acknowledged as they unerringly crossed the sea of heads to find her – his heady flash of triumph driving the breath from her body . . .

Bastard, she silently screamed, fighting the urge to cry. Playing games. Poor Dee. Lucky Stevie. Because Jared had kissed her, touched her, roused her, wanted her, needed her, and Stevie had denied him. Not a conscious decision on her part maybe, but she *had* pulled back, had ultimately denied him – a lasting insult to a man with an ego the size of the moon. So this was Jared's revenge – flaunting Dee, vulnerable, lonely, man-hungry Dee, for all the world, and especially Stevie, to see.

'On the prowl she may be,' Lorna conceded, coming up behind Stevie and helping herself to a glass of dry white wine. 'But no man's a catch unless he's ready to be caught. You mark my words; Dee won't hold him.'

'And who on earth is that supposed to reassure?' Stevie challenged crossly. 'I've told you before, Lorna Deighton, but since you clearly weren't listening I'll say it again. Loudly. Stop meddling. I'm single, I'm happy, I'm sane. I'm answerable to no man and that's the way it's staying.'

'Stevie –'

'Now what?' she bit out.

'Don't fight it, hey?' Lorna stunned her by suggesting. 'Don't fight what nature intended.'

'Oh – fiddlesticks!' Stevie muttered, stomping away, heading for the open windows and a breath of fresh air.

Catching the low murmur of voices – lovers, she supposed, with a snort of derision – she swung right, slipping round the corner to the short arm of the L-shaped terrace with its magnificent view of Lord Street. A different view from her own – from Andrew's, she corrected automatically – which faced west and caught the vast stretch of sand with the silver gleam of Liverpool Bay beyond.

Elegant, tree-lined Lord Street, with its glass-topped verandas, outdoor cafés, its gardens and fountains and charming arcades that sprang from secret alleys. A nightmare to cross in season, with the traffic nose to tail, but a world-class boulevard – and home. For now. For, with Andrew flying back within the month, Stevie was looking for something in a more downmarket part of town. A blessing in disguise if it took her away from Jared. A shrug of resignation, a bitter twist of lips. Because it wouldn't, of course. But away from the confines of the office at least she'd be able to breathe.

Breathe. Deep gulps of salt-tang air. Peace and quiet ten storeys high. And, since all too soon she'd have to go back inside, join the fray, make small talk, smile, listen, smile again, feign interest in some mind-numbingly boring conversation while carrying the ALITANI flag for Jared, she leaned her arms on the still warm stone of the parapet and emptied her mind.

'I thought I might find you hiding away out here.'

Stevie froze, the hairs on the back of her neck rising like the hackles of a cat.

'Hardly hiding,' she murmured coolly, not bothering to turn, not even surprised that he'd managed to track her down. On the other hand, fleeting surprise that Dee had let him off the leash she *could* allow, and the thought was vaguely amusing. Sensing a movement behind her, Stevie stiffened, banished the smile in a trice.

'No?' he queried sceptically. 'So what exactly are you doing?'

'Just partaking of the night air,' she explained. 'Alone. No law against that, surely?'

'Manners, Stevie,' he pointed out mildly. 'A party needs its hostess.'

'And don't tell me? Dee's finally come to her senses, given you the slip and disappeared for a drive along the beach with a richer, more handsome, more powerful model?' she tossed out absurdly. 'I would have tagged on younger,' she explained, turning her head, lowering her voice, assuming an air of concern, 'but age is a touchy subject, so I've heard, and I guess it must hurt to find yourself on the losing end for once.'

'Never having been in that position,' he contradicted her coolly, 'I wouldn't know. And, furthermore, I haven't the least intention of losing out to any man – ever.'

'Bully for you,' Stevie scorned, beginning to see that where men like Jared were concerned it was the thrill of the chase that mattered, that the moment the prey was caught was the moment it lost its charm.

Poor Dee. In love with a man who would take her, use her, ultimately discard her. And if that included a brief sortie into the realms of matrimony, then more fool Dee for thinking she could hold him. Rich, powerful, ruthless, the Jared Wildes of this world didn't make a lasting commitment. They took what they could, when they could, how they could. Oh, yes, Stevie had come across his sort before. Rich, powerful, ruthless – and callous. Just like Rosa's father. Poor Mae. Poor Dee. But never, ever poor Stevie.

Not that she was likely to be tempted – or, heaven forbid, play the temptress. Because men didn't fall for Stevie. They took one look at the outrageous hairstyle, the outrageous clothes, the outrageous mask of make-up, and then they ran a mile. Safer that way. Lonely too, a composite voice intruded. Dee's voice, Lorna's voice, Mae's voice. Not Stevie's voice, she reassured herself fiercely. She didn't need a man, any man, and, despite the shocking physical pull, most definitely not this man.

'Stevie –'

'No!' she breathed, recoiling from the touch of skin on skin. 'Don't touch me. I'm an employee not a plaything,' she rasped. 'And I'm here tonight to work. Work, Jared. Nothing more, nothing less.'

'As I was saying,' he drawled, with the merest hint of annoyance, 'hiding away in the shadows isn't quite what I expect of my hostess.'

'Hostess? Me?' she mouthed incredulously, spinning round to face him. 'Oh, no. No. No. No. Dee's the lady on your arm; Dee can play the lady of the house. I –'

'You will walk back through that door and mix. You'll smile, sparkle, shine and give everything you've got for me and my company. *Our* company, Stevie,' he emphasized grimly. 'And tonight could make or break us. Nicky Sanders. I assume the name rings a bell?'

'It might do,' she conceded huffily. 'Though I can't see why.'

'You will. When he arrives.' He pointedly

177

checked his watch. 'Five minutes. You've five minutes precisely. Because the moment Sanders arrives, he's all yours.'

'Meaning?'

He folded his arms, allowed his lazy gaze to travel the length of her body, appraising, assessing, insulting – like a dealer weighing up the merits of a horse for auction, Stevie decided, resisting the urge to land him one on the shins with an elegant, stiletto-shod hoof. 'Use your imagination,' he entreated, lips curling. 'The guy's an important prospective client, and you can take it from me, tonight you're all woman.'

'So is Dee, in case it's slipped your notice, and Dee knows the rules of the game. Naïve of me, I know,' she scorned, 'but Little Red Riding Hood's clean out of practice.'

'Ah, yes, but then naïveté is part of the appeal. Besides, Dee knows nothing about the business.'

'And, since I don't work for ALITANI *yet*,' she reminded him coolly, 'neither do I.'

'Correction. Italian Impressions is your creation, Stevie. All you have to do is sell it to Sanders.'

'And if I don't?'

Jared nodded, smiled – another cold and mirthless flash of white teeth. 'You will.'

Or else. He didn't say it, of course, but then he didn't have to. It was written loud and clear across that arrogant forehead.

CHAPTER 10

Nine o'clock. An informal supper. A hot and cold buffet – an impressive selection of the best ALITANI had to offer. Not Italian Impressions, Stevie assumed, since the range wasn't in production, but sure to be impressive.

'Sicilian Casserole? If seeing is believing, that is. But since the proof of the English pudding is in the eating . . .'

The man who'd been clinging onto Stevie like a leech from the moment he'd arrived darted forward suddenly, giving her space, space to breathe, but, mindful of Jared's orders, she stifled the urge to bolt and approached the magnificent spread of food, taking the plate that was proffered and edging round, putting the width of the table between them and fervently hoping to keep it that way.

Heaping an obscene amount of food upon his plate, Nicky Sanders inhaled deeply, savoured the aroma, swallowed a generous forkful and smiled. 'Exquisite. If I closed my eyes,' he almost drooled, 'I could smell the essence of Sicily itself.'

Wrong again, Stevie silently acknowledged, and since she'd practically lived on Sicilian Casserole for the past three months, helped herself to a selection of vegetables and pasta in every shape and size and colour.

Trust Jared not to miss a trick, to know the man was Italian, to order the dish Stevie had been working on. An Italian. She might have known. Along with their English-sounding names, Sanders and Jared had so much in common. Italian. Somewhere along the way. Arrogant, good-looking, powerful. And, judging by that gleam in his eye, heading straight back to invade her personal body space.

Stevie's appetite withered and died.

'My dear.' A fastidious lift of an eyebrow, a critical gaze switching from the barely touched food on her plate to her face, and down, following the lines of her body, just like Jared thirty minutes earlier, assessing, appraising, mentally undressing, Stevie realized, smothering a ripple of distaste as he homed in on the pert thrust of breasts – the rise and fall of her clearly braless breasts – the film of perspiration across his top lip enough to turn even a cast-iron stomach off its food.

Leaning across, he patted her arm. 'My dear,' he repeated thickly, 'you can take it from me, hot-blooded men like a little meat on their women. It gives them something to hold onto in love-play, something to keep them warm on those cold winter nights. Eat up,' he entreated huskily, lowering his voice, leaning forward, allowing his glance to drop to her cleavage in an almost tangible caress that made Stevie's flesh crawl. 'Eat up and later maybe, just maybe, you'll discover what you're missing.'

'Creep,' she murmured vehemently, escaping to the bathroom and taking her time. And if Jared noticed and objected, then tough. She'd plead a headache and go home. Not that Jared would, she conceded, touching up her lipstick and blotting the excess on a tissue before casting a critical eye over the face that came back at her – a face she barely recognized without the generous layer of make-up. Understated, like the dress, like the rest of her appearance in fact.

For Jared? she fleetingly wondered, running her fingers through the wisps of her hair. Or had she dressed to please herself? Might as well please herself, since no one else seemed to notice. And yet Tom had been pleased, Lorna delighted and a starry-eyed Dee had smiled her approval across a sea of heads. As for Jared – Jared had eyes for no one but Dee. Not strictly true, since those heavy-lidded eyes missed little with their deceptively lazy appraisal of a room. And in that case, she was wrong. Jared would know precisely where to find her and precisely how long she'd been gone. Not to mention why.

'Hiding, Stevie? Feeling the strain?' he drawled as she emerged from the bathroom, her furtive glance right and left confirming her suspicion as the familiar shape stepped out of the shadows. 'Don't tell me you've overdone the wine? Or maybe it's the food – not that you managed to eat much,' he scathingly acknowledged. 'So maybe it's the company the lady finds irksome?'

'She certainly does,' she conceded sweetly. 'Present company, Jared. And as for that creep, Sanders –'

'All you have to do is smile, feed his face and feed his ego. In short, make him feel important.'

'I'd rather consort with a rat,' she retorted, attempting to sweep past and brought up short by a hand on her arm. A hand. Jared's hand. Tanned. Naturally dark to start with, given his Italian heritage, and standing out starkly against her own fair, lightly freckled skin.

'I –'

'Don't fret, Jared,' she sneeringly reminded him, pointedly shaking free. 'Duty calls. Sweet you want him, sweet he'll be. All in the name of business.'

A dizzy hour, more wine than was wise, but it helped dull the pain. The pain of watching Jared, wanting Jared – oh, yes, she wanted him, she acknowledged, the knife-blade twisting in her belly. Loved him, wanted him, needed him. Needed him like a bear needed a sore head, maybe, but the need wasn't about to go away. And seeing him with Dee, touching Dee, dancing with Dee, dipping his head to nuzzle at her temples was more than Stevie could stand.

Dance. Dance, dance, dance the night away, and why not? The man cradling her close was tall, dark and handsome. Italian, too, she added sourly, somewhere along the way. And he was holding, touching, nuzzling with his mouth, stroking with his fingers. Insidious fingers that managed to slip into nooks and crannies that would surely be off-limits to any gentleman worthy of the name. Unless, of course, Stevie allowed, it happened to be Jared.

But it wasn't Jared, wouldn't be Jared, and she swallowed the surge of hysteria along with the waves of nausea. For Nicky Sanders had pulled her close, was nuzzling her neck with those lamprey lips while his hands swept over her buttocks, tugging her hard against him. And he was hard. And he was grunting softly. And sweating. And grinding his hips against hers as they shuffled around in time to the music, the discreet lighting and the push-shove of the other couples all the camouflage he needed to indulge his need. His need. But not Stevie's. Unfair, her mind screamed. Because had it been Jared –

'My dance, I believe.' A brittle smile from Jared; Sanders' flash of anger instantly controlled.

'My pleasure,' he murmured with a calculating

glance at the rapid rise and fall of Stevie's agitated breasts. A fleeting smile, a theatrical bow. 'Until later, my dear.'

Over my dead body, she spat, only silently, aware of Jared's anger and suddenly confused. Suddenly angry. Worse than angry, livid.

'What the *hell* do you think you're doing?' Jared demanded, having manoeuvred them out onto the terrace, amazingly, thankfully empty.

'Keep him sweet, *you* said,' she hissed as he thrust her against the parapet.

'Precisely. Keep him sweet, feed his ego. His ego, Stevie. Not ravish him in public, damn you –'

'And damn you,' she spat, twisting free of his vice-like grip, her eyes pools of hate in a stark white face. 'Damn you for ever, Jared Wilde. The man's revolting. He's got more arms than an octopus and he clearly thinks Stevie Cooper's part of the deal. Only I'm not – hey, Jared?'

A careless shrug of shoulders. 'A moot point. If you're asking my opinion, I'd say it normally depends on the point of view. But if that's what Sanders thinks . . .' Another shrug, those heavy-lidded eyes giving nothing away. 'Then that's the message you're putting across. You're available.'

'Jealous, Jared? Peeved?' she demanded, crying inside, dying inside, but damned if she'd let it show. 'Did the Big Bad Wolf get his paw slapped when he tried the same tactic? Poor Jared,' she scorned. 'Poor little rich boy. Conditioned from birth to think he can buy what he wants, take what he wants, do what he wants, when he wants. Well, maybe you can,' she conceded tersely. 'But not with me. I'm not for sale. Not to you, or Sanders, or the entire male population. And if that job at ALITANI depends on Stevie Cooper hopping into bed with every man who fancies his chances —'

'Wishful thinking?' he interrupted slyly, folding his arms and treating her to one of those infuriating, lazy smiles. 'Bed?' he reminded her. 'Monday evening? And if it hadn't been me —'

'It wasn't, unless somewhere along the way I blinked and missed it,' she scoffed. 'And what a massive blow to an ego that would be. Now, a common or garden spot of rejection —'

'Hardly common or garden,' he reminded her tersely. 'More a case of sheer necessity, since you were clearly expecting company. Male company?' he insinuated slyly. 'The sort of male company you'd greet in a bathrobe? So much more convenient than a full set of clothes. One tug of the belt and you're raring to go. And you're quite a goer, hey, Stevie? For on the verge of making love to me you recall a prior engagement and can't get rid of me fast enough.'

'Like I said — jealous, Jared?'

'Just relieved. Glad I didn't succumb to your not inconsiderable charms. And, *yes*, I wanted you,' he surprised her by admitting, catching her gasp of amazement. 'Briefly. Ridiculous though it seems, for a moment of madness I nearly made love to a tramp.'

Stevie hit him. Hard. Horrified, she saw the imprint of her hand across his cheek, caught Jared's flash of amazement, the follow-on flash of amusement, and, choking back the tears, she stumbled backwards, came up against the rapidly cooling stonework of the parapet and froze.

'Unwise,' he murmured softly, rubbing his cheek with the back of his hand. 'And definitely not in the Queensberry rules. So – having over-stepped the mark, now comes the question of the penalty.'

'You wouldn't –'

'I wouldn't?' he queried, moving closer by degrees. Stevie's fight-flight surge of adrenaline was a conflict of signals. 'I wouldn't – what? Pay you back in kind? Put you over my knee and tan your pretty little hide? Lady,' he drawled, with a solemn shake of the head, 'if I were you, I sure as hell wouldn't bank on it. And yet, no –'

He broke off, smiled, moved closer again – so close she could breathe the spicy tang of his aftershave, even in the half-light catch the pinpricks of light dancing in his eyes. Because, far from being angry, Jared was highly amused, was laughing at Stevie, had been laughing all along. And though she stiffened, priming herself for flight, when Jared's hands fastened on her near naked shoulders she simply closed her eyes, closed her mind, and wanted him to kiss her.

Kiss her. Touch her. Take her, she realized hysterically. For if Jared was miles wrong about her lifestyle, when it came to the needs of her body his insight was unnerving. She wanted him, needed him, loved him.

'Woman, woman, woman,' he crooned, his face against her cheek as he cradled her close, the anger and the heated words and the vile accusations for the moment pushed aside. 'Oh, woman, you drive me insane.'

Insanity. Allowing him to kiss her, to touch her, to move against her. Wanting him, needing him, craving him, the battle in her mind fought and lost, shameless to the end, Stevie simply gave in to the need, parting her lips, allowing Jared to taste, to savour, his tongue sweeping through into the secret moist depths, an intimate sweep of the tender nooks and crannies of her mouth.

Somewhere far away a woman was moaning; Stevie was moaning. Her heated response fanned the flames, Jared's hiss of indrawn breath music to her ears.

A scything of pain as Jared pulled away, his glance of enquiry fleeting, fleetingly uncertain, and then he was smiling, his arms going around her as he gathered her close, kissed her. Hands and mouth creating havoc. Wonderful hands on the near naked skin of her shoulders, a feather light brush of thumbs little more than sheer imagination as Jared slid the tiny shoe string straps over the curves before turning his attention to the zipper.

Madness. A step away from a roomful of people and prissy Stevie Cooper was half naked in the arms of a man, was kissing a man, wanting a man, the tug in her belly a bitter-sweet craving.

Breasts, tiny but perfect, just right for hands, for mouth, for hands again, her straining nipples eloquent invitation for Jared to dip his head. And so he did, a darting tongue flicking from one to the other and back again until, almost on his knees, he fastened his hungry mouth on one, cradled the second in his palm, the growl of approval in the back of his throat filling her with heat.

Lost to the world, Stevie swayed backwards from the pivot of her waist and thrust tingling breasts into Jared's hungry mouth, his waiting palm, a perfect fit for both, she decided, smiling inside. Warm inside. The thrill of excitement was giving way to the glow of knowledge. For if Stevie's need was exquisite, Jared's need was every bit as fierce.

Back on his feet, he was kissing her again, holding her, thrusting against her, and locked against the stonework Stevie was powerless to move – not that she wanted to move, she hastily reassured herself, the swirl of her hips an erotic contradiction.

'Stevie! Hell, woman,' he groaned in anguish,

tugging her closer still, the heat of him, the need of him, the strength of him sending fear rippling through her. Fear, want, need. The need was eating away at her mind, creating havoc in her body. A weak woman's body that was craving a man's touch; and more, the sudden dampness at her groin eloquent proof of how much more. Paradise, heaven on earth. The wealth of emotion was endless, the knowledge too shocking to face. Man and woman. Stevie and Jared. Dee and Jared. Mae –

Stevie froze. Mae. In love with a man, dependent on a man, rejected by a man, ruined by a man. No!

Open palms connected with his shoulders and, with surprise her only advantage, Stevie pushed against him, twisting free, the sudden release a bitter-sweet triumph.

'Stevie? *No*, Stevie!' Jared insisted, snatching at her shoulders and twisting her round to face him.

'Oh, but, yes,' she contradicted, the angle of her chin unwittingly aggressive. And she folded her arms across her naked breasts, shivered despite the warmth of the evening, and held his gaze with a massive surge of will.

'But – *why*?' he demanded, eyes nuggets of jet in the rapidly approaching dusk. 'Why, Stevie, why? We –'

'Have guests,' she reminded him dully. 'Important guests who'll be wondering where we are.' Not to mention man-hungry Dee, abandoned by her man and sure to be on the prowl. And, less in shame for her own behaviour as hate for the hurt she'd cause if Dee's worried face suddenly appeared in the doorway, Stevie swallowed her embarrassment and wriggled back into the bodice of her dress, pushing the barely adequate straps over her shoulders before reaching with clumsy fingers for the zipper.

'Here, let me. I can –'

'I can manage perfectly well, thank you,' she murmured primly, quickly discovering she couldn't as the teeth of the zipper connected, interlocked, jammed and, despite Stevie's frantic tuggings, proved impossible to budge.

With an anguished glance at Jared, she turned her back, braced herself. The skin to skin contact was searing as Jared freed the offending fold of fabric before tugging the zipper back into place.

'Stevie –'

'Duty calls,' she reminded him over-brightly, eyes bright with unshed tears. Tears? she silently scorned. Because he'd kissed her, touched her, wanted her. Yet most of all – she forced herself to swallow – because she wanted him.

'Why, Stevie?'

No heat in the words, no trace of anger, she noted, her own anger surging. Just idle curiosity. Because Stevie had pushed him away and men like Jared Wilde weren't programmed for rejection.

'Why?' she queried coldly, angling her head, ice-cold eyes locking with simmering black pools. 'Surely it isn't so much why, as how dare I?' she sneered. 'How dare I say no to Jared Wilde? Rich, handsome, powerful, irresistible Jared Wilde. Well, have I got news for you,' she scorned, hitting out, hating him, hating herself more. 'Because the simple answer to both is I don't have to explain. My reasons, my decision. End of discussion.'

'Oh, no –'

'Yes!' she hissed. 'Queensberry rules or Stevie Cooper's; I can simply say no. The prerogative of every woman, Mr Wilde, from the grandest lady in the land to the tartiest of tramps. No, no and no.'

'Ah.'

'Ah, what?' Stevie bit out, aware of a sudden flash of amusement and irrationally annoyed.

'Just, ah, I see. I see, therefore I begin to understand,' he conceded lightly, spreading his hands and dazzling her with the brilliance of his smile. 'The *lady*,' he emphasized lightly, 'is annoyed. Understandably so. The remark was uncalled for and I apologize unreservedly.'

'Big of you,' she needled, not in the least impressed by his lightning change of mood – a dangerous change of mood, given Jared's undoubted charm.

'So – since the lady in question is precisely that, needless to say she'll accept my humble apology.'

'Humble, my foot. If I thought for one moment you even knew how to spell it, I'd probably die of shock.'

'H-U-M-'

'A-R-R-O-G'

'Guilty as charged, he interrupted dryly. 'Sometimes. But not now. Right now I'm sorry. More than sorry. I'm mortified, ashamed, abashed, disconcerted, chastened, lowly, meek, bowed and thoroughly broken. Unless, of course,' he added hopefully, 'the lady's in a forgiving mood?'

'And if the lady isn't? Always assuming she's qualified,' she challenged

'She is, on all counts,' he reassured her swiftly. 'So I guess we can take it as read.'

'Words. Easy words.' She gave a disdainful snap of the fingers. 'And, along with an easy smile, the mechanics of an apology.'

'I could always go down on my knees?' he offered.

'Forget it. If the wind changed direction you'd be stuck there.'

'Another quaint northern phrase?' he needled.

'The place positively drips them,' she conceded, smiling grimly, logging his annoyance, barely perceptible but there nonetheless. Because Stevie was winning. Little more than a war of words, but she'd salvaged her pride and regained the upper hand. Quit while you're ahead, girl, she silently entreated, beginning to walk away, back to the open doorway and the noisy crush of a party that beckoned anything but cosily.

'Stevie?'

'Jared?' she queried politely, halting, not bothering to turn.

'Give a repentant wolf a clue, hey?'

'Give me one good reason why I should,' she stalled, smiling and glad he couldn't see it. 'And, since you'll take it as read in any case, why bother asking?'

'Because I was wrong. Because I hit out in anger. Because –'

'You need to keep me sweet so I can sweet-talk Sanders into signing on the dotted line?'

'Hardly, since the deal with Sanders is off – my decision, not his,' he tagged on swiftly, catching Stevie's flash of surprise as she spun round.

'But – you needed that contract,' she pointed out calmly, a lot more calmly than she was feeling.

'Correction, I *wanted* that contract.'

'Same difference,' she murmured, suddenly unsure and stifling the panic. No need to panic. If Jared gave her the sack before the job had begun, she'd simply go back to Deighton's. If. If Jared could be trusted to keep his word.

'Not at all,' he contradicted mildly. 'My company, my contract, my decision. And especially when it affects the welfare of my staff.'

'Meaning me?'

He nodded. 'Don't sound so surprised.'

'Less surprised than available – remember? My fault, not Sanders',' she reminded him bitterly.

'Hardly. The guy's an out and out creep – remember?'

'Oh, I remember all right,' Stevie acknowledged, swallowing the pain. 'Believe me, Jared, I remember each and every word.'

'Words, Stevie. Angry words. I was annoyed and I hit out –'

'You simply said what you believed.' Then and now. And nothing he could say would change the way he felt. Stevie was available. She'd read it in his eyes, in his blatant contempt at Tom and Lorna's, in the sly digs about the man she'd been expecting the other night, in Jared's own words less than an hour ago. An hour ago? A lifetime ago, she decided as the tears began to well. Virginal Stevie Cooper. Prim and proper Stevie Cooper. A tramp. Her lips twisted. If it wasn't so pathetically amusing she'd cry.

She walked away, back into the noisy, heated room, half expecting an accusing turn of heads, silent disapproval from a sea of knowing, hostile eyes. Only it didn't happen, it was simply her guilty conscience pricking her, and she scanned the crowd, looking for Dee, looking for Sanders, finding neither, and she was instantly reassured as she threaded her way to the drinks tray. One small glass of wine and then she'd stick to fruit juice, keep her wits – might even hold onto that job, she acknowledged, spotting Lorna and Tom shuffling round in time to the music and raising her glass in acknowledgement.

No sign of Sanders, still no sign of Dee. An awful thought was occurring. Ridiculous, in any case. Because if Sanders *had* trapped Dee in some secluded corner, Dee could take care of herself, would eat a man like Sanders for breakfast. Unlike Stevie.

'Stevie! Darling, you look wonderful! A new job, a new image?' Dee probed, appearing out of nowhere. 'Or are you finally breaking out of that shell you've built around yourself?'

Stevie smiled, aware that Dee was teasing, that she'd long since given up hope of seeing Stevie follow her example by tripping down the aisle even once on the rocky road to married bliss.

'Just doing my bit for the firm,' she explained, pouring a second glass for Dee. 'First impressions and all that jazz. I thought the boss might expect it. Not that I could hope to compete with the lady on his arm,' she added, smothering a twinge of guilt as Dee positively beamed.

'Like it?' she queried, indicating the dress that fitted where it touched and treating Stevie to a twirl on the spot.

'Hmm. There's not an awful lot to like,' Stevie observed dryly.

Dee's smile broadened. 'I guess there isn't at that,' she conceded and, spotting Jared framed in the door to the hallway, flashed Stevie another bright smile before sidling across.

Stevie watched her go, smothering another pang of unease. For if Stevie's comparatively sober outfit could be said to render her available, how far would the same irrefutable male logic be applied to Dee? Vulnerable, lonely Dee, who was simply looking for love. Available she wasn't, not in the derogatory sense that Jared was implying, but available she certainly was – for love, and all its exploitations.

Still looking on as Dee reached her goal, Stevie braced herself, and sure enough Jared smiled, opened his arms, caught Dee to him, wrapped his arms around her, the hands caressing her near naked back bringing painful recollection of his hands on Stevie's skin. Severing the connection, she blinked back the tears, yet couldn't resist another blurred glance. Fatal. Jared's muted flash of triumph was unmistakable, and Stevie's head snapped up as something vital died.

Playing games. With Stevie, with Dee, with countless dozens of others, she silently derided. Available? Strange how the insult didn't apply to the male of the species. Superstud. Playboy. Man about town. Nudge-nudge, wink-wink and it's another well-deserved conquest, another maiden bowled over by a heated glance, a silver tongue, a touch of mouth and fingers.

Still, no time to brood, she had a job to do – circlulate, talk, smile, listen, dance, though with Sanders clearly out of the way thankfully no more wandering hands. Stand, talk, smile, move around. Lounge to dining room, to kitchen, to drawing room and back again.

The apartment was bigger than Stevie's – Andrew's, she corrected automatically – and would have cost a pretty penny. Another pretty penny to furnish, judging by the look of things.

Like Andrew, Jared had selected a basic colour and carried the scheme throughout. The palest of salmon-pink walls were perfectly offset by a sculptured jade carpet, the sort of Oriental rugs that wouldn't be on sale even in Southport's more exclusive shops. And as for the furniture itself . . . From that enormous Italian marquetry table in the dining room, its highly polished surface reflecting a stunning array of crystal and silver and expensively fluted crockery, through to the elegant jade and cream striped sofas in the lounge, the whole effect was welcoming and warm, unlike Andrew's stark expanse of white. And whilst the drawing room was clearly more formal, the winged chairs and scattering of occasional tables held more than a hint of invitation.

A place to live and a place to entertain. A perfect combination, thanks to money. And along with money, the power to control, to destroy. A man's control over a woman. Unfair, her mind screamed. But then, no one had ever pretended that life was even remotely fair.

So, make the most of it, girl. Smile, circulate, talk, listen, pretend. Be happy. Pretend. Fool the world. And with the chimes of midnight beginning to trill from some exquisite clock in the corner, surely the interminable night must soon draw to an end?

And, with Anna sure to be wondering where she'd got to, it was high time Stevie headed for home. So – decision time. Risk the boss's wrath and leave without permission, or simply melt away while Jared wasn't looking? Yet why not simply be bold? Other people had begun to drift away and so would Stevie. Now. But first she'd locate her wrap, little more than a shawl to cover her bare shoulders.

Easier said than done, she realized, popping her head round a bedroom door – the spare bedroom, she surmised, given its position, like Rosa's, next to the bathroom.

No sign of the wrap or anyone else's light-weight jackets, so another pause outside a door. Jared's bedroom. The master bedroom. The firmly closed door unmistakably hostile. So, knock and put her head round? Or knock and wait, listen, strain her ears for the hasty rustle of clothing? Ridiculous in any case. It was a party, a flat warming party; the place – warts and all – was open house. And if Jared hadn't the sense to know it, then tough.

Fingers closing round the handle, Stevie paused, and, taking a deep breath, followed through. Empty. The waves of relief rippled over her, and then she caught a sound, a woman's low laugh, and froze.

It came from the bathroom, the *en suite* bathroom, an eerie echo through the chink of the slightly open door.

'Jared –' A hint of protest in the single word, Jared's reply little more than a growl.

Spying her wrap among the others tossed nonchalantly on the bed, yet caught fast in no man's land, a frantic Stevie weighed her options. Tiptoe forward and make a grab, or effect a tactical retreat? Retreat? She'd done nothing wrong, for heaven's sake, and if Jared and Dee had to cavort in the bathroom when they were supposed to be entertaining, they'd simply have to face the consequences of detection.

She was halfway across the rich pile of the carpet when the bathroom door began to swing open. Stevie stopped dead, catching Dee's mew of protest, another throaty growl from Jared, her eyes darting of their own volition to the gap in the jamb and beyond, to the figures reflected in the bronze of the mirror. Man and woman, kissing, holding, touching. Fully dressed, her mind logged automatically. At least, she amended painfully, Jared was. And he was smiling, smiling down at Dee, who reached her arms behind her back to tug with slow and deliberate movements at the zipper of her dress. To release the zipper, to shrug the dress from her shoulders, to step out of the dress clad in nothing but her panties. To smile, and then move forward into Jared's waiting arms.

CHAPTER 11

Knowing she wouldn't sleep, Stevie didn't bother with the pretence of getting ready for bed. Anna, heavy-lidded and tired, had taken herself off at once, and for this Stevie was grateful. Dry-eyed, despite the turmoil raging in her heart, she poured herself a weak brandy and Coke and then tiptoed into Rosa, standing for long, long moments before brushing a wisp of damp hair off the sleeping child's forehead. And smiling. And crying inside. And dying inside.

It wouldn't work. Not day in, day out, being with Jared, yet not being with Jared. Wanting, needing, aching, craving. Knowing. Ah, yes, the knowing. Imagining, seeing, picturing, remembering. Jared and Dee. Together. Kissing, touching, loving.

Because if sheer imagination wasn't enough to start with, Stevie had seen for herself. Jared and Dee. Together. On the verge of making love. As they would be now, she acknowledged, automatically checking her watch as the knife-blade twisted. Twenty minutes. A lifetime in Stevie's mind. And she'd bolted, leaving the wrap for another day, vaguely aware that Jared's guests were using the midnight hour as the benchmark and taking themselves off. Leaving Jared and Dee alone. Leaving Stevie alone with the knowledge.

Damned if she did and damned if she didn't. For whilst the job at Deighton's was still an option, it was a luxury she couldn't afford. Because Jared would know. She'd be running away. And clever, clever Jared would know why. So – Stevie was trapped, caught fast in a web of Jared's making, and there wasn't a thing she could do about it. Except grin and bear it, work her passage, and the moment she judged she'd proved herself – in her own mind at least – she'd quit. Six months, she calculated, draining her glass and refilling it, with Coke this time, and, curling her legs under her body, she wriggled down into the cushions.

Closing her eyes, she squeezed back the tears, fighting for control, aware that if she let go now, she'd weep for the rest of her life. Only she mustn't. There was Rosa to think about, not to mention her own self-respect.

A sniff. A hasty smother of the sobs that were starting to build, a hasty brush of a salt-damp cheek. Damn Jared Wilde. Damn, damn and damn the man for ever.

The shrill sound of the door bell shattered the

silence, shattered her nerves, the near empty glass almost slipping from her grasp. Who on earth –?

'Jared!'

'Don't sound so surprised,' he drawled, his lazy glance travelling the length of her in one of those intimate appraisals that set the blood boiling in her veins, not really any different from the glances she'd suffered from Sanders, yet not so much insulting as caressing. 'You left your wrap,' he smilingly explained, holding it out. 'An invitation to call, perhaps?'

'At this hour of the night? What the *hell* do you take me for?' Stevie hissed, snatching the shawl from his outstretched hand and flouncing back into the lounge.

He followed, ignoring her seething silence. 'A wee nightcap, Jared? How kind of you to ask,' he improvised absurdly, logging her glass and hazarding a guess at the contents. 'And whilst brandy would be lovely, Stevie, I find that it generally pays to come prepared. Champagne. I trust it meets with madam's approval?' And before she had time to reply, he'd whipped a well-chilled bottle from behind his back and produced two delicate crystal flutes from the pockets of his jacket.

'I –'

'You don't have to say a word. Just sit, sip, savour and relax. Relax,' he entreated, and, seeing her hesitation, he off-loaded the bottle and glasses before placing his open palms on

202

her shoulders, urging her gently but firmly back onto the cushions. 'Relax, Stevie,' he repeated, a single finger tucked beneath her chin. 'Believe it or not, the Big Bad Wolf hasn't come to ravish you.'

'Heaven forbid,' she murmured dryly. 'Not to mention Dee. And talking of Dee –'

'We're not. I'm not. You're not. It was your night, Stevie, it's you I've come to thank.'

'Like I said, at this hour?'

'Why not? I noticed the light was on as I was passing, and guessed – hoped,' he amended swiftly, 'that you wouldn't be too tired for company.'

'And if I am?'

'Then naturally I'll leave?'

Question, not statement, Stevie noted, logging the single raised brow. Pause. Time enough for Stevie to reply, yet not so long that the moment grew awkward. A rueful smile, a shrug of powerful shoulders and Jared took the hint, spinning on his heels and strolling lazily to the door.

A pause again as he turned, raised a hand to his temple in jaunty salute. 'So long, Stevie. See you bright and early Monday mor –'

'No! Don't go.'

Another raised brow, a flicker of emotion masked in an instant. 'No? But only if you're sure?'

Stevie nodded. Madness, she realized as the hope in her heart sparked into life. For if Jared *had* been passing her door, the implication was obvious. Dee. On her way home. Alone. And, since barely thirty minutes had passed since the scene she'd unwittingly witnessed in Jared's bathroom . . . Hope. Vain hope, she'd doubtless discover in the fullness of time, but in the meanwhile . . .

'To a job well done?' Jared queried softly, raising his glass. 'And to my very lovely hostess.'

'Yes. Dee did look divine,' Stevie reminded him, with belated loyalty to her friend. A very good friend. A trusting friend. And all the more reason to keep Jared at a distance.

'She did indeed,' he smilingly acknowledged, taking his place beside her, unexpectedly, unnervingly close. 'And so did you. Better than divine, in fact.'

'I think "presentable" is the word you're looking for,' she reminded him slyly.

'And one of those remarks a guy won't be allowed to live down,' he ruefully admitted.

'Forgiven but not forgotten,' she agreed. 'This time.'

'Sounds ominous?' he queried, eyes narrowing.

'Not so much a warning shot across the bows as the truth. My wardrobe,' she said. 'If you're expecting designer outfits by the dozen, you'll be sorely disappointed. Now Dee, on the other hand –'

'Doesn't work for me. Worry not, Stevie, you'll do.'

'I'll have to,' she returned tartly.

Jared smiled, one of those smiles that turned her blood to water, sent rivers of heat flooding her veins, and, suddenly hot and bothered, Stevie dropped her gaze, sipped the well-chilled wine with its after-taste of bubbles and waited, and waited, and found the sudden silence unbearable. And risked a glance through the veil of her lashes.

More confusion. He was watching her, the expression in his eyes unfathomable. Stevie shivered, shifted position, a shoestring strap slipping over her shoulder and drawing his gaze. Drawing his gaze, drawing his touch as he reached out to hook it back into place, just a single finger but scalding nonetheless. Stevie went rigid. Yet another overreaction, she discovered, as Jared removed his hand, drained his glass, refilled it, angled the bottle in silent enquiry.

Stevie shook her head. She needed to keep her wits. Champagne on top of brandy on top of wine would do little for her self-control, not that she was feeling *in* control having Jared within touching distance. Touch. A finger sliding beneath her chin, tilting her chin, forcing her gaze.

'I was wrong,' he acknowledged huskily.

She nodded. Heaven only knew what he was saying but those eyes, such wonderful eyes, were locked onto hers, and there was passion swirling in their depths. So easy to melt against him, to open her mouth beneath his, to feel his arms close around her. Oh, so easy. Only she mustn't. Dee.

205

Remember Dee. Lovely, trusting Dee. Trust. A futile emotion where men were concerned. Think of Dee. Think of Mae. Think of herself.

'No, Jared!'

He released her, another flash of emotion veiled in an instant, and then he was sitting back against the arm of the settee, cradling the glass in his hands. Glancing across and sensing her confusion, he smiled. 'Not so much wrong, as very wrong. On several counts – hey, Stevie?'

'Who knows?' she retorted flippantly. 'Two weeks from now, two months from now, and you might be in a position to judge. As it is, you barely know me.'

'No.' A ghost of a smile was playing about the corners of his mouth. 'But I'm learning and I'm learning fast.' He raised his glass. 'Here's to what the next two weeks reveal.'

'Don't build up your hopes,' she warned. 'What you see is basically it.'

'Young, beautiful, touchy, fiercely loyal to her friends. Not to mention hard-working. Sounds a pretty good basis to me.'

'For what?'

'Oh, you know . . .' He shrugged, smiled, waved his glass. 'For life, Stevie Cooper. And not a bad life at that,' he mused, glancing round as if the thought had suddenly struck him.

His gaze travelled the room, missing not a thing, Stevie was sure – the exquisitely stark decor, the sumptuous white leather suite, the collection of objets d'art carefully out of Rosa's reach behind the glass-fronted cabinets, Jared's nod of approval was silent endorsement of Andrew's taste. 'A good job,' he murmured, eyes coming back to lock with hers. 'A beautiful home. A very beautiful home. For a woman of twenty-six, you've done well.'

'And a man of twenty six? Would he have done well? Or do the Jared Wildes of the world take a man's success for granted?' she heard herself needling.

'Only one, Stevie. Jared Wilde, singular. And by twenty-six I'd made my first million.'

'Pounds?' she sneered. 'Or lire?'

'Oh, definitely pounds,' he informed her solemnly. 'A different breed entirely. At the risk of sounding smug, lire millionaires are ten a penny.'

'I wouldn't know,' she conceded.

'No? Strange,' he added, with another loaded glance. 'I thought all things Italian were the lady's speciality.'

'Meaning?'

'Italian Impressions. More than just a name, hey, Stevie?'

'Since I devised the range, I could hardly hope to deny it,' she retorted carefully, swirling the wine around her glass and watching the bubbles form and pop and swirl again.

'And that other connection? The source of inspiration? Not so much a recipe book as a man. Right?'

'Wrong!' Intuition? she wondered, vaguely alarmed. Had the vibes of hostility on the night they'd first met really been such a give-away? Or had some little bird been talking out of turn? Unlikely, given the loyalty of her friends. Discretion. Sensitivity. Loyalty. She'd stake her life on it.

Jared shrugged. 'If you say so,' he allowed, clearly disbelieving.

'I do. But you needn't take my word for it. Make some enquiries, Jared. Ask around. Put your mind at rest. After all, as from nine o'clock Monday morning this humble employee is at your beck and call twenty-four hours a day, three hundred and sixty-five days a year, and I should hate you to doubt my integrity.'

'I'm your employer, not your keeper. Worry not, Stevie, your private life's your own concern.'

'Good.'

'Just so long as it stays that way,' he tagged on slyly.

'And what the hell is that supposed to mean?' Stevie challenged, her head snapping up.

He waved an airy hand. 'This. You. A good job, Stevie. On the salary I'm paying I could begin to understand it. But . . .'

'But nothing,' she snapped. His meaning was unmistakable. 'It's private; it's none of your business — remember? My life, my lifestyle. And I won't — repeat, won't — be making front-page news as call girl of the year.'

'I didn't –'

'Oh, yes, you did,' she rasped, up in an instant and towering over him, toweringly angry. 'You know what you're implying, and every snide, revolting word has been carefully selected. I'm available. I'm a tramp. I clearly live beyond my means and a child of six could put two and two together and come up with the magic number of conclusions.'

A child of six. Oh, God! Rosa. Beautiful, innocent Rosa, sleeping peacefully just beyond a closed door. Sleeping peacefully until World War Three broke out in the lounge, that was. And Stevie was stinging, was crying inside, was openly crying, she realized, swinging away before Jared could see, could add scorn to his contempt.

'Stevie –'

'No! Just go. Leave me alone,' she rasped, struggling for control, folding her arms and going rigid as he moved to stand behind her. 'Because despite what you think, Mr Wilde, there's nothing to keep you here. I'm available to no one. *No one*,' she emphasized grimly. 'And, like it or not, that includes you. Now go. Get out of my house.'

'Stevie –'

'Will – you – please – leave – me – alone?' she enunciated carefully, unheeding of the stream of tears. Because she didn't care any more. Because he'd hurt her. He'd insulted her once too often and he'd hurt her. And she'd cry, and she'd purge the hurt. And damn Jared Wilde but he could go to hell. She swung round.

'Stevie! Oh, hell, Stevie –'

'No! No, no, no!' she bit out, the expression on his face tugging at her heartstrings. As if! As if the arrogant Jared Wilde would care that he'd hurt her. And he had. And he was holding her, touching her, rocking her, was pressing her face against his shoulder and was rocking Stevie just as she did Rosa, whispering words, soothing words, meaningless words.

'No, Stevie. No, no, no,' he crooned. 'You're too young, too beautiful, too pure –'

'Pure as the devil in hell,' she scorned, struggling to free herself, her open palms pushing against his chest, and yet Jared simply laughed, caught her flailing wrists, forcing her arms down and pinning them to her sides. And then he was holding her, kissing her, lapping away the tears, kissing her salt-stained cheeks, nuzzling her lips.

Madness. Because he despised her. Wanted her as a man did a woman but despised her all the same. Because Stevie was available.

'No, no, no,' he insisted as Stevie continued to resist. 'I want you. I want to hold you. I want to kiss you. Hell, woman, you must know that I want you. And I'm wrong. Right and wrong both, but most of all wrong,' he told her fiercely, enigmatically, half shaking her, kissing her again.

'But I'm a tramp,' she bit out, twisting her head

away in a vain attempt to evade the nuzzle of his lips.

'No, Stevie. No, no, no,' he repeated, cupping her face in his hands, holding her face, holding her gaze. 'For God's sake, woman, will you listen to me?'

'Give me one good reason why?' she challenged as the fight began to drain from her body.

'Tom,' he murmured unexpectedly, the anguish in his eyes tearing her apart – wonderful black pools that fastened onto hers and refused to let her look away. 'Lorna. Kelly. Dee. Love, Stevie. Friendship, loyalty, love. I might not know you well,' he acknowledged tersely, 'but that doesn't mean that I don't know you at all. I know you through your friends. Don't you see?' he demanded, shaking her. '*They* love you. And what's good enough for Tom and Lorna is good enough for me. They know the real Stevie Cooper. It's enough, more than enough.'

He kissed her then, Stevie's mew of protest buried beneath the onslaught of his lips, his mouth, and Stevie was drowning, drowning, was kissing Jared, was shamelessly pushing her body into the hard lines of his, and Jared was wonderfully hard, wanted her, wanted Stevie every bit as much as she wanted him.

Only she mustn't. No, no, no, she told herself, chanting the word in her mind. Easy. Too easy. Just like the tramp he believed her to be. Not true, she consoled herself. She was pure. As pure as the

211

devil in hell, she contradicted swiftly. In mind, at least. Because she wanted him. Shameless. So Jared *was* right and wrong both, she realized – realized too that his hands were ranging her body in a most delightful way, touching, caressing, kneading, stroking, stoking, enflaming, moving on, and down and round, and cupping breasts that were aching for his touch, flicking nipples that hardened and pushed against his lazy thumbs. And Jared laughed, dipped his head, put his mouth to the straining nubs, the flimsy barrier of fabric heightening the need, honing the tension.

More kisses, lips suckling, teeth gently biting, and his hands were gliding over her hips and bottom, down, down, down as Jared sank to his knees before her. And still his mouth created chaos, sucking, lapping, teasing, while Stevie stood and trembled, running her fingers through the silky locks of his hair, cradling his head to her aching breasts, a wonderfully tactile sensation but so easily matched by the hands that were exploring.

A gentle tickle of the sensitized skin at the back of her knees before the hands began to climb, gliding over the sheerest of sheathings. Upwards, slowly, relentlessly, reaching the tops of the self-holding stockings. Skin. Skin against skin. And Stevie was well on the road to paradise.

'Oh, God, Jared!' she moaned as his hands connected with the lace of her flimsy panties, curved round her bottom, swirled around again, allowing twin thumbs to brush against the mound.

'Oh, Stevie,' he crooned, barely lifting his mouth from her straining, aching breasts to glance upwards, the fire in his eyes fanning the flames. 'Oh, woman!' he growled. 'I want you. And I'm going to take you. Here. Now. I'm going to place you down in the middle of this wonderfully soft, wonderfully inviting expanse of carpet and I'm going to take you. I want you. I want you so much it hurts. And now I'm going to touch you. Touch you, taste you, take you,' he insisted, reaching for the hem of her panties, his eyes fastened on her face.

A single finger slid beneath the lace and paused. And as he paused Stevie flooded, caught Jared's throaty growl of approval and trembled. And waited. And waited. And Jared, tantalizing, tormenting Jared, barely moved. Moved a finger. Imperceptible. Impossible. Unbelievable. Moved again.

Stevie closed her eyes, smiled, caught the sound of a child crying out in her sleep and froze.

Jared stiffened. 'You're married!'

'Something else you don't know about me?' Stevie quipped, the flame extinguished in an instant. And she should have known, should have realized she was clutching at straws, imagining Jared should want her. And, since Jared had loosened his hold with almost indecent haste, she

213

took a step backwards, angled her head, met his incredulous gaze full on. 'But no,' she conceded tightly as Jared came hurriedly to his feet. 'I'm not, never have been, never will be.'

'Then –'

'Yes, then.' Stevie smiled, a mocking, goading smile that helped mask the pain, and, folding her arms across her chest in an unconscious gesture of protection, she lifted her chin, part-defiance, part-aggression, part-pride.

'Shocking, isn't it?' she derided, logging the expression in his eyes and crying inside, dying inside. 'In the fun-loving nineties Stevie Cooper's an unmarried mother.' She leaned forward, lowered her voice, her outward composure at odds with the turmoil raging inside. 'Looks like that assessment of yours was right in the first place,' she told him confidentially. 'How did it go again? No, don't bother repeating it,' she sneeringly entreated. 'The word's engraved in stone upon my heart. Tramp.'

Not the truth, the whole truth and nothing but the truth, but enough to keep the fastidious Jared Wilde at arm's length. And it worked. Because if that moue of distaste was masked in an instant, it was an instant too late. Stevie had seen. Stevie understood. And it hurt.

'I –'

'Exit stage left?' she supplied dully, glancing pointedly to the door. She waved a hand. 'Be my guest,' she invited, instinctively aware that Jared was caught between the devil and the deep blue sea, that the urge to walk away was set against another emotion, an emotion Stevie couldn't hope to understand. The gentleman in Jared, she vaguely supposed, not wanting to be seen to overreact. After all, it was the fun-loving, liberated nineties . . .

'Goodnight, Jared,' she murmured, speeding his decision. 'See you bright and early Monday morning. Unless, of course, you're about to change your mind?'

'About the job? And why should I do that?' he queried, back in control as he reached for his glass, abandoned half a lifetime ago, it seemed, drained it refilled it, drained the bottle as, un-asked, he topped up Stevie's.

So, maybe not fully in control after all, Stevie decided, her gaze drawn to the pulse beating a rapid tattoo at his temple.

She shrugged. 'Oh, you know. Bad for the company's image,' she scorned. 'Family values and all that jazz.'

'Deighton's survived.'

'Ah, yes, but then Deighton's is British through and through. And Tom knew what he was getting from the start.'

Jared's turn to shrug. 'Fine. Tom's endorse-ment is good enough for me.' He gave a tight smile, raised his glass in a mockery of a toast. 'Bright and early Monday morning it is.'

He quaffed the champagne in one, placed the

crystal flute down on the table beside Stevie's with a theatrical flourish and strolled across the vast expanse of carpet without a care in the world, scooping up his carelessly discarded jacket along the way.

Framed in the doorway that led through to the hall, he paused and glanced back at Stevie, who hadn't moved, except to hug herself even tighter, fingers digging into the skin of her upper arms as she struggled for control. Sensing he had something to say, she angled her head in enquiry.

'About your – family commitments,' he murmured carefully. 'I assume there's nothing to stop you working late, if and when required?'

'Twenty-four hours a day, three hundred and sixty-five days a year,' she reminded him bitterly. 'Fear not, Jared, my private life won't stand in the way of ALITANI's profits.'

'Good. But if there did happen to be a problem –'

'Then I'll do what I've done for the past six years,' she hissed with unexpected vehemence. 'I'll cope. I'll manage. And I won't, repeat won't, be asking any favours.'

'Then more fool you, Stevie Cooper. In Italy, of course, the needs of the child would prevail. Still, she's your daughter; I guess you know what you're doing.'

'I do. Believe it or not, Rosa's living proof of it.' Something struck her. *Daughter.* An educated guess? Or had Jared known all along?

'I just followed the string of clues,' he conceded, uncannily reading her mind. 'Carelessly missed at the time, I admit. But, as my nine-year-old nephew would surely confirm, pink frilled bears are strictly for girls.' He gave a fleeting smile that even managed to reach his eyes, she noted absurdly, melting inside. 'Oh, yes,' he added lightly, reaching into a pocket for his door keys, which he swung around his finger before palming them neatly. 'And their mothers. So long, Red. Enjoy the rest of your weekend. See you Monday.'

CHAPTER 12

Monday. A tense day. An interminable day. Over now, thank goodness, and barely a hiccup. Just work, work and more work, and nothing glaringly different from Deighton's. The obligatory guided tour, of course, along with the endless introductions – pointless, in Stevie's mind, since she'd never been good with names. But at least everyone would know who Stevie was. The boss's right hand. Almost the boss's lover, she amended tersely, not wanting to remember, attempting to close her mind and failing miserably.

But if the weekend had been hell, it could have been so much worse. If they'd really made love. If Jared's disappointment – disgust, she contradicted starkly – had given way to anger, to naked contempt. If. So many ifs. Try not to brood. Try to fill the waking hours.

Saturday. A feverish round of cleaning and polishing an apartment that had been aesthetically clean to start with. Only Rosa's bedroom had been spared, Jared's parting remark about the needs of the child still festering. Guilt, she'd acknowledged. Guilt, when she'd done nothing wrong, for heaven's sake. And so the clutter in Rosa's room was left untouched. Time enough for a spring clean there when Andrew arrived home and Stevie needed to find space for the put-you-up bed alongside Rosa's.

With not even the shopping to distract her, Stevie had settled for a ramble round the park with Rosa and Kelly, feeding bread to the ducks before heading for McDonald's. Happy Meals for the girls while Stevie hand-delivered her booking form. Twenty-five children for four weeks on Sunday. A new dress for Rosa? Stevie had mused, mentally adding the cost to the party bill. Why not? Rosa asked for little, expected little, seemed to know with an instinct beyond her years that money was tight. And, since money wouldn't be quite so tight from now on, thanks to the job with Jared, all the more reason to make a small child's birthday special.

Jared. Did each and every thought have to lead back to Jared? Stevie had wondered, scowling visibly.

Sunday. Ten o'clock mass at St Marie's, a pink and shining Rosa in tow. More guilt. It was the first time Stevie had shown her face in church for over a month, and filling the time hadn't helped because her mind had refused to conform. Prayers. Silent pleas, pitiful orisons, mingling with the faint smell of incense and swirling round her mind. And Jared Wilde at the centre of each. Escape. No escape from the man and everything he stood for. Not even at Nanna's nursing home.

'Stevie! And Rosa. Oh, love, I didn't expect to see you this week. But, oh, sweetheart, what a lovely surprise.'

A hug for Stevie, a big kiss for Rosa, and if Nanna's eyes had been suspiciously bright, they had been more than matched by Stevie's.

'And how was the party?' Nanna asked when a beaming Rosa handed over a precious slice of cake, crumbling and stale by now, despite Stevie's efforts to keep it wrapped in foil and airtight. But, since the thought was worth more than the deed, Nanna was touched.

'I had a new dress,' Rosa confided, perching on a stool beside Nanna and swinging her legs. 'I wanted to wear it today to show you but one of the boys spilled juice down the front and Mummy had to send it to the cleaners. Of course, when I have my party,' she loftily informed her, 'I won't invite boys.'

'And what about your old nan? Does she deserve an invite?'

Rosa grinned, aware that Nanna was teasing, that excursions from the nursing home were few and far between these days.

'McDonald's!' Nanna echoed when Rosa had finished explaining. 'Well, I never. Whatever will they think of next?'

'Trips to the moon?' Stevie suggested, tongue in cheek. 'It would never have happened in your day, hey, Nan?'

'Nor yours, love, more's the pity. When I think –'

'Don't,' Stevie entreated tightly, aware that whilst Rosa had skipped out through the open window she was still within earshot. No point filling her innocent mind with the horrors of Mae and Stevie's childhood, no need to resurrect it in her own. And as for Nanna's pangs of guilt for having let them down, as Stevie unfailingly reminded her, living in Liverpool, she hadn't been on hand to witness things herself.

Precious little to witness, in fact. No outward signs, no physical abuse. Just an over-strict regime centred on school and church, being seen but not heard when at home, and eating the food the good Lord had provided. Plain food. Unappetizing food. Food that had stuck in Stevie's throat and caused a white-faced Mae to heave. Food that couldn't be wasted and which would be served up for breakfast, lunch and tea for days on end, until it was finally consumed.

Easier to eat at the very first sitting, Stevie had learned early, closing her mind and swallowing without tasting. But Mae, delicate, fastidious Mae, had grown thinner and thinner and thinner, and even as an adult had loathed the sight and smell of food.

'My fault –'

'No, Nan,' Stevie interrupted. 'You didn't know. How could you? And if you had, you'd only have worried yourself sick. Much better you didn't know. Besides, it's water under the bridge now.'

'Aye.' A heavy sigh. 'Poor Mae. Still, we have got Rosa.'

Rosa, skipping happily around the flowerbeds in the bright June sunshine. Mae's child. Dark-haired, dark-eyed, dark-skinned. Mae's child – and Dino's. The unknown Italian whose handsome face had smiled out from the handful of photos Stevie had found in Mae's box of treasures. Young, handsome, rich – and married. And he'd turned his back, had left Mae and the baby to rot. May he rot in hell, Stevie decided sourly, and, banishing the shadows with a huge effort of will, wheeled Nanna's chair out into the sunshine.

'You didn't ask Mummy about her party,' Rosa reminded her thoughtfully, dropping to sit cross-legged on the grass.

'Maybe that's because I didn't know about her party,' Nanna observed tartly, sharp eyes switching to Stevie.

'Can I help it if my social life's so hectic a party or two can slip by without notice?' Stevie chided, colouring despite herself.

'Knowing you? Chance would be a fine thing,' Nanna retorted. 'Well?'

Stevie shrugged. 'Nothing to report. Housewarming. The new neighbour.' The new boss too, but she'd keep that piece of news for later.

'Ah!'

'Ah, what?' Stevie challenged, blushing again.

'Not married, I seem to recall.'

'There's nothing wrong with your memory, Nan.'

'And precious little wrong with my eyesight, my girl. You're smitten.'

'Chance would be a fine thing,' Stevie jeered, with a warning glance in Rosa's direction. 'If you must know, he's a friend of Lorna and Tom's, and we disliked one another on sight.'

'Love and hate,' Nanna murmured smugly.

'Exactly. Poles apart.'

'That's what I thought the day I met your grandad. And first impressions can be wrong; you mark my words.'

Stevie swallowed a smile. 'Yes, Nan.'

'So?'

'So?' Stevie stalled, green eyes wide and innocent.

'So how did you get on?' Nanna probed, her expression suddenly thoughtful. 'He must be worth a bob or two if he's living at Parklands?'

'Not necessarily. I live at Parklands and I'm as poor as the proverbial church mouse.' Not strictly true, and, given the salary Jared would soon be paying, now even more inaccurate.

'Fiddlesticks. And you needn't bother trying to change the subject, because I know.'

'Yes, Nan. You probably do at that,' Stevie conceded good-naturedly. 'Which means you won't need to hassle me for details.'

'Stevie Cooper, for two pins I'd wring your pretty little neck.'

Stevie laughed outright. 'Only you won't. Because you love me. And you've never given up hope of seeing me walk down the aisle on the arm of a man. Wishful thinking, Nan,' she reminded her softly, leaning across to hug her. 'And where this man's concerned you're so wide of the mark you're not even hitting the target. But, if it's any consolation, you're right about one thing. The guy's well-heeled, all right. Rich, handsome and every girl's dream – every girl but me,' she tagged on defiantly.

'So sure, Stevie?'

'About Jared? Does the sun rise? Do the birds sing in the sky? Does night follow day?' she scorned, fingers crossed she was giving her the truth.

'Jared, hmm? Footloose, fancy-free, and practically living on your doorstep.'

'Well, one out of three isn't bad,' Stevie conceded wryly. 'He lives across the hall, he's in the same line of business as Tom, and I for one wouldn't trust him as far as I could throw him. Oh, yes. I almost forgot,' she added, features impassive. 'He's offered me a job.'

'And, let me guess, you've turned him down?'

'Have I?' Stevie challenged softly. 'Well, if you say so.'

The job. Not so much a routine, nine-to-five existence as Jared taking her at her word. Overtime at the drop of a hat, early starts sprung out of the blue and hours and hours spent closeted with Jared, planning, talking, discussing, disagreeing, bouncing ideas before finally agreeing to disagree when Stevie stubbornly stuck to her guns on the thorny subject of packaging. Because Italian Impressions was her baby, and, change of company notwithstanding, the layout she'd envisaged was the layout she'd endorse.

'Fine.'

Jared, tight-lipped and weary, leaning back in his chair. And, since it was nudging ten p.m., he wasn't the only one feeling the strain.

Working with Jared, being with Jared, battling with Jared, Stevie's nerves were in a permanent churn, and the string of sleepless nights didn't help.

'Okay, Stevie,' he barked, tossing his pen onto the desk – like a boxer throwing in the towel, Stevie decided absurdly, smothering an equally absurd surge of pride. 'You win. But only because we're running out of time,' he amended tersely. 'Which means the original mock-ups can be adapted for the food fayre. Congratulations, Stevie. It's not often I'm persuaded to change my mind.'

'Persuasion?' she challenged slyly. 'Or expediency?'

'A rose by any other name . . .' he snapped, face muscles tightening. 'And, since Friday is Press day at the fayre, we'll just about make it.'

'You mean the Earl's Court convention?' Stevie queried, shockingly aware of Jared little more than a knee's width away. 'In London?'

'London, as in the capital of England,' he agreed sarcastically. 'And where better to launch ALITANI's new product?'

Where indeed? Stevie echoed, only silently, her heart sinking as she second guessed what was coming next.

'And, since it's a fair drive down, I assume an overnight stay won't be a problem?'

'Not at all,' she lied, forcing a smile. 'If you feel it's really necessary?'

'The trip?' he queried politely. 'Or the stay?'

Stevie shrugged. 'Not so much the stay as the time it wastes,' she pointed out sweetly. 'Why drive when you can fly?'

'Why indeed?' he echoed, eyes narrowing thoughtfully. He nodded. 'You're right – again. And, though it goes against the grain to admit it, I'd say you're beginning to deserve every penny of that exorbitant salary you bullied your way into.'

'So the labourer is worthy of her hire?' Stevie scorned. 'Don't sound so surprised.'

'Less surprise than vindication,' he corrected.

'I expect the best; you're giving the best. And if by some fluke you hadn't . . .'

Back to Deighton's, Stevie supplied silently, beginning to realize that working for Tom could never be the same. If Tom agreed to have her back in the first place. And as for the corresponding drop in salary . . . She could wave goodbye to that house for a start.

Nothing definite at this stage, more a picture in her mind. A house. Hers and Rosa's. With a garden and space – space to run, space to play, space to hide. No place to hide now, with Andrew expected any day and Jared's front door just a hop, skip and a jump across the hallway – literally, given Rosa's preferred means of travel. So, nothing to do but grin and bear it, work the hours, justify the wages, and bury the pain of wanting Jared deep in her heart.

'Stevie?'

She started, blinked, froze. Completely lost in thought, she hadn't noticed that Jared had moved, was now perched on the desk in front of her, arms folded across his chest, a quizzical smile playing about the corners of his mouth.

'Good heavens, is that the time?' she queried, pointedly checking her watch and swivelling the chair away from his devastating nearness before coming to her feet. Halfway across the room, something struck her. She halted, half turned. 'I take it we have finished for the day?'

'Maybe,' he replied enigmatically. 'And maybe not.'

'Meaning?' she queried, logging the expression in his eyes and going hot, then cold, then hot again.

Jared smiled, one of those lazy smiles that tugged at her heartstrings, and, rooted to the spot, Stevie could only watch as he slid from the desk, closing the gap between them in three easy strides.

'I know it's late,' he conceded softly, 'and I know you'll want to get home to Rosa. But another half-hour won't hurt, surely?'

Stevie swallowed hard. Unfair. She'd been working since eight and would be back in the office in ten hours' time, and yet Jared was suggesting they work on? Hoist with her own petard, she realized. Twenty-four hours a day, three hundred and sixty-five days a year left precious little room for manoeuvre, and since she was damned if she'd ask for favours . . .

Stifling a sigh, she retraced her steps, regained her place, crossed her legs primly at the ankle and angled her head in polite enquiry.

To her surprise she saw the gamut of expressions chase across his face: faint amusement, disbelief, anger – though heaven alone knew why – before that vaguely amused, vaguely mocking smile settled again.

'Not work, Stevie,' Jared insisted, moving back within distance. Touching distance. Touch. Reach out, trace the angle of his jaw, feel the faint rasp of stubble beneath her fingers . . . Lest the thought should lead to the deed, she clamped her hands to her sides and smothered the waves of panic.

'For God's sake, woman,' he castigated tersely. 'What do you take me for? Slave-driver? Tyrant? A modern-day Mr Gradgrind?'

'It – had crossed my mind,' she admitted, a fleeting smile lighting up her features.

'Well, thank you, Stevie Cooper, for that honest response. You'll be telling me next you're voting me in as Employer of the Year.'

'Hardly,' she demurred, dropping her gaze, tracing the pattern of the carpet beneath her feet – a bold black and white design, vaguely reminiscent of the carpet that graced Parklands' hallway.

'Precisely. I'm working you too hard and you're too full of pride to complain. Only you should. You should shout it from the rooftops. "No, no and no" is how you normally phrase it.'

'Fine.' She nodded, risked a glance through the veil of her lashes, caught another expression she couldn't quite place and slammed the lid on the panic. Stay calm. She mustn't overreact. He was her boss, nothing more, nothing less, and if Jared overstepped the mark she'd simply take him at his word, shout no, no and no loud and clear.

'No, Jared!'

A hand sliding beneath her chin, forcing her head up. The very touch was a brand and Stevie was looking anywhere but at Jared.

'Yes, Stevie. A drink. Now. At The Mount Pleasant, since it's on the way home. You can leave your car here for the night, and I'll pick you up in the morning. A drink. Nothing more, nothing less. I promise.'

Easy enough to say, easy enough to agree to, but with Jared's lazy thumb stroking the soft underside of her jaw, with Jared himself just a hair's breadth away, the sight of him, the smell of him driving her insane, Stevie knew she had to be strong, had to resist, had to say no.

'Thanks, but no, thanks,' she insisted pleasantly, pressing down on her heels and propelling the chair backwards on its castors.

Jared's response was lightning, his hands closing on her shoulders before Stevie had time to breathe. Difficult to breathe with the breath driven from her body, yet as her head snapped up in alarm she caught a flare of emotion in Jared's velvet eyes and her heart soared. Want. Need. Desire, she told herself, willing herself to be strong, to resist, to deny. And, since the shutters had dropped into place over Jared's eyes, probably sheer wishful thinking on her part.

'I could always make that an order,' he said softly, another strange smile playing about the corners of his mouth.

'You're the boss,' she pointed out calmly, a lot more calmly than she felt.

'So humour me, play it safe, let your hair down for once.'

'Or else?' she challenged oh, so softly.

Another flash of anger, just as quickly controlled. 'Let's just say I might be forced to turn up on your doorstep with a bottle of consolation. Champagne, Stevie. Well-chilled – remember?'

Oh, yes, she remembered. She remembered each and every touch, every kiss, every nuance of expression. And that included the contempt he hadn't been able to hide. And in that case –

'Like I said,' she retorted coolly. 'The lady says no, the lady means no. I trust the gentleman understands?'

'Perfectly,' he conceded tightly, releasing her at once.

Stevie flashed him a bright, brittle smile, came to her feet, crossed to the desk for her briefcase. Bone-weary or not, she had work to do – the finishing touches to the Italian Impressions range. Another half-hour should see it finished, but she'd take it home, take a shower, take a peek at the sleeping Rosa and, having thanked Anna for her efforts, she'd settle down with a well-earned glass of wine, *red* wine, she decided defiantly, and finish her sketches.

'Oh, no!' Jared. Another lightning move as he blocked the doorway, his gaze dropping from her startled face to the briefcase clutched in rigid fingers. 'Go home, Stevie,' he insisted tightly. 'If that's what you've decided. But the bag stays here. It's late and you've already done enough.'

'I –'

'Go. Now,' he insisted, prising the case from her grip. 'Go home, go to bed and take tomorrow morning off. And that, Miss Cooper, is an order.'

'No –'

'Don't argue. No favours asked, no favours given,' he insisted, uncannily reading her mind. 'Just part of the staff welfare plan – introduced a mite belatedly, perhaps, but up and running as of this moment.'

Shades of Nicky Sanders, she silently acknowledged, and, since she hadn't summoned up the nerve to raise the subject before, she took the bit between her teeth and asked now.

'Simple, Stevie,' Jared retorted with a flash of humour that even managed to reach his eyes, helped ease away the strain of the past ten minutes. 'I simply grabbed him by the seat of the pants and ran him out of town.'

'Not literally, Jared?' Stevie queried, smiling despite herself.

'Literally, my dear. Out of Parklands, at least. And as for the rest, once the news begins to spread in the trade, he'll get no more than he deserves.'

Stevie shivered. Power. The power to destroy. And hand in hand with money, a devastating combination. A devastating man, she was beginning to see.

She made to move past. Had to force herself not to shrink away from the man who was all but blocking the doorway. She brushed against his powerful body, gasped as Jared gasped, as his arms came round her, and she was kissing him, wanting him, fighting him, the threads of common sense snapping one by one. Need. Want. Lust. Not love, she told herself, not on Jared's part at least.

So good, so right – so wrong! the voice of her conscience pointed out. 'Please, Jared,' she insisted, twisting her mouth away, but Jared simply laughed, cupped her face in his hands and kissed her, and held her, and murmured words she couldn't quite catch, and nuzzled her temples with his lips, and kissed her again.

And Stevie was weakening. Because she wanted him. Kiss, touch, taste and kiss again. Shameless. A tramp, in Jared's eyes, so maybe a tramp in nature as well as name, because heaven help her she wanted him, and, pressed against the powerful lines of his body, the proof that Jared wanted her every bit as badly was the most wonderful sensation in the world.

'Stevie? Aw, hell, Stevie,' he murmured in anguish, pulling her hard against him. 'I want you. I want you, but not here. Let's go home, hey, my love?'

Home, with his love, to make love. Love. The most overworked word in the world when it came to a man getting what he wanted. Want. Nothing more, nothing less.

Something vital in Stevie's mind died, and, sensing some of her reaction, Jared loosened his hold.

'I –' A door slammed nearby and she broke off,

her startled gaze darting to Jared's face, logging the strain – the shock of rejection, more like, she told herself – smothering a hysterical sob and attempting to pull herself together.

And with footsteps growing nearer, the tap of stiletto heels echoing eerily round the stairwell, louder and louder the length of the corridor, Stevie obeyed a compelling stab of instinct and retreated into the room.

'Dee! Good heavens,' Jared railed as Dee stepped into the frame, taking Stevie's place the doorway. 'What on earth are you doing here at this time of night?'

'If Mohammed won't come to the mountain,' Dee teased, flashing Stevie an open smile as she slid into his arms, raised a face for the kiss that Jared could hardly have avoided if he'd wanted to – not that he'd want to, Stevie acknowledged silently, sourly, shockingly aware that a peck on the cheek it wasn't. 'Why, then the mountain must come to Mohammed, my love. Home, Jared,' Dee insisted smokily, the message in her eyes unmistakable. 'Now. My place. Supper's ready and waiting, and later –'

'Later,' he interrupted thickly, darting a loaded glance at Stevie as he dipped his face, nuzzled Dee's temples, pulled her close. 'Later we'll do just whatever the fancy takes us – all night long.'

CHAPTER 13

All night long. Tossing and turning, imagining, thinking, wanting, hating. Because she loved him. Because if the common sense side of her was glad she'd called a halt, the other side, the vulnerable side, the erotic side, was screaming out for Jared. Fool, fool, fool, she silently berated herself. For loving him, for turning him down. And it was only a matter of time, she was beginning to realize. Might as well get it over and done with. A quick tumble between the sheets, and with the thrill of the chase over and his masculine pride restored Jared would be happy to see the back of her. Not so Stevie, who wanted this man with a pain too exquisite to describe.

'You'll know, one day,' Mae had insisted. 'You'll know, you'll understand and you'll forgive.'

'Nothing to forgive,' Stevie had insisted, terribly afraid that her sister was dying before her eyes. Pining away for love. A ridiculous notion in this day and age, but the thought had stubbornly refused to go away. Pneumonia. The official verdict, at least. But Stevie knew better – now. Stevie and Mae. And, as she finally made sense of the demons that had driven her sister, she knew they had far more in common than Stevie had ever realized.

'Italian men. The most wonderful lovers in the world,' Mae had dreamily informed her.

Men. As in plural. How many men? Stevie now wondered, wondering, too, if taking sips from the honey pot of love was addictive, if once she'd surrendered her body to a man she'd crave a man's touch for evermore. Irrelevant, since the craving for Jared refused to go away.

Jared, Jared and more Jared. Wanting, needing, aching for him. Working with Jared, travelling with Jared. Knees shockingly close in the confines of the aeroplane, the thirty-minute flight a nightmare – but less of a nightmare than a drive would have been, not to mention an overnight stop.

A successful day. Another nightmare in its way, but over at last. And a surprisingly thoughtful Jared drove them home from the airport, stood by her side in silence in the confines of the lift, walked Stevie to her door, waved her across the threshold and solemnly thanked her.

And then he walked away, back to the lifts – back to Dee, Stevie realized instinctively, crying inside as she closed the door and slumped against it. Home. Alone. For, with Rosa staying over at Kelly's, just the weary chimes of the clock rang out to greet her.

'You're working too hard.'

'Am I?' Sensing the concern in Lorna's cloudy blue eyes, Stevie forced a smile.

'Either that or there's something on your mind. Am I right or am I right?'

'Oh, heaven forbid you could ever be wrong,' Stevie acknowledged dryly. 'So where shall I begin?'

'What's wrong with the beginning? "Once upon a time" is how it normally goes.'

'Ah, yes, but this is life, Lorna, not a fairy story,' Stevie reminded her as the knife-blade twisted.

'So?' Lorna probed, a quizzical smile playing about the corners of her mouth.

'So – nothing, I suppose,' Stevie allowed doubtfully. 'Just everything and nothing. House-hunting, the new job, worries about Rosa and Nanna. All the usuals, really,' she acknowledged. 'Like I said, nothing in particular. Just –'

'Just?' Lorna echoed softly.

Stevie shrugged. 'I don't know,' she conceded warily. 'Nothing I can put my finger on. Just a big black cloud hanging over me. Because things are going well for once and I'm terrified it can't last. Crazy, huh?'

'Not crazy, understandable. You've come through a lot and you've had to fight every inch of the way. And now that everything's going right –' Lorna broke off, paused, reached for a truffle from the half-eaten box on the table and shot Stevie an unusually perceptive glance. 'I suppose *everything* does include Jared?' she probed, nibbling at the chocolate.

'Meaning?' Stevie stalled.

'You know, the new boss. The new neighbour. The new hunk in your life.'

'Not my life, Lorna – Dee's, remember?' Stevie pointed out with a sudden surge of colour.

'Yes. And a certain young lady not a million miles across this table made a point of throwing them together. I told you at the time you'd regret it.'

'Oh, no, you didn't,' Stevie protested huffily.

'And I don't. Well, only because Dee's unbelievably smitten and she's bound to get hurt,' she allowed doubtfully.

'So what's new?'

Stevie laughed despite herself. 'Unfair, Lorna Deighton, if not uncannily right. But Dee can take care of herself. She'll bounce back.' She'd have to. If Jared grew tired. When Jared grew tired.

'So?' Lorna persisted, absent-mindedly nudging the box towards Stevie.

'So . . .' Stevie shrugged, logged the concern in her friend's cloudy eyes and racked her brains for the means to set her mind at rest. 'I guess you were right in the first place,' she stalled. 'I'm working too hard. Fact, not whinge,' she insisted briskly, helping herself to a chocolate. 'I'm not complaining. Long hours go with the job – as someone not a million miles away is about to discover for herself.'

'Ah yes, but I'm married to the boss,' Lorna reminded her. 'With all the perks that that entails. Not to mention strict instructions to stick to part-time while Kelly's small. And, talking of Kelly, I never had the chance to thank you. Anna's a treasure, and knowing Kelly's with Rosa is a weight off my mind, especially with the long school holidays looming.'

Stevie smiled. 'Good.' She was glad. Glad Lorna had something to occupy her mind. For with Mrs Hunter on the mend there was little enough to keep Lorna busy, and nibbling her way through a mountain of chocolate or trawling the shops for outfits she didn't need and would probably never wear was a waste.

'Just one of life's little ironies,' Lorna allowed, when Stevie gave voice to her thoughts. 'I thought Mum would hit the roof when I told her I was working but she didn't even bat an eyelid. She's tougher than she looks and that's for sure.'

'She'd need to be,' Stevie observed. 'A heart attack's a pretty grim experience for anyone.'

'Yes. And though she has to take it easy, she's

determined to make the best of things and wants everyone else to do the same. Luckily for me, that means working for Deighton's. It couldn't have worked out better.'

Yes. Working for Deighton's. The ideal solution. Only not for Stevie. Not any more. But then, neither was working for Jared.

'Work, work, work. I've barely seen Jared in days. If I didn't know you better, Stevie Cooper –'

'Only you do. And you were right first time,' Stevie reassured her softly. 'It's work, Dee. Nothing more, nothing less. Cross my heart and hope to die.'

'I know. It's just . . .'

'Just?'

'Oh, nothing,' Dee insisted, forcing a smile. 'Just me, hellbent on rushing things as usual. But I had hoped . . .'

'Oh?' Stevie probed with a shiver of premonition.

An eloquent shrug, another scowl, another attempt to banish the shadows. 'You know me. Ever the optimist. With my divorce from Anton all signed, sealed and legal in six weeks' time, I guess I'm jumping the gun.'

'Not to mention out of the frying pan into the fire. Delia Fields, will you never learn?'

'Oh, but I'm learning all the time,' she insisted saucily. 'Experience *is* the best teacher.'

'And practice makes perfect – hey?' Stevie couldn't resist needling.

'Maybe, maybe not,' Dee conceded, eyes dancing. 'But it sure is fun trying, and especially with a man like Jared.'

'I wouldn't know,' Stevie reminded her tartly. 'And before you offer to fill me in, that's the way it's staying.'

'Spare your blushes along with the finer details? Don't worry, Stevie, my lips are sealed.'

She rummaged through the debris of her bag while Stevie scanned the menu. Not Café Matisse today, because there simply wasn't time. Work, work and more work. But if Jared drove Stevie hard, he drove himself even harder. Understandable, Stevie supposed, with the launch of a new range testing the mettle of a fledgling operation. But, fingers crossed, things were going well, and hopefully in a month or two things would settle down.

They'd certainly be different, Stevie acknowledged, cradling her glass and sipping the mineral water slowly. Andrew would be home, maybe even for good this time, and Stevie and Rosa would have a house of their own. And as for Dee –

Dee showed a flash of defiance as she broke the seal an all too familiar packet.

'Oh, Dee,' Stevie chided softly. 'I thought you'd given up.'

Dee shrugged, placed the cigarette between her lips and glanced round for a light. Sure enough, Stevie noted, vaguely amused, the man seated alone at a table nearby was up on his feet in a flash.

'Allow me.'

Inhaling deeply, Dee smiled brightly up into his face before filtering the smoke through her nostrils. 'Thanks.'

'My pleasure.' A dismissive glance at Stevie as he dropped the lighter into a pocket, drew a card from a bulging wallet. Scribbling a number on the back, he leaned towards Dee, lowered his voice. 'I'm new in town. And from what I've seen of it so far, I'm inclined to stick around. Why not give me a call? Show me the high spots and, who knows? A lovely lady could have the time of her life.'

Dee preened, took the card, idly checked the details before tucking it with slow deliberation into her cleavage. 'You never know,' she allowed with an obscene flutter of lashes. 'I might do exactly that.'

'Dee!' Stevie glanced across, caught the man's amused expression and immediately dropped her voice. 'What about Jared?'

'What the head doesn't know the heart can't pine for,' Dee retorted placidly. 'And who's to know what Jared's getting up to the moment I turn my back? He's a man,' she scathingly reminded her. 'And you can take it from me, there's not a full-blooded male alive who can resist temptation when it's offered.'

'You don't believe that any more than I do,' Stevie insisted, smothering pangs of guilt.

'Oh, but I do,' she contradicted harshly. 'Because practice not only makes perfect, it's also the key to the mire of the average guy's mind. I wouldn't trust Jared, or any man for that matter, as far as I could throw him.'

'It's your life, your decision,' Stevie pointed out softly. 'But I wouldn't want to be in your shoes when Jared gets wind you've been cheating him.'

'He won't. I won't. I'm a one-man woman, not a tart,' she reminded her huffily. 'But it doesn't hurt to dream once in a while, hey, Stevie?' she tagged on wistfully.

Food for thought. Because despite the brave words, the air of defiance, Dee wasn't happy. Jared. That man, Stevie decided sourly, sure had a lot to answer for.

'Good morning, Stevie. You're up and about bright and early.'

'Duty calls,' she retorted, colouring, scowling, and praying Jared would reach the lifts and disappear before Rosa appeared. Irrational, she knew, but keeping work and home-life separate helped to keep her sane.

The doors slid silently open and Jared smiled, stepped into the tiny compartment, raised a lazy hand.

Stevie ignored him, waiting for the soft whirr of the lift drive before diving back inside.

243

'Rosa! What on earth are you doing now? Come on, love. Anna will wondering where we've got to.'

'Coming, Mummy.' A ghostly echo from the depths of the bathroom.

An impatient Stevie resisted the urge to open the door, chivvy her along, aware that the need to be at her desk before eight was all tied up with the need to prove herself in Jared's eyes. And, since she clearly wouldn't make it by eight this morning, why break her neck by even trying?

The door swung open and Rosa sidled out. 'Ready now,' she insisted brightly, half defiantly, the over-generous application of Stevie's favourite lipstick reminiscent of Coco the Clown.

Stevie swallowed a smile, shook her head, folded her arms. 'You know the rules. Miss Atherton won't like it. Not even the big girls are allowed to wear make-up,' she reminded her, but as Rosa's features began to crumple Stevie relented. Crouching down, she pulled her into her arms. 'I know,' she insisted, hugging her, stroking her hair, the beautiful long black tresses that Anna would later tease into a ponytail. 'There's plenty of time. How about we leave it for Anna and Kelly to admire and you can wipe it clean before you set off for school? And if you take the lipstick with you —'

'Yippee! I can practise at Anna's. Oh, Mummy, you're the bestest mummy in the whole wide world,' she insisted, throwing her arms around

Stevie's neck and half strangling her in the process.

Stevie gently disengaged her. 'But you're not to take it to school – not even to show the others. Deal?'

'You bet! Come on, Mummy,' Rosa insisted, grabbing her wrist and tugging Stevie to the door. 'I can't wait to show Kelly and – oh!' She pulled up sharp as a shadow crossed her path.

'Oh, indeed,' Jared echoed with a barely perceptible twitch of lips. His curious gaze passed from Stevie to Rosa and back again, Stevie's silent plea managing to make itself felt.

Dropping to his knees, he brought his head on a level with Rosa's. 'Miss Rosa Cooper, I presume?' he solemnly acknowledged, holding out a hand. 'How do you do? I'm Jared Wilde. I expect you might have heard of me?'

Rosa nodded. 'Um. Mummy's new boss,' she allowed, and, with a doubtful glance in Stevie's direction, equally solemnly placed her hand in his.

'Don't tell me it's time for school already?' Jared enquired, pointedly checking his watch.

'Not exact –'

'Don't be silly,' Rosa cut across Stevie with a scornful toss of the head. 'Mummy's taking me to Anna's. School isn't for ages and ages yet. We start at nine and finish at half past three,' she explained, as if talking to a five-year-old. 'And sometimes Mummy picks me up instead of Anna

245

and takes me to McDonald's for – Oh! I forgot!'
She broke off in a fluster, eyes fleetingly cloudy.
'Mummy works for you now. But does she have to
work late *every* single Friday?' she ended plain-
tively.

'I guess not,' Jared conceded, a tightening of
the muscles at the corners of his mouth betraying
his annoyance. 'So, what time would madam
suggest?'

'Oh, no! Madam wouldn't dream of imposing,'
Stevie insisted. Grabbing Rosa by the wrist and
slamming shut her door, she made to push past.

'Maybe not,' Jared allowed, back on his feet in
an instant, his powerful body filling the hallway.
'But it's a reasonable suggestion and I'm a reasonable man. In fact, now that I come to think of
it, we'll all finish at three on Fridays. Is it a deal?'

'No, Jared, it is not a deal. You run a business,
not a crèche,' Stevie exclaimed. 'The idea's
absurd.'

'A crèche? Hmm. Now there's a thought.
Thank you, Stevie. We'll have it up and running
in time for the school holidays. And thank you,
Rosa,' he pointedly added. 'You're a very clever
young lady. I guess your mummy's proud of you.'

'Amongst other things,' Stevie acknowledged,
gritting her teeth as she tugged her daughter
down the hall.

Reaching the lift, she jammed her finger on the
button and prayed for the door to open. The
indicator button flickered into life. Ground

floor. It would be ages and ages yet, she calculated swiftly, half toying with the idea of taking the stairs. Ten flights of stairs with Rosa in tow? She'd wait.

Sensing Jared hadn't moved, she turned her head. 'I know it's Friday,' she all but hissed. 'But we can hardly finish at three if we don't turn up for work in the first place.'

'So I forgot my briefcase,' he explained mildly. 'It's hardly the crime of the year. If I'm late, then I'm late. Call it one of the perks of being in charge.' A fleeting smile crossed his features. 'Bye, Rosa. See you again sometime.' He nodded at Stevie. 'See *you* at the office.'

He did.

'The decision's made. And before you claim I've taken leave of my senses, it might even lead to a rise in productivity.'

'And how do you work that out?' Stevie scorned, tossing her pencil onto the desk – her desk, brand-new and groaning beneath the weight of the latest batch of sketches and photographs, not to mention the state of the art computer on the short arm of the L. And, left with nothing to do with her hands, she lightly clenched her fingers, resisted the urge to fold her arms, adopt a defensive position.

'Research,' he clipped out, taking the chair opposite. 'American research maybe, but the psychology's just as valid. End of weekitis. The Friday malaise. And, with the weekend looming,

247

the temptation to call in sick, take the whole day off. So what we do instead –'

'Is down tools at three and lose hours and hours while the place shuts down completely?' she put in saccharine sweetly.

'Toss in a productivity bonus to counter lost time and bingo! We've cracked it – all thanks to Rosa.'

'Now you're being ridiculous. She's a child, for heaven's sake –'

'Precisely. Your child. And worth a bit of your time, wouldn't you say?'

Stevie went cold. 'Meaning?'

Jared shrugged. 'Meaning exactly that. She's a child. She needs her mother. And who does she see instead?'

'Lorna, Kelly, Anna,' she bit out. 'She's looked after and she's loved – not that it's any of your business,' she pointedly reminded him.

'Oh, but it is. All part of the ALITANI staff welfare programme. If something's affecting your performance I've a right to be concerned.'

'Concerned, maybe,' she scoffed. 'But my private life's private and the arrangements for Rosa have been in place for years. And Rosa does not, repeat not, affect my performance.'

'Ah, yes, but then that begs the question, do you affect hers?'

'I beg your pardon?'

'Rosa. Her performance. With no father in the

frame from what I can see, Rosa's need of her mother is all the more pressing.'

'I don't believe I'm hearing this.'

'I bet you don't. Because it's easier to bury your head in the sand than face the truth.'

'What truth? That I work for a living like the rest of the nation? Strange, I was under the impression it was all above board and legal these days – in this part of the world at least. I'm a mother, not a leper,' she reminded him. 'I don't have to stay home baking cookies or darning socks. Or doesn't sir approve?'

'Of course I approve, within reason –'

'Oh, I see,' she interrupted silkily. 'Well, that makes everything all right, then. "Within reason." And what does *that* mean precisely? Let the little woman go out to work so long the man of the house isn't threatened? A spot of part-time, perhaps? Nothing too strenuous or mentally taxing. Just an hour or two to keep her busy. Not so much for the money as the need to while away an idle hour. My, we have come a long way since the Dark Ages.'

'You don't believe that any more than I do,' he pointed out mildly. 'And you're missing the point. No – correction you're side-stepping neatly. Time – and money – and the need for a balance. So, tell me,' he invited, spreading his hands, 'just out of idle curiosity, of course. On an average weekday, how many hours does Rosa get to spend with her mother?'

'Irrelevant. It's quality that counts, not quantity. Fact, Jared. Research,' she sneered. 'The latest British research, in fact. And Rosa's living proof of it. She's a happy, well-adjusted six-year-old.'

'Precisely. A little girl. She needs her mother –'

'She needs,' Stevie hissed, 'All the love and care that I already give her. Not to mention food on her plate and a roof over her head. But maybe I've got it wrong,' she scorned, eyes shooting flames. 'Maybe she'd do better in a squalid little bedsit –'

'Go from the sublime to the ridiculous? Now you're being absurd. But, since a mortgage on Parklands doesn't come cheap . . .' He paused, shrugged, an eloquent lift of the shoulders. 'Find someplace else to live and you'd save a small fortune. And with fewer commitments you could think about part-time –'

'Not interested, Jared,' Stevie cut in. 'Rosa's happy, I'm happy. The job, the hours, the overtime, the salary. Niggles from the boss I can happily live without,' she couldn't resist adding, 'but the rest of the package suits me – and Rosa – down to the ground.'

'Fine. Time to put your money where your mouth is. Rome. The flight's provisionally booked for Sunday. I assume a couple of days away won't strain those arrangements for Rosa?'

'Next Sunday?' Stevie stalled, suddenly cold, icy cold. Rome, of all places. And Rosa's birthday.

Jared leaned back, folded his arms, nodded. 'Next Sunday.'

Stevie clenched her fists, the skin across her knuckles taut and white as she struggled for control. She raised her head, meeting his gaze full on, the thrust of her chin unwittingly aggressive. 'You bastard,' she castigated softly, deliberately, beginning to suspect that the package that suited her down to the ground was about to go flying out of the window, and that for once in her life she really didn't care.

Because Jared had baited the trap, and gullible Stevie Cooper had jumped in with both feet. 'You bastard,' she repeated, with a curious lack of emotion. 'You have the nerve to sit there and lecture me about my childcare arrangements, practically hang, draw and quarter me for wilful neglect, and then coolly suggest I take off for Rome at the drop of a hat? You really are an out and out bastard.'

'And you're the one with a point to prove,' he countered coolly, his mouth a thin and angry line. 'I'm simply giving you the chance. Oh, yes, and just to show that I'm not entirely the villain you're painting me, it's worth a week off in lieu. Add it to the two weeks' leave that's owing,' he informed her tersely, 'and that's half the school holidays neatly catered for. You and Rosa. Together. Quality time – remember?'

'Maybe so,' she acknowledged tightly. 'But aren't you overlooking one tiny but significant detail? Holiday entitlement. Like most of the staff, in fact, I haven't been here long enough to have earned it.'

'No problem. It was part and parcel of the Deighton's deal. Didn't Tom mention it?'

'Since Tom probably didn't know,' she ground out. 'I guess my answer's no.'

'And your other answer, Stevie?' he queried politely, angling his head.

'How does go to hell sound?' she enquired, saccharine sweetly.

'Suspiciously like pique to me. Like cutting off your nose to spite your face. But you're the career woman, *you* decide. A three-day trip to Italy set against three whole weeks in August. Your decision. Career woman or mother. Stevie – the choice is yours. All you have to do is decide.'

CHAPTER 14

No contest, for any other weekend in the year, that was. Damned if she did, damned if she didn't, Stevie acknowledged, swallowing the bile. Because whatever she decided it would be Rosa who would suffer.

Insides churning, she glanced across at Jared, handsome, arrogant Jared, who'd backed her into a corner and who was sprawled in the chair without a care in the world while Stevie went to hell and back.

Career woman or mother, he'd goaded, when for years she'd done what countless thousands of others had done and combined the role. Guilt. She was riddled with the stuff. But she'd coped. She'd picked herself up, dusted herself down and got on with the task of providing a home for Rosa.

Rosa. Product of Mae's love for a man like Jared; rich, handsome, powerful – and thoroughly unscrupulous. Because the Jared Wildes of this world had no concern for the misery they caused, the broken hearts they scattered along the way. Life. A laugh a minute for a man like Jared. And to think he'd had the nerve to question her commitment to Rosa.

Out-manoeuvred, out-thought, out-*talked*. Stevie squeezed back the tears, damned if she'd cry, betray the least sign of weakness, give this man the chance to despise her even more. She'd do it. It wasn't ideal but it couldn't be helped. She'd mention it to Lorna, knew with an instinct born of friendship that she wouldn't even need to ask, that the party at McDonald's would go ahead as planned. And, come hell or high water, Stevie vowed, she'd make it up to Rosa later.

And so she nodded, and the flicker of light in Jared's eyes was surely sheer imagination.

'Good.' Brusque. A nod of approval. Conversation over, decision made, subject closed. It was back to the serious business of earning pots and pots of money for the ALITANI organization as Jared swung himself upright, pointedly checked the time. 'Any questions?' he tagged on belatedly.

'Only one,' she murmured, the thought just occurring. 'Why Sunday? In a Catholic country like Italy, surely Sunday's a day of rest? If the trip's business –'

'Business and pleasure both,' he mockingly informed her. 'Since I'm practically passing the door, naturally enough, Stevie, I'd planned to drop in on my family.'

Fine. She nodded, smiled a bitter smile. The irony was clearly lost on Jared, who could drag her away from Rosa without so much as a qualm yet timed his own arrival in Italy to suit the needs of his family.

'Monday?' she queried absurdly, afraid she'd misheard, horribly afraid it was sheer wishful thinking on her part, or that Jared was indulging a hitherto unsuspected warped sense of humour. Smothering the surge of elation, she shrugged. 'You're the boss,' she reminded him, vaguely aware that it was anger that was simmering beneath the surface – anger not derision – and it was clearly linked to the sudden change of plan, but, since it was nothing to do with Stevie, she wasn't about to let it worry her.

'You run the show, you make the decisions,' she declared. 'Sunday, Monday. This year, next year, sometime, never.' Emotions in a churn, she gave a disdainful snap of the fingers, unwittingly rubbing salt into a wound. 'It's all the same to me,' she conceded flippantly. 'And twenty-four hours is neither here nor there.'

'No, I don't suppose it is,' Jared hissed. 'But it damn well should be.' And Stevie flinched, smothered a different surge of emotion and stumbled away from him, the breakfast bar behind pulling her up sharp. 'And just for the record,' he informed her coldly. 'It was never my decision in the first place. Rosa,' he bit out, towering over her, his face black as thunder. 'Sunday is Rosa's birthday and any mother

255

worthy of the name would know she'd have to be there.'

'Who told you?'

'Does it matter? Tom, Lorna, Kelly, Dee – or half the town itself,' he scoffed. 'The glaringly obvious fact is *you* didn't think to mention it.'

Stevie shrugged. 'My daughter, my problem,' she retorted. 'Not that Rosa is ever a problem to me,' she pointed out, inwardly wincing at the fury in his eyes.

'No.' A loaded pause, a sneering curl of the lips. 'Obviously.'

'And what the hell is that supposed to mean?' Stevie demanded, catching his drift.

'Latchkey kid – or as good as. An expensive latchkey maybe,' he conceded. 'But it doesn't alter the facts. When the child is in the way, the child is pushed to one side. You really are a cold and calculating –'

'Oh, no!' Stevie cut in, her own anger flaring. 'Not here,' she insisted, with a hysterical sweep of her arm. 'This is my home,' she reminded him icily. 'And there isn't a man alive who has the right to walk in univited and insult me.'

'Madam,' he snarled, snatching at her arms, fingers biting deep, almost bruising in their strength. 'Since there isn't a man alive who could manage to insult you, your prissy protestations won't wash. *Why*, Stevie?' he demanded on a different note. 'Why didn't you say? Why didn't you explain?'

256

'You know why. You. The job. The small print. That cunning little clause that covers twenty-four hours a day, three hundred and sixty-five days a year.'

'But not literally, you little fool. I was annoyed. Can't you see?' he demanded tersely, shaking her. 'You'd been playing hard to get and I was paying you back in kind. For God's sake, Stevie, what on earth do you take me for? No!' He cut her off with an imperative wave of the arm. 'Don't. I really don't want to know. Just this once,' he conceded wearily, pushing her away, 'ignorance is bliss.'

'Like I said, you're the boss,' she reminded him aware that when it came to trading insults they were quits, that Jared was toweringly angry for some reason of his own, yet in hitting out at Stevie he was punishing himself. An absurd thought, maybe, but not beyond the realms of credibility.

'The boss. Nothing more, nothing less, hey, Stevie?'

'To me? What do you expect?' she challenged coolly, unconsciously rubbing at her arms where his fingers had bitten. 'I barely know you. Five weeks, Jared. Now give it five months or five years – not that we stand a chance of lasting that long – and maybe, just maybe, we'll both know enough to judge. But in the meantime –'

'You're prepared to put the job before your family. My fault, Stevie – or yours?'

'Neither,' she conceded as the anger died. 'You weren't to know and I was too proud to ask.' Her lips twisted bitterly. 'Which neatly answers the question. My fault. Pride. One of the deadly sins, so I'm told, and the stuff that goes before a fall. Coffee?' she queried absurdly, grabbing the jar of instant and waving it under his nose.

'An olive branch?' He gave a rueful grin, rubbing his chin with the back of his hand, the dark shadow of stubble drawing her gaze. 'I'm impressed.'

'I'll take that as a yes, then?' she murmured over-brightly, nerves in shreds, the strains of the past twenty-four hours beginning to take their toll.

Breaking the news to Rosa, watching the shadows chase across her face, then watching the smile spread at the thought of sleeping over at Kelly's, the promise of a weekend of fun at Disneyland Paris ample compensation, yet nothing like enough for Stevie, who'd felt like the Wicked Witch of the West for spoiling her daughter's big day.

'Black, no sugar,' Jared reminded her. 'Though heaven knows why you're offering.'

'Manners, Jared. I'm simply being neighbourly. And you have taken a load from my shoulders.'

'Only fair,' he pointed out. 'Since I piled it on in the first place.'

'Hardly,' Stevie countered mildly. 'You're the boss. You're entitled to an honest hour's work for an honest hour's pay.'

'Which doesn't include the proverbial pound of flesh.'

Stevie smiled. 'Not even in the small print, Jared?'

'Not even then. Why, Stevie? Why didn't you say?'

Teaspoon heaped with coffee, Stevie paused, shrugged, dropped the granules into a cup before adding the scalding water. 'Who knows?' she finally conceded, pushing Jared's across the counter towards him. 'Pride. Stubbornness. Anger. The need to sort things out for myself. I'm –'

'Too independent for your own good. Understandable, I suppose, but next time, Stevie, do us both a favour and ask. No . . .' Generous lips twitched. 'Correction. Do what you're good at. Make a decision, fight your corner, and against all the odds stand your ground.'

An up and down day, like most of her days, in fact. Thanks to Jared. Strange how much turmoil a few short weeks could bring. A change of job, though less a change of job than a change of employer, and never a dull moment. Thanks to Jared. And as for the last twenty-four hours, Stevie had been to hell and back – twice, she seemed to recall. All thanks to the man sprawled on the cushions, long, jean-clad legs stretched out beneath the coffee table, perfectly at home, perfectly relaxed, while Stevie's nerves in contrast tied themselves in knots.

Devastating. Casually dressed, assuming designer jeans belonged in that particular category, there was no denying the impact he made – crisp cotton shirt, carelessly unbuttoned at the neck, the dark shadow of hair at his throat a tantalizing glimpse of the mass that covered his chest, Stevie recalled with a shiver of desire.

Give and take. An easy banter for once, and they'd finally cleared the air. Stevie would continue to give one hundred percent plus to her job, but on the strict understanding that Rosa's needs would come first. Flexibility. Not charity. No favours asked, no favours given. Just Stevie's entitlement.

'It can't be easy, coping with a child single handed?' Jared mused casually – too casually Stevie decided, wondering just how much of Rosa's history Jared had been treated to. Pillow-talk, courtesy of Dee, she wondered? The idea was vaguely alarming.

'It's – not such a big deal these days,' Stevie allowed, swirling the dregs of her coffee round the base of her cup. 'Single mothers are ten a penny.'

'Maybe so. But a child's a big commitment – time, patience, love, security, not to mention money,' he tagged on thoughtfully. 'I take it Rosa's father is happy to pay his way? Not that it's any of my business,' he added swiftly, catching Stevie's reaction. He raised his hands in mock surrender. 'Not idle curiosity, Stevie. Just concern, I promise.'

'All part of the staff welfare plan?' Stevie mocked, though not unkindly, aware that a girl could drown in those dark velvet eyes. Continental chocolate, she decided absurdly. A bit like Jared himself. Hard on the outside, rich creamy velvet at the centre. Concern? Possibly. Not nosiness; she could allow that. And, since Jared clearly didn't know, Dee equally clearly hadn't been speaking out of turn. Not that she'd really expect Dee to waste time discussing another woman when she had a hunk like Jared in her bed.

Bed. An exquisite stab of pain. The vivid image banished in a trice. She angled her head. 'No, Jared,' she murmured matter-of-factly. 'Rosa's father doesn't pay his way. Never has, never will. As far as he's concerned, Rosa doesn't exist. Fact,' she added crisply, defiantly, daring him to contradict. 'And that's the way I like it.'

'It's – your life,' he conceded softly. 'And Rosa's, of course.'

'Meaning?' Stevie challenged, colouring.

Another of those eloquent shrugs. 'Nothing. You've coped, and you've coped well. You don't need the benefit of my advice.'

'Precisely.' Stevie bared her teeth in the semblance of a smile. 'Agony Aunts – or Uncles – I can well do without.'

'Unlike friends.'

'Yes.' Close friends. Dee, Tom, Lorna. More family than friends. Unlike colleagues at Deighton's and a host of people from her schooldays. Not friends. Passing acquaintances, mostly.

'Are we friends, Stevie?' Jared murmured softly.

'Hardly,' she demurred, amazed he could consider it. 'Like I said, five weeks. I barely know you. Ask me again in another five years –'

'Not that you seriously believe we'll get that far,' he conceded dryly.

'Miracles have been known to happen,' she reminded him flippantly. And if Dee did succeed in dragging Jared to the altar –

Too cruel. Impossible to face. Time enough to face it when it happened. If it happened. If.

The grandmother clock in the corner began to chime the hour. Four o'clock. She was picking Rosa up at half past, bringing Kelly and two other friends back to stay the night – a treat for the girls and a dress rehearsal for next weekend when Rosa would go to Kelly's. No, correction. That would be a day later now, thanks to Jared.

'All part of the Jared Wilde, Big Bad Wolf newly reformed, School of Domestic Service,' he demurred when Stevie brought the subject up again. 'I – er – took the liberty of mentioning it to Rosa. I hope you don't mind?'

'Rosa?' Stevie queried absurdly.

'I had lunch at Tom and Lorna's today. The girls were full of the party,' he explained awkwardly. 'Lorna did suggest that I phone you first –'

'But, surprise, surprise, arrogant Jared Wilde took it upon himself to spill the beans. Well, fine,' she conceded tightly, hanging onto her temper with a massive surge of will. 'The decision, yes, since the decision was yours to make. But not the cosy little chat with my daughter. My daughter, Jared – remember?'

'Ah, yes. Your daughter. The daughter you were happy to abandon on her birthday. The daughter who doesn't see her mother during working hours – or any other hour of the day from what I can see. Quality time? *Any* time would doubtless be a bonus,' he sneered as the temperature plummeted to zero. And as Stevie sprang to her feet, eyes blazing, cheeks on fire, he raised a single, sneering eyebrow. 'What's the matter?' he queried nastily. 'Does the truth hurt?'

'Your truth, Jared? Not one bit,' Stevie scorned with a defiant toss of the head. 'Rosa –'

'Isn't here. Again. She's over at Tom and Lorna's.'

'With Kelly,' she bit out. 'She's a child. She needs company her own age – other children, room to play, a garden. The apartment –'

'Ah, yes, the apartment . . .' His thoughtful gaze travelled the room in a shrewd assessment of the decor, the sumptuous leather sofas, the carpet deep enough to drown in, not to mention the artwork gracing the walls – local artists, mostly, but still worth a small fortune.

White. Stark. Minimalist. And not a speck of

dust to be seen, not so much as a magazine to spoil the lines of a room that would never pass for cosy. A showcase. A place for Andrew to entertain his influential friends. Pristine.

A nightmare for Stevie, who'd practically lived in the kitchen for months, terrified of the damage sticky fingers could cause. No place for a child. Such a well-behaved child – unnaturally so? she wondered with another stab of guilt. No. No, no, no! A healthy child. Rosa. Her Rosa. Wise beyond her nearly seven years, but a normal, healthy, exuberant child who chose to let off steam in the park, or at school, or at Kelly's.

Yet as Jared finished his long and silent perusal, brought his gaze back to Stevie, something in the set of his mouth, the angle of his head froze the blood in her veins.

'Most impressive,' he acknowledged with a sneering curl of the lips. 'But . . .'

'But, what?' Stevie stalled, horribly afraid she knew what was coming.

He shrugged. 'The place is a museum. Expensive. Undoubtedly tasteful,' he allowed. 'If that's the way your preferences lie. But a home for a child?' He shook his head. 'Lady, from where I'm standing, Mother of the Year you're –'

'Get out,' she said softly, viciously, biting back the tears. 'Get out of my house and don't ever bother coming back. Are you listening, Jared Wilde? Get out and stay out.'

His lips formed a parody of a smile. 'Closing

time, huh? Sure. Thanks for the coffee,' he murmured pleasantly, coming lazily to his feet. 'And thanks for the guided tour. It was – most enlightening.' Reaching into a pocket, he pulled out a handful of change and dropped the coins carelessly down into the centre of the table.

'W-what are doing?' she queried absurdly, hugging her chest as she struggled for control.

'Doing? Why, paying my way, of course. Upkeep of the building. Since a place like this doesn't come cheap . . .' A careless shrug of powerful shoulders. 'Call it payment for services rendered,' he tagged on slyly.

'Meaning?'

'Meaning precisely that, my dear. But, being the lady you are, you'll no doubt be quick to deny it.'

'Nothing to deny,' she insisted, choking back the pain.

'No, Stevie?'

Control hanging by a thread, fingernails gouging the skin of her upper arms, Stevie held his gaze. 'No, Jared.'

'No?' Lips curling in derision, the single word echoed round the room. 'Since the truth is glaringly obvious, I don't suppose there is. So long, Stevie. See you bright and early Monday morning. After all, the earlier the better for Rosa, who can then spend her time with people who really care.'

'You're wrong, Jared,' Stevie heard herself

pleading, hating herself, needing to explain yet despising herself for the weakness.

He paused, turned – turned her heart to stone with the expression in his eyes, the blast of condemnation from each and every pore. 'Am I?' he queried. 'I doubt it. I've come across your sort before, you see,' he explained confidentially. 'But if I'm wrong – *if*,' he underlined softly, 'then the Big Bad Wolf will willingly put his head on the block and wait for the axe to fall.'

He began to walk away, footsteps muffled in the thick pile of carpet. An eternity to cross the room, to reach the door to the hall. A lifetime for Stevie to stand and watch, to hold back the torrent of tears. Tears. For this man who clearly thought the worst. For Jared despised her, despised everything about her. Only Jared was wrong.

Stevie knew. And Lorna, and Tom, and Dee. But not Jared. And it hurt. And one day maybe Jared would learn the truth and then he'd know that he'd misjudged her. And maybe, just maybe, she consoled herself, maybe by then it simply wouldn't matter any more. Not to Stevie.

Ten seconds. Five, four, three, two. Precious little time to hang onto the threads of self-control. The tears were beginning to ooze between her clamped lashes.

Fool! she berated herself silently, viciously. For caring. For hurting. For allowing Jared's contempt to matter. And then she caught a sound she couldn't quite place, a metallic sound, the rattle of a key – the click of a lock disengaging, she identified, her mind going into overdrive. And, convinced she'd stepped from nightmare to nightmare, she could only watch in open-mouthed amazement as the door swung slowly open on its hinges. Who on earth –?

'Andrew!'

'Stevie –'

'Oh, Andrew!' The surge of joy melted faster than a flake of snow in a desert, withered clean away beneath the blast of Jared's contempt. Because Jared saw, and Jared judged, his gaze slipping from Stevie to Andrew to the key that Andrew held. Exhibit one. Proof. The expression in his eyes was one of fleeting condemnation, and then the shutters came down and the gaze that locked with Stevie's was curiously blank.

'Oh, Stevie,' he castigated softly. 'Who'd have believed it?'

CHAPTER 15

'Drink, Stevie?'

'Thank you, Jared. Brandy, please.'

A raised eyebrow, a surreptitious glance at his watch; a defiant Stevie held her ground. In silence. An icy silence she'd maintained for each and every minute of the week she'd just endured. When Jared had been around, that was. Unless Jared had required a direct answer, that was. And then she'd been icily polite.

Work. A nightmare. Because Jared misunderstood and Stevie was too stuffed up with pride to explain.

Andrew . . .

'Darling, why on earth didn't you let me know?' she'd berated him, throwing herself into his arms and sobbing against his shoulder the moment the door had closed to behind Jared. And Andrew had laughed, holding her tight, soothing, rocking and wiping away the tears before pouring the first of the brandies. Brandy. Hot and fiery. Not Stevie's drink at all, but it sure helped numb the pain.

Threading his fingers through hers and drawing her down onto the cushions, Andrew had smiled. 'I thought I'd surprise you. Pleasantly. Didn't think you'd secretly want to drown me. Tears, Stevie? The happy sort? Or are you worried I'm about to turn you and Rosa out on the streets? And talking of Rosa, where is the birthday girl?'

'You remembered?'

'As if I'm likely to forget. Like her mother, she's special.' Another fierce hug, and then, twisting Stevie round to face him, 'So – why the over-reaction? The Stevie Cooper we all know and love doesn't let go in public. She waits till she's alone and then sobs into her pillow. Intuition,' he'd explained as Stevie's head shot up. 'Rare in a man, I know, but you and I go back a long way. So, what is it? What's really bothering you?'

'Hormones,' she'd insisted, crossing her fingers at the tiny white lie. 'And the trials and tribulations of a new job.'

'Promotion? And about time too. Tom Deighton's been selling you short for years.'

'Hardly,' she'd demurred, smiling despite herself, wiping her eyes and blowing her nose, just tears of happiness hovering on her lashes as she'd allowed her hungry gaze to travel the lines of Andrew's face, logging the tracery of lines that hadn't been there two years earlier – a legacy of that high-powered job, she supposed – along with the sprinkling of grey at his temples.

269

Seven years older than Stevie, footloose, fancy-free and single, Andrew was every girl's dream – had once had a soft spot for Dee, Stevie recalled, wondering how Jared would take to the notion of Andrew turning up on Dee's doorstep, bottle of duty-free in one hand, froth of Chinese silk in the other.

Andrew and Jared. Same age, same height, same aura of power. Dark-haired, dark-eyed – and too good-looking for comfort. And they'd come face to face in Stevie's hallway – Andrew's hallway, though Jared didn't know it – and the spark of animosity could have powered a season of lights at Blackpool.

'Andrew Roxton,' she'd murmured on the verge of hysteria. 'I'd like you to meet –'

'I think not,' Jared had cut in, the contempt in his tone enough to slice through steel. And with a flash of white teeth that would have done a wolf proud, he'd made his escape.

'So much for that famously warm northern welcome,' Andrew had drawled with a careless shrug of the shoulders. Only Stevie had crumpled then, the sobs racking her body, and a stunned Andrew had drawn her into his arms and allowed her to ruin the jacket of an expensive lightweight suit.

'Little more than a dishrag,' he'd insisted, when Stevie had bewailed the damage. 'And ten a penny in a place like Hong Kong.'

'So –' She'd forced a watery smile, allowed

Andrew to top up her glass. 'What are your plans?'

'You *are* worried you'll be sleeping on the streets?'

'Hardly,' she'd demurred, sensing he was teasing. 'And if the worst came to the worst and you did show us the door, I'm poised to sign a contract on a place of our own.' A house in Churchtown, tiny but perfect, and close to Rosa's school. Not that it would make any difference to Anna's arrangements with Rosa. Rosa! 'Oh, hell!' Frantic eyes had swivelled to the clock. She should have collected Rosa from Kelly's an hour ago. And with two large brandies under her belt –

'No problem,' Andrew had soothed. 'Call Lorna. Surely she won't mind if you explain?'

'Ah, yes, but . . .'

'But what?' he'd probed, eyes dancing merrily, nuggets of jet in a sunburnt face.

'Rosa and Kelly. There's a sleep-over planned. Here. Tonight. With a couple of girls from school.'

'And wicked Uncle Andrew's about to spoil the fun?' Andrew had grinned, the fingers threading hers giving a squeeze of reassurance. 'Like I said, no problem. Even I could hardly turn up out of the blue, snap my fingers and demand my bed back, Stevie, so I took the precaution of checking my luggage in at the Scarisbrick. Talking of which, I'll make myself scarce –'

'Don't run away on our account,' Stevie had interrupted. 'Why not stay and say hello to Rosa?'

'Exhaustion,' he'd explained, smothering a yawn. 'I'm bushed. Once my head hits the pillow, I'll sleep the clock round. But the moment I wake I'll give you a call and you can come over for a drink. Or, if it's awkward for Rosa, I'll come to you.' He'd grinned, eyes crinkling at the corners. 'I can't wait to catch up on the gossip. Promotion, huh? I'm impressed. See you tomorrow? Or will it be today? Or, by the time my body clock's back to normal, who knows? It might even turn out to be yesterday!'

And, too overwrought to protest that she was turning Andrew out of his home, Stevie had nodded, the prospect of four giggling girls in the bedroom next to hers the last thing she needed right now. Only she'd cope. For Rosa's sake. And, damn Jared Wilde, but it really was none of his business.

Business. A week of hell. Just Andrew's intermittent presence keeping Stevie sane. And Lorna and Tom, who seemed to sense things were wrong but had too much tact to comment.

A strange week; an even stranger ending. The birthday treat at McDonald's, with almost as many adults as children: Stevie, of course, Lorna, Tom, Andrew and Anna, and one or two of the other mums. And then, large as life and twice as devastating, Jared, with an exquisitely wrapped box under his arm, the expression in his eyes unfathomable.

'Jared! How kind of you to drop by,' Stevie had exclaimed, going hot, then cold, then hot again.

Jared had smiled, his glance sliding from Stevie to the noisy knot of children at the 'play' end of the restaurant, and he'd nodded at Tom, raised a hand to his lips to blow a careless kiss at Lorna. The light reached his eyes as their glances locked, yet as his idle gaze had travelled the knot of people Jared had stiffened, his expression darkening, and Stevie hadn't needed to turn her head to know that he'd spotted Andrew.

'Mummy, Mummy, Mummy, look what Uncle Andrew's bought.' An over-excited seven-year-old in a brand-new party dress whom Stevie had swept into her arms, hugging, holding, squeezing, squeezing back the tears. Because Jared had heard and Jared had judged.

'Uncle'. The name covered a wealth of relationships, but none so eloquent as the picture Jared's mind had painted.

Only Rosa, wonderful Rosa, had smoothed the awkward moment, taking the box that Jared proffered with a shy smile of thanks and then: 'Oh, Mummy, look. A teddy bear. Isn't he beautiful?'

Exquisitely beautiful. The sentiment alone was worth a wealth of thanks. Thanks from Rosa. But as for Rosa's mother – Stevie had been too wound up to indulge the inanities of small talk, and so

Jared had taken himself off – back to Dee, Stevie supposed, not really surprised Dee had given the party a miss. Not her scene at all. Now a cosy candlelit dinner for two . . .

Stevie drained her glass, checked the time, allowed the magazine on her lap to close to under its own momentum. Another hour before they'd land. Another hour of silence and then three whole days of Jared in a country she'd long learned to despise. The man and the country both, she decided, and, smothering a weary sigh, risked a sideways glance.

He was watching her, eyes black as night, but the shutters came down at once.

Stevie moistened her lips, forced herself to meet his gaze. 'I – didn't have chance to thank you,' she murmured awkwardly. 'For Rosa's present. And for taking the time to drop by. It was good of you to make the effort.'

'Believe me, Stevie, the pleasure was all mine. I miss my little nephew,' he surprised her by explaining. 'And Rosa's a nice kid. Unspoiled.' He paused, held her gaze, seemed to be choosing his words with care, and Stevie held her breath, sensing it was make or break time, that whatever Jared said next would set the tone not only for the trip but for the rest of her life.

'About Rosa,' he murmured softly. 'I'd like to apologize. I was wrong. The idea that she's neglected is nothing short of lunacy.'

'Yes.' Stevie swallowed hard, craved another

brandy, wondered if Jared's eyebrows would disappear into his hairline if she dared to suggest it.

They did. But he didn't deliver the expected reproof – for which small mercy she was grateful.

'Stevie?'

'Jared?'

'Can we bury the hatchet – for the next three days at least? Once we're back home, of course, you can revert to sulking if that's what you want.'

'Sulking? For two pins, Jared Wilde,' she told him silkily, the block of ice around her heart beginning to thaw, 'I'd bury the hatchet all right – smack in the middle of that handsome forehead.'

'Handsome, huh? Progress indeed. In which case,' he entreated, smiling broadly and spreading his hands. 'Be my guest.'

Business. So much to cram into three short days – three and bit, Stevie amended automatically, aware that she could hardly be churlish by objecting to *that* change of plan. Business lunches, business dinners – she had food coming out of her ears – and in between visits to dusty villages on the outskirts of the city, to markets and factories – small, family-run concerns mostly, she quickly discovered – and then more factories, not to mention farms, restaurants and hotel kitchens.

'Research,' Jared explained when Stevie sank into a chair for a well-earned coffee break.

'There's never any substitute for first-hand experience. Besides, if we intend shipping our product over here . . .'

'Coals to Newcastle?' Stevie teased, impressed. 'But if you really want to sell Italian food in Italy, why not simply set up here in the first place?'

'Red tape. Rules and regulations.' Jared made a moue of resignation. 'With forty-two separate permits required the last time I enquired, and little foreign investment even now, the task is a labour of Hercules. Much easier this way,' he insisted.

Stevie shrugged – just another endearing Italian custom, she supposed, surprisingly unsurprised. For if a simple thing like popping into a café managed to involve queuing for twenty minutes to pay for the food at one end, and twenty minutes at another to proffer the receipt, and only then collect the order, who was she to complain?

'What happens if you change your mind?' she mused, swirling the grains of chocolate into the cream and watching them sink into the coffee.

'Not allowed,' Jared informed her, features impassive. 'Too much red tape. All those forms you'd have to submit.'

'You are joking?' Stevie queried, wrinkling her nose.

'Only mildly,' he allowed, smiling, his hand sliding across the table to capture hers.

Stevie froze. Touch. The touch of skin on skin.

Scalding, branding. Unfair, her mind screamed. Because she wanted him to stop, didn't want him to stop, that erotic swirl of thumb on her back of her hand stirring the blood in her veins.

'I —'

'You don't need to say a word,' he interrupted softly, huskily, his fingers closing round her hand the instant he sensed she was about to pull away. 'And if you did, Stevie Cooper, you'd be lying.'

'Ah, yes, but you don't know what I was thinking,' she teased, shockingly aware she was playing with fire.

A fleeting smile lit up his features. 'Want a bet?'

Stevie swallowed her smile. No. The coward's way out, she'd be the first to admit, but safer. And in the meantime Jared was speaking, and Stevie was horribly afraid she hadn't misheard.

'Dinner with your family? But —'

'Hush. No buts,' he insisted, the finger he put to her lips stifling the rest of her protest. 'Business and pleasure both,' he reminded her, the finger replaced by that lazy swirl of thumb as Jared's hand traced the angle of her jawline, his palm cupping her chin. And as rivers of heat began to stir in her veins, Stevie had to fight the urge to part her lips, draw the thumb into the delicate vice of her teeth and suck. And nibble. And nuzzle. And set a train of events in motion that she knew could only lead to disaster.

'No arguments,' Jared declared. 'You've

worked long and hard these past few days, and don't think I haven't noticed. So –' Abruptly he released her. 'I've one or two things of my own to catch up on and you deserve a break. Take the rest of the day off and I'll see you back here for pre-dinner drinks.' He checked his watch. 'Say – seven for seven-thirty?' he mused. 'And don't look so worried. Whilst Caterina's a bit of a tartar, her bark is worse than her bite.'

'Caterina?'

'My grandmother. As old as the hills and every bit as wise. She'll love you.'

A moot point, but one Stevie didn't stop to argue. The rest of the day. Three whole hours of solitude before she needed to head back to the hotel to change for dinner. Dinner with Jared's family, whatever that was supposed to mean, and, given the contents of her suitcase, she had nothing remotely suitable to wear.

A business trip, he'd told her, and a business trip she'd grimly packed for. Two summer suits she'd recently bought for work, a couple of lightweight dresses more suited to the beach than the boardroom, and, in a moment of defiance, that skimpy red number she'd worn the night they'd met. So – head for the shops and waste money she could ill afford on an outfit she didn't want and would probably never wear again? Or make do?

No harm in looking, she supposed, taking a white-knuckle taxi ride to Piazza di Spagna, after the perils of a lone female wandering the streets of Rome had been sternly underlined by Jared.

Via Condotti. Heaven alone knew why she'd chosen to come here. Hardly Stevie's scene at all. Only one of the world's more exclusive shopping streets, she acknowledged bitterly as the memories flooded back.

Mae, dragging Stevie from one exclusive display to another – money no object, thanks to Dino. Stevie groaning under the weight of the designer label bags. Oh, yes, Stevie remembered them all. And little had changed, each discreet window display matched by the next, and the next, hinting at an opulence that didn't merit the vulgar intrusion of a price tag.

'If a girl has to ask, a girl can't afford it,' Mae had informed her airily.

'A girl – or Dino?' Stevie had slipped in slyly. And Mae had simply grinned. Because Dino was besotted and Dino would pay – then.

It was later the rot had set in, when Mae had discovered she was pregnant and discovered too that the man she loved not only refused to have anything more to do with Mae or the baby, but had a wife and a clutch of *bambinos* happily ensconced in a villa in Tivoli. But, no . . . Stevie's lips twisted. How could she have forgotten? The pay-off. Enough for that one-way ticket to London and a couple of hundred spare to cover the cost of the abortion. Only Mae, beautiful, heartbroken Mae, had chosen to stay close to the man who'd betrayed her in the hope that he'd change his mind.

Men. Italian men. The most wonderful lovers in the world. And, standing at the foot of the Spanish Steps with the sound of the fountain tinkling in her ears, Stevie watched the passers-by, the lovers old and young, hand in hand, Italian, French, English, lovers from Mars for all Stevie knew, but of one thing at least she was grimly sure. Men were trouble with a capital T, and if she had even half of the sense she'd been born with, she'd continue to give men, and Jared Wilde in particular, that mile-wide berth. In the meanwhile, she'd pop round the corner to Via del Babuino and hope it was sale time in some of the less upmarket salons.

'Stevie?' A discreet knock at her bedroom door.

Stevie stiffened, blotting her lipstick and casting a final glance at the figure in the glass. Time to face the wrath of the Big Bad Wolf and put another of Mae's theories the test. Because ten times out of ten, her sister had insisted, a man would judge the woman not so much on merit as by the cut of her clothes and the depth of her make-up.

Head up, shoulders back, Stevie took a deep breath, stifled a last-minute twinge of conscience, flung open the door and marched through into the shared sitting room.

'Well, well, well,' Jared drawled. 'If it isn't Little Red Riding Hood herself.'

'It certainly is,' Stevie agreed, darting him a glance of pure defiance.

And though Jared smiled, stepped forward, offered his arm, Stevie had caught the flash of annoyance he couldn't quite mask and wished she had the grace to look ashamed.

CHAPTER 16

'Not such an ordeal after all, hey, Stevie?'

Stevie smiled, nodded, allowed Jared to take her hand beneath the table, the squeeze of reassurance bringing a glow to her cheeks, and yet, discreet though the gesture had been, it wasn't missed by the beautiful young woman seated opposite.

'Stevie?' Franca Wilde's pert nose wrinkled in puzzlement. 'A boy's name, surely?' she scorned, black eyes flashing from Stevie to Jared and back again.

'Not at all,' Jared insisted pleasantly, treating her to one of those deceptively dazzling smiles that Stevie was just beginning to recognize for what they were. A warning. An eloquent warning. 'Stevie's a diminutive. Like Gian for Giancarlo, or Matt for Matthew.'

'Matteo,' Franca corrected, her fleeting glance going to the man on her right, an older, coarser version of Jared, over-fond of his food, not to mention the *vino*, Stevie decided. She decided, too, that a fiercely loyal wife shouldn't cast such openly hungry glances at another man, any man, let alone her brother-in-law. 'My husband's Italian, Jared,' Franca reminded him. 'And proud of it.'

'As I am,' Jared allowed. 'But since my father – and Matt's,' he pointed out coolly, 'was British through and through, let's not forget our English heritage. Matt's, mine, and Gian's. Even here in Italy,' he reminded her, 'the name of Wilde is one to be proud of.'

'Thanks to Matteo.'

'I don't –'

'Jared! More wine for our guests, please.'

An imperative. Stevie swallowed a smile as the entire table jumped to attention.

Caterina Mancini, as formidable a woman as Stevie had ever met. Ninety-two and in possession of all her faculties, she clearly ruled with a rod of iron. 'Stevie – Stephanie,' she corrected, breaking the name into heavily accented syllables. 'Tell me, how are you enjoying your visit to Italy?'

'Stevie's hardly had time to sample the local colour,' Jared put in mildly.

'Which means my unthinking grandson has been working you too hard. Next time, of course, I shall take steps to ensure it doesn't happen. Naturally you'll both stay with me. No, Jared –' She raised a hand, smiled, nodded, leaned forward to pat her grandson on the cheek. 'One of the privileges of age,' she reminded him dryly, 'probably the only privilege, in fact, is that cantankerous old ladies can demand the unreasonable.'

'Hardly unreasonable, Nonna,' he demurred, capturing her hand and dropping a light kiss into the upturned palm. 'But, since the trip was business, I didn't like to impose.'

'Nonsense. I like to have my family around – what's left of it, that is. It keeps me young. And *you* don't fool me for an instant,' she scorned, with an admonitory wag of a finger. 'Like that fusspot of a brother of yours, you're afraid the excitement will finish me off.'

'Remember what the doctor said,' Matthew tossed in mildly, draining his glass and automatically refilling it.

'Doctors? Pah! I want a life, not an existence. Eat little, drink even less. What with pills to make me sleep and pills to wake me up, and pills to cover my every ache and pain, it's a wonder my heart doesn't rattle instead of tick.'

'Hearts don't tick, silly,' nine-year-old Gian interrupted.

'Mine does,' Stevie confided, onto her second glass of wine by now, with the tensions of the day beginning to drain away.

'Tick-tock, tick-tock – just like a clock?' Gian's smile broadened as the idea caught his fancy. 'What happens when the battery runs out?'

'You grow old, just like me,' Caterina reminded him tartly. 'But give it another year or so and there's sure to be a pill to cope with that too.'

'Caterina –'

'Don't fuss, Jared. You don't have to tell me. I'm sure to pay for it later, but for now I simply want to enjoy myself. And you can leave that jug of water where it is,' she told him sharply. 'I'm about to propose a toast – with wine. So . . .' She smiled, nodded, beamed around the table, waited patiently for Jared to pour her a glass, to top up the others, to pour Gian a well-diluted cupful, and then she raised her glass, the hand that held it as steady as a rock. 'To Jared's new venture. To Jared and Stevie and whatever the future may bring.'

Jared and Stevie. The names rang out around the room, a small, private room that led out onto the terrace, with its strip of lawn beyond and across the valley, to the silver gleam of the river just visible in the distance. Stevie and Jared. Almost a couple. Only they never would be. And yet, how ironic. To be spending time in Rome with a man like Jared, being wined and dined in style as part of his family. Hardly, she demurred, intercepting yet another speculative glance from Franca. Only this time, as Stevie caught and held the other woman's gaze, the devil inside her surfaced.

Swallowing a smile, she leaned forward. 'Franca,' she implored in a confidential whisper, 'be honest. If I've managed to smudge my lipstick –'

'But – how would I know?' Franca demurred, spreading her hands along with her sly smile. 'Given the quaint English fashion for laying it on with a trowel . . .'

An audible gasp. Caterina, Stevie identified, as, too late, she silently deplored the contribution she'd made to the spat of bad manners.

'What's a trowel?' Gian enquired in all innocence.

'It's – a tool for spreading mortar,' Stevie explained, her voice not quite steady.

'But Mamma said –'

'Yes. Your mother was making a joke. Because Italian ladies are known for their style and English ladies have a lot of catching up to do. Leastways,' she amended tightly, 'this one does.'

'Nonsense,' Caterina Mancini declared, in a tone that brooked no denials. 'Milan and Paris have had their day. London's the centre of the fashion world now. And quite rightly. So . . .' She was leaning forward, inviting confidence. 'Tell me, my dear, who designed your dress? The style's so unusual and the colour's simply perfect. It really ought to clash with your hair,' she allowed, her age-wise eyes brimming with silent apology, 'but it doesn't in the least. So charming, so refreshing, so liberating.'

Stevie smiled despite herself. The tensions round the table eased and suddenly everyone was talking at once – even Franca, Stevie noticed, was forced to banish her scowl under the sharp gaze of Jared's formidable grandmother.

'You're nice,' Gian confided, pulling his chair closer to Stevie's on the terrace, leaving the debris on the table for the hotel staff to discreetly clear away.

'Why, thank you kindly,' Stevie retorted. 'You're kind of nice yourself. And your English is perfect. Do all Italian children learn it at school?'

'And at home.' He pulled a wry face. 'Homework. Do English children do homework?' he asked confidentially.

'I'm afraid so,' Stevie confirmed. 'Even the little ones. Rosa's only seven, but she –'

'Rosa?'

Stevie glanced across, uncomfortably aware of several sets of eyes fastened on her face, with concern, indifference, curiosity – an intense curiosity from Franca.

'My daughter,' she replied, risking a glance at Jared, who'd made a point of dropping the lightest of kisses on the top of Stevie's head as they'd settled onto the terrace, a gesture she'd cherish for the rest of her life. Unvoiced support – then. Now his face was unreadable.

'So you're married?' Franca said.

'It doesn't have to follow,' Stevie retorted coolly, annoyed at the woman's blatant rudeness. 'But, as it happens, no.'

'I see.'

Stevie inclined her head. 'I doubt it,' she murmured, but she smiled as she spoke and another awkward moment passed, and yet with Franca hell-bent on monopolizing Jared, Stevie was sharply conscious of the dangerous swirl of undercurrents.

Nine o'clock. Way past Gian's bedtime, Stevie wouldn't mind betting, watching the boy kicking a ball around the grass, enjoying the sight of Jared in opposition, expensive dinner jacket doubling as one of the goalposts, Stevie's handbag pressed into service as the second.

'Goal!'

'Offside!' Jared, the beaten defender, appealed to the crowd. 'Come on, Stevie, you're the referee. Make a decision.'

Stevie grinned, pointed to what she guessed would be the centre spot.

'Easy, easy,' Gian chanted when the scoreline reached double figures.

'Speak for yourself, young man,' Jared playfully retorted, blowing the final, imaginary, whistle. 'Enough. You win. This time. And talking of time —'

'Yes, Jared. I haven't had a night like this in months,' Caterina confided wistfully. 'And, though I'll doubtless pay for it tomorrow, I wouldn't have missed it for the world. Thank you, Stevie. Thank you all. But Jared's right, as usual . . .'

'Do we *have* to go home?' Gian wailed as Jared swung him up onto his shoulders.

'Afraid so,' Jared replied. 'All good things have to come to an end.'

'Why?'

'Because they do. It stops you taking them for granted. Like eating a box of candy,' he explained. 'A small one doesn't fill you, but a big one makes you sick. Much better not to overdo it in the first place.'

'Yes, but how do you know?'

'I just do. And when you're my age, you'll know too. Now, a kiss for Stevie and it's time to go.'

Kisses all round before they headed through the foyer, Caterina walking heavily, an arm linked through each of her grandsons', Jared and Matthew, so alike and yet so vastly different.

More kisses at the foot of the steps, where the car was waiting – a huge limousine with uniformed chauffeur, Stevie couldn't help but notice, impressed. Warm hugs from Caterina and Gian, a peck on each cheek from Matthew, and a cool kiss of the air from Franca, who then smiled, raised her face to Jared, offering her mouth in a long, lingering kiss. Not the least bit sisterly, Stevie decided, scowling, so caught up in disapproval that she missed Franca's flash of anger as Jared gently but firmly put her away from him.

A spat of voluble Italian, and Franca's exquisite features were fleetingly ugly.

'Helena?' Jared echoed, with a strange glance at Stevie. Something about the set of his mouth hinted at an anger she couldn't begin to understand, and yet for some inexplicable reason the hairs on the back of her neck began to stand on end. 'Ah, yes,' he mused, the words barely audible. 'And how is – your sister?'

'Helena is fine, all things considered,' Franca bit out, with a venomous glance at Stevie, who'd moved tactfully back to the steps.

Jared rejoined her, and, logging the iron set of his jaw, Stevie felt her heart sink. Still, nothing ventured, nothing gained . . . She took a deep breath, counted to five and took the plunge. 'I'm sorry.'

'*You're* sorry? Oh, no!' An arm closed round her shoulders, tugging her close, and the conflict of emotion was almost too much to take: the undercurrents, the anger, the sudden warmth of Jared's body.

He raised a hand as the car pulled away, the occupants little more than shadows behind the smoked glass panels, barely waited for the car to draw level with the wrought-iron exit gates before swinging Stevie round to face him, the expression in his eyes unreadable.

'*I'm* sorry,' he insisted, iron fingers closing round her shoulders and sending fresh rivers of heat running through her veins. 'Sorry that I dragged you away from Rosa in the first place. Sorry I didn't take you to stay with Caterina, as I

290

should have done. Sorry I put you to the trouble of making polite conversation with a woman not good enough to lick your shoes. But most of all,' he said thickly, almost shaking her, 'I'm sorry as hell that beautiful, kind, considerate, yet vulnerable Stevie Cooper feels the need to apologize for anything.'

'I let you down. The dress –'

'You heard Caterina –'

'Manners, Jared. She was simply being polite.'

'She meant every word,' he bit out. 'And it's the woman that's important, not the wrappings.'

'My, you've changed your tune,' Stevie scorned, aware that she was hitting out, hitting back at Jared for a slight delivered in anger almost seven weeks before.

Bullseye. Jared's face darkened, but yet another flash of anger was banished in a trice. 'Maybe,' he conceded tightly. 'But I'm man enough to own when I'm wrong. You're –'

'Available?' she jeered, as another barb hit its target, and she shook herself free, took a step away from him, laughed – laughed when deep down inside she was crying. Crying for this man who could blow hot and cold, who could admire and despise both within the same draw of breath. 'Don't!' she spat as he made to speak. 'Don't lie, don't toss out another wrong in the hope of making things right. I know what you think; I know what you believe –'

'Past tense, Stevie. Because the woman I know –'

'Hah!' she interrupted shrilly, aware of heads beginning to turn, aware that raised voices in the foyer of such a prestigious hotel were bound to meet with disapproval even in a hot-blooded country like Italy. And, choking back hysterical gurgles of laughter, she swung away, set off for the bank of lifts, praying Jared would take the hint and allow her to go, give her time to cool off. Cool down. Regain some self-control before she talked herself out of a job she needed now more than ever.

Hell. Heaven and hell both. And the moment they returned she'd tender her notice, work her notice, and take whatever job she could as long as it paid the bills.

'Stevie —'

'Time for bed,' she told him brightly, jabbing her finger at the illuminated button. 'Alone. Surprised?' she trilled. 'Amazed? Or a teensy bit piqued that a lady could choose to sleep alone two nights in a row when there's a full-blooded male in the room next door? A *lady*,' she emphasized grimly. 'And, since lady of leisure I'll never be, I guess lady of the night must fit the bill. Trollop,' she underlined, stepping into the confines of the lift, shockingly aware of a grim-faced Jared following.

'Third floor, I believe. The Hermitage Suite. Wall-to wall opulence. Only the best for a lady, you know. Tramp!' she bit out as she marched stiff-backed the length of the corridor, tears

292

hovering on her lashes. Only she mustn't cry. Not here, not now. Because once the floodgates opened, she'd cry enough to fill the Tiber.

Half-blind with tears, she struggled to insert the key in the lock, was forced to hand it over to Jared, the sudden touch of skin on skin searing, unnerving, and she snatched her hand away, waited for Jared to step to one side before risking pushing past.

'Like I said, very impressive.' Pirouetting on the spot, she let her outstretched arm sweep the room, taking in the exquisitely understated decor, all white and gold, and yet nothing like as stark as Stevie's apartment. Not her apartment in the first place, she silently corrected, and, spotting the open door of the mini-bar beckoning like a siren, she danced across.

'Brandy, Jared? Or should we be devils, crack open the champagne, toast a successful evening?'

'*Why*, Stevie?' he breathed incredulously, waving away the glass that she'd poured. 'Why punish me? Why punish us both?'

'You know why,' she reminded him tightly. 'Me. Mother of the Year, I ain't, so switch the label to "hussy" and I guess you've got the picture. Stevie Cooper, the Southport Strumpet. Oh, very efficient at her job, no doubt – the *day* job that is,' she emphasized sweetly. 'But a lady with a past. Rosa. Living proof of the folly of falling for the charms of a man. And so I don't do it,' she informed him tersely, giving him the truth, though Jared couldn't know it. 'It's called survival. No man's allowed to sweet-talk his way into my bed – ever. Which means, well –' she broke off, shrugged, smiled, took a generous slug of the brandy and waved an airy arm.

'I was going to say work it out for yourself, but you managed that weeks ago. First impressions, and the delights of proving them right all along. Floozie, mopsy, doxy, hussy. Take your pick,' she entreated, beginning to crumble, Jared's flash of contempt proof and more that he believed what she was saying. 'Tramp. Trollop. Slut. Only tonight I'm not for sale – not to you.'

'Precisely. I don't buy,' he informed her, lips curling in derision as he folded his arms and looked her up and down, from the streaks of mascara beneath her eyes to the tips of her crimson-painted toes in the strappy summer shoes. Up and down. Down over the lines of a dress that fitted where it touched, the tiny bodice that did little to hide the pert thrust of breasts, the nipples that tightened with an ache she stubbornly refused to acknowledge. Jared's expression was more than eloquent proof that he'd noticed, and that he really didn't care that he could manage to provoke such a heated response.

Down lower his glance slid, skimming her hips much as the dress did, over the curve of her thighs – and such an awful lot of skin exposed between hemline and knee, Stevie acknowledged, lips twisting bitterly. Because the dress was a compromise, in every sense of the word. So near, so far.

Standing on the pavement in Via del Babuino, the money in her purse, the dress in the window had been simply perfect: the right size, the right colour, the right style. Discreet. A calf-length, midnight blue evening dress, off the shoulder, maybe, but demure enough for dinner with the Pope himself, should the occasion ever arise, and if the price tag had made her blink, she'd swallowed hard, taken a deep breath and headed for the door, her eyes automatically sliding to the colourful display of children's wear in the next window along.

No contest. Rosa. First and always. And so Stevie had tossed a mental coin, weighed a travel-stained suit against a sundress and had finally gone to the ball in rags. Red rags to a charging bull, judging from Jared's reaction.

'I don't buy,' he repeated, black eyes oozing scorn. 'I don't beg, I don't ask, and I sure as hell don't pay.'

Stevie squeezed back the tears, took an unsteady step forward. 'Jared —'

'Go to bed,' he insisted wearily. 'Top up your glass by all means, Stevie, but get out of my sight before I'm forced to say something we'll both regret.'

'I — don't want to go to bed,' she contradicted

tersely, almost squeezing the life out of the glass she was holding. 'Not alone. Not tonight.'

'Fine.' He gave a contemptuous toss of the head, raised the shutters on those dark, glowering eyes and looked through her, not at her, she couldn't help but notice, dying inside. Jared's turn to wave a hand. 'There's the door,' he reminded her coolly. 'Don't let me stop you. You're a big girl now and Rome's a cosmopolitan city. There's sure to be a man to your taste out there somewhere. Or two, or three or –'

'Don't!'

'Don't, what?' he queried frigidly, eyes pools of hate in a thunderous face. 'Don't speak the truth? The *truth*, madam,' he repeated cruelly. 'And by your own admission at that. Slut? The word doesn't even come close,' he informed her nastily. And before she had time to fathom his intentions, he'd crossed the room, snared her wrist in a grip of tempered steel and dragged her across to the open door of her bedroom. The glass she'd been clutching slipped from her grasp and shattered, spattering her bare legs and feet.

Halting in front of the floor-to-ceiling mirrors, he twisted her round, moved in tight behind her and fastened his hands on her shoulders.

'Look at me,' he ordered in a voice chill enough to freeze the Tiber. 'Look at me.'

And when Stevie continued to focus her tear-blurred gaze anywhere but at the figures cruelly outlined in the glass, he swore lightly under his breath, slid a rough hand beneath her chin and forced her head up.

Eyes closed, Stevie stubbornly refused to do as Jared wanted, and the grip on her chin tightened as he moved in closer still.

'Look, damn you,' he growled, loosening his grip for an instant, and as Stevie swayed unsteadily his arms came round her, pulling her into the hard lines of his body. Hard. Oh, God! Her lids flew open, the shock of desire in her eyes matched by a fleeting shock of recognition in Jared's. Because he wanted her. Because, hate and despise her though he did, still the need refused to go away.

'Stevie –'

'No!' she insisted, attempting to pull away. Not like this. Not in anger, in hate. Most of all not in hate. 'Please God, Jared, no.'

'Yes!' he breathed, his hands sliding from her shoulders, pushing away the tiny straps of Stevie's dress and tugging impatiently at the zipper.

Braless, as always, Stevie closed her eyes as the fabric dropped away, closed her mind to the shame. Shame because she wanted him. Shame because tonight she'd give herself to a man. And Jared would take her – in anger, in hate, when all Stevie craved was his love.

Love! As if, she silently derided. The stuff that makes the world go round, according to the songs, the stuff that Mae had revelled in – and died for. Love. The most overworked word in the English language. But this is Italy, she remembered, absurdly, hysterically. Italian men, the most wonderful lovers in the world. Jared.

'Jared! Oh, God, Jared.' Hands cupped her breasts; twin thumbs stroked her nipples – nipples that hardened, swelled, thrust shamelessly into the palms of his hands. And, *yes*, Stevie was watching, watching the tableau as if in a dream. Man and woman. Caught fast in the web of love. The man's dark head cradled against the woman's slender neck as his mouth nuzzled the warm, fragrant skin. The woman's breasts tightening as she clenched her fingers, struggled to deny him, to deny them both, while the swirl of heat in her belly made mockery of her resolve.

Want. Need. Lust. So wrong. Too exquisite to fight. And as the man raised his head, locked his gaze onto the woman in the glass, Stevie knew with an instinct primeval and true that to struggle was futile, that she wanted Jared and Jared wanted Stevie. Want. The threads of common sense were dissolving one by one. *Want*, she emphasized cruelly. Never love.

'No, Jared!' One last desperate attempt at denial.

'Oh, but yes,' he contradicted thickly, pushing the crumpled skirt over her hips and allowing the final flimsy barrier to fall.

Not quite, Stevie amended silently, tersely, logging the triangle of lace that made a mockery of her modesty. Yet even as Jared pulled her hard against him, ground his manhood against her, driving the breath from her body, the fingers at her groin were tugging the shamefully skimpy, shamefully damp panties over her hips.

CHAPTER 17

'Stevie, Stevie, Stevie! No! Stevie,' he groaned in anguish as she pulled away, spun round to face him.

But Stevie was smiling, was dancing on air. Because he wanted her, and oh, God, how she wanted him. Naked and thoroughly shameless, she danced back into his stunned embrace, offered her mouth for a kiss, pouted prettily instead, then danced quickly away, denying him, denying them both.

'Witch!' he breathed, an arm shooting out to pull her up short. And Jared smiled, and Stevie smiled, and the man and woman reflected in the bronze-tinted mirror smiled.

'Not tramp, trollop, slut?' she challenged softly, hands on hips, her body language saucy.

'No, Stevie. Not tonight, not ever. At least,' he amended thickly, 'not ever again. And never, ever as far as I'm concerned.'

'Wrong, Jared,' she contradicted smokily, reaching out to touch him, to run her fingers the length of his manhood. And as the heat of desire pulsed through her body Jared groaned, grabbed at her wrist, refused to allow her to draw away.

'Fine. Prove it,' he commanded, rubbing himself against her open palm. 'I'm a man. And I want you. And I want you to seduce me. Though dear God, Stevie,' he acknowledged tersely. 'It won't take much to bring me to the brink. And – whoa, there, lady!' he insisted, arching out of Stevie's reach in an effort to temper the pace.

Stevie laughed, danced around him, moved in behind him and slid her arms around his waist, her hands roving round and across the powerful barrel of his chest, impatient fingers tugging at the buttons of the dress shirt.

'Oh, no,' she insisted, slapping his hands away as Jared attempted to help. 'A seduction sir asked for; a seduction sir is getting. Understand?'

'Yes, maam!' he retorted briskly. 'Only soon. Make it soon, hey, Stevie,' he pleaded, in another tone, an anguished tone, as Stevie's dancing fingers reached the waistband of his trousers.

A tantalizing pause as Stevie smiled, pushed herself against him, body to body, the curves perfectly matched as insinuating fingers snapped the top button, tugged oh, so slowly at the zipper, slid inside, paused, barely hinted at a connection before following the trail of curls – upwards.

Another anguished groan. 'No, Stevie.'

'No, sir,' she agreed, totally unrepentant as she plundered the curls of his chest, a wonderfully thick mass just right for fingers to explore, for a mouth to nuzzle. And, since thought has a habit of leading naturally on to deed, in no time at all she'd moved round, was rubbing her cheek against the thick scrunchy mass, loving the texture, loving the smell of him, the touch of him, the taste of him.

Taste. Stevie parted the curls with her fingers, sucking greedily at first one nipple then the other while Jared's hands ranged the silky skin of her back. Touch. Jared pulled her against him, forcing Stevie to raise her face, raise her mouth, give another anguished groan as he scooped her completely into his embrace, fastened his mouth onto hers and kissed her, all but dived into the secret, sensitive recesses of her mouth.

Unbelievable. Jared's tongue was exploring, triggering thrill upon thrill, now a languished sweep, now an urgent dart, and as the blood in her veins began to boil he made yet another slow and lazy sweep of her mouth, of the soft, sensitive skin of her inner lips, before sweeping back in frantic search, a fruitful search.

Tongue entwined with tongue and Stevie was drowning, aware of every touch, every shiver of emotion. Jared was kissing her, touching her, driving her wild, wild, wild, when *she'd* been intent on seducing Jared.

'Stevie!'

'My bedroom, my seduction,' she reminded him, her heart soaring at the wealth of emotion in the depths of his eyes, such wonderful eyes, pools of dark, swirling chocolate, irresistible – no, no, no. She would be strong, she would resist – for now. Deny herself, deny them both, and when they did finally come together . . . When. Soon, she promised herself, as Jared spread his hands in silent submission. Very, very soon.

Unexpectedly acquiescent, Jared shrugged – shrugged the now crumpled shirt carelessly over his shoulders and, naked from the waist up, drew himself to his full height, folded his arms across his chest, and, other features impassive, raised an eyebrow. And waited. And waited.

Not a breath, not a movement. Just man and woman, alone, the atmosphere electric. Man. All man. Feet planted well apart, long, long legs drawing her gaze upwards. But she'd been wrong about no movement, she realized with another thrill of pleasure. Proof. His manhood. Straining at the zipper. The zipper she'd partly lowered. A zipper now unzipping of its own volition. Because Jared – oh, God, Jared!

Stevie closed her eyes, swayed against him, was vaguely aware of the room spinning dizzily as Jared scooped her into his arms.

'My bedroom, *my* seduction,' he growled, crossing the sitting room in a dozen easy strides. 'Understand?'

He placed her down, the fingers on her

303

shoulders digging deep in passion, not anger, she identified, convinced she was dreaming – such wonderful dreams, because Jared was kneeling before her, his glance reverential as he raised his head, locked his gaze onto hers. 'Because I want you, Stevie,' he told her thickly. 'Because I've wanted you from the moment I set eyes on you. Because that night at Tom and Lorna's you appeared in the doorway like a vision from my dreams and I wanted you. Then, and now, and every moment since. And every moment since has been leading us to this. This, Stevie!' he insisted, snatching her to him and holding her, hugging her, his cheek against her belly, the rasp of stubble strangely erotic. 'Stevie, Stevie, Stevie!'

Kissing, touching, tasting, hands and fingers exploring, a hot mouth covering her breast, an impatient tongue swirling across the pink swollen nub at the centre, lapping, sucking, teasing, hungrily, greedily, and the currents of heat swirled through her as Jared's mouth wreaked havoc, first one apple-firm breast, then another, lips, tongue, teeth – teeth biting.

'Jared! Oh, my love!' she exclaimed at the exquisite dart of pain, and she swayed forward, shamelessly offering her breasts, her hands cradling his head, urging him into her body, fingers ranging the thick mass of hair.

Side to side and backwards and forwards, a gentle undulation because Jared's mouth had moved on, his finger and thumb tweaking nipples in its stead, and, shameless through and through, Stevie groaned, nipples swelling, thrusting, aching.

'Oh, my love,' she moaned, swaying back from the pivot of her waist while Jared explored the plains of her belly, raining devastating kisses across and up and down, his hands sliding into the curve of her waist as he tugged her even closer. Nuzzling, kissing, lapping, an erotic tongue swirling into the hollow of her navel, sweeping round and out and down, down, down, his lips nuzzling the curls, his hands cupping her bottom, holding, caressing, kneading, round and over the soft skin of her inner thighs.

Shower a million kisses the length of her slender legs; pause to tickle the sensitive spot behind her knees before trailing onwards, down, and then up again, infinitely slowly, not a single pore of skin on Stevie's trembling legs neglected, fingers exciting, lips and mouth igniting.

'Stevie, oh, Stevie, you're the most wonderful woman in the world,' he groaned, pausing, sitting back on his heels and angling his head, black eyes locking with hers, a rebellious lock of hair falling over one eye, roguishly appealing.

'Maybe,' she teased, cupping her breasts, breasts that needed no support but craved the touch of this man who was kneeling in reverence before her, and, leaning forward, she made silent offer, saw the hunger in his eyes, a hunger reflected in her own, and something infinitely precious at the centre of her existence burst into life. Want. Desire. Love – on her part at least. Need. An exquisitely bitter craving. She wanted him. Oh, God, how she wanted him.

She flooded with desire, felt the trickle of damp on her inner thighs, saw the man's eyes darken, and as if in a dream watched him reach out oh, so slowly to slide a single finger into the give-away shimmer of dew.

'Stevie? Now, Stevie?' he queried softly, moving the finger back and forth, so near and yet so far, because he was scalding her, driving her crazy with the touch of skin on skin when she was screaming out for the finger to plunge into the heart of her. 'Too soon,' he growled smokily. 'And yet nowhere near soon enough. But I want you, and you want me, and we've all the time in the world. Now, and later, and again and again and again,' he insisted thickly. 'Woman,' he breathed. 'I want you. I want you now.'

And then he paused, and he angled his head, and he allowed that finger to slide to the very brim, and then he halted. 'Now, Stevie?' he challenged softly, angling his head. 'Say it, Stevie. Tell me you want me. Show me you want me – now!'

'Now! Now, now, now,' she moaned, and she was thrusting shamelessly against the hand, nudging the finger to make the connection she craved. Jared's audible gasp as he located the tiny ridge of pleasure was music to her ears.

'Jared. Please, Jared,' she implored, swaying back and forth, the shivers of heat beginning to ripple through her, and Stevie was moaning, her body trembling as the tidal wave of pleasure began to build, threatening to engulf her, so near, so far because Jared knew. Enough, no more. Enough to incite, to enflame and then –

'No!' she screamed in anguish as the finger withdrew, but Jared simply laughed, spanned her waist with his hands and urged her to her knees, his mouth devouring hers, his hands wreaking havoc on her body.

Crushing her to him, he held her, kissed her hair, her face, her neck, her fragrant shoulders, held her tight enough to squeeze the very life from her body. And all the time he was kissing her he was whispering words, words of love, she told herself, imagining, believing, not understanding the urgent flow of Italian and yet knowing with an instinct born of love that he was telling her he loved her.

Italian men, the most wonderful lovers in the world. Singular, she told herself, her heart soaring. Only one. This man. And she loved him. Now and always, and if Jared's love proved transitory –

No, no, no. Too awful to comprehend, to allow. Don't even think it, she implored herself, her mouth opening like the petals of a flower beneath his, her tongue darting between his lips, finding his tongue, sucking, biting, teasing, drawing his tongue back into the warm dark recesses of her mouth as she began to turn the tables.

'My bedroom, my seduction,' he reminded her, shockingly attuned to her every thought, and Stevie angled her head, glanced smokily up into his eyes, eyes she could happily drown in, and parted her lips but a fraction of an inch, allowing the pink tip of her tongue to protrude.

An electric pause, and with slow deliberation she ran the exposed tip across her bottom lip, stoking the flames of desire in coal-black eyes and proud of it. Logging Jared's reaction, her mind smiled.

'Fine.' She released him abruptly and, sitting back on her haunches, spread her hands. 'Your bedroom, your seduction,' she agreed huskily. 'Come on, Jared. What are you waiting for? Seduce me – if you can catch me, sir.'

And Jared growled, lunged forward, cursed as Stevie dived to one side, fleet as a deer, up on her feet and out of reach, darting through the door before Jared had time to fathom her intentions.

Mid-way between the two bedrooms she halted, hands on hips, her expression smoky.

'Whose seduction now?' she growled. 'Yours – or mine?'

'Ours,' he groaned, peeling his trousers the endless length of his legs. 'Ours, woman. Now.

Now this minute. Come here,' he commanded. 'Come here, Stevie, I want you.'

Want, she silently repeated, the knife-blade twisting. Too late, her mind screamed. Because if Jared wanted Stevie, then, shameless to the end, she wanted Jared. Magnificent, naked Jared, who was inching imperceptibly nearer. Wonderful, naked Jared, who saw Stevie's eyes go to his groin, caught the flicker of fear mingled with desire in her startled gaze and halted, a wealth of emotion chasing across his face.

'Stevie?'

Unsure. Impossible to believe in this day and age. He didn't need to put thoughts into words; Stevie understood. Fool that she was, she'd betrayed herself, and Jared, man of the world Jared, understood, yet didn't understand, and suddenly he couldn't make sense of it.

He took a step back. 'Stevie?' he said again, shaking his head in disbelief.

A conflict of evidence. Rosa. Stevie's own admission. Trollop. Tramp. Slut. So near, so far. Love, lust, want, desire, need. But most of all love. She loved him, she wanted him, and heaven help her just this once she'd follow the dictates of her heart.

Stevie's turn to shake her head. 'Afraid, Jared?' she teased, inching forward, holding his gaze, her expression smoky. 'Of making love? Man and woman, mouth to mouth, body to body. Body to body,' she repeated huskily, halting in front of him, aware of the battle raging in his mind. He didn't know. How could he know? But Stevie's scent of fear had caught him unawares, sowing the seeds of doubt, and so now it was down to Stevie.

She reached out, ran her finger the length of his shaft –

'Don't!' he insisted, attempting to pull away, but Stevie had come too far to risk losing him now, and the very instant Jared moved her fingers closed round him. And held.

'No, Stevie!'

'Yes, yes, yes!' she contradicted. 'Now, Jared. Take me, Jared. Now,' she repeated, shockingly aware that Jared's rigid control couldn't last, that the pressure was building beneath her fingers, that he was losing the mental battle.

'Hell, woman –'

'Yes. Woman. All woman. Your woman,' she insisted. 'Ready for love. Now. Because heaven help you, Jared Wilde, if you don't I'll –'

'Yes, Stevie?' he interrupted huskily, tugging her into his arms, and Stevie's mind soared. 'You'll what, my little minx?' he whispered against her ear. 'You'll turn around and walk away? Walk alone into that bedroom and close the door. Because if you do –'

'Why, naturally, sir, you'll follow,' she told him saucily, the awkward moment banished, never to return. 'Because I want you and you want me – here, now. Our seduction, Jared,' she reminded

310

him, sinking to the floor and pulling him down beside her, her fingers scrunching the mass of curls that covered his chest, tapered downwards in a natural invitation for hands to follow the trail, for fingers to close round him, to discover afresh just how badly Jared wanted her. 'Kiss me,' she said simply, raising her face, eyes brimming with emotion. 'Kiss me, take me, love me.'

'Well, only if madam insists,' he teased, reaching for her shoulders. And he held her, and he kissed her, and he pushed her gently down onto the rug, pausing to tuck a cushion beneath her head. And with his unblinking gaze fastened on her face, he parted her legs and slid with slow deliberation into the very essence of Stevie's heart and soul.

'Rosa?'

'Mine,' she told him proudly a lifetime later. 'All mine. For the past six and three-quarter years, that is.'

'Ah! I do believe I'm beginning to see. She's adopted?'

'Not exactly,' Stevie explained, only didn't explain, tucking her body close in to his. There was precious little room in a single bed, but it was infinitely more comfortable than the floor, she could allow.

'So . . . ?'

'All will be revealed in time,' she murmured sleepily. 'Tomorrow – or maybe it's today. But then, tomorrow never comes, I suppose,' she mused doubtfully. 'Better tell you now, then.'

She did. Little more than the bare essentials. No histrionics, no embellishments, not even a hint of the father's nationality. Because it really wasn't important. Not any more.

Sleep. The threads of daylight were beginning to intrude as the man curled around her body began to stir, and grow, and harden, and –

'Stevie?'

'Mmm?' she replied sleepily, wide awake in an instant and smiling inside.

'I'm sorry.'

'I'm not,' she retorted with deliberate misunderstanding. Because all the insults, the sly insinuations, the bitter words, were suddenly not important.

'I –'

'Hush,' she insisted, wriggling her bottom into his groin, and Jared growled, ground himself against her, caught Stevie's gurgle of delight and growled again.

'Witch,' he murmured throatily, his hands closing round her breast, a finger and thumb playing havoc with her nipple. 'Seducing an innocent man, and in his own bed at that . . .'

'Complaining, my love?'

'Only at the length of time it's taken you to manage it. Those two nights, Stevie,' he groaned in anguish. 'Two whole nights of tossing and turning alone in my bed, knowing you were sleeping soundly in the room next door. Have you any idea what that was doing to me?'

'I can probably hazard a guess,' she allowed, twisting round in his arms, face to face, belly to belly, lips to lips as she raised her face, began to nibble at the corners of his mouth. 'And, since two long nights means a hell of a lot of making up to do, I guess I can't afford to waste a single moment. Still, my sin, my punishment,' she insisted mournfully, wriggling upright, placing her hands on his shoulders and pushing him firmly down into the pillows.

Jared smiled, made to reach out, was brought up short by an imperative wave of Stevie's hand.

'No, sir! Touch me at your peril,' she warned, arching away.

Straddling his lower legs, she raised her face, locked her gaze onto his, saw the need, the naked desire, the passion stirring in the bottomless depths of Jared's eyes, and with slow deliberation raised her hands to her breasts, brushing a lazy thumb across each nipple.

'Stevie —'

'Mine?' she challenged smokily. 'Or yours?'

'Since a guy's allowed to look, but not touch, a moot point, Stevie. This is supposed to be your punishment, remember?'

'So it is,' she allowed, completely unrepentant, pouting, thinking, plotting. She smiled. Putting her thumbs to her mouth, she moistened the tip of each, rubbed each dark and swollen tip, then leaned forward to circle Jared's areolae, all but lost in the tangle of curls.

'Woman –'

'Mine,' she insisted, dipping her head, running the tip of her tongue across first one and then the other. 'All mine. Understand?'

'I – think I'm beginning to get the picture,' he allowed, raising his hands to the back of his neck – calling her bluff, Stevie decided, the evidence springing lustily into life before her eyes stark contradiction of Jared's carefully assumed insouciance.

Arching carefully over his body, she kissed him, Jared's clamped lips no challenge for Stevie's swirling tongue, and yet the moment he relented, groaned, allowed her tongue to slip through, was the moment she pulled away, raining tiny kisses from the corner of his mouth to the cleft of his chin, and on into the stem of his neck, feathering, teasing, tormenting.

'No!' she reminded him as he raised his hips from the sheet, attempting to make a connection. 'Touch me now,' she reminded him huskily, 'and sir will be forced to pay a forfeit.'

'Another moot point, since it can't be worse than the hell you're putting me through already,' he groaned in anguish. But he was smiling, his eyes going from her face to her breasts and back again, Stevie's thrusting nipples all the proof he needed that it was only a matter of time.

Because if he wanted Stevie, she wanted him

every bit as badly. He had his proof, he was content – for now. And, seeing Jared's secret smile, instinctively attuned to the workings of his mind, Stevie lowered her body, rubbed her breasts against his chest, felt the strain of his manhood and pushed down, the long, hard length of him brushing the curve of her belly.

An exquisite pause, and then she pushed again, shimmied her hips a tantalizing fraction, and just as swiftly pulled away.

'Oh, no!' he insisted, snatching at her wrist.

'Oh, yes,' she contradicted, tugging free, moving to kneel beside him on the covers. 'Don't forget,' she reminded him saucily, 'this is hurting me more than it's hurting you. I'm the one working hard, Jared Wilde. All you have to do is grin and bear it.'

'So I'm grinning. So seduce me. So stop wasting time and get on with the job in hand,' he retorted crisply.

'In hand, huh? Yes, why not?' Stevie mused, finger and thumb closing round him, Jared's electric response sending shivers of heat swirling though her.

'Easy, lady,' Jared growled, arching upwards in an attempt to ease the pressure.

Stevie laughed, loosened her grip just a fraction, and Jared's undulating hips gave instinct a nudge as Stevie discovered the delights of taking a man to the brink of heaven and back again.

'You can't –'

'Just watch me,' she contradicted, bending, running her tongue over the plains of his belly, hands and mouth wreaking havoc where they touched, where they didn't touch, barely an inch of him untouched.

Heaven and hell. Both for both. Stevie's need was almost driving her insane and yet still she denied him, stretching out beside him, craving a touch, craving so much more, hands, mouth, lips, fingers; nuzzling, teasing, stroking.

She cupped his face in her hands and kissed him, her smouldering gaze fastened on his as her tender fingers traced the angles and planes, brushed the curve of cheekbone, explored the rasp of stubble . . .

Explored the powerful muscles that rippled with pain and pleasure, fingers scrunching the thick mass of hair. Chest to belly, belly to groin. So easy to give in, to touch him, work him, bring Jared to the brink again and again and again. And again she denied him, denied herself just as badly, for if Jared was groaning and writhing, Stevie was on fire. Body to body, not touching. She wanted him, she needed him; she needed him so badly that it hurt.

'Now!' she insisted thickly, pushing against him, rubbing her breasts against his chest and wriggling her hips in close to his. 'Now! Now! Now! Oh, yes!

She howled in anguish as he pulled away. '*Jared*!'

But Jared was simply teasing, paying her back for keeping him waiting. And Jared had flipped her over onto her back, was kissing her, straddling her, denying her, teasing, kissing, touching, tasting, punishing, until Stevie simply couldn't take any more. And the moment he detected the first give-away tremble of her body was the moment he drove himself inside her. Stevie and Jared, man and woman, out of control in perfect synchronization.

'Now what?'

'Breakfast?' she enquired, opening her eyes to find fingers of sunlight chasing across the floor of the room. She checked the time on her wristwatch. Nine-thirty. Which meant . . .

'Business – and pleasure,' he reminded her as she jerked bolt-upright, kneeling behind her to cradle her against him, a lazy hand cupping her breast, triggering the currents in an over-sensitized body.

'But you're late –'

'Only if I intend turning up in the first place, my love.'

'But –'

'No buts,' he insisted, his other hand at her mouth, cutting off her protest. 'I'm here, I'm with you, and, since the plane doesn't leave until two, that leaves hours and hours to do what we want. Any ideas?'

'Breakfast?' she repeated brightly.

'Breakfast?' he echoed, trying and failing miserably to keep the note of disappointment at bay.

'But of course,' she insisted, nibbling at his finger. 'It's at least an hour since I sipped from the honey-pot of love. I need feeding, Jared. Ambrosia. The food of the gods. Feed me, Jared,' she pleaded softly, wriggling round in his embrace, sliding her arms up and around his neck and rubbing her breasts against his chest. 'Feed me.'

He did. An exquisite meal. 'Little more than a taste of things to come,' he informed her, running the flat of his hand over the plains of her belly. 'Stevie –'

'Hush, Jared. No words. Not now. Not yet. Just love and more love . . .'

'I'm not sure I have the means just yet,' he chuckled.

'You will,' she insisted, smiling up into his face, seeing all the love she'd never dreamt could be hers. She patted the hand that was ranging her body. 'And soon,' she added thoughtfully, nudging the hand in a southerly direction, praying he'd take the hint.

Jared growled, threaded the curls, slid a finger into the warm moistness and –

'Woman, you're insatiable!'

'Complaining?' she teased, shockingly close to losing control all over again.

'Heaven forbid. But when we do finally come up for air, you and I must talk. Today, Stevie. I –'

318

'Later,' she insisted thickly. 'Later. We have all the time in the world.'

A strange noise, a strident intrusion – the telephone, Stevie realized as Jared smothered a curse, raised his head, locked his sultry gaze onto Stevie's.

'I should have cancelled that appointment,' he confided ruefully. 'Still, give me half a minute and it's done. Thirty seconds,' he reminded her, climbing out of bed and padding through the open door.

A voluble barrage of Italian, and the note of urgency in Jared's tone was clearly nothing to do with business. Suddenly afraid, though she didn't know why, Stevie wriggled upright, pulled the crumpled sheet up under her chin and fastened her eyes on the door.

'Jared?'

He gave her a reassuring smile that did nothing of the kind. 'It was Matthew,' he explained, coming to sit beside her, take her by the shoulders and hold her tight. 'He –'

'Caterina?' she interrupted shrilly. 'Oh, Jared –'

'Hush,' he murmured, absent-mindedly kissing her. He forced a rueful smile. 'Knowing my brother, he's probably overreacting. Too much excitement last night, I guess. But –'

'Of course you must go. Now. At once, Jared. Caterina needs you. I'd come too, but I'd only be in the way. Go, Jared. I'm a big girl, remember, and I'm perfectly capable of making my own way home.'

'I lo –'

'Hush,' she insisted, her finger on his mouth, cutting him off short. 'I know. And I also know how much Caterina means to you.'

'Yes. And you, Stevie,' he insisted. 'And the minute I'm home, I'll prove it.'

CHAPTER 18

Love. The stuff that makes the world go round. He loved her. He'd proved it again and again, and if he hadn't quite said it then she had no one to blame but herself. Only he didn't need to say the words. Proof. Stevie's aching, tingling body was all the proof she needed.

She checked the time. Ten past twelve. Another twenty minutes and the taxi would arrive, and, since Jared hadn't phoned back, she'd be making the trip alone. Caterina. Apparently not one of Matthew's overreactions, though, please God, she would be fine.

'I'll phone,' Jared had insisted. 'If I don't call here, I'll phone you at home tonight.'

'If you have time,' Stevie had insisted, pushing him gently away, waving him towards the waiting car and standing and watching till it was long out of sight.

With hours to kill, yet reluctant to go for a walk in case she missed Jared's call, Stevie had showered, dressed, packed, and curled up on the balcony with a magazine she'd read from cover to cover without taking in a single word.

Love. The most wonderful sensation in the world. Stevie and Jared. Jared and Stevie. Love. Here in this room, and for ever in her heart. One last glance around, one last smile at the woman in the bronze-tinted glass, and simply by closing her eyes she could relive the night all over in her mind.

She was still smiling as she stepped out of the lift, allowed the porter to dart forward and take her suitcase, place it by the open door.

A glance at the clock on the wall. Twelve-twenty. Far too early for that taxi, she'd sit in the foyer and watch for the car arriving, but first she'd return her room key.

She crossed the marble-tiled foyer, reaching the counter, smiling, catching sight of a woman reflected in the mirror behind the receptionist's chair and swinging round in disbelief –

'Franca!' But no, how silly. And yet the resemblance was uncanny. 'I'm sorry,' Stevie murmured, racking her brains for the Italian translation and forced to settle for the language she knew. 'I thought –'

'Yes, Miss Cooper?' the woman interrupted, her beautiful face fleetingly ugly. 'You thought?'

Franca. The same build, the same height, the same colouring, the same exquisite taste in clothes, the same sneering contempt in her eyes. Franca, only not Franca, which meant –

'Helena Wilde,' she introduced herself, generous lips curling in derision. 'As in Mrs Helena Wilde. So perhaps, Miss Stephanie Cooper,' she entreated in perfect if frigid English. 'You wouldn't mind explaining what the hell you think you're doing playing around with my husband.'

Making love – love, she told herself. Not sex. Not a cold-blooded seduction. Because Stevie had wanted Jared and Jared –

Yes, Jared. A man. A normal, healthy man with a normal healthy appetite. Sex. Practically on a plate, since Stevie had needed little persuasion. And when it came to replaying the tape in her mind, hadn't Stevie done all the running? Every word, every glance, each and every touch and Stevie was guilty as hell. Because Jared had realized and he'd tried to back away. Only Stevie hadn't allowed it.

Her lips twisted bitterly. Shameless. *She'd* seduced Jared. Which made her every bit and more the slut he'd believed her to be in the first place. More tears, enough to fill the Tiber and the Marine Lake both, although the sobs that choked her body night after night were beginning to subside. She'd cried herself dry.

Not before time, she realized, with a shiver of apprehension. For with Dee dropping by for supper, it was high time Stevie took control. Control? Some chance, given the state of her emotions. Time for a fortifying drink, then. Not the first of the day by any means, and probably not the last, given the ordeal to come.

The phone rang the moment she settled back down and she jumped, the wine slopping over the rim of her glass, an obscene splash of red on Andrew's stark white settee.

Smothering a curse, Stevie snatched at a box of tissues, thrust a generous handful into the spreading pool and flung open the door to the hall.

'Sorry there's no one in. If you leave your name and number after the tone,' the outgoing message trilled brightly, 'I'll get back to you.'

'*Liar*!' Jared's voice, the anger barely contained.

Because Jared had called, and called, and called, and Stevie had stubbornly refused to pick up the receiver. Not at home, not at work, her terse instructions not to be disturbed causing delicately raised eyebrows. And when Jared's harassed PA had burst into tears at yet another tirade down the phone line, Stevie had put a finger to her lips, shaken her head and melted quietly away, allowing the poor woman to speak the truth for once.

Miss Cooper wasn't in. Miss Cooper was touring the factory. Miss Cooper was making a demonstration video. Miss Cooper had an appointment with the butcher, the baker, the candlestick-maker . . . was wining and dining clients

at The Scarisbrick . . . the Prince of Wales . . .
Valentino's . . . Lies, all lies, but Jared wouldn't
know, and if the thought of Stevie entertaining
men – and they were definitely men, she decided
grimly – happened to upset him, then tough.

'Pick up the phone, damn you,' he ground out
tersely, and Stevie winced at the anguish in his
tone. 'Now, Stevie. Or tomorrow. Or the next
day. Or bury your head in the sand and wait until
I come home. And then we'll talk. You and me.
Alone. No hiding place, Stevie, because in less
than forty-eight hours I'll be home.'

Silence. Just the sound of the tape resetting,
the single red eye of the 'message waiting' light
blinking balefully up at her. No hiding place.
Escape. She needed to escape. Time to take Jared
up on that holiday entitlement and buy a precious
bit of time. Only first she'd have to face him.
Worse than that, she realized, logging the time
and moving with wooden footsteps into the
kitchen, first she had to look her best friend
squarely in the eye and pretend there was nothing wrong.

'But it doesn't make sense,' Dee insisted, grinding a half-inch stub into the overflowing ashtray
and immediately lighting another cigarette. 'His
grandmother's on the mend, Stevie. A heart
attack, a mild one at that, and Jared –'

'Doubtless has his hands full propping up his
family. Give the guy a chance, Dee,' Stevie

entreated softly, exchanging the plateful of half-eaten food for a raspberry cheesecake that Dee pushed away without tasting. 'You know Jared. He's hardly likely to head for home unless he's sure Caterina is strong enough to leave.'

'Wednesday,' she muttered, blonde curls quivering in indignation. 'According to the super-efficient Miss Tracey, that is. Ten days,' she informed Stevie sulkily. 'And not once has he managed to pick up the phone.'

'He —'

'Can go run and jump in the lake,' she interrupted scathingly, exhaling a cloud of smoke. 'I've had enough. If Jared Wilde thinks he can simply turn up on my doorstep with a bottle of champagne in one hand and a dozen red roses in the other and expect me to climb into bed at the drop of a hat, he's about to get his eye wiped.' An impish grin split her features. 'Now a drop of something else . . .' she allowed enigmatically, reaching for the bottle and topping up her glass. 'And since absence makes the heart grow fonder, not to mention the body —' She broke off, eyes narrowing behind the veil of blue haze. 'I don't suppose, Stevie Cooper —'

'No, I don't suppose you do at that,' Stevie interrupted, catching her drift. Stevie and Jared. Miles from home and footloose and fancy-free. Little more than an idle thought but not beyond the realms of possibility.

Stevie smothered the panic. For Dee was no

326

fool, and when it came to telling lies, squeaky clean Stevie Cooper had never been in practice in the first place. And since the truth was out of the question . . . Might as well get it over and done with, cross her fingers, take the bull by the horns – and bluff. 'Now, come on, Dee,' she challenged softly, holding her gaze with a massive surge of will. 'Would I? Would Jared?' she added, praying the ludicrous idea of prim and proper Stevie Cooper allowing a man, any man, into her bed would prove a novel diversion.

'Jared? Who knows?' Dee derided, draining her glass and promptly refilling it. 'He's a man, and you take it from me,' she tagged on nastily, 'when it comes to men and sex, anything in skirts will do.'

'Maybe so,' Stevie conceded, inwardly wincing. 'But where Jared's concerned I'm sure you're overreacting. Face it, Dee,' she pleaded softly. 'You're peeved he hasn't called and you're hitting out blindly. But go for the jugular the moment he shows his face and you can wave goodbye to that cosy reconciliation.'

'Cosy? Winceyette pyjamas, slippers and steaming mug of cocoa in front of the fire?' Dee grinned, shook her head, leaned across to pat Stevie's clenched hand. 'Oh, no. Not quite what I had in mind at all. You're right, as always. Silly me's overreacting.'

'Not to mention over-indulging in the wine,'

Stevie observed sternly. 'And since you're driving –'

'One teensy little glass won't hurt, and then I'll
head for home and that cold, empty bed.'

Eleven o'clock. The strains of the night were
beginning to tell, and Stevie's stifled yawn finally
registered.

'You're showing your age,' Dee observed
mildly. 'It's nowhere near midnight and you're
ready for sleep. Not like the old days, hey, when
we'd be heading into town with the rest of the
gang to dance the night away?'

'Don't let me stop you,' Stevie entreated,
taking the dig in good part. 'In fact, if it wasn't
for the need of a sitter for Rosa, I'd be tempted to
join you.'

'Liar.' Dee tempered her derision with a smile,
at the same time rummaging through the debris of
her bag in search of lipstick and mirror. 'Even in
the old days you loathed each and every moment.'

'As obvious as that, huh? And I thought I'd
been discreet.' Stevie shrugged. 'The noise, the
heat, the flashing lights, the heaving crush of
bodies, not to mention the groping hands.
Sounds divine.'

'Chance would be a fine thing,' Dee retorted
wistfully, straightening her dress, a fitted black
sheath that plunged daringly into a vee at the
front. Not so much neckline as navel-line, Stevie
decided, and far more suited to a night on the tiles
than a cosy supper in with a girlfriend.

'You know, for two pins,' Dee mused, with a speculative glance at her wristwatch, 'I'd take myself down to Maymies. Only I can't. Where a man can turn up on his own, of course, an unescorted woman's on the make. Oh, look.' She halted by the phone, by that blinking red eye that Stevie hadn't had the nerve to cancel. 'I didn't hear it ring,' she part queried, part acknowledged, a tiny frown creasing her forehead. 'You must have switched the tone down. Someone's called. Better play it back,' she entreated in all innocence, a crimson-taloned finger hovering over the button. 'You never know, it might be –'

'No!' Stevie dived forward, pushed her hand away, turned the colour of Dee's nails as their glances locked, and, aware she'd overreacted – and how! – forced an apologetic smile. 'It's – been playing up,' she explained. 'You wouldn't believe the row that it makes. And since Rosa's fast asleep . . .' Another shrug, another apologetic smile. 'It's sure to have been Andrew in any case,' she lied with a mental cross of the fingers. 'Calling to say he'll be late. And speaking of the devil . . .'

A key rattled in the lock, the door swing open on its hinges – Stevie's cousin, large as life and –

'Dee! Leaving already? But the night's still young,' he observed, dropping a light kiss on the top of Stevie's head in passing.

Reaching the doorway, he halted, spun on his heels and pocketed his keys, his gaze sliding past

Stevie and on to Dee. A thoughtful gaze, an appraising gaze, and, sure enough, Stevie noted, amused despite it all, Dee visibly preened.

'Tell you what,' Andrew mused, raising his eyes the length of Dee's body and homing in the generous show of cleavage beneath her open jacket. 'I'll walk you to your car. A woman alone can't afford to take any chances, not in this day and age.'

'But it doesn't make sense,' Lorna insisted briskly. 'You had dinner with his family. If Jared was happily married, his wife would have been there. He can hardly pass himself off as footloose and fancy-free in front of his doting gran. Talking of whom –'

'She's fine. A heart attack, and, like your mother, a mild one, thank goodness. Jared's flying home tomorrow, and Dee –'

'Not a good idea,' Lorna warned. 'And, since we don't know the truth, we don't have the right to interfere. Not you, not me, not anyone. Besides, Dee can take care of herself.'

A moot point, Stevie mused, since Dee was the original little girl lost and managed to fall for the age-old patter time and time again. Men. How many men? Stevie wondered, not for the first time, aware too that Andrew's bed hadn't been slept in. None of her business, she knew. But if Andrew *had* spent the night with Dee . . .

Stevie mentally shrugged. As Andrew had

330

observed at the time, the night was young and they were grown adults. What could be more natural than to dance the night away? Sex? Stevie mused, stifling a twinge of conscience. Not love. Just like Stevie. And, just like Stevie, all Dee craved was love. And Jared. The waves of disgust rippled through her. Ugly. Whichever way she viewed it, she'd let Dee down, let herself down just as badly. And as for Jared, Lorna was right. If Jared *was* married, Helena would have joined the family dinner.

Which meant Helena Wilde had been sparing with the truth. Another irrelevance, Stevie realized as the knife blade twisted. Separated, divorced or happily married, Jared's marital status didn't matter in the least. Not to Stevie. Poor besotted Dee. Let down by the man she loved, if only she but knew it, but, worst of all, betrayed by her best friend.

Wednesday. Three forty-five. The day was interminable. And, try though she did to keep mind and body busy, it was little more than an exercise in marking time. Jared. No hiding place. Sorely tempted to call in sick, Stevie had changed her mind. Home or work; it would be all the same to Jared. In which case, safety in numbers. She'd go to work. Not even Jared would risk a scene in public.

'Ah, Miss Tracey.' A deceptively dazzling smile as he appeared in the open doorway, swept into the room, flung his briefcase into a corner and lifted his prim and proper PA bodily from the chair where she'd been sitting taking notes. 'Business. Such a lot of catching up to do,' he explained with a flash of white teeth that didn't fool Stevie in the least. 'So, come fire, flood or Biblical pestilence, or the outbreak of World War Three,' he outlined silkily, 'on no account are we to be disturbed. Thank you, Miss Tracey. I know I can rely on your discretion.' Placing the astonished woman down in the corridor outside, he firmly closed the door, turned the key in a lock that had never been used to Stevie's knowledge, dropped the key into his pocket and swung round to face her.

'Well?'

Stevie swallowed hard, saw the pain and the anguish and the disbelief etched upon his features and wanted to place her head down on the desk and cry. Cry for this man who could hop from Dee's bed to Helena's to Stevie's and who had the nerve to think he could keep the peace.

'No,' Stevie conceded icily. 'Assuming you're enquiring about my health, of course. I feel sick. Sick, Jared. Sick up to here.' She gestured as she spoke, the slice of her hand going to the top of her head.

'Why?'

'*Why?*' she breathed incredulously.

'Yes, why?' he roared, crossing the room to stand before her, tower above her, six feet three inches of blazingly angry man. 'Why did you walk away? Why have you refused to take my calls? Why are you behaving like a skittish adolescent. We made love, damn it. All night long. And you –'

'Enjoyed each and every moment?' she tossed out mildly. 'Don't worry Jared, there's precious little wrong with your technique. After all, practice makes perfect, so I'm told, and you're sure as hell not short of that.'

'Dee –'

'No!' She cut him off, the thought of discussing Dee and Jared's nights of love with Jared himself almost the last straw. 'Not Dee,' she countered frigidly. 'Not even the sultry Franca, as it happens. And, yes,' she insisted as his head shot up, 'I noticed. Since she was openly panting for the chance to get her hands inside your trousers, difficult not to. I noticed, Caterina noticed and worst of all,' she reminded him icily, 'her mild-tempered husband noticed. Poor Matthew. Anyone with half a brain could see which of the brothers she preferred.'

'Irrelevant. We didn't, we haven't, I wouldn't.'

'No.' Stevie smiled grimly, Helena Wilde's features swimming before her eyes. The same height, the same build, the same taste in clothes – and men, she tagged on sourly, driving the knife-blade into her belly and twisting it round and round. Only younger than Franca, and with some strange appeal in those enormous black eyes. A fragility. Yes. A worldly-wise, brittle fragility that hadn't fooled Stevie one bit. For if Franca was a prize bitch, Helena was doubly so.

'If you say so,' she demurred, smiling, wincing as Jared's features darkened and he leaned across the desk, cutting the distance between them to a whisker.

'I do. Fact, Stevie. Next accusation?'

'What makes you so sure there is one?'

'You. And some snotty remark about practice making perfect. Talking of which, I'd say you're quite a girl. So tell me,' he invited confidentially, 'just for the record, of course. Are you really a fast learner, or did I blink and miss something important?'

'Meaning?'

'You. That impressive vestal virgin routine. It almost had me fooled. Quite an act. A first-class performance, in fact, and –'

Stevie hit him.

'Hellcat!' he bit out venomously, snatching at her wrists, tugging her to her feet. Just the width of the desk stood between them, and his eyes were pools of hate in a face contorted with anger. 'Oh, yes,' he sneeringly conceded, the vivid imprint of her hand standing out against his tan and drawing her gaze. 'You had me fooled all right. I swallowed the bait – hook, line and sinker. Not to mention that impressive line in pillow talk. Rosa –'

'No!' The howl of a wounded animal. Stevie struggled to be free. 'You won't – you can't. She's

334

an innocent child, for heaven's sake. Don't drag Rosa into the mires of your mind. Not Rosa. Me. Insult me, Jared. I'm the one you're angry with. Stevie Cooper,' she reminded him, eyes shooting flames. 'Tramp. Trollop. Slut –'

'The art of understatement, madam? Because when it comes to plumbing the depths, you can take it from me, there isn't a name for a woman like you. You know something, Stevie?' he enquired with a lightning change of tone, lips curling in derision. 'You disgust me. I believed in you. I fell for every word, every glance, every touch –'

'I didn't notice the fastidious Jared Wilde complaining at the time.'

'I'm a man. I'm human. I simply –'

'Couldn't resist a bargain when it was offered on a plate? Sex, Jared. Nothing more, nothing less. Nothing underhand or sordid. I'm not ashamed to admit that I enjoyed it, and if you were even half the man you claim to be you'd –'

'Be going back for seconds? Oh, yes.' Another sneering curl of the lips as he pointedly thrust her away. 'Second helpings, and third, and the rest. Like I said, it was quite a performance. Congratulations, Stevie. But as for enjoying myself . . .' He paused, spread his hands, raised his shoulders in careless unconcern. 'You *were* good,' he sneeringly conceded, 'but not that good. Marks out of ten?' He paused, pursed his lips, made a pretence of considering. 'I'd say seven or eight should cover it.'

335

'Bastard.'

'Just being honest. And you did ask.'

'Ah, yes, but if the performance was disappointing,' she countered silkily, 'maybe the gentleman in question should have lent more of a helping hand. Only it wasn't. I know.'

'Well, you would, wouldn't you, my dear?'

Words. Angry, bitter words. Not the truth, she consoled herself, dropping her gaze, the objects on the desk swimming out focus. Insults. Jared's anger. Jared's disgust. Because Jared wanted to believe and Stevie had too much pride to give him the truth.

Besides, she owed it to Dee. Beautiful, vulnerable Dee, who loved this man and who'd no idea that he'd betrayed her, had bedded her best friend the moment her back was turned. Or, since Stevie *had* done all the running, maybe it was the other way round. In which case, she conceded bitterly, Jared had known Stevie better than she'd known herself. How did it go again? Tramp. Because from the moment they'd met, she'd wanted him. First impressions. And, as Nanna had slyly reminded her, the shades of love and hate.

Hate. Lashings of the stuff. When all she'd ever wanted was his love.

Squeezing back the tears, she moved over to the window, pushed aside the blind, allowing fingers of sunlight with their shafts of dancing dust motes to pour into the room. Summer.

Long, hot days; long, lazy nights. Nights alone in the uncomfortable guest bed in the corner of Rosa's bedroom. Because Andrew was home and it was only right that he had the master bedroom. Still, in another few weeks, and with the ink dry on that contract, she and Rosa would be settled in a place of their own. Assuming Stevie had the means to pay the mortgage that was. Jared —

Her chin shot up, her startled gaze colliding with Jared's. He was perched on the edge of the desk, Stevie's desk, arms folded across a powerful chest, and for a fleeting moment of madness she caught a glimmer of emotion in the depths of his eyes and her mind soared. Love —

Loathing, she countered sternly. Disgust. Hate. And he was her boss. Difficult to justify a sacking, since Stevie was good at her job, but an easy enough task to make life intolerable. Jared wouldn't. No, she acknowledged, recognizing the truth and swallowing hard. Jared wouldn't. But then, he really wouldn't need to. Working for Jared, talking to Jared, just being under the same roof as Jared simply wasn't an option. Not any more.

Stifling a weary sigh, she raised her arms, running her fingers through the feathers of her hair, stretching the fabric of her blouse tight across her breasts, the gesture unwittingly erotic. Decision time, resignation time. Worries about the mortgage would have to keep. She took a deep breath. 'Jared —'

'No!' He dropped his gaze, eyes going to the curve of breast, the shameless thrust of nipples that had a life of their own where Jared was concerned.

A flash of naked emotion. Want. Need. Desire. And *yes*, the shutters had come down, but not before Stevie had time to notice. Her cheeks flamed. He wanted her. Tramp of the Year, yet even now he wanted her. Time to turn the tables. Time to pay him back for those twisted accusations, the snide remarks. Stevie's revenge. After all, might as well be hung for a sheep as a lamb . . .

Sidling across, she came to halt before him, glanced up into those treacherous brown pools and smiled. 'What's the matter?' she breathed, a lazy hand going to the chain at her throat and tugging, an absent-minded gesture carefully designed to draw his gaze. 'Something wrong?' she challenged smokily, dropping the hand but a fraction and deftly snapping a button in the process. 'Afraid, Jared? Afraid I'm about to seduce you, perhaps?'

A double distraction. The pink tip of her tongue tracing the outline of her lips, slowly, deliberately.

'Afraid you won't be able to resist?' she probed as another button gaped, giving a tantalizing glimpse of Stevie's breasts, perfect blush peaches with their dark buds straining at the centre. She moved her head from side to side in slow but silent admonition. 'Surely not,' she taunted, eyes raking his face, a face she loved, a face now dark with anger – or desire. 'Resist. Easy to resist, hey, Jared?' she repeated. 'Look – but don't touch. So . . .' Another exquisite pause. Stevie's hand hovered, and then snapped the last of the buttons in perfect synchronization with the words, 'Look – but don't touch.'

'Don't –'

'Exactly.' A shake of the head, an imperceptible inching closer. 'Don't. Don't touch. Just look.' And, angling her chin, she stifled the ripples of disgust and held his gaze with a massive surge of will. 'Look, Jared,' she entreated softly, freeing the fabric from the waistband of her skirt and tugging it taut across her breasts, the shameless thrust of her nipples. 'Yours,' she insisted, green eyes oozing hate, meeting hate full-on and returning it unblinkingly. 'All yours,' she invited smokily, and, pulling the gaping edges of her blouse apart, she thrust her upper body forward in defiance. 'Here you are, Jared. Feast your eyes.'

Silence. The atmosphere so thick she could have cut it with a knife. And Jared staring at her, staring through her, just the tightly clenched fists hinting at a chink in that rigid self-control.

Stevie's mind smiled. Shameless to the end, she parted her lips, opened her mouth a fraction, moistened twin thumbs with her tongue and allowed the thumbs to circle the swollen buds at the centre of her breasts.

'No!'

'Yes!' she insisted as the eye contact severed. 'Yes, yes, yes! Because you want me –'

'Fine! Here! Now!'

Stevie's head shot up, and, catching her start of panic, Jared laughed, snaring her wrist and tugging her hard against him.

'What's the matter?' he scorned in turn, grinding his hips against hers, the shock of his arousal driving the breath from her lungs. 'Had a change of mind?' he queried silkily, twisting her round to pin her against the desk. Not with hands, not vicious fingers, not even the contempt blasting out from those frigid black eyes, just hip to hip contact that triggered the heat of desire in Stevie's wayward mind and body. 'About to back away like the teasing little madam we both know you are?' he queried nastily, moving against her. 'Oh, no! Too late, lady. No one, but no one,' he emphasiszed frigidly, 'plays games with Jared Wilde. You want me,' he insisted matter-of-factly. 'You've got me.'

He kissed her. Stevie's mouth parting of its own accord, his tongue sweeping into the warm moistness beyond, sweeping round, finding her tongue and repulsing her tongue, an insulting invasion that was over in a fraction of a moment. Stevie's gasp of protest as Jared raised his head provoked a throaty laugh.

Another kiss, another fleeting exploration. Stevie's newly clamped lips were all the spur he needed to punish her, and punish her he did, relaxing the pressure of his mouth, lips persuading, caressing, coaxing, barely touching, a feather-light brush that was almost sheer imagination, and Stevie was moaning, was pushing against him, the fabric of his shirt frustrating her need. Skin against skin – oh, God, Yes! Fingers. Hands moulding the curves, thumbs nudging the nipples. Too right to be wrong. She loved him, she wanted him, she needed him – No! she silently screamed as Jared pulled away.

'Look but don't touch?' he scorned. 'And who do you think you're kidding? You're insatiable.'

'You and me both, hey, Jared?'

'I go for quality, not quantity,' he reminded her, eyes raining hate. 'And, whilst you clearly offer the latter . . .' An eloquent shrug, a sneering curl of the lips before he thrust her away in disgust. Snatching her jacket from the back of the chair where an over-warm Stevie had earlier draped it, he tossed it carelessly onto the desk beside her. 'Put it on,' he ordered icily. 'Make yourself decent.'

Left trembling in the middle of the room while Jared pointedly turned his back, Stevie folded her arms across her naked breasts, the waves of loathing threatening to swamp her. Hate. Stevie's hate, not Jared's. Hate. Disgust. Contempt. Shame. Most of all shame. But not for Jared. Not even for that single night of love. Because she loved him, had worshipped him with mind, soul and body and would treasure the memory for the rest of her life. No regrets – or leastways, she amended, facing the truth, not for loving Jared. It was living with the hurt she'd unwittingly done to Dee that was eating away her.

Catching a hot trickle of salt on her cheeks, she brushed it away with the back of her hand, reaching for her bag, not caring that Jared would note the soft rustle of tissue, the give-away blowing of her nose. She buttoned the blouse with fingers that shook before shrugging the jacket over her shoulders, and then suddenly in need of some support, sank down into the chair behind the desk.

Go, Jared, she silently pleaded, eyes fastened on that rigid, unforgiving spine. Go.

As if sensing her silent scrutiny, Jared moved, spinning one of the swivel chairs around and straddling the seat in reverse, leaning forward to rest his arms on the back-rest, black eyes full of hate.

'You know something, Stevie?' he entreated confidentially. 'Do you know what really hurt? Do you? *Do* you?' he repeated frigidly. 'No,' he scorned, with a contemptuous shake of the head, 'I don't suppose you do know – or care. But you're going to hear it anyway. Caterina. She's a thousand times the woman you'll ever be and yet you didn't even give her so much as a second thought.'

'Wrong, Jared. I phoned the villa, spoke to Franca – Ah, yes, Franca,' Stevie mused, lips twisting bitterly. And the flare of emotion in Jared's eyes was surely wishful thinking on her part. 'I might have known she'd keep it to herself. Not that it matters,' she reminded him tightly. 'Caterina was getting better and that's all I needed to know.'

She paused, moistened her dry lips, searched his face, searching for the words to reach him. A waste of time maybe, but she had to try, had to make the effort for her own peace of mind.

'I know you really won't care one way or another,' she said softly, imploringly, aware that Jared had already dropped the shutters, pointedly shutting her out, 'but I liked her. She's a very special lady and she made me feel at home.'

'Part of the family? And quite a family at that,' he conceded bitterly. 'With my sultry sister-in-law batting come-to-bed eyes across the antipasto. Though, come to think of it, since you and Franca are cast from the same mould, it's hardly surprising you felt at home.' His smile spread, an ugly flash of brilliant white teeth. 'Welcome to the family,' he mockingly entreated. 'Which makes you what, I wonder? Honorary sister? Honorary cousin? Honorary aunt to Gian, perhaps? Or how about –?'

'Wife, Jared? Not that I'm offering. I was thinking more in terms of the one you have already.'

A sharp hiss of indrawn breath. That had thrown him.

'Helena –'

'Ah, you recall the lady's name? How reassuring.'

'Who the hell's –'

'Been speaking out of turn? Why, no one, Jared,' she soothed, saccharine-sweetly. 'Only Helena. And, since the lady is your wife, I'd say she's entitled to her views. Strong views too.'

'I can imagine. But you can spare me the gory details because I really don't want to know. And for your information,' he tagged on frigidly, 'my marriage was over years ago.'

'The marriage – but not the relationship, hey, Jared?' Stevie scorned.

'Meaning?'

'Meaning sex. A cosy afternoon in bed. Bed. With Helena. And then, six hours later, insatiable Jared Wilde has the nerve to switch his attentions to me.'

'I didn't –'

'Spend the afternoon with Helena? Don't lie, Jared. How else did she know you were in town?'

'Franca –'

'She simply filled in the gaps. Telephoned Helena like the loyal sister she is and told her about Jared's under-dressed, over-painted English plaything. Hardly surprising she had to come along and see the exhibition for herself. Would you believe, the word "tart" managed to creep into the conversation?'

'Knowing Helena, nothing would surprise me. So?'

Stevie shrugged. 'I guess Franca hit the nail on the head in the first place,' she acknowledged tersely. 'I'm your current bit of stuff. Correction. Past tense. Over and done with but good while it lasted. A bit like your marriage, according to Helena. Not to mention a certain afternoon,' she tagged on slyly. 'And before you trot out another denial, there were too many details for Helena – or Franca – to have stumbled on them by chance. You –'

'Fine!' The roar of an angry animal as Jared thumped the desk with the heel of his fist, set the paperweight jangling. Horrible, grating noises that set Stevie's teeth on edge, would ring in her ears for days to come. 'You want the truth, then I'll give you the truth. Yes, Stevie,' he carelessly informed her. 'I spent the afternoon with Helena and I enjoyed each and every moment. Satisfied now?'

CHAPTER 19

Satisfied? Oh, definitely satisfied. After all, she'd finally succeeded in dragging the admission out of Jared. An afternoon of fun with his ex-wife. Not that it mattered to Stevie. It was Dee he'd really been cheating on. With Helena. With Stevie herself. So – as far as Stevie was concerned, Helena didn't count at all. So why did it hurt? she asked herself. Why did Jared's whole sneering condemnation of Stevie matter in the least? Tramp, trollop, slut. And she'd allowed him to believe it, willed him believe it. Safer that way, she acknowledged, surreptitiously brushing away a rogue tear. Because Jared wouldn't want her any more, and so Jared would leave her alone, would focus his attention on Dee.

'I'd sooner you than me,' Dee had gleefully conceded, helping Lorna and Stevie shepherd the girls onto the train, settle their luggage in the spaces between the seats. 'Disneyland Paris.

346

Now, Paris on its own I could take, assuming Jared was feeling romantic. But Disneyland?' She'd pulled a wry face. 'All those children,' she'd confided. 'Not to mention the forty-fives and over who've never grown up. Not my idea of fun at all. Still, I guess you know what you're doing.'

Escaping, Stevie could have told her. Only didn't And she *had* promised Rosa, and, whilst Stevie hadn't missed her daughter's birthday after all, thanks to Jared, a promise was a promise, and especially to a child.

'Say hello to Dumbo for me,' Dee had reminded them, hugging Rosa and Kelly in turn. 'And Mickey and Minnie and each and every one of those hundred and one Dalmatians. And, just in case you step into your favouritest story of all,' she'd added, blowing a kiss as the train shunted into life, 'watch out for the Big Bad Wolf.'

Too late, Stevie could have cried. Could have cried and cried and cried. And, when no one was looking, that was exactly what she did.

'You're losing weight.'

'Jealous, Lorna?'

'As hell. I only have to think the word "diet" and my waistline starts to explode. I thought going back to work would have helped,' she confided wistfully. 'But the moment Tom and I reach home, we crack open a bottle of wine.'

Stevie grinned. 'Welcome to the real world, Lorna. I believe it's called stress. Some of us have suffered it for years. But don't worry, she reassured her airily. 'Once the job settles down, so will your weight. Assuming you're prepared to give up that mountain of chocolate, that is.'

'So what's your excuse?'

'For what?'

'The waistline. Twenty-four inches and shrinking. Something's on your mind, and before you smile and bat those luminous green eyes and pretend there's nothing wrong, I know. I've known you too long. Andrew?' she mused. 'And the trials of sharing a bathroom with a man who spends more time in there than you do? Or . . .?'

'Or?' Stevie smiled despite herself. Lorna's scathing assessment of Andrew was uncannily accurate, and, since Stevie herself was daily uncovering aspects of her cousin she'd never remotely suspected, Lorna's insight was nothing short of amazing.

Lorna shrugged, blue eyes full of hidden knowledge. 'Just, or. You're a big girl, Stevie, you can probably work it out for yourself.'

'Jared.' Statement. Fact. Because if Dee was Stevie's oldest friend, Lorna came a very close second. Very close indeed. Perceptive too. All in all, thoroughly unnerving.

'And?'

'And nothing.' Literally, thank heavens, the stomach cramps she'd been praying for having put in a belated appearance. A whole week of wondering, watching, waiting, praying, the thought of history repeating itself nothing short of madness. An Italian man, an Italian affair, an Italian baby. Devastating. But luckily, for Stevie at least, not true.

'Stevie Cooper,' Lorna berated softly. 'You're a liar, and a bad one at that.'

'Yes, Lorna.'

'So – sit yourself down, pour us both a well-earned glass of wine and spill the beans.'

'You won't like it.'

'If that man's been leading you a dance, playing fast and loose with your emotions, too right I won't. Only he hasn't.'

'No.' Stevie smiled. 'Got it in one. Which means there's nothing to confess. Just . . .'

'Rome?' Lorna supplied with another flash of insight. 'Three nights alone with a hunk like Jared, and surprise, surprise, nature takes its course.' Lorna's eyes sparkled like the bubbles in the glass she was cradling. 'Oh, Stevie,' she breathed. 'How wonderful.'

'Yes.' Another smile, a tender smile. Stevie remembering, savouring, each and every moment. Precious. Not sordid or sullied. Because the angry words, like Stevie's pangs of conscience, hadn't come into play until later.

'And? Come on, Stevie,' Lorna chivvied eagerly. 'You can't keep a girl in suspense. It's inhuman. After all,' she reminded her with a very winning smile, 'I am your best friend.'

'Yes,' Stevie acknowledged, raising her glass in

a mockery of a toast. 'And in case it's slipped your mind, Lorna Deighton, the same can be said for Dee.'

'Dee. Oh, hell.' Lorna's eyes were fleetingly cloudy. 'Poor Dee. What on earth are you going to tell her?'

Nothing. She was over the worst, had thankfully faced Dee before the ordeal of facing Jared. Nothing to say, nothing to do. Just hope. Hope that Dee didn't get hurt. Hope that Jared wouldn't tell her – ever. Unlikely, Stevie supposed, clutching the straw of reassurance like a lifeline. More likely he'd continue to play fast and loose with Dee's affections and trade her in when someone new took his fancy.

'Stevie Cooper! You're as bad as that cousin of yours.'

Nanna's voice, jolting Stevie rudely back to the present.

'What is it, girl? Judging by the look on your face, I'd say you were miles away. And unless my eyes are deceiving me,' she added with a lightning change of tone, 'you're losing weight.' She reached across to pat Stevie's clenched hand, her own hand parchment-dry and shrivelled from the muscle-wasting disease that had stolen her mobility but thankfully left her mind unimpaired. 'Oh, Stevie,' she probed, a lifetime of knowledge in the depth of her eyes. 'What is it? What's the matter, love?'

Seeing the concern, the worry, the love, Stevie banished the shadows, opened her fingers and captured Nanna's hand in hers. 'Nothing. *Nothing*,' she insisted with a squeeze of reassurance. 'Nothing for you to worry about, Nan. Just the age-old story,' she insisted briskly, crossing her fingers at the tiny white lie. 'Too much to do and never enough hours in the day. And, since I am on the verge of moving house . . .'

An audible sniff, eyes as sharp as needles raking the lines of Stevie's face. 'But you are eating?'

'Yes, Nan. Three square meals a day.'

'And there's nothing wrong with Rosa?'

'No, Nan. Rosa's fine. She'd be here this afternoon but she's out for the day with Anna and Kelly. But if it helps to put your mind at rest, we'll pop in and say hello first thing tomorrow.'

'There's no need to bother. I know how busy you are. But I was wondering . . .'

'Mmm?' A wide-eyed Stevie swallowed a smile; the smell of burnt martyr hung tangibly on the air.

Another strange, speculative, probing glance. 'I –'

'No, Nan,' Stevie cut in swiftly. 'I know what you're thinking and you're wrong. I'm fine. I promise I'm eating,' she insisted softly. 'And I'm not about to fade away to nothing. Honestly. I'm simply overdoing things.'

And, since Nanna wasn't the only one concerned about her weight loss, it was time to shake off the pain of losing Jared and pull herself together. No more wallowing in misery, pushing the forkfuls of food around her plate until the food was cold and congealed. Mae. The shadow of anorexia. Only Stevie wasn't Mae, had never suffered the same torments as a child, had somehow found the strength to cope when life was dealing out more than its share of pain. Until now. Fiddlesticks, she told herself, and lots of other highly colourful words beginning with the letter F that would make the devil himself blush to hear. Fade away? For the love of a man? Any man? Not a cat in hell's chance.

'So –' Back in control and pouring the tea, reaching for the platefuls of sandwiches and cakes that appeared as if by magic at four o'clock sharp every afternoon, her mind seized on Nanna's opening comment. 'You're turn to come clean,' she insisted, biting into a delicate salmon pâté roll and savouring the taste on her tongue. 'What has Andrew done to upset you this time?'

'Nothing,' Nanna bit out. 'Hardly surprising since there's been neither sight nor sound of him. Expect him to drop in and see his old nan? Aye, and pigs might fly,' she derided. 'Not that I'm bothered. He's bad news, is Andrew Roxton, and between you, me and the gatepost, I'll be glad when you and Rosa have finally moved out.'

Stevie didn't reply, allowing Nan to vent her spleen, nodding, murmuring, only half attending. Definitely burnt martyr, she decided. Understandable, she supposed, since Andrew hadn't been around for months on end, and wasn't falling over to visit her now that he was. But bad news?

'Selfish. Self-centred. If you could trust Andrew Roxton with one thing,' Nanna railed, 'it's the ability to take care of number one. Heaven help the woman he marries. He's –'

'He's been good to me and Rosa,' Stevie reminded her, eyes silently pleading. For Nanna was feeling hurt, was hitting out, hurting Stevie in the process.

'Aye,' she agreed, in a different tone, not so much scathing as worried, Stevie decided, smothering a pang of alarm. 'You're right. But did it ever cross your mind to stop and wonder why?'

Because she was doing Andrew a favour, of course. A mutual favour. He'd needed to let the apartment and hadn't wanted to risk being landed with the tenants from hell. Offering it to Stevie had been the obvious thing to do. A base for Stevie and Rosa at a rent she could afford, while Andrew could rest assured the place was in good hands. An ideal arrangement.

Less ideal now that Andrew was home for good. Despite its size, the apartment was too small for the three of them. Or maybe Stevie was simply conscious that the needs of a lively seven-year-old didn't tie in with Andrew's sophisticated lifestyle. Two weeks. Two more weeks and they'd be moving into a house of their own. Escape from Jared in one respect, but with work on Monday morning looming like a shadow . . .

Stepping out of the shower, Stevie reached for the towel she'd left draped on the radiator, silently cursed the fact it had obviously slipped down the back, and, planing the water from her eyes, groped blindly at the rail.

'Allow me.'

'Andrew!' Cheeks on fire, Stevie's startled gaze locked with his, logging the amusement, the glance of approval as he dropped his eyes, allowed his heated gaze to travel the lines of her body in a slow, appraising glance that seemed to reach out to touch her, the almost imperceptible nod of Andrew's head chilling the blood in her veins.

Snatching the towel from his outstretched fingers, she pointedly turned her back, wrapped the towel around her shivering, damp body and waited for the click of the door that would tell her she was alone.

Only she wasn't. Her own hazy outline in the steamed up mirror was clearly flanked by another.

Andrew moved, slid his arms around her waist, his lips nuzzling the warm, fragrant skin of her shoulders.

'For God's sake, Andrew, what on earth do you

think you're doing?' she demanded, shaking free and pointedly pushing past, heading for the safety of her bedroom.

Halfway across the lounge, something awful struck her, and she pulled up sharp, allowing Andrew to run full pelt into her.

'That's my girl,' he growled, his arms going round her as he pulled her against him, began to nibble the sensitive skin at the nape of her neck.

'Andrew!' Stevie bit out, attempting to pull away without resorting to the instinctive use of her elbow. 'Have some sense. We're practically brother and sister.'

'Only we're not. And if it didn't stop Mae,' he carelessly informed her, the grip of his fingers tightening imperceptibly, 'I don't see why you should object.'

Stevie licked her dry lips. 'Mae?'

'But of course, Don't sound so surprised. It's practically the third millennium, Stevie. People do, you know.'

'Yes, but not when they're closely related. It's —'

'Fun?' he interrupted slyly.

'Practically indecent,' Stevie hissed, pulling free and swinging round to face him. 'It's —'

'All above board and legal, my dear. In fact, the same can be said for marriage. Not that I'm proposing, you understand.'

'Oh, but you are,' Stevie rasped, pulling the towel tight across her chest, her heart thumping

355

nineteen to the dozen as she struggled to stay calm. 'Sex. That is what you're proposing?' she queried icily. 'Nothing more, nothing less.'

'But lots of fun, Stevie.'

'Fine. Have fun if that's what you want. But not with me.'

'Why?'

'You *know* why. Legal or not, it's wrong, and there's not a thing you can say to make me think otherwise. Besides,' she tossed out absurdly, 'I don't love you—not in that sense.' Not in any sense, she was beginning to see, beginning to understand, too, some of Nanna's unvoiced concerns.

'Love?' A fastidious eyebrow disappeared into his hairline. 'Love?' he repeated incredulously, folding his arms and regarding her with thinly veiled amusement. 'Grow up, Stevie. You're a woman. You have needs. You can't reach the age of twenty-six and still be spouting all that adolescent tripe about love and marriage and roses around the doorframe. You'll be telling me next that you're still a virgin,' he sneered. 'How does that silly phrase go again? Convent-qualified and proud of it?'

Stevie went hot, then cold, the colour flooding her cheeks before draining away, leaving her eyes luminous pools in a chalk-white face. 'It's none of your damn business,' she rasped.

'Just idle curiosity,' he explained confidentially. 'Since I've never bedded a virgin, I was wondering how it would feel.'

'Sordid – with you at least. The very thought's enough to make me heave. Besides –' She broke off, horrified at what she'd nearly blurted out. And, no, it wasn't shame that kept her silent, more the need to protect something precious. For if her night of love with Jared had taught her nothing else, the knowledge that man and woman could give pleasure, receive pleasure, share pleasure, share love, was too precious to share with another living soul. Love – in Stevie's mind at least. And a moment to savour in the long, lonely years that lay ahead.

'Besides?' Andrew queried, eyes narrowing suddenly as they rested on her face, clearly not missing the guilty stain of colour.

'Nothing,' Stevie snapped. 'Nothing you'd understand.

He moved in, unnervingly close, so close she caught the faint whiff of brandy and smothered her distaste. 'So, try me,' he invited, dazzling her with the brilliance of his smile, a flash of white teeth that would have done a basking shark proud. 'Explain. Start off with, "Besides". Or the lead-in to it. Something about you and your over-sensitive sensibilities. The thought of sex – with me – or any man. Though maybe I was right in the first place,' he conceded grimly. 'Not so much the sex as the man. This man.

'Oh, Stevie, Stevie, Stevie,' he berated softly, moving his head from side to side. 'You really don't understand, do you, my dear? Well, let me spell it out for you. You're a big girl now, and this is the game of life. Life, Stevie. Man and woman. Alone. Together. Forget the skittish virgin routine; you've given yourself away. And, since you've nothing left to lose, why not simply cut your losses and come to bed with me? Who knows? You might even enjoy it. Besides,' he tossed out slyly, 'we both know that you owe me.'

'*Owe* you? And what the hell is that supposed to mean?' she demanded incredulously, the waves of nausea beginning to wash over her. Because she knew what he was hinting at, and, heaven help her, it was true – up to a point. But never, ever in the way Andrew was implying. She owed him. A luxury apartment at a rent she could afford, and now Andrew wanted his reward. Sex. Andrew and Stevie. Andrew and Mae. Which meant Rosa –

Oh, God! Stevie stuffed her fist into her mouth in an effort not to cry. Mae and Andrew. Handsome, dark-haired, dark-eyed Andrew. And Stevie had never known, had never suspected, never dreamed . . .

Unwittingly, she turned her head, focused on the photograph of Rosa, the end-of-school-year portrait given pride of place above the mantelpiece.

'Not guilty,' he lazily informed her, following the line of her gaze and uncannily reading her mind.

'Disappointed?' he queried slyly. 'Or relieved?'

'Disappointed, disgusted, disenchanted, disillusioned – with you. You're revolting. But as far as Rosa's concerned, I couldn't be more relieved.'

'Better the devil you know than the devil you don't, and talking of devils, Mr ALITANI himself dropped by –'

'His name,' she hissed, 'is Jared. Jared Wilde. And not that it makes a pennyworth of difference, but he's as British as you and me.'

'Maybe so – technically. But you can take it from me, there's more than a touch of the da –'

'Don't!' she bit out. 'Don't use that revolting word.'

'Don't speak the truth, you mean?' He shrugged. 'Now why, I wonder? Unless . . .' Black eyes narrowed in speculation as Stevie held her breath, half afraid that he'd guess, half hoping he'd guess so that she could use the knowledge to taunt him.

Because Andrew Roxton wasn't good enough to lick the boots of a man like Jared, yet still he had the nerve to despise him. Because Jared was everything Andrew was not: kind, considerate, caring, loving. Because Stevie was proud of Jared and everything he stood for, and far from being a source of shame, sleeping with Jared was something she could be proud of for the rest of her life. And in that case she'd be damned if she'd allow Andrew's racist taunts to goad her into giving him the truth. She knew; it was enough. And as for Andrew –

'Sleeping with the boss, Stevie?' he stunned her by asking. 'I'm right, aren't I, you little tramp? That's why you can afford to turn me down. That's why you've money enough to turn your back and walk away. Money, Stevie. And sex.'

'And if you believe that, Andrew Roxton, you need to see a shrink. Jared's seeing Dee, remember? He has been for weeks.'

He shrugged. 'Seeing, but not bedding, Stevie. You can take it from me; I know. Which means –'

'No! I don't want to know.' Stevie closed her eyes, blocking out the man, but not the truth. Not Dee. Please God, don't let Andrew hurt Dee – and yet please God he was telling the truth. Jared and Dee. Together – yet not together. And, hungry for love, Dee would trust Andrew in much the same way Stevie had, would look at this handsome, dark-haired, dark-eyed man and for a fleeting moment of madness would see Jared. A pale comparison, a ludicrous comparison in Stevie's mind. But Stevie wasn't Dee. And Dee had slept with Andrew. Not Jared, she consoled herself. A pyrrhic victory in its way. Because it really didn't matter any more. Jared and Dee, or Jared and countless dozens of others. Because if Jared really wanted Stevie, she'd hop into his bed so fast her feet wouldn't touch the ground. Only he didn't. Not even for sex.

She swung away, her mind teeming with thoughts. She had to get away – now, today. She couldn't stay. Not now. Not knowing. Andrew. The man she'd treated as a brother, loved as a brother. And he'd let her down, had clearly been in the apartment when Stevie had returned home and run herself a shower. Silent. Lurking. Deliberate. He'd misled her. And now his solid form was suddenly blocking her way, filling the doorway, the expression in his eyes sending a chill of premonition running the length of her spine.

'No!'

'Yes!' Snatching at her arms, his fingers bit deep as he pulled her roughly against him, his mouth searching for hers. A frantic Stevie moved her head from side to side in an effort to deny him.

Only Andrew simply laughed, folded his arms around her, pinning her arms to her sides as he played kiss-chase across her cheeks, his warm, wet mouth branding. With the nausea back with a vengeance, Stevie swayed dizzily, caught a sound she vaguely recognized and strained to make her mind penetrate the muzzy fog of hate and panic.

A bell. The doorbell. Short. Sharp. Impatient.

'No!' Andrew bit out as she made to pull away.

'Oh, but yes!' Stevie contradicted, and, silently blessing Dee for those self-defence classes they'd attended in the sole hope of Dee meeting a hunky Mr Right, she raised her knee, aiming for his groin. The satisfyingly dull thud of connection was almost drowned out by Andrew's howl of pain as he jack-knifed.

Free, for a precious few moments, she darted the length of the hallway and flung open the door without so much as a backward glance.

'Jared! Oh, thank God!' she blurted hysterically, Jared's stunned expression turning her sob into a giggle. 'I – he – I –'

'Rosa?' he queried tightly, his sharp gaze taking everything in at a glance.

She shook her head. 'Anna. with Kelly. She –'

'Hush,' he insisted with a reassuring squeeze of her shoulders. 'Later.'

Five giant steps to reach the figure doubled up and moaning in the middle of the floor. Hands reaching for his collar, jerking him roughly to his feet.

'What the hell –'

'Time to leave,' Jared explained grimly, iron fingers grabbing his lower arm. 'Now. Move!' A deft twist and in a matter of seconds Andrew's arm was pinned behind his back as Jared frog-marched him with brutal unconcern out through the door.

Don't let him hit him. Please God, don't let him hit him, Stevie silently prayed, sinking to the cushions, the thought of Jared on an assault charge more than she could bear.

The door swung open. 'Jared –'

He crossed to kneel before her, eyes fastened on

her face, their expression unreadable. 'He didn't hurt you?'

'Only my pride,' Stevie conceded, shivering, trembling, the tears beginning to stream down her cheeks when she realized how close she'd been to disaster. 'I – didn't know, never dreamed –'

'Hush. Later,' he repeated, hugging her, holding her, the warmth of his body pouring life into her veins. And yet the moment he sensed that she'd calmed, Jared gently pulled away. 'Here.' He thrust a handkerchief between her clenched fingers. 'Dry your eyes. I'll fix you a brandy.'

Brandy. Towelling robe. Though heaven alone knew why he'd gone into the master bedroom in search of them. Oh, no? Stevie froze, the implication shaming. But at least now Jared would know. Not a bathrobe, not a hairbrush, not a trace of Stevie in Andrew's room.

She began to giggle, part relief, part shame, part nerves.

'Feeling better?' Jared queried dryly, having taken the chair opposite, the gesture speaking volumes. She was on her own. Jared had stepped in to help a neighbour in need and now she was on her own. 'Finding something amusing, Stevie?'

'You,' she explained, making an effort to pull herself together. 'Charging in like Sir Galahad despite thinking the worst, picking a man up off the floor, dusting him down and throwing him out of his own home.'

'So –' A sharp hiss of indrawn breath. 'I was right. He has moved in. No – don't bother trying to deny it,' he entreated tersely. 'I've seen him around often enough, and since I called round earlier . . .'

'Yes.' Stevie risked a glance from beneath her lashes, logged the expression in a set of dark, brooding pools and wished she hadn't bothered. 'Andrew mentioned that you'd called. Something to do with work on Monday?' she queried politely, and then, since the thought had been chasing about in her mind for the past three weeks, 'Always assuming you want me?'

'I – naturally the firm wants you,' he conceded coolly. 'You're good at your job – first-class, in fact. Why else would I bother to poach you from Tom in the first place?'

Why else indeed? Stevie scorned, only silently, wondering just how long she could stand working for Jared, loving Jared, wanting Jared, and yet enduring his tangible contempt.

She sipped at the brandy, an over-generous, undiluted measure that was beginning to put some colour back into her cheeks.

Jared had joined her, she realized as he raised his glass, his hand cradling the balloon.

'You're hurt.'

'Just a scratch,' he insisted, following the line of her gaze, and he smiled grimly, switched the brandy balloon to his left hand and flexed the fingers of his right. 'See?' He held the hand up for Stevie's inspection. 'Nothing broken.'

'I don't agree. You've grazed the skin.' She placed her glass on the table beside her, stumbled awkwardly to her feet. 'I'll fetch the first-aid box –'

'*I'll* fetch the first aid box,' Jared insisted, up on his feet in an instant. 'If you'll tell me where to find it?'

'I – easier to do it myself,' she explained, heading for the kitchen and shockingly aware of Jared just a step or two behind.

She stood and watched as Jared rinsed his hand under cold running water, Stevie's offer to bathe it having been politely and firmly declined.

'Here.' She offered a square of kitchen paper, hardly antiseptic, she could allow, but better than making a fuss, and then pointedly removed the top from the tube of ointment normally kept for Rosa's grazed knees.

Jared took the hint, smeared a pearl of cream over his knuckle and grinned. 'I'll live,' he explained with a flash of wry humour. 'And, no, I didn't kill him, much though I wanted to. Just put a dent or two in his ego to match the dent or two in his head. He'll live. Disappointed, Stevie?' he queried slyly. 'Or relieved?'

That was twice today she'd heard those words. First Andrew and now Jared.

'Relieved – on your account,' she told him, smiling despite herself.

Seeing the smile, Jared's face darkened. 'How typical,' he jeered. 'Trust a woman to relish the thought of two grown men squabbling over her.'

'Only you weren't, hey, Jared?' she reminded him coolly. 'Your visit was strictly business.'

'Since I like my women a little less shop-soiled,' he sneeringly conceded, 'too true. But a word of warning. Play about with a thug like Roxton and you could end up with more than you bargained for.'

'As if you care.'

'I care. Believe it or not.'

'Fine. You can stop worrying. I'm moving out. Now. Tonight.'

'That's what they all say,' Jared informed her grimly. 'But I've seen it before and I'll doubtless see it again. You'll be back – assuming you ever leave, that is. It's like an addiction. A guy turns on his macho act and intelligent women go weak at the knees. But you –' He broke off, his contemptuous gaze flicking over her – less of an appraisal than a dismissal, Stevie realized, going cold, oh, so cold. 'You disappoint me. I thought Little Red Riding Hood was made of sterner stuff.'

Stevie shrugged. Let him think the worst. Jared was peeved. He wasn't the only Big Bad Wolf in the woods and Stevie's rejection stung, all the more because Jared believed that Stevie had rejected him for Andrew.

Simmering silence. Footsteps muffled in the thick pile of the carpet, that interminable length of the hall.

Reaching the front door, Jared halted, a quizzical eyebrow raised. 'Monday morning bright and early?' he queried politely.

'Of course,' she insisted equally politely, and then, unable to bear the sudden proximity, she pushed past him, reaching for the handle. Jared's low growl at the body to body contact was music to her ears.

'No!' Stevie pulled away, shrank back against the wall. 'Not here,' she said simply, imploringly, eyes fastened on his face. 'This is Andrew's home, remember?'

Thunder and lightning, both in his eyes. Not to mention the contempt. 'Oh, yes. And you're leaving – tonight. So, tell me, Stevie, where will you go exactly?' Polite. Clearly unbelieving.

'Lorna and Tom's. Or Dee's,' she murmured defiantly, daring him to contradict her. 'Or, if all else fails, we'll find ourselves a guest house. There's no shortage of accommodation in a seaside resort.'

'In high summer? I wouldn't bank on it. Still, it shouldn't be a problem. I'm sure your . . .' pause, a deliberate choice of words '. . . friends will be happy to oblige. Though heaven knows what you'll tell them.'

'The truth, Jared. Andrew and I have quarrelled. Nothing more, nothing less. They know

367

the set-up: you can take it from me they'll understand.'

'You surprise me. Dee, yes, she's naïve enough
to think you could love the guy. But Tom and
Lorna?' A shrug of powerful shoulders spoke
volumes.

He reached the door, paused, turned. Their
glances locked and Stevie clenched her fingers,
digging her nails into her palms, aware of her
control hanging by a thread. Because she loved
him. And he despised her. And the nightmare
events of the afternoon were beginning to take
their toll.

'Stevie?'

'Jared?'

'Nothing. It's not important, not any more.
You've made your decision and I guess I'll learn
to live with it. But just for the record, that
afternoon with Helena – oh, yes, it really did
happen,' he explained as her head snapped up,
the knife-blade twisting in her belly. 'Helena, me
and half a dozen lawyers. The divorce. The final
settlement. Signed, sealed and legal, and if it cost
me my share of the family business, it was worth
every penny and more. Leastways,' he amended
tersely, his voice full of pain. 'that's how it
seemed later, spending the night with you.
And, then – ah, yes, then,' he reminded her
harshly, black eyes pinning her, full of silent,
simmering hate. 'Then.'

Another eloquent shrug as he swung away, and

Stevie watched, crying, dying as Jared walked away, never to return. Not her Jared. Not the man she loved, wanted, needed. They were strangers. Neighbours – briefly, since Stevie would go the moment the door closed behind him – colleagues. Polite. Icily polite. Because a single night of love had gone so drastically wrong. No. Not the love, she told herself. The lies. Helena's lies tied to Stevie's belated pangs of conscience.

'Jared –'

'*I loved you*,' he revealed with devastating frankness, thumping the door with the heel of his fist. 'I'd loved you almost from the moment we'd met. First impressions,' he reminded her cruelly, angling his head, the contempt in eyes freezing the blood in her veins. 'Ironic, hey? Because Helena knew, as did Franca. And as for Caterina – No –' He broke off, shook his head, clenched his fists, banishing the demons of his mind with a massive surge of will.

'Oh, Stevie, Stevie,' he berated softly. 'You swallowed Helena's scorned little wife act hook, line and sinker and destroyed us both along the way. Why, Stevie? *Why?*' he repeated incredulously. 'After everything we'd shared. The loving, the kissing, the touching, the sharing, the belonging. I loved you. I worshipped you. And yet you chose to believe that woman's lies. Oh, Stevie,' he repeated, moving his head from side to side in dreadful condemnation. 'Why?'

And then he smiled, a mocking, taunting,

goading smile that froze the blood in her veins. 'But then, I was forgetting. It doesn't really matter, hey, Stevie?' he conceded tersely. 'You, me, Helena, the lies.' He raised a hand, gave a derisory snap of the fingers. 'Irrelevant. You and Roxton. You and Roxton all along. Only gullible Jared Wilde hadn't the sense to see it. So, tell me – just for the record, of course – tell me, Stevie, how long precisely?'

'Andrew and I? We go back a long time,' she conceded thickly. 'And, yes, I've loved him since the moment we met. But when it comes to first impressions, Jared, I'd say that makes us quits.'

'Oh, yes? And how do you make that out?' he scorned.

'Andrew,' she told him simply. 'He's my cousin.'

CHAPTER 20

A soft click as the door pulled to. Stevie didn't look, didn't want to watch him go, wouldn't see in any case, not with the tears already streaming down her cheeks. He loved her. Past tense, she amended, choking, sliding down the wall and sinking to her bottom, hugging her knees, fighting for control. He had loved her. Then. And now? Now he hated and despised her. For believing Helena's lies and destroying something precious.

Not true, she consoled herself. Helena's clever manipulations had simply jolted Stevie's conscience belatedly into life. Dee. Betrayed by her best friend. Another irrelevance, given Andrew's less than subtle hints. So – all for nothing. She loved him. She'd lost him.

A sudden whoosh of air as the door swung open on its hinges. Stevie's head jerked up in alarm, the blur of tears blinding. Andrew.

'No!' Panic. Stumbling to her feet, too late –
'Stevie. No, Stevie.' Hands restraining, arms

going round her, tugging her into the solid lines of his body. 'It's all right, sweetheart, it's me. You're safe. It's over now. You're safe with me. Oh, Stevie, Stevie, Stevie,' he crooned in anguish, almost squeezing the breath from her lungs. 'I'm sorry. Every word, every insult, each and every revolting accusation –'

'Words, Jared. My fault as much as yours.'

'Hurtful words, my love, but if it's any consolation I didn't for a minute believe. I –'

'Jared –'

'No,' he insisted tersely, 'let me finish. Let me explain. My fault, Stevie, and I should have known, should have realized. The most wonderful night of my life,' he conceded, black eyes pinning her and swirling with emotion. 'And I should have believed. Only –'

'I froze you out, wouldn't let you close.'

'And because I didn't understand,' he explained, holding her, hugging her, squeezing her, 'I hit back at the woman I love. I love you, Stevie,' he told her simply, softly, gazing down into her eyes and seeing to the centre of her soul. 'And I think, hope, *believe* that you love me, that you can somehow forgive me for putting us through hell. I love you, woman,' he repeated fiercely. 'And nothing and no one is ever going to come between us. Not Helena, not Roxton, not Dee.'

'Dee?' Stevie raised her tear-stained face, a nervous tongue moistening her parched lips.

He nodded, the hope in his eyes shadowed by doubt. 'Dee,' he repeated. 'The missing link. And, unless I'm reading things wrong again, the key to your rejection. You love me – or at least,' he amended tersely, 'that night in Rome you loved me enough to give me something precious.'

'And me the original vestal virgin?' Stevie teased, her mind beginning to smile as her body began to melt.

Jared winced, his pain Stevie's pain, and she reached up, tracing the angles and plains of his face with her fingers, exploring each and every pore of skin, every rasp of stubble, love in her eyes, love in her fingers. Hands and fingers sliding around his neck. Fingers plunging into the thick mass of hair and urging his head down.

'Stevie –'

'Hush,' she insisted, her words an unwitting echo of Jared's. 'Later. We've all the time in the world, my love. And since actions,' she reminded him smokily, her mouth against his, 'are said to speak louder than words, here's your chance to prove it.'

She was kissing him, pushing her body into the hard lines of his, savouring the taste of him, the smell of him, the feel of him. Jared's arms enfolded her, his hands caressing, pushing the bathrobe free of her shoulders, just the towel she'd wrapped around herself and practically double-knotted, standing between Stevie and her modesty.

Precious little modesty as Stevie smiled, saw the pain in his eyes, the love in his eyes, the need in his eyes and loosened the towel, allowed it to drop to the floor, unwanted, unneeded. Jared's hiss of indrawn breath was music to her ears. He wanted her. He loved her. Love, want, need, but most of all the love.

She opened her arms. 'All yours,' she told him thickly. 'Now and always.'

'Here? Hell, Stevie, we can't,' he reminded her as she danced back into his arms, rubbed herself against him. He caught her to him, kissed her, caressed her, urging her body to meld with his, and, yes, he wanted her! Hard, wonderfully hard, and straining against her. A shameless Stevie pushed against him, a slow swirl of hips guaranteed to enflame and –

'Jared! What are you doing? Put me down,' she insisted as he scooped her into his arms, began to stride the length of the hall. 'Jared!'

'Not here,' he growled, dipping his head to kiss her, briefly, urgently. 'And, since I refuse to wait so much as another moment –'

'You can't!' she insisted as he reached the open doorway. 'No!' She was wriggling like a worm on the end of the line. 'Put me down,' she squealed. 'Jared! Let me grab the towel at least.'

'No time,' he informed her thickly. A waste of time in any case, since he'd already crossed the threshold, and Stevie closed her eyes, praying the neighbours wouldn't choose that particular moment to arrive at their front door. Not to mention a host of visitors via the lifts.

A dozen fast paces and they'd be safe, she calculated swiftly. After all, hadn't Rosa hop-skipped the distance often enough?

Five, six, seven and Jared had swung her down, Stevie's bare feet connecting with a carpet sure enough, but not the inches-thick pile in Jared's sumptuous lounge.

Her lids flew open, the thrill of panic gripping her, for Jared simply smiled a lazy smile, spread his hands. 'Here?' he suggested absurdly, the laughter dancing in his eyes. 'Or, if madam could control her baser instincts –'

'Murder in the vestibule?' Stevie queried, shivering – part cold, part with desire, part with the thrill of possible discovery. 'And don't assume it wouldn't cross my mind. You, sir, will get us both arrested. Have you no shame?'

'*I'm* decently dressed,' he reminded her.

'Not for much longer,' she informed him grimly. And then, calling his bluff, 'I'm game if you are.'

A single eyebrow disappeared into his hairline. A hand was at his throat, snapping the buttons of his shirt in much the way Stevie had popped the buttons of her blouse that dreadful afternoon in her office. The very thought was enough to make her cheeks flame. Angry words, insults, goadings, not to mention her own shameless behaviour.

Shameless now. Jared, carelessly shrugging

free of the shirt, tossing it away, his hands already snapping the button at his waistband and reaching for the zipper.

'You wouldn't, Jared?' Stevie breathed, eyes enormous green pools.

'Wouldn't I?' he challenged, tugging slowly but deliberately. Stevie's eyes were riveted on the bulge beneath the boxers. 'Well, if you say so . . .'

'Jared! No! Have some sense,' she cried, and, catching the sound she'd been straining her ears for, the low hum of the lift, she made to dart past.

'Hey, not so fast!' He snared her wrist, pulling her up short, tugging her against him, and his mouth was on hers, his tongue sweeping through, exploring, an exceedingly thorough exploration. Stevie collapsed against him, relaxing, responding – only the moment he sensed her co-operation, of course, Jared pulled away.

'Shameless,' he hissed gleefully. 'For if anyone gets us arrested –'

No time for threats. A mad dash the last couple of yards as the lift doors swung open, and a giggling Stevie tumbled over the threshold of Jared's front door to the sound of drifting voices.

'Stevie?'

'Jared?' Sober now, the passion controlled, the tension mounting as his eyes locked with hers.

'I love you, Stevie.'

'I know,' she told him simply, opening her arms in silent invitation, and when Jared closed his eyes, leaned back against the wall, Stevie read a wealth of remorse in each and every angle of the face she loved, and she cried inside. And smiled. Because she had the means to heal the pain.

'Sweetheart —'

Stepping close, she placed her head against his chest, feeling the rapid beat of his heart beneath her cheek. 'Words, Jared,' she reminded him softly, her fingers scrunching the curls, nudging a hidden nipple. 'Just words. Anger, hurt, pain, misunderstanding. I hit out at you, you hit out at me and the vicious circle is forged. Only not any more. Because I love you. Because you love me. Show me how much you love me,' she implored, her hand travelling downwards and sliding beneath the waistband of the boxer shorts, the shock of connection thrilling her.

'Please, Stevie,' Jared groaned, snaring her wrist in an effort to halt her.

Stevie simply smiled, reaching up on tiptoe to kiss him, her left hand sliding down to take its place.

'Oh, God, Stevie,' he moaned, moving against her. 'I love you, I want you, I need you —'

'Fine! Here! Now!' she all but barked, and Jared's head snapped back in alarm. 'Oh, yes,' she told him solemnly. 'I remember every word, every insult, every nuance of distaste. And I love you. Because of it, in spite of it — take your pick,' she invited calmly, far more calmly than she felt, but she was determined to lay the ghost of that dreadful afternoon once and for all. 'I love you.

Here, now, always. And believe me, Jared Wilde,'
she insisted in a different tone, a saucy tone, 'if
you don't place me down upon that hearth-rug
and take me and love me and pleasure me, and
take me again, and soon, then –'

'Yes, Stevie?' he interrupted, sweeping her
back into his arms and striding into the bedroom, where he dropped her into the centre of
the magnificent double bed. Quick as a flash he
was covering her body, pinning her arms against
the pillows, his eyes full of dancing lights. 'Yes,
Stevie?' he prompted as she tried to wriggle free.
'You were saying? If I don't –'

'Oh, but you will,' she told him smokily.
'Later. It's a date. You, me and that hearth-
rug. So in the meantime, Mr Wilde, might I
suggest that you dispense with the trappings of
modesty and –'

'Take you, pleasure you, love you?' he queried,
dropping his remaining clothes onto the floor and
stretching out beside her, the long length of his
body melding with hers. 'Love you, love you, love
you,' he murmured, kissing her, touching her,
tasting her. Mouth to mouth, lips to lips, skin
against skin and Stevie was writhing, every touch
a brand, every touch a pleasure.

'Oh, God, Jared. Jared!' she protested as he
pulled away, knelt between her legs, his very
glance paying homage.

Eyes, the mirrors of his soul, swirled with
emotion. Exploring her face, her neck, the hol-

low in her throat. A reverent sweep downwards, over breasts that tightened and strained for a touch that Jared continued to deny her. Down again, to the lush triangle of curls at the apex of her legs, a pressing invitation for fingers to thread, to explore, to caress. Only Jared didn't. Simply looked. Touching with a glance, scorching with a glance. Thigh to knee, knee to toe and back again, over the lazy sweep of creamy white thighs that were beginning to tremble. And still Jared didn't touch. Except with his eyes. Loving, caressing, worshipping.

'Please, Jared,' Stevie urged, aware that the moment he touched her she'd explode.

He shook his head. 'Too soon,' he murmured in anguish. 'I want you. Hell, woman, how I want you. But –'

'No! Take me. Now! Here! Please, Jared,' she entreated. 'And again and again and all night long. Only make it soon. Please, love, make it soon.'

'Too soon,' he crooned, but he was kissing her, eyes, cheeks, mouth, and down. An erotic swirl of tongue into the hollow of her throat, and down. Hands and fingers creating havoc, mouth creating havoc, and Stevie was writhing, was shamelessly lifting her hips in an effort to make the connection she craved. Only Jared, tantalizing Jared, was holding himself aloof, his self-control hanging by a thread, his journey barely begun.

A shower of tiny kisses from throat to navel, a

379

pause to explore the valley between her breasts along the way, lips nuzzling, tongue lapping, licking and then darting into the puckered dimple . . . And down, nudging aside the curls, a fleeting touch that triggered the first of the explosions in her mind. Mind and body both, because Jared's hands had followed the trail his mouth had blazed and Jared –

'Oh, God, Jared,' she breathed, lifting her hips, nudging the hand to continue. 'Oh, Jared.'

'Nice?' he enquired smokily, a single finger threading the curls, locating the tiny ridge of pleasure and moving slowly backwards and forwards.

'Just – oh, hell!' she exclaimed, the spasms racking her body robbing her of conscious thought. 'Unfair!' she screamed as he paused, touched, triggered all over again.

'Nice?' he repeated, smiling, eyes smouldering coals. 'Tell me, Stevie. Say it, Stevie,' he insisted. 'Tell me. Tell me what you want.'

'You! I want you. Now. I love you, Jared Wilde. I want you. Please, Jared. Love me. Take me. Just love me,' she said softly, simply, holding herself still with a massive effort of will. 'Just love me.'

'I do,' he told her solemnly. 'But, since actions speak louder than words, so I'm told . . .'

He was stretching out beside her, moving against her, with her, the tension building, the pain too exquisite to prolong, and if Stevie was thrashing from side to side in a matter of moments, Jared's iron control was beginning to break too, and Jared was moaning, a great tidal wave of pleasure gathering momentum and sweeping both into the oblivion of a whole new dimension.

'Pride,' he conceded wryly a lifetime later. 'You believed Helena's lies, so it seemed, and, fool that I am, I had too much pride to explain. Instead I went for the jugular.'

'Not quite,' Stevie conceded, leaning back against the pillows, decadent glass of champagne in hand, the bubbles exploding in the back of her throat miniature reminders of other recent explosions. 'I froze you out, remember? My fault, Jared, as much as yours.

'Hardly, given those revolting accusations. But if it's any consolation, my love,' he informed her, hugging her fiercely, 'I never for an instant believed what I was saying. I was hitting out, hurting, punishing –'

'You certainly managed that,' she acknowledged, chuckling, catching his grimace of pain and relenting.

Kisses. Consolation kisses. Champagne kisses.

'I –'

'Hush,' Stevie interrupted. 'It doesn't matter any more. 'We're here, we're together, we belong.'

'No thanks to me.'

'Jared Wilde, will you please stop blaming yourself?' she entreated sternly. 'These things happen. It's all part and parcel of the fun of falling in love. Only not any more,' she reminded him, rubbing her cheek against his chest, the coarse curls tickling, the beat of his heart reassuring. 'Because I love you and you love me. Love, Jared. And trust. So, no more secrets, hey, my love?'

'Only the odd teensy weenie little ones,' he contradicted, features impassive. 'Just the usual things a husband keeps to himself, you understand. Diamonds or pearls for your birthday? Earrings, bracelet or brooch? But if you'd rather choose for yourself –'

'Nope,' she conceded, wriggling into the hollow of his shoulder, Jared's arm coming round to hold and enfold her. 'I'm sure your taste is impeccable. After all,' she reminded him pertly, 'you've chosen me.'

'A moot point, given your line in seduction. And even then I nearly blew it –'

'Only you didn't. *We* didn't,' she pointedly reminded him. 'Only nearly. Besides, we belong. Sooner or later,' she informed him, slightly tongue in cheek, 'you'd have realized your mistake and come clothes in hand to apologize.'

'Shouldn't that be cap in hand?' he observed mildly.

'Less fun that way,' she explained, smiling

broadly. 'But a safer option in public. Only we're not, and you didn't.'

'No. Chiefly because a certain little lady couldn't wait to get her hands inside my pants.'

'I didn't notice you raising any objections at the time.'

'I didn't. I'm not. I won't. Private or public; it's all the same to me.'

'And if I call your bluff on that one . . .'

'You won't.'

'Ah, but I might,' she contradicted mildly. 'In which case, sir, you'd better be prepared.'

'Woman,' he castigated sternly, 'have you no shame?'

'Apparently not,' Stevie cheerfully conceded. 'Not where you're concerned at least.'

'I don't deserve you, do I?' he groaned. 'And when I think how close I came to losing you –'

'Subject closed,' she reminded him sternly.

'All thanks to Roxton,' he surprised her by conceding. 'His parting shot. A string of abuse not fit for a woman's ears but raw enough to make me stop and think. Dee. The reason you froze me out. You thought you were cheating on your best friend, only –'

'I know it isn't true – now,' she interrupted softly.

'Hmm. No prizes for guessing,' Jared supplied dryly. 'Roxton. I should have known.'

'You and me both,' she conceded. 'He and Dee are – old friends,' she explained diplomatically.

'Then more fool Dee. And, talking of Dee, what on earth are we going to tell her?'

'I don't think we'll need to, my love. Andrew. He's bound to get to her first. But as to how she'll take it –'

'Knowing Dee – and most definitely not in the Biblical sense, you understand,' he insisted mock severely, 'with her usual aplomb. So, next problem. Rosa.'

'*Is* Rosa a problem?' Stevie queried with a stab of apprehension.

'Not for me. But now that I've found you I'm not inclined to let you go. You and me. Sleeping together. Tonight and tomorrow and for ever and always. Think, Stevie. A strange man in her mother's bed. Quite an adjustment for the average seven-year-old. Unless . . .'

'Unless?' she mused, settling down again. The moment of panic had been absurd, she decided, nuzzling against him, scrunching the curls, shamelessly nudging the nipples.

'Unless we arrange the wedding at once,' he explained. 'How about Tuesday? Plenty of time to pick up the special licence, ring round our friends and ask a couple of little girls to do us the honour of being bridesmaids. Unless you think I'm rushing things?'

'Positively indecent, I'd say,' she agreed solemnly. 'But, since the blushing bride is as eager as the groom, I guess we'll just have to grin and bear it.'

'Oh, good. Wedding here, honeymoon in Italy. And with lots of room at the villa, Rosa and Kelly could tag along too. A sort of happy family affair, with one delighted grandma at the centre.'

'Two,' Stevie contradicted, seeing Nanna's face in her mind and smiling. 'If you're sure Caterina's up to having visitors?'

'Doctor's orders,' he assured her. 'Everything's under control so long as she takes it easy. Hang on a minute. What did you say?'

'Grandmas. Plural. And surprisingly alike, wouldn't you know? Probably just as well, really. Mine can go to the wedding, yours can preside over the honeymoon arrangements, and nobody's nose is pushed out of joint.'

'Hmm. Kind of unconventional, though,' Jared mused doubtfully.

'Ah, yes, but in case you hadn't noticed,' Stevie reminded her, 'I'm an unconventional sort of girl. Take it or leave it.'

'I'll take it. And you. Now,' he growled. 'Because, in case you'd forgotten, a certain hearth-rug beckons. If madam would care to step this way?'

'Madam wouldn't. So if sir wants me,' she informed him pertly, 'sir will just have to do something about it, won't he?'

Sir did.

More love. The pile of the hearth-rug was almost as comfortable as the bed and simply perfect for a warm summer afternoon. Simply perfect, full stop.

The phone rang, nudging a reluctant Stevie out of a wonderfully erotic dream. Not a dream, she discovered, opening her eyes to find Jared stretched out beside her, propped up on an elbow, gazing down with love in his eyes. So much love, she acknowledged happily.

'Leave it,' he instructed as she made to wriggle upright. 'The answer machine's on. If it's important,' he conceded, dipping his head to kiss her, taste her, kiss her again, 'we'll deal with it next week. Or next month,' he added, an exploring tongue pushing through into the secret moist depths and sending rivers of heat swirling through her veins. 'Or next year. Maybe.'

Important it wasn't. More a case of vital.

'Okay, Stevie Cooper, the game's up.'

A familiar voice, a mournful voice. Stevie went cold, oh, so cold, her startled gaze locking with Jared's.

'I know you're there, Stevie Cooper, and furthermore, you shameless little minx, I know precisely what you're doing. At least,' Dee amended with a lightning change of tone, 'I hope you are. Because if I had to lose out to someone,' she cheerfully conceded, 'I really am glad that it's you. So – assuming the role of matron of honour is mine,' she pointedly reminded her, 'I guess I can find it in my heart to forgive you – this time.'

'This time?' Jared growled, seizing on the words and pouncing on Stevie, a smiling Stevie sprawled shamelessly across the hearth-rug, straddling her and pinning her to the floor with his knees. 'And what, pray,' he enquired mock severely, folding his arms and regarding her from under hooded eyes, 'exactly does that mean?'

'Oh – you know,' Stevie replied airily. 'Just a short, sharp reminder to keep you on your toes. Keep the lady in your life happily pleasured,' she explained, 'or else.'

'Or else . . . ?'

'Or else, Jared Wilde,' she smokily informed him, reaching for her breasts, idle thumbs brushing her nipples, dark buds already straining for Jared's touch, Jared's lips, Jared's teeth. And, sensing his reaction, she allowed her hands to slide with slow deliberation over the curves and across the plains of her belly. Jared's manhood stirred into life and thrust eagerly forward to meet her. 'Or else,' she insisted with a tantalizing hint of a connection, 'she might just be forced to teach you a lesson you won't forget.'

'Heads I win, tails I can't lose, hey?' he drawled, with definite shades of another time, another place, another playful exchange of words. First impressions. And the delights of proving them right – or wrong.

Stevie smiled. 'You and me both, hey, Jared?'

she challenged smokily. But she didn't wait for an answer, didn't really need an answer. Jared's groan of pleasure as her fingers closed round him, and the echoing thrill in Stevie's mind and body were all the proof she needed.

THE EXCITING NEW NAME
IN WOMEN'S FICTION!

PLEASE HELP ME TO HELP YOU!

Dear *Scarlet* Reader,

As Editor of *Scarlet* Books I want to make sure that the books I offer you every month are up to the high standards *Scarlet* readers expect. And to do that I need to know a little more about you and your reading likes and dislikes. So please spare a few minutes to fill in the short questionnaire on the following pages and send it to me.

Looking forward to hearing from you,

Sally Cooper

Editor-in-Chief, *Scarlet*

QUESTIONNAIRE

Please tick the appropriate boxes to indicate your answers

1 Where did you get this Scarlet title?
Bought in supermarket ☐
Bought at my local bookstore ☐ Bought at chain bookstore ☐
Bought at book exchange or used bookstore ☐
Borrowed from a friend ☐
Other (please indicate) _____

2 Did you enjoy reading it?
A lot ☐   A little ☐   Not at all ☐

3 What did you particularly like about this book?
Believable characters ☐   Easy to read ☐
Good value for money ☐   Enjoyable locations ☐
Interesting story ☐   Modern setting ☐
Other _____

4 What did you particularly dislike about this book?
_____

5 Would you buy another Scarlet book?
Yes ☐   No ☐

6 What other kinds of book do you enjoy reading?
Horror ☐   Puzzle books ☐   Historical fiction ☐
General fiction ☐   Crime/Detective ☐   Cookery ☐
Other (please indicate) _____

7 Which magazines do you enjoy reading?
1. _____
2. _____
3. _____

And now a little about you –
8 How old are you?
Under 25 ☐   25–34 ☐   35–44 ☐
45–54 ☐   55–64 ☐   over 65 ☐

cont.

9 What is your marital status?
   Single ☐   Married/living with partner ☐
   Widowed ☐   Separated/divorced ☐

10 What is your current occupation?
   Employed full-time ☐   Employed part-time ☐
   Student ☐   Housewife full-time ☐
   Unemployed ☐   Retired ☐

11 Do you have children? If so, how many and how old are they?
   _____
   _____

12 What is your annual household income?
   under $15,000 ☐ or £10,000   ☐
   $15–25,000   ☐ or £10–20,000   ☐
   $25–35,000   ☐ or £20–30,000   ☐
   $35–50,000   ☐ or £30–40,000   ☐
   over $50,000   ☐ or £40,000   ☐

Miss/Mrs/Ms _____

Address _____

_____

_____

Thank you for completing this questionnaire. Now tear it out – put it in an envelope and send it, before 30 June 1998, to:

Sally Cooper, Editor-in-Chief

USA/Can. address
SCARLET c/o London Bridge
85 River Rock Drive
Suite 202
Buffalo
NY 14207
USA

UK address/No stamp required
SCARLET
FREEPOST LON 3335
LONDON W8 4BR
Please use block capitals for address

WIAFF/12/97

Scarlet titles coming next month:

MARRIAGE DANCE Jillian James
Anni Ross is totally committed to her career in dance. She's positive that she's got no time to spare for falling in love! But attractive lawyer Steve Hunter has other plans for Anni's future . . .

SLOW DANCING Elizabeth Smith
Hallie Prescott is plunged into the world of glitter and glamour when she accompanies her screenwriter husband to Hollywood. But it's not long before the dream goes sour. Can Grant Keeler help Hallie rebuild her life?

THAT CINDERELLA FEELING Anne Styles
Out of work actress Casey Taylor will take any job she can find. Which is how she ends up delivering a kissagram to the offices of Alex Havilland, a businessman who has no time for frivolity and who is definitely *not* amused!

A DARKER SHADOW Patricia Wilson
Amy Scott can handle any problem that the world of computers throws at her. But when it comes to coping with sudden and frightening events in her private life, she doesn't know where to turn. Until her arrogant and disapproving boss Luc Martell decides to intervene . . .